EMMANUEL

J.R. Bacon

First published by On the Write Path Publishing
5023 W. 120th Ave. #228
Broomfield, CO 80020
martinmcleanlit@aol.com

On The Write Path
PUBLISHING

Paperback ISBN: 978-1-63837-075-8
eBook ISBN: 978-1-63837-076-5

This book is a work of fiction. Places, events and situations in this book are purely fictional and any resemblance to actual person, living or dead, is coincidental.

This book is printed on acid-free paper.
Printed in the United States of America

I dedicate this novel to my mother, Doretta Reed Bacon. When I was a kid, I always thought she unfairly expected more of me than she did of my brother or sister - in fact, very often too much more.

After living through many years of marriage, children and hundreds of other things, I have come to realize that her "Great Expectations" were probably the reason I have accomplished as much as I have in this life.

She wasn't loud or brash. In fact, in a crowd she was pretty much transparent. However, with quiet dignity, she moved through life, doing the best she could with what she had.

It has befuddled and amused me that I chose a woman to be my wife who was not unlike her. Mother probably figured that out because, when she met this woman I was to marry, she took to her immediately. In fact, they became fast friends, banding together to keep me in line.

After my first year of teaching, I did something I have been thankful I did ever since that day so many years ago. I wrote my mother a letter in longhand, telling her that I finally realized what a great mother she had been.

Four years and four months later she was dead. She died of cancer at much too young an age, fifty-five. She left this world quietly and gracefully, much like she had lived in it.

There are some things we do in this life which are just right. That letter to my mother was the most right of all the things I have ever done.

Acknowledgments

I would like to take this opportunity to acknowledge several people who made it possible for me to write and publish this science fiction novel.

First, and foremost, I would like to thank my son, John, for his thorough feedback about my writing and his faithful support of my writing career.

I would also like to thank my daughter, Jane, for encouraging me to pursue my dreams.

My special thanks goes to Lisa Martin, my agent, for her good advice, her encouragement and her faith in my talent.

Finally, I thank Dave Petty for the excellent photo on the back cover of this novel.

Cast of Characters

Starship Cygnus
Green Shift
    Commander Seth Okanata – pilot
    Captain Salathiel Tikal – pilot
    Lieutenant Elaina Djoser – navigator

Orange Shift
    Captain Chan Caracol – pilot
    Lieutenant Lindos Lycastus - navigator

Starship Security
    Lieutenant Alto Bucolus – lieutenant and security chief
    Private Osiris Imhotep
    Private Mases Astrides

Rocket Engineers
    Lieutenant Masal Djoser
    Sergeant Hector Copan

Onboard Professionals
    Doctor Bokar Neleus – psychiatrist
    Doctor Orus Nestor – medical doctor
    Doctor Colonus Meander – astrophysicist
    Doctor Jak Eloi – anthropologist
    Doctor Kan Naranjo - geologist
    Doctor Garm Rahotpe - teleporting

Megall Pirates
    Calchus – captain & commander of pirate fleet
    Scarphe
    Halios
    Delos
    Balius
    Casus

Planet Hyksos, city of Memphis

- Lycia Copan – Hector's wife
- Charis & Aten – Hector and Lycia's children
- Dax Copan – Hector's father
- Themis Copan – Hector's mother
- Niobe Lysander – Hector Copan's babysitter
- Cadmus Menon – Lycia Copan's lover
- Canace Bucolus – Alto's wife
- Balder Clio - detective Memphis Police Department
- Wexal Luxor – startup company investor
- Alba Thoth – Seth Okanata's cleaning lady

CHAPTER ONE
"FATE"

Hyksos
Memphis
1889 Bay Street
9M, Day 24, 6572
9:18 a.m.

Commander Seth Okanata descended the stairs to the front foyer. He could hear Mrs. Thoth vacuuming in the living room.

Seth had used a robotic service to clean his house for several years, but he always felt that the work was never quite thorough enough. Mrs. Thoth had come recommended by Kara Borg, a woman down the street.

And why had he acted upon Kara Borg's recommendation for a cleaning person? It was simple. Kara Borg's house was so clean one felt that he or she could eat off the floors. Well, not really, but the house was unusually clean.

Kara Borg had Mrs. Alba Thoth clean her house once a week. Seth wasn't quite that fanatical about clean. He had Mrs. Thoth out here twice a month. After all, Seth was the only soul living in this house and, if he did say so himself, he was extremely neat.

Ahead of him, he could see the large woman shoving the vacuum cleaner back and forth, almost as if she was attacking any nasty little bits of dust which might be hiding from sight inside the living room carpet.

When Seth neared her, she jumped back. She flicked off the vacuum switch.

The humming tone subsided downward toward a deep bass, then ceased.

"You startled me, Mister Okanata."

"Sorry, Mrs. Thoth. I just wanted to tell you that I'm leaving now. I have to get out to the base. I'll be starting my journey the thirteenth of next month. If I remember correctly, you're not due until the fifteenth, so I won't be seeing you again until I'm back."

"Mister Okanata, how come I haven't seen anything on the news about this space journey?"

Seth shrugged. "I suppose because we haven't released any information about it."

"If you don't mind me sayin' so, sir, that's a mite strange."

"I don't make those decisions, Mrs. Thoth. It's people farther up the Mayan Space Administration ladder who are responsible for those decisions."

Actually, Seth had thought the upper brass was being a little too secretive about this. He had been told that they were afraid there might be demonstrations by some of the radical groups and these same people said they didn't need any bad press.

He supposed the real reason was that the Mayan Space Administration always seemed to have difficulty wrenching money out of the government coffers. Any kind of bad press didn't help these matters because there would inevitably be questions about how they were managing the money they had already been given. A demonstration would only start a political war between the liberals and the conservatives and that could lead to challenges about their annual budget.

"You know, sir, there's somethin' I wanted to pass on to you." Mrs. Thoth slung her right hip upward and rested her open hand on it. "You see, sir, the ladies in my book club were wonderin' how come a good lookin' man like yourself who has a big house and a good job isn't married to some nice woman."

Seth could feel his face heat up. "So what brought on that subject?"

"Oh, I'm so sorry, Mister Okanata. Didn't mean to embarrass you like that. Cathy, my friend, says I'm a bit blunt. Don't mean any harm. Just always say what's on my mind. I've wondered about this, sir. Then some of my friends was askin' about it too."

Seth nodded. "I'm very flattered that your friends are concerned, Mrs. Thoth, but I guess what it comes down to is that I've spent a lot of my time focused on my career."

"Must get kinda lonely at times, sir."

"I've gotten quite used to it, Mrs. Thoth." Seth glanced at his wrist control. "Well, I do have to be going. While I'm gone on my journey, I don't think you need to clean except, perhaps, once a month. . . beginning next month, of course. Lights will come on in the house when it gets dark each night. So don't be surprised, if you happen to be around here after dark.

"As usual, my bank account will pay you each month while I'm gone. And, as I've said, I do believe just once a month will be adequate."

Mrs. Alba Thoth nodded several times. "Same as always. That will be just fine, sir. You have yourself a nice trip, Mister Okanata."

Seth made a smile. "Thank you very much, Mrs. Thoth."

He turned around and walked into the foyer. There he opened the house door and stepped out to the teleporteco.

Once he had closed the door, Seth turned to face the house. He was about to tap his wrist control in order to teleport, but just at that moment, he thought about what Mrs. Thoth had said. It made him feel like an oddball and, actually, he felt a little lonely.

He had lonely times like this – not often – but he did have them. It was as if he would suddenly be aware that he really was alone.

These events happened most often when he was here at the house and, of course, especially when he was on furlough. He supposed that was because his furloughs lasted two weeks and that meant he was not working for two weeks. Usually, when he was on a furlough, he would plan a trip of some kind, something to keep him busy.

He really did enjoy traveling. However, it did occur to him, just now, that actually this might be his way of avoiding his real problem - loneliness.

But he wasn't a social man. He wasn't someone who could easily approach a woman and ask her if she would like to have dinner. In fact, because he was single, he didn't have a social circle of married friends. Therefore he wasn't exposed to women in the first place, except sometimes when he was working.

There were women assigned to his starships, doing various things. Most of them were much younger than he was, so they weren't interested in this older guy.

Well, enough of this. He had to get to the MSA base. He had things to do today.

He tapped his wrist control, then scrolled down to "MSA" and he touched that.

Blue bubbles appeared around him, then gold.

During the brief teleporting journey, Commander Seth Okanata could not shake off the feeling of loneliness.

He hated moments like this. He would much rather be in front of his crew preparing them for their journey.

Maybe, someday, there would be a woman, but it hadn't happened so far and he was forty-eight years old.

Probably he would be a bachelor for his whole life. Maybe that was his fate.

CHAPTER TWO

"In His Bones"

4281 Aswan Street
Memphis
9M, Day 24, 6572
10:03 a.m.

Sergeant Hector Copan had seen this change in his wife lately. Most of the time it had been little things, hardly noticeable.

Other times it was more obvious. But those things didn't happen very often. He just could not figure out what was going on.

That was the thing about working for the Mayan Space Administration. You were gone a lot and that made it hard to stay connected to your family. Of course, most of it had to do with the way you handled it, but there were a lot of divorces with people who worked for the MSA. Most of it was about being gone for months. That was hard on any marriage, no matter how good it was. But he didn't want a divorce. That would be hard on the kids.

As far as his kids were concerned, being away seemed to be pretty good. Sure, they were upset when he left, but you just had to work to stay connected to them.

What Hector did was text them from the starship out in space, sometimes sending silly pictures of himself doing dumb things like pretending to make repairs to beds, or lamps or toilets. One time he unscrewed the stand from a safety chair and sat on the post. He did that to make his kids laugh. Sometimes he made goofy faces – did things the kids thought were funny.

He was a mechanic aboard the ship, but a rocket mechanic, not some kind of repair man or something. Being a rocket mechanic was much more complicated than fixing lamps and shit like that.

Of course he and Masal Djoser did go on some EVAs because both of them knew how to weld. When there were meteorite strikes, sometimes damage happened to the outer hull of the starship. Most of the time repairing the outer hull required welding.

The kids seemed proud of him working on a starship. With his wife, Lycia, it was different. She didn't handle it as well as they did, and Hector had no idea why she seemed to get real upset when he left.

He just kept working on that, trying to make her happy. He didn't seem to be making much progress, but he was trying.

"Daddy, I have something to tell you," said a whispering child's voice off to Hector's left.

Hector turned.

His daughter, Charis, was standing next to the dining room table. The eight year old scurried across the hardwood floor to the entrance into the living room. She leaned through the wide archway. Then she scurried back to her father's side.

"Did you want to tell me somethin', honey?"

Charis glanced toward the archway again. "Yes," she whispered.

Hector could not imagine what it was that his daughter was going to tell him. Charis was his girl, much more than she was her mother's. They just seemed to bond better or something. He also noticed that once in a while Charis would show some jealousy when her mother was with him.

Charis ran over to the archway again and leaned to look into the living room.

"So, what's up, honey? Somethin' you want to tell me? I've gotta write down my thoughts before Masal gets here so I don't miss somethin'."

Charis ran back to him and moved up close. "It's about Mommy," she whispered.

"What about your mommy?"

Charis put her finger to her lips. "Shhh, Daddy. Not so loud."

This was really odd. Hector had no idea what was going on. "You can tell me anythin', honey," he whispered.

"I know, Daddy."

"So, what do you have to tell me?"

"Yesterday Mommy was acting weird."

"What do you mean, honey?"

"When Mommy was at Super Mart she talked to this man and she giggled a lot like she was in high school."

"Who was she talkin' to in the grocery store, honey?"

"I don't know. He was a really pretty man and he smiled a lot and they talked."

"What were they talkin' about?"

"Just silly stuff. And Mommy giggled a lot. Then when I said I wanted to go home, she stopped giggling and she was kind of grumpy."

"I'm sure it's nothin', sweetheart. Don't worry about it." Hector made a smile for his daughter and he leaned and kissed her cheek. "You go play. School starts again tomorrow so you should spend your time outside today, honey. You're gonna be all cooped up in that school buildin' tomorrow."

Charis stood in front of him. "I just thought I ought to tell you, Daddy. It was because Mommy was so weird."

"Don't you worry, honey. I'll take care of it."

Charis wrapped her arms around the neck and kissed his cheek. Then she charged away into the kitchen.

He heard the house door to the back yard open, then close.

Hector could feel tension in his body. What was going on with his wife? She'd been acting different lately.

When Hector thought about his daughter, he suddenly felt sad. He would be away from her again for a couple of months. He had another starship journey.

This one he didn't know much about. Nobody seemed to know. Hector wondered what the MSA was up to this time. He would have to ask Masal about it.

He sure missed his kids when he was away. They changed so much, especially the little one, Aten. Every time Hector returned from a starship journey, little Aten seemed to have grown more. It just happened so fast. Of course, he was away for months at a time.

Hector turned and stared out the bay window. What his daughter had just said made him uneasy. Normally, because she was a young child he wouldn't have worried about it much. But Charis was a smart kid and he had never known her to lie to him. Then there was the fact that lately Lycia had been acting strange.

Was his wife flirting with some other man? Is that what Charis meant when she said her mother was "acting like she was in high school?"

Hector was convinced that he would need to have a face-to-face talk with Lycia. There was probably nothing to this, but she was behaving kind of odd lately.

There was a loud buzz.

Hector rose out of the dining room chair and moved out into the living room. "Got it!"

He crossed the living room to the front door.

The foyer overhead light flicked on.

Just before his hand touched the door handle, there was another buzz.

Hector pressed down the lever handle and pulled open the door.

It was Masal, the mechanic who worked with him on the starship. Masal pulled open the screen door and stepped through the doorway. "Hey, Hector, how're they hangin'?"

"Come on in, Masal." Hector pulled the inside door back.

The other starship mechanic walked by him into the foyer.

Hector pushed the inside door closed. He nodded toward the living room. "I'm set up at the dinin' room table. Say, Masal, do you know anythin' about this next journey were goin' on?"

Masal looked at him. "No, nothin' at all. Kind of strange if you ask me. We usually know where we're goin' and what we're carrying. This time nothin'. I even called Caracol, that younger pilot. He said he didn't know either."

Hector nodded. "I hope were not goin' where there are pirates or somethin'."

"Naw. . . the MSA wouldn't do that. They wouldn't want to lose a starship."

Masal moved into the living room, then the dining room.

Hector was behind him.

Masal swung a folder out from under his right arm. He glanced back over his shoulder. "About our business project here. . . I've been talkin' to my cousin, Nestor. Called him first thing this mornin'. He says we could probably get a loan for about four percent interest. If our credit was real good, we might get three and a half percent."

Hector motioned to the right side of the table in front of the window. "Take a load off, Masal."

The taller man pulled out the nearest chair in front of the window and sat down. He dropped his folder on the wooden tabletop. "You know, Hector, I really think we can do this antique car restoration thing. Nestor says the worst part is fillin' out the paperwork and then waitin'. The waitin' period is sometimes about a month or more."

"What did he say about our chances?"

"He didn't. He did say the real thing was doin' a proposal, a business plan, and then the credit check. He said the business plan was real important. He said if we never did it before that we might want to hire somebody to write up a plan for us."

"How much is that gonna cost?"

Masal shrugged. "I have no idea. We'll have to check all this out."

"I've been thinkin' about this, Masal, and this is what I decided. . ."

At that moment Lycia appeared in the living room. "I'm goin' over to my mother's."

Hector stared at his wife. He noticed that she was wearing a lot of makeup and he could smell perfume. "Why are you goin' over there?"

"We're plannin' a big birthday party for Charis."

"Her birthday is two months away."

Lycia didn't respond. Finally she said, "I'll be back in a couple of hours." She pivoted around and hurried across the living room into the foyer.

The light flickered on.

The front door opened, then shut.

"Your wife's sure dressed up nice. If I didn't know better, I'd say she was on the prowl or somethin'."

"Shit, Masal! Why would you say somethin' like that?"

The other man shrugged. "Just sayin'."

Hector could see his wife standing on the concrete pad under the teleportico just outside the front door. She seemed to be studying her wrist control. If it was her mother's place, why would Lycia have to study her wrist control? She should be able to find the address easily. She went there often enough.

A blue glow appeared around Lycia Copan. Then she vanished.

"You okay, Hector?"

He looked to his right. "Yeah, I'm okay. Wife's just been actin' odd lately."

"The way she looks and smells, Hector, I'd say she's on the prowl."

"Come on, Masal, you know it's because you were comin' over here."

Hector had meant that as a light, humorous remark, but what he got from Masal was kind of weird. The man stared at him like he was in shock.

Then he seemed to collect himself. "I've got to tell you, Hector, I'd check that out. I've never heard of any woman dressin' up like that to go see her mother."

There was the thumping of a fist beating on the front door and distant howling and crying.

Hector rose from his chair. "Shit, somethin's goin' on with Aten. I've got to see what's wrong. Give me just a minute, Masal."

"Sure, take your time."

Hector hurried across the living room to the foyer.

The overhead light flicked on.

He pulled open the front door.

Aten was standing outside the screen door crying. "Charis hit me!"

Hector carefully pushed open the front door and crouched down next to the four year old. This was not going to be a good day. He could feel it in his bones.

CHAPTER THREE
"Downward Slope"

Driving Range
Memphis
9M, Day 30, 6572
11:42 a.m.

Masal had been right about this Lynx. It really had the get-up-and-go.

Hector pressed the accelerator and the long, grey sedan climbed the gradual slope up toward the plateau.

Of course, this time Lycia wasn't here. She said she was going out with her girlfriends. Hector had met only one of them, a woman named Kora.

But, anyway, he had the kids and that was fine. There was another MSA assignment in a couple of weeks. He would be gone for months. This was a weekend, so he wanted to be with them.

He had come out here to try out Masal's Lynx. He was going to help him restore it. Masal was one of these guys who had the skill to repair stuff. He just didn't have the eye for color and style. And, besides, he wanted it to look like the original and Hector knew a lot more about that than Masal.

In a way, it was relaxing to be away from his wife. She had been leaving the house lately wearing that perfume and tight slacks. He wasn't sure what was going on, but he could make a guess that it didn't have to do with going to her mother's.

Today, she was with her girlfriends. Apparently they went out for lunch, then did some shopping at the mall. At least, she had said she was going to be with her girlfriends.

Lycia had left the house again this morning – same scenario. She was wearing tight slacks and a tee shirt that made her boobs show. In fact, it kind of looked like she wasn't wearing a bra, although she probably was. She got embarrassed about things like that.

Hector had been cruising the driving range out here for almost a half an hour. He had been all over this place, down every side road.

Most of those led to restaurants or repair shops. Some were scenic lookouts. They were all labeled with electronic signs. The signs were virtual, hanging in the air just before the intersection with the main road.

"Daddy, when are we gonna stop for lunch?"

Hector glanced over the edge of the driver's seat. "In a few minutes, Charis. Daddy's just drivin' around to get a feel for how Mister Djoser's car works so he'll know what to fix."

"Why are you going to fix Mister Djoser's car?"

"Well, honey, I know more about what to fix than he does and, besides, we're gonna start a business together fixin' these old cars. Then Daddy won't be goin' on any long journeys anymore. He'll be home every night."

"I'd like that, Daddy."

"Me too, honey. How's Aten doin' back there?"

"He's sucking his thumb."

"Shouldn't do that, Aten."

"Don't do that!" yelled a boy's voice.

"What happened, Charis?"

"He won't stop sucking his thumb."

"Don't bother him. He's not hurtin' you, honey."

"But he's not supposed to do it."

"Let Daddy handle it, honey."

Up ahead on the right Hector spotted the sign. The white letters glowed above the shoulder as if they were suspended by some invisible wire from the sky.

It read, "Ocean View Road."

Hector was pretty sure this was the one that he remembered from long ago. There was a bluff over a beach. He and his wife used to climb down off the bluff to the beach and neck - and do other things.

He pressed the brake pedal. He didn't know why he did this. Maybe old memories. He hadn't been up on that bluff for years.

The large grey sedan slowed and the electric motor descended downward to a deeper hum.

He checked his rearview mirror. There was a car behind him about two miles back.

He was thinking about pushing up the turn signal, but he decided not to do that. He wasn't sure why. Maybe he didn't want the person behind him to notice he was turning. That was kind of stupid because that person probably couldn't see his direction signal lights from that far away.

Again, he didn't know why he was so concerned about that other car knowing where he was going, except maybe he was feeling kind of sentimental about those times years ago and wanted to be up there alone.

Hector pressed the brake harder.

The long sedan slowed.

Hector spun the wheel to the right.

The Lynx turned onto Ocean View Road.

Hector pushed down the accelerator. He wanted to be far down this road before that car behind him passed the turnoff.

The road descended in a gradual slope between two areas of tall wild grass toward a steep downward hill into a valley of leafy hardwood trees. Beyond the valley was a rise and at the top of the rise were stunted angular pines, some of them looking like the work of some crazed artist.

When Hector reached the crest of the steep descent into the valley, he checked his rearview mirror.

No car yet.

He checked his right side mirror.

Nothing there either.

Just as the Lynx tipped over the lip of the hill crest, a shadow crossed his rearview mirror.

He hoped that person didn't notice the Lynx. Of course it wasn't his to begin with, but he still didn't want anyone to know he was out here on this road. It was something about the way his wife was behaving and some old memories.

At the bottom of the hill the long grey sedan was racing at almost seventy miles an hour.

Hector wasn't concerned because Masal had said that the vehicle was sound, and it did seem sound enough. It was just the interior that needed work – a lot of work.

Hector glanced to his right as the grey sedan rose up the steep incline toward the short angular pines at the top.

The passenger door was almost bare of leather covering. The only complete remnant was a torn leather armrest. Hector could see into the interior of the door.

Yes, this car needed work. He would give Masal a hand with the repairs.

At the crest of this second steep hill the Lynx was moving at only forty-two miles an hour.

Hector pressed the brake to slow it even more.

Once over the rise, he turned right and rolled into a fenced-in parking lot.

He pressed the brake.

The grey sedan rolled to a stop.

At the far end of the lot was a single car, a red Ajax sport convertible. Well, he wasn't the only one up here.

Hector glanced around to see if anyone was nearby.

Nobody.

He lifted his foot off the brake pedal and pressed the accelerator. Then he turned the Lynx to the left and came to a stop across several vertical parking places under a squat, angular pine tree.

He pushed the shift lever up into PARK, then twisted off the ignition key.

Hector unbuckled his seatbelt and slid out the key.

"I want a burger."

Hector turned toward the back seat. "You can have one, Aten. Daddy just wants to get out and look around."

"I want to get out."

"Sure, but you're gonna have to hold onto my hand. It's real pretty up here, but that bluff's dangerous."

Hector leaned to the right, opened the glovebox and brought out a binocular case. This was a great view. Sometimes you could see ships out on the Poseidon Sea. The kids would love something like that.

He pulled the binoculars out of the case and slipped the strap over his head down to his neck. Then he opened the door. "Okay, we can get out now. Charis, can you unbuckle Aten?"

"Sure thing, Daddy."

Hector rose out of the car.

Now he could hear the distant sound of the waves crashing onto the beach below the bluff.

A breeze blew against his face and a tuft of his hair wiggled over the left side of his forehead.

Yes, he remembered this place from way back. And it was before even Charis was born and certainly before little Aten.

His natural reaction was to just slam the car door, but something stopped him from doing that. Maybe it was the beauty of this place.

He pushed the driver's door up against the opening until he heard a subtle click of the latch.

Charis and Aten scrambled out of the back seat of the car. Charis slammed the door.

Together they walked slowly across the blacktop parking lot toward the high black iron fence bordering the far edge of the pavement. Hector held onto Aten's hand.

Beyond the fence was the edge of the bluff and the shiny blue water of the Poseidon Sea.

Hector had seen this sea when it was calm like a mirror, but today it was full of rows and rows of curling whitecaps.

The closer he came to the iron fence, the more he could see the water near the beach. Up close, it was curling rollers, sweeping inward and splaying white foam in tongue-like patterns onto the brown sand.

Near the fence Hector looked to his right to check on Charis. "Now, don't play with this fence. Stay right here with me, you two. That's a very high bluff out there and it's very dangerous."

"I know that Daddy."

Hector released Aten's hand and smiled down at his daughter.

"You're smart enough to know, honey, aren't you?"

Charis nodded. "Yes, Daddy."

"Keep your eye on your brother."

"I am, Daddy."

Aten was gripping the iron bars of the fence and pressing his face between them.

"Oh, look, Daddy, there are people down there." Charis pointed.

Hector turned to his left. At this distance, it appeared to be a man and a woman wrapped up in a blanket. He wondered if maybe Charis shouldn't see this.

But then he noticed something. The woman's hair was dark brown and curly – like Lycia's. Just then, he had a creepy feeling and he shivered.

"Are you cold, Daddy?"

"No, honey." Hector didn't want to know, actually, but he raised the binoculars anyway and touched the ribbed focus wheel between the two barrels.

Yes, it was Lycia and her bare shoulders showed above the edge of the blanket. She was on her back and the guy was on top of her.

Hector lowered the binoculars.

"What's wrong, Daddy?"

Hector could feel his eyes welling up with tears. "Nothin', honey."

"I want a burger."

Hector turned.

"Daddy, why are you crying?"

CHAPTER FOUR
"The Quiet House"

Hyksos
1821 Park Place
Building #8
Memphis
10M, Day 3, 6572
10:19 a.m.

Hector Copan did not like this kind of thing at all. He had been warned by his father about setting up a business with a friend. Unfortunately, Dax Copan was right. Hector had learned that when it came to business, his father was pretty smart.

He stared at the front door of the house he had just teleported to. It was Masal's place.

Hector hadn't been here in three years. He and his wife used to socialize with Masal and Elaina. But Elaina was always having these accidents. Finally, in private, Hector's wife had said something like "Masal isn't a nice person, Hector. I don't think I want to come here anymore."

Now, for his wife to say that was unusual because Lycia was always up for partying and socializing. So, he finally figured out that Lycia was hinting that Masal was abusing his wife – beating her or something.

Did he believe that? He wasn't sure, or really, he was sure but he didn't want to think about it. After all, he worked with this guy in the Mayan Space Administration.

Hector straightened his shoulders, then reached out and pressed the doorbell.

There was a muffled buzz inside the house.

Then Hector heard two voices. The first was a man. "Hey, get the door!"

Hector could hear that very clearly. What the female voice said after that, he couldn't hear.

He really hated coming here. So far, Masal hadn't lived up to his end of the bargain. If he didn't come through, this loan application was never going to make it. They would be right back where they had started from or, really, he would be back there up to his ass in debt with no chance to start this business.

Hector pressed the black button again.

The door opened.

"Hi, Elaina."

"Hello, Hector. Do you want to see Masal?"

"Yeah."

"He's in the dining room."

Hector noticed, when he walked by Elaina, that the side of her face was swollen.

She caught him looking.

Hector averted his eyes and moved past her into the foyer. All he could think of was what his wife had said, and that was, probably, three years ago. "So, how's it goin', Elaina?"

She shrugged. "Everything's fine." She moved to his right. "He's in here, working on your business project." She nodded toward the dining room.

Hector noticed that she wasn't making eye contact. He figured small talk wouldn't hurt. "I heard you and Masal are gonna be together on the next MSA journey."

Elaina glanced at him. A quick smile appeared on her face, then vanished. She nodded. "That's true." She began walking toward the dining room.

Hector followed. "Well, at least you won't be separated from him. I hate this leavin' and bein' gone for three or four months. . . sometimes longer. Guess most of us get damned tired of it."

Elaina stopped at the entrance in the doorway. "Masal, Hector's here."

The muscular man looked up from the dining room table. "Hector. . . take a load off." Masal averted his eyes.

Hector was pretty sure Masal knew why he was here.

"Can you go upstairs, Elaina. We need some privacy." Masal stared at his wife.

"Sure." She pivoted around and hurried out of the dining room into the foyer.

Behind him, Hector could hear Elaina climbing the stairs to the second floor.

"So, Hector, what brings you here this mornin'?"

Hector didn't like getting into people's faces. Maybe he should start this on a lighter tone. "Hey, Masal, remember I said I was gonna fix that Cadmus Menon asshole?"

Masal leaned closer. "The one who was messin' with your wife?" he said in a low voice.

"One and the same."

"Did you really do somethin' to him?" Masal's voice was just above a whisper.

Hector smiled and nodded. "I fixed him fine." He moved closer to Masal. "Screwed up the wirin' in his car," he whispered.

"No shit?"

"Oh, yeah. He's gonna be getting' all kinds of electric shocks when he drives that piece of shit."

Masal shrugged. "Hey, messin' with your wife? He's got it comin'."

The man on the other side of the table leaned back and folded his arms across his chest. "Hey, buddy, what's the real reason you came over? It wasn't to tell me about that fuckin' prank."

Hector pulled out a chair and sat down. "I think you know the reason, Masal."

The muscular man nodded. "I figured that was it."

"Mister Luxor won't work with us unless we come up with half a million dollars. But you already know that."

"I don't have it, Hector."

"I've wired my share to him. Had to borrow it."

Masal looked across the corner of the table. "Two hundred fifty thousand dollars is a lot of money, Hector."

"Hey, I understand, but you said you could get it. This thing's gonna fall through if you don't come up with your half. Luxor doesn't need us, Masal. He'll just find an investment somewhere else."

"He needs us. That's how he makes his fuckin' money. . . puttin' the screws to chumps like us and collectin' his high interest."

Hector didn't know where to go from here. Finally he said, "Can you get it? I don't mean in three months. I mean in a week or two."

"I can't come up with that kind of money that fast."

"Take out a loan, Masal. That's what I did. . . a business loan from Memphis National. Now I'm up to my ass in debt. You've got to come through or this is gonna fall apart."

"Don't fuckin' tell me what I have to do!"

Hector was startled by Masal's anger. It took him a minute to get his head together. Then he said, "Look, Masal, I'm not tryin' to bust your balls here. It's just that it's gonna be a real moneymaker because there are hundreds of people who have antique cars. If you count people who might come from out of town, it might be thousands. There's lots of people who get into that hobby. We've got a great opportunity here."

Masal jumped up out of his chair. "Don't you think I know that? Are you tryin' to tell me I'm stupid?"

Hector had never seen Masal this angry. What popped into his mind was the swelling on the side of Elaina's face.

He wasn't going to get anywhere today. Hector rose from his chair, then turned and moved toward the doorway. He spun around. "If you could get the money by next week, Masal, that would be good. Otherwise, I don't think it's gonna work."

"Get the fuck out of here!"

Hector shrugged. "Sure. . . okay." He moved through the doorway into the foyer. For just a second he was tempted to try one more time. He even stopped in the foyer and looked back.

When he turned his head, he noticed Elaina in the balcony on the second floor.

She made eye contact, then hurried away toward the enclosed hallway on her right.

Hector walked to the front door. He looked back one more time.

In the dining room, Masal seemed to be studying some papers lying on the table in front of him. He looked up and stared.

Hector reached for the door lever. He was half expecting that someone would let him out or at least say something – maybe something apologetic or maybe just something friendly.

When he pressed down the door lever, the click of the latch was loud in the quiet house.

Once he was outside on the teleportico, Hector actually felt relief.

He faced the house and pulled the door closed. At this moment, he realized that if he was going to have a repair garage for antique cars, he needed to do it himself.

And there was something else. He never wanted to be a business partner with Masal Djoser – absolutely never.

CHAPTER FIVE

"The Mystery"

Hyksos
1725 River Street
Memphis
10M, Day 13, 6572
1:06 p.m.

Lieutenant Alto Bucolus did not want to leave Hyksos this time. He was due for a furlough after this next trip. He was really looking forward to that. All this bouncing around the galaxy months at a time got kind of tiring after a while.

It was good that the MSA required downtime for the crew members. Three journeys, then a furlough.

Then he could spend some time with his kids, Cova and Dax. He really enjoyed that. He didn't want to be one of those fathers who later wakes up to the fact he should have spent more time with his kids. He already had guilt feelings about missing birthdays and things like that.

Alto didn't often get assigned to Chan's starship, but this time it had happened. It was the second time in a row and he was grateful for that.

He really liked the kid a lot and he felt almost like his older brother. Alto had his own family. Canace was a terrific wife and his kids were great, Cova and little Dax.

But he had taken Chan Caracol under his wing a long time ago. If he remembered right, it was nine years. The guy was the nicest person, but he was running around aimlessly like he didn't know where he was going. For some reason, that bothered Alto.

Well, what it came down to was that he hated seeing this nice young guy running from woman to woman and never settling down.

Sure it was hard to lead what was seen as a "normal" life when you worked for the Mayan Space Administration. But Alto knew from his own experience that having a family gave you an anchor. There was someone to come home to. Well, it wasn't exactly that simple, yet that was an important part of it.

If you were on for three journeys at a time, you were gone for most of a year crisscrossing the galaxy. It was crazy.

It wasn't that he didn't like his job. Alto did. It was a good fit. He liked police work. Sure it was sometimes boring, but when it was good, it was very good and he got this sense of doing the right thing when he put some asshole behind bars.

Of course, on a starship it might be just standing by some door with an assault rifle looking dangerous in your camouflage field issue. But, even then, you were doing an important thing. You were making sure everybody was safe.

His young friend, Chan needed a good woman and then maybe some children. He was a damned nice guy. As far as Alto was concerned, nice people should be the ones to have children.

Alto Bucolus checked his duffle bag one more time to make sure he had everything packed. Then he pulled the zipper down the full length and pressed the Velcro strap across the end.

There, he was packed.

Canace appeared at the top of the stairs. As usual, she looked great. She had to wear a suit at work. She was the junior partner in a law firm, Chiron, Oeta and Bucolus.

Whenever he was going on a journey, she teleported home to be here when he left the house. This was the surprising thing about his wife. She was actually one tough lawyer. He had seen her working in a courtroom.

However, with Canace, it was like she had two personalities, one was the tough lawyer. The other was a sweet, caring person. She had a whole string of friends who probably had no idea what a tough woman she really was.

The beautiful redhead descended the stairs. She was making eye contact with him. What was strange about the eye contact thing was that Alto found it to be very stimulating, in a sexual way.

Canace behaved that same way before those very private moments they shared, but then, once things were moving along, she would become this sweet, accepting woman who was not the initiator. But she did get into sex and she was passionate about it.

Simply put, she was complicated and Alto was crazy about her for that very reason. He figured that he was the one who got the beautiful princess.

"So, you're leaving again."

"Yup."

She put her hands on his shoulders. "You be careful out there. I want you back here in three months."

"Three months. . . maybe."

"Tell Okanata that your wife says three months or he's going to have to deal with me."

Without warning, she pulled him up against her body and planted a kiss on his lips.

Alto knew she would probably do this, but he was always surprised and always stimulated.

She pulled away. "I love you, Alto. You'd better come back here in one piece."

He smiled. "I wouldn't dare do anything else."

Now she was smiling and she nodded. "The kids always miss you."

"I miss them, too. Someday I'll retire from this job or put in for a desk job at the MSA installation west of town."

"You'd be bored with that."

"I know, but I'd be around you and the kids."

She brushed his hair back off his forehead. "I know you've got to get rolling. I'll miss you, honey."

Alto could feel a rush of emotion. "Same here." At that moment he was remembering this sometimes crazy girl he had met right after college. She had walked up to him in a bar and introduced herself.

Prior to that, he had noticed her in the room and he had also noticed that she was beautiful and tall and nicely built. But after he had checked her out, he had thought she was a whole lot above his level.

And the next thing he knew, she was at his bar stool, introducing herself.

"What're you thinking about?"

"The night I met you."

Canace grinned. "Bold chick. . . right?"

"Yeah, and a big surprise."

Her head canted to the left. "Really. . . you were surprised?"

"You were just too beautiful to be interested in a guy like me."

"I thought you were cute. And, besides, you had a good face."

"A good face?"

Canace shrugged. "Honest. . . good person. My daddy always said that's what I should look for. And there you were, Mister Good Guy. I could tell that you were into me right away."

"Sure. . . of course, absolutely."

"No, really. I can read people."

Alto nodded. Yes, he knew that for sure. "Well, I have to get moving."

Her face became serious. "Really, Alto, be careful out there. Don't do anything crazy."

"I won't, honey." Alto slung his duffle bag over his right shoulder, opened the inside door and pushed open the screen door.

He stepped out onto the teleportico and turned.

Canace smiled and made a finger wave. "Good bye, honey. Say hello to Chan."

"I will." He pushed the screen door shut.

He could see Canace turn and hurry toward the stairs to the second floor. He supposed she would go up to the master bathroom, check her makeup and pick up her briefcase. Then she would come back down here and teleport to the law firm downtown.

Alto raised his left wrist. Then he tapped the ADDRESS button on his control.

With his index finger he swiped downward across the face of the wrist control until he saw "Chan Caracol, 2732 Sea View."

He tapped that address.

The area around him glowed blue. Gold bubbles appeared.

In a split second he was standing in another teleportico. The address to the left of the door was 2732.

The door opened and a beautiful young female stepped out. She pulled the door closed. "Hi. You must be Alto."

"Yes." Alto smiled and held out his right hand. "What's your name?"

"Olenus." She clasped Alto's hand.

He bowed slightly. "Good to meet you, Olenus."

"Same here, I'm sure. I have to go." She released his hand and stepped farther out onto the concrete pad.

She pivoted around and waved. Then she tapped her wrist control.

A blue column glowed around her, then gold. She vanished.

As usual, a good looking girl. But this one didn't seem to be the marrying type. Alto shrugged. "Maybe next time," he said in a low voice.

He stepped over to the door and touched the black button to the right of the casing.

From inside he could hear a muffled buzz.

Alto had been hoping that Chan would find himself a nice girl to marry. Of all the people Alto had ever met, this guy seemed to have a truly good heart. However, Chan didn't have any luck with women, and that was too bad.

The kid definitely dated a lot and he always seemed to find really pretty girls. Most of them were nice girls, but none of them seemed to be the type that would marry any time soon.

Chan was twenty-nine, which wasn't the end of the world of course. As you moved into your thirties, however, your options began to narrow. Alto was pretty sure that was true.

He wouldn't be so focused on getting Chan married, but he had worked in law enforcement long enough to see an awful lot of people - who really shouldn't be allowed to marry - get married. Then these same people would raise kids that were problems.

Sure, he had this attitude because he was a cop, but it did work that way. And one of the problems he had seen over and over again was that these couples who shouldn't have kids - not only had kids - they had lots of them.

The door opened. "Hey, Alto!"

"How's the kid doin'?"

"I'm good, Alto."

Alto pulled open the screen door and stepped inside. He swung his duffle bag to the tile floor of the foyer. "You don't mind if I leave this here, do you?"

Chan shrugged. "No, that's fine."

Alto slid the huge bag over to the side and dropped the strap. "I saw that cute chick you had here last night."

"Olenus?"

"Yeah. Man, she was real cute."

"Sure – she's cute. And she's pretty nice. I don't know if there's anything permanent with her."

Alto made a smile. "Hey, kid, time will tell."

Chan shrugged. "I guess." He placed his hand on Alto's shoulder. "Want some coffee before we teleport out of here?"

"Sure. I could use some. I ran short and forgot to buy a new bag of coffee beans. When I'm home, I do the shoppin' to give Canace a break and I screwed up. It was so bad, she wouldn't drink any."

Chan grinned. "I swear, Alto, your mind's getting weak. You're going to ruin your marriage over a bag of coffee beans."

"Now, don't give me any shit about bein' older than you and, by the way, my marriage is fine."

"Well you are older. You're not senile, but you are older. And I will admit that Canace is a beautiful, cool woman."

Alto chuckled. "You're always bustin' my balls."

Chan slapped his back. "Any chance I can get."

"Of course, the wife compliment helps. I tell you what. You should have a good woman like that for yourself."

Chan didn't reply to this remark. Instead, he led Alto through the living room into the dining room and finally into the kitchen.

Once there, he pointed toward the stools next to the breakfast bar. "Take a load off, old man." He winked at Alto.

"Hey, kid, there are advantages to bein' older and married – like we don't fuck around with every woman who's breathin'. That must get kind of complicated. Do you actually remember their names?"

Chan's white face turned pink. "Now that was a low shot, Alto."

"Hey, kid, this place is like a revolvin' door. I've met more cute girls out on your teleportico than anywhere else in the galaxy, and I've been to a lot of places in this galaxy."

"How do you like your coffee?"

"Black with one sugar."

Chan pulled the coffee pot out from under the brewer and poured coffee into a white mug. Then he placed the pot back and picked up the sugar bowl with a spoon sticking out of it.

He carried both of them over to the breakfast bar and placed them in front of Alto. "Olenus likes sugar too. Maybe you should ask her out, Alto."

"No, thanks. She's young enough to be my daughter. Besides I'm married to a cool, beautiful woman."

"Maybe Olenus is even young enough to be your granddaughter."

Alto grinned. "Hey, wise guy, that would mean that I got it on with some chick when I was only two years old."

"That's a disgusting idea." Chan poured a mug for himself. Then he walked around the end of the counter and sat next to Alto. "Have you heard anything about this journey?"

"Not a thing. Everybody's been mum about it. Can't figure out why, unless nobody else knows anythin' either." Alto dumped a heaping teaspoon of sugar into his mug of coffee. "Makes you wonder what this is all about."

Chan put his mug down on the counter. "Usually they tell the pilots, but I've been told exactly nothing."

"I sure as shit hope we're not goin' into one of those goddamn wormholes to nowhere."

"Why would the MSA do that to us?"

Alto shrugged. "Damned if I know, but I've heard scuttlebutt about the MSA settin' up some kind of program to try and figure out where those wormholes lead to."

"Nowhere."

"Oh, I know that's where they're supposed to go. Why else would they call them Wormholes to Nowhere or WTN? But what I'm sayin', Chan, is that I've been hearin' that some of these crazy-ass astrophysicists want some ships to do some explorin'."

"Where'd you hear that?"

"On my last assignment. There was talk all over the starship about it."

"I was on that starship and I didn't hear anything."

"Sometimes the pilots don't hear things the rest of us do."

"It may just be loose talk."

Alto shrugged. "Could be. I know I don't want to go into one of those damned WTNs again. Went into one with the crew of the Draconis Starship a couple of years back.

"We backed out the way we went in. Was strange because the damned time pieces on the starship got all screwed up. It was like we went ahead in time by a few minutes or somethin'. Real strange."

Captain Chan Carocol checked his wrist control. "We should get going."

Alto gulped down some of his coffee. "This is good, a lot better than mine was."

"I'm glad it is." Chan motioned with his head. "Go out to the teleportico. I'll be out in a minute. I have to set the lights and lock up."

"Sure thing." Alto gulped some more of the rich coffee and swallowed. This was really good stuff.

He slid off the stool and moved across the tile floor to the doorway to the dining room.

What surprised Alto was that even Chan didn't know where they were going. That was kind of odd. Usually the pilots knew everything.

The fact that Chan didn't know made him just a little uncomfortable. Alto wondered if maybe he should ask the commander.

Okanata was a good guy. Oh, he went by the book, but he didn't pull any crap on you.

Yeah, he'd ask Commander Okanata. He probably wouldn't get an answer, but it was worth a try.

CHAPTER SIX
"First Impressions"

Hyksos
MSA Base
Briefing Room #5
10M, Day 13, 6572
8:32 a.m.

Commander Seth Okanata scanned the briefing room. He noticed that one of the men appeared to be pale and tired. He tried to remember this guy's name.

He picked up the roster on the clipboard from its position on the table and studied it. It was either that Lieutenant Bucolus, the one in security or it was the mechanic, Sergeant Copan.

Then he remembered that Bucolus was a huge man. It was definitely Copan. The commander wondered what Copan had been doing last night. Probably a big party or some such thing.

He checked the roster again. He was a married man. Of course things at home might not be going so well. These people who worked in this business were gone for months at a time. That could be hard on marriages.

The door to the briefing room opened and Congressman Rahotpe stepped in and closed the door behind him.

Commander Okanata was going to invite the congressman up to the front row, but before he could do that Armant Rahotpe sat down in the back of the room.

The commander switched on the combination microphone, earphone angling out from the left side of his face. "Good morning." He nodded toward the back row. "Congressman Rahotpe, one of our ardent supporters is here to witness the briefing this morning."

Everyone in the room turned around to look.

"I would just ask the congressman not to discuss the details of this briefing with anyone until we have launched out of our retention orbit above the planet."

The congressman waved and smiled. "Of course, Seth!"

"Thank you, Congressman." Seth Okanata glanced around at the crew of his starship. "You might notice that we have a superb crew for this mission."

He swept his hand from left to right above the lectern. "So, where are we going? I'm sure that's the question on most of your minds.

"We have kept that from you for a very good reason. The last mission to this particular part of the galaxy occurred over fourteen hundred years ago. Yes, you heard me right – fourteen hundred years."

He scanned the faces in the room. "That mission was pretty close to a disaster. Several lives were lost, discipline on the starship, Orion Four, collapsed. There was a virtual mutiny and the first commander, a fellow named Zeus, was shot."

He smiled. "You can see why we would keep our destination a secret until this morning. Where are we going?" He waited for effect. Then he continued, "To planet Earth in the Orion Arm of the Milky Way Galaxy."

A hand shot up.

"Yes, Lieutenant Bucolus?"

"Isn't that Megall pirate territory?"

"Not exactly, Lieutenant."

"But, sir, they live in the Perseus Arm of the galaxy. Isn't that just outside the Orion Arm?"

"Yes, it is, Lieutenant."

Another hand went up.

"Yes, Captain Caracol?"

"Sir, I believe the last mission lost a shuttle to some kind of natural phenomenon on the planet Earth."

"That's correct, Captain. A volcano."

Commander Seth Okanata did not like the direction this briefing was going. Things were getting negative here. "Let me remind you of something. This is fourteen hundred years later. Unless that very primitive planet has prodigiously blazed forward to an age commensurate with our own, and therefore has our technology, I don't see any real difficulties for us.

"Frankly, the reason we have been hush, hush about this is because of the public perception that there is some kind of curse in that region of the galaxy because of the Orion Four mission. Curses are not real, at least that kind."

A chuckle scattered across the briefing room. Some people were smiling.

"I wanted to also inform you that we're going to stop at the planet of origin for the Mayan people, the planet Mars. We have to return a fallen comrade there to his home planet, Hyksos, a Lieutenant Coptos Gurab. He was lost and died in a giant sandstorm on Mars during the last journey into that solar system.

"Lieutenant Gurab deserves to be buried properly on his home planet, Hyksos, even if it is fourteen hundred years later."

The room was very silent.

"Those were much more primitive times and there were accidents. Apparently Lieutenant Gurab was a victim of one of those accidents."

Captain Caracol raised his hand again.

"Yes, Captain?"

"Sir, weren't the circumstances surrounding Gurab's death somewhat suspicious?"

"Yes, they were, Captain."

Commander Seth Okanata didn't want to dwell on these negative things. He turned to face the wall behind him and pressed a button on his narrow microphone.

The back wall lit up with a field of stars.

He glanced back over his right shoulder. "This is the area of the galaxy where we will be going."

He pointed his finger at the wall and a red laser dot appeared in a dark area among the stars. "We will be searching for a wormhole in this area of the Sagittarius Arm, the one we live in, to transport us over here to the Orion Arm."

The red dot moved to the right on the wall.

"The red dot is now at the current location of the planet Earth."

He turned around to face the small audience. "So why are we going to Earth? We will be assessing Earth's minerals and other raw materials to determine if it would be profitable to set up a colony on that planet and establish trade. We hope to trade raw materials for manufactured goods from Hyksos and other planets in the Grand Alliance."

He turned to face the picture on the wall.

The red dot moved outward in the galaxy. "This area out here is the Perseus Arm and, as Lieutenant Bucolus pointed out, is the home of the Megall pirates."

He faced the audience again. "Once we move through the wormhole into the Orion Arm of the galaxy we will put up our cloaking device immediately. I would do it sooner but, as you all know, our astrophysicists tell us that our cloaking devices might just interfere with our passage through wormholes.

"The starship must pass through with a clean hull – no obstacles, electronic or otherwise."

Commander Okanata pivoted around. "Are there any questions or comments?"

In the last row a hand shot up.

Seth Okanata moved to see who it was. "Yes, Congressman Rahotpe?"

"May I come up there, Seth, and address the crew?"

Seth felt a little uneasy about this. He realized that it was his typical desire to have control, but this congressman was a friend of the MSA. "Certainly, Congressman."

The tall, dark-skinned man rose from the back row and moved down the aisle to Seth's left. He walked with long and smooth confident strides.

It was at that moment Seth was reminded that the congressman had played professional soccer before entering politics.

Armant Rahotpe stepped up onto the dais. He reached out. "Could I borrow your microphone, Seth?"

"Sure." Seth fumbled with the lightweight bar attached to his ear and finally lifted it off and handed it to the congressman.

Then he stepped back away from the front of the dais.

The congressman slipped the microphone piece onto his left ear and moved forward toward the lectern. "Good morning. As you know by this time, I'm Congressman Rahotpe. I wanted to speak to you briefly this morning because there are some people in the legislature who are ready to make huge cuts to the MSA budget.

"You and I know that what the Mayan Space Administration does on a daily basis feeds the economy for all of Hyksos. What we need to do is have everyone we know – cousins, ex-wives, brothers, sisters, parents call their congressmen and tell them to vote against Congressional Bill number eight, one, three. . . nine one. Write that down – eight, one, three. . . nine, one.

"Believe me, this is important." The congressman waved and smiled. "Thank you and keep up the good work." He pulled the microphone, earpiece combination off of his ear and handed it back to Seth Okanata. Then he stepped off the dais and moved down the aisle.

Commander Seth Okanata clipped the microphone on his left ear. "If there are no other questions, this briefing is over."

Captain Caracol rose from his seat in the front row. "Attention!" He saluted.

The other crew members rose from their seats and saluted.

Seth Okanata raised the tip of his right hand to his right eyebrow and returned the salute.

The salutes in the room dropped.

Captain Caracol pivoted around. "Dismissed!"

Commander Seth Okanata noticed Lieutenant Masal Djoser and Lieutenant Elaina Djoser walking down the aisle side by side.

Seth didn't know how they happened to be assigned to the same starship. That was normally considered improper. Of course, Elaina Djoser had been recommended by Captain Sal Tikal and Seth had chosen her as a navigator.

Seth wondered if he shouldn't have a little chat with them about how to deal with this. There might be emergency situations where this could be a problem.

Commander Okanata had worked with Lieutenant Masal Djoser before. He was a very competent mechanic. But he had never worked with Lieutenant Elaina Djoser, the wife.

She certainly was an attractive woman. For some reason, they didn't really act like a married couple. Of course, first impressions were sometimes misleading.

CHAPTER SEVEN
"Secure"

Starship Cygnus
Bridge
10M, Day 20, 6572
9:01 a.m.

"We were supposed to be launched one minute ago. What's the problem?"

Lieutenant Elaina Djoser sat facing the navigation console. Sitting in front of her were the two pilots, Commander Okanata and Captain Sal Tikal.

She had journeyed with Tikal before. He was a very competent pilot in the manual sense. He had great hands and good instincts. She had seen him in action when there was trouble in a braking flyby one time, several years back.

They had gotten too close to the intended braking planet. Tikal had acted instinctively while the commander had just sat dumbfounded. She was trying to remember that commander's name. Was it Menelaus? Yes, she believed it was.

"Sir, the engines aren't at the proper power level," said the speaker in the overhead above the pilots' consoles.

"Why not, Lieutenant?"

"We had some last minute adjustments, sir."

"Fine tuning the engine, Lieutenant Djoser?"

"Yes, sir."

"Very good, Lieutenant."

"We should be ready in just a few seconds, sir. I will give you a heads-up when we're at full power."

"Very good, Lieutenant."

For Elaina, it was strange to hear her husband's voice over the radio system in the starship. She had never journeyed with him before.

Her relationship with Masal had been very different. Back when they first got together, he had been this attentive, sweet guy. However, over the last four years or so, he had become this strange, angry person.

She didn't know where that came from. She had suggested that they go to a marriage counselor. He had refused. To a certain point, she could tolerate the occasional outbursts of anger, but sometimes when he was angry, he would hit her.

"All systems ready for launch, Commander."

"Very good, Lieutenant." The commander flicked a black switch. "All crew members, this is your commander. We will begin the launch in ten minutes and counting. Make sure you are strapped into a proper safety seat." The commander stared at his console. "Will begin countdown in eight minutes."

There was silence.

Elaina thought that going back to their home planet in the Orion Belt of the galaxy would be pretty neat. There was a problem, however. They had to find a wormhole that would move them from the Sagittarius Belt out to the Orion Belt and wormholes were unpredictable. Some of them led to blackness – Wormholes to Nowhere or WTN. She had dealt with them before. They were dangerous and frightening.

"This is your commander. Beginning countdown. . . ten, nine, eight, seven, six, five, four, three, two, one – fire!"

Elaina heard the loud click of a switch on the pilots' console.

There was a rumble and the starship shook.

Elaina was slammed into the seat cushion. She felt pain in her left side. It was that rib again. Masal had punched her really hard there several months ago. She wondered if it would ever heal properly.

The MSA doctor, who had seen her recent X-rays, said she had a cracked rib and it would heal eventually. Then he had asked about her marriage. Finally, he had told her the crack was in an odd place and that none of the other ribs in that area were damaged.

He had asked her if she had run into some pointed object. She didn't answer. Then he said, "I'd see a marriage counselor, Mrs. Djoser."

Unfortunately, that was out of the question. Masal wouldn't do it. Elaina just hoped there wasn't an incident during this journey. It would be so embarrassing.

She had learned to live with the occasional abuse. Yet it was as if her life had come to a halt. She had wondered about children. He didn't want any.

Elaina sometimes found herself staring at other married couples she would see in shopping centers or at grocery stores. They were friendly partners, sometimes with small children.

She would find herself smiling when she saw them. Then the smile would turn to sadness. She would realize that she could never have that, not with Masal.

She had considered asking him for divorce, but she was afraid of him. Maybe she should just file for divorce after this journey. She had a furlough coming when this was over. Maybe that would be the time to act.

Without warning, the pressure let up and the pain in Elaina's side eased to a pointed burn.

She knew what would happen next. The burn would morph into a kind of hot numbness. Then by the end of the shift it would be gone.

She supposed she should take some time off to let that heal. However, she needed to keep working so her navigation skills were up to date. She was a good navigator and she wanted to keep that reputation. She was sure her reputation was the reason Commander Okanata had requested her for this journey.

"Lieutenant Elaina Djoser, are we on course for the wormhole portal?"

"I will check, sir." Elaina's fingers rattled across the keyboard. She stared at the new screen in front of her. "Yes, sir. We're directly on course. We should arrive there in sixty-two hours, nineteen point three minutes."

"Have you entered this portal in any of your recent journeys, Lieutenant?"

"No, sir."

"Then you don't know the characteristics of this wormhole?"

"No I don't, sir."

"I can't find anybody else who knows anything about it either, Lieutenant."

"May I make a suggestion, sir?"

"Of course, Lieutenant."

"Perhaps, sir, it would be wise to seek out another portal with our sensors."

"For the time being, Lieutenant, let's make this our target. If this portal proves useless, then we'll adjust our course to an alternative one."

"Yes, sir."

"And, Lieutenant. . ."

"Yes, sir."

"Thank you for the constructive suggestion."

"You're welcome, sir." Elaina was baffled by this last remark. She had never had a commander say that kind of thing before. Maybe this guy was going to actually be nice, even polite.

Her first impression of Commander Okanata was that he looked conservative and straight laced, a by-the-book starship commander. Maybe she had been wrong.

She didn't mind the by-the-book commanders. At least you knew where you stood, but some of them were really rigid. Sometimes they were that way because they were young - probably a little insecure. Okanata didn't seem that young – maybe in his mid-forties.

"Activate the cloaking device, Captain Tikal."

"Yes, sir, Commander."

There was a subtle humming sound. It dissipated gradually into silence.

"Can you take the helm, Captain?"

"Yes, sir."

Commander Okanata rose from the left seat and walked around the console in front of Elaina. Now he was standing on her left.

She turned to him. "Is there something you wanted to see me about, sir?"

"Yes, Lieutenant." The commander crouched down next to her. "I wanted to arrange a time when you and your husband could come to Conference Room #3 on our off shift," he said in a low voice.

Elaina's stomach tightened. "Is there a problem, sir?"

He shook his head. "No, no, nothing like that, Lieutenant. It's just rather odd that a married couple is serving aboard the same starship." He reached out and patted her back. "Don't worry. It's just that we have to discuss some things. That's all." He smiled. "Okay?"

She smiled back. "Sure, Commander."

Commander Okanata patted her back again. "Good." He rose to his feet. "Carry on, Lieutenant."

"Yes, sir."

At that moment, what struck Elaina in a very deep way was how kind this commander seemed to be. She felt warm and secure.

Actually she hadn't felt that warm and secure in a very long time. Oh, she was an independent woman, right enough. Yet sometimes she liked the feeling that someone had her back, like a husband for instance.

But with Masal she didn't feel that anymore. In fact, sometimes her husband scared her.

CHAPTER EIGHT
"Chicken"

Hyksos
Memphis
Driving Range
10M, Day 20, 6572
10:14 a.m.

Lycia had never had so much fun. Well, maybe she had a lot of fun back when she was in high school, although she had not come out here to the driving range until she met Hector her senior year.

The thing with Hector was that it was always about the car, not her. Or at least that's the way she remembered it.

With Cadmus it was all about the fun. He didn't give a shit about his car. He had fixed it up just enough to drive and have fun. To hell with whether the parts were genuine antiques. He was going to drive it and have a good time.

Did she feel guilty about doing this with Cadmus? Well, maybe a little, but she had given nine long years to that marriage with Hector and what did she have to show for it? Her husband was never home. She didn't have any social life.

So, here she was on a sunny morning with a fun guy out at the driving range. It was really quite harmless.

A green car whizzed by the parking lot. This lot was one of the areas where you could teleport to the driving range. They had just arrived here.

Lycia watched that green car sweep along at high speed upward on the long gradual grade.

Off to the right was a patch of woods. She had often wondered what it would be like to get it on with Cadmus in those woods – kind of wild like, the way the animals did it.

Lycia realized she had better stop thinking about those things or she and Cadmus really could end up in the woods doing the dirty boogie.

But she had been a good mother through all this. She couldn't feel guilty about that part. The kids had a good babysitter. It was the one who cost more, the one that was really good with both kids. Lycia may have done that out of guilt, or maybe she did it just because she was a good mom.

She liked to believe she was a good mom. That was an important part of the way she thought about herself. At the same time, she did need to have fun. Everybody needed fun once in a while and with Hector, she wasn't having a whole lot of it.

When Hector was home it sure as hell wasn't fun. It was all about the antique cars and the kids, never about her. Honestly, they had no damned social life at all.

Cadmus wanted to spend time with her. Sure – sometimes they did the dirty boogie together, but there were other things they did too. They had danced together at this one club out here on the driving range. They had just had themselves the best damn time that night when they danced. Hell, she always had a good time with Cadmus, no matter what.

"So, beautiful, where do you want to go today?"

Lycia shrugged. "I don't know. What about that straightaway up on the plateau. Have you ever tried to see what this little piece of shit can do up there?"

"Hey, don't call my car a piece of shit, but, no, I never took her above eighty."

"I'll bet this little bugger will go over a hundred twenty kilometers an hour."

"Maybe at one time, but I don't know about now."

"You chicken, Cadmus?"

The big man smirked. "Come on, don't pull that stuff with me. You know what I'll do." Cadmus opened the driver's door and dropped into the bucket seat. "Come on, babe." He stared at her. "You scared or somethin'?" He slammed the door.

Now that she thought about it, Lycia was just a little bit scared. Maybe she shouldn't have gotten on his case like that. Cadmus tended to overreact when she ripped on him about anything to do with his strength or manhood.

She pulled open the passenger door. Then she dropped into the bucket seat and slammed the door.

With her left hand, Lycia reached over her right shoulder for the safety belt.

"You gonna belt yourself in?"

"Don't you think it's a smart idea?"

He shrugged. "I guess, but I wouldn't want to be belted into this thing if it caught fire or went into the water or somethin'. Hey – just suppose it flipped over. Would you want to be hangin' upside down?"

"Okay, let me just say, Cadmus, I hope I can trust you not to do somethin' stupid."

He turned the ignition. "Of course I won't do anythin' stupid."

He flipped the shifter back into DRIVE and jammed down the accelerator.

The little car lurched forward and sped out of the parking lot onto the blacktop road.

Lycia reached over with her left hand and pressed down the lock on her door. It was just a matter of feeling safer. She didn't want a door to fly open, or something worse.

The little car raced up the long, sloping grade.

Lycia glanced at the speedometer. They were traveling at just below seventy kilometers an hour. That was all right.

She leaned forward and checked the right outside mirror.

There was nobody behind them. That was good because Cadmus liked to race with people who passed him.

Lycia leaned back in the seat and let her hair blow in the wind. That was the neat thing about a convertible. Being out in the air and feeling the sunshine and the wind. That was great.

The sky above was blue and it was not going to rain. Things were good. She would just sit here and let the wind blow her hair and she would enjoy the ride.

The little car rose up over the crest of the hill.

Ahead of them was a flat strip of black pavement with tall grass on either side. On the right, far off in the distance, were clusters of leafy softwood trees and pines.

Lycia tried to remember what Hector had said about how long this was. Maybe seven kilometers – something like that. She didn't remember exactly.

"Okay – so here's the trick. I'm gonna speed up and I'm gonna keep on speedin' up until you beg me to stop. Got it?"

Lycia grinned. "You're on." When she said that, she felt a little flutter of excitement, but that's the way it was with this guy – exciting.

Cadmus tromped down on the accelerator.

The electric motor whined and the little convertible lurched forward.

Lycia checked the speedometer. The black needle was creeping up toward one hundred kilometers an hour.

"Hey, this little bugger's still got some juice."

Even though they were going fast, Lycia felt very safe. The road ahead was straight and there didn't appear to be anyone in front of them. That might complicate things.

At that moment a larger blue car traveling in the other direction whizzed by in the left lane.

"How fast was he goin'?" she shouted.

Cadmus shrugged. "Maybe a hundred! Maybe a hundred ten!" He glanced over at her. There was a smirk on his mouth. "Any time, babe!"

Lycia turned away and stared out the windshield as if she didn't care how fast they were going. Before she turned she had noticed the speedometer was reading just a little bit over a hundred kilometers an hour.

The air above the windshield roared and her hair was twisting around her face. It felt like someone was pulling it, not hard, just pulling a little bit.

She glanced at the speedometer again. The little black needle was approaching one hundred twenty kilometers an hour. What was strange was that Lycia felt very safe. The car seemed to be steady. The only thing was the roar of the wind around her ears.

Cadmus jerked his right hand away from the wheel. "Shocks!"

"What?"

He glanced at her. "I'm gettin' shocks!"

Lycia wondered if that wasn't his way of chickening out. She turned away and stared out the windshield.

Up ahead she could see the road curve to the left, but it was still quite far away. Beyond the curve was the bluff. She remembered that because there was a road that led off this road into the parking lot right up to the fence that overlooked that bluff above the Poseidon Sea.

"They stopped!"

"The shocks?"

"Yeah!"

Lycia faced the windshield again. She was sure that Cadmus was going to push this little car right up to that curve before he slowed down.

The curve was coming toward them faster now.

Lycia was beginning to wonder if Cadmus was going to slow down at all. Maybe he was going to just shoot off on this side road to the parking lot and come to a screeching halt near the fence or some other stupid thing.

"It won't slow down!"

Lycia turned. "What?"

"My foot's off the accelerator. It won't slow down!"

"Shut it off!" She pointed at the ignition key on the steering column.

Cadmus reached around the wheel to turn the key.

A blue bolt of light shot across to his index finger.

"God!"

His body thrashed.

The car jerked to the left and flipped.

Lycia was sure the little convertible was airborne. She felt like she was flying below it. She could see black pavement over her right shoulder. It was very close.

Her shoulder slammed. Pain shot through her whole body. Her head jerked and smashed hard. Pain radiated through her skull.

CHAPTER NINE
"The Next Furlough"

Starship Cygnus
Conference Room #3
10M, Day 20, 6572
6:23 p.m.

"**A**re you havin' trouble with the commander?"

Elaina shook her head. "No. Are you?"

Masal stared at her. "You've got to be kiddin'. I'm the best mechanic in the MSA."

"I was just asking." Elaina stared at the closed door on the far side of Conference Room #3. There was a security guard standing there.

She was sure that the guard wasn't there normally. The commander had apparently ordered him here for this occasion.

She had just finished her shift, the Green Shift. The Orange Shift began at 6:00 p.m.

Why the commander wanted to see them was not at all clear to Elaina. She hoped it had to do with the fact that normally a married couple was not assigned to the same starship at the same time. "I think it has to do with us being married."

Masal stared at her. Then he shrugged. "Could be."

She knew that was his way of agreeing with her without giving her credit for coming up with the right answer.

"I told Hector it was kind of weird that they let us on the same starship at the same time. I never heard of it before. He said he hadn't either."

Hector was the other mechanic onboard. They were friends back on Hyksos too. They were both into antique cars. In fact, they were planning to start a company for rebuilding antique cars. From what she could tell, however, that wasn't going so well.

The door to the conference room slid into the wall to the right and Commander Okanata stepped over the curved threshold and moved into the conference room.

Elaina rose to her feet.

Masal did as well, but he stood up more slowly.

Elaina recognized it as his way of saying that he was really very smart and shouldn't have to stand up for a starship commander.

The commander turned to the soldier at the door. "Private, step outside and don't let anyone in unless it's an emergency."

The soldier saluted. "Yes, sir."

Okanata returned the salute and moved across the conference room toward Elaina and Masal. He smiled. "Good evening. I won't keep you two very long. I realize that both of you just finished your shift."

The commander nodded toward them. "Sit down, please."

Elaina sat in the second seat from the end of the table, where she had sat before. Masal always liked the end seat, but this time he was next to her in the last one on this side. Of course that was a better seat than hers. He always seemed to get those better seats.

"You're both on the Green Shift due to my editing the shift order." He looked at Masal. "I wanted your wife on with me because she's an excellent navigator." He turned to Elaina. "And I thought that the two of you would be much more comfortable working on the same shift. If you were both assigned to the bridge, it would be a different matter."

"Thank you, Commander." Elaina made a smile for him.

His blue eyes met hers. "You're more than welcome, Lieutenant Djoser."

Masal said nothing.

Elaina thought it was kind of rude of him not to thank the commander, but she had and she was happy she had because it was the right thing to do. The commander had done something kind for them.

"I wanted to bring you two here, this evening, just to go over some basic things. I don't know how you both got assigned to the same starship, but I found out so late that I couldn't make a change without getting a lot of flak from the MSA. These days they don't like a lot of problems because they're watching their budget so closely. Everyone is paranoid about spending."

He put his fist to his mouth and cleared his throat. "Enough said about that. What I want to remind you of is that in emergency situations, you may be separated and you may have to sit and wait while your better half is in danger."

He gestured toward Masal with his right hand. "For instance, Masal might have to do some dangerous repair work, even an EVA, which can be very dangerous, and you, Elaina, will have to function to full capacity, even though he might be in danger."

He looked at Elaina, then Masal. "And, Masal, you might have to be alone for a whole shift in your compartment if Elaina is needed past her shift on the bridge."

He held up both hands, palms outward. "Now, I do fully realize that you are aware of these things. However, we are running a starship and I must have your complete compliance with these stringent guidelines. When you are on duty, you are on duty and that is your primary responsibility. At that time, your spouse is not your primary responsibility. Is that clear?"

Elaina nodded. "Yes, sir."

Masal didn't respond.

"Do you have a question, Masal?"

He shook his head.

Commander Okanata focused on Masal's eyes for several seconds. Then he turned to Elaina. "I know both of you have served on several starships, but serving together is unique. It poses new challenges."

He faced Masal again. "Both of you are top people in your fields. That's why you were assigned to this journey." He looked back and forth between them. "This might just be a rather challenging journey. We hope everything is nominal, but you know that nominal is not always what happens."

He looked at Elaina again. "Are there any questions?"

"No, sir."

He smiled at her. "Very good." He turned to Masal. "You, Masal?"

Masal shook his head.

Commander Okanata rose from his seat. "Then you are dismissed."

Elaina rose to her feet. "Yes, sir." She saluted.

The commander smiled and returned the salute. "Have a good off shift. Get some rest."

"Yes, sir." Elaina dropped her salute hand. She was aware that Masal had risen next to her. She didn't know whether he had saluted or not. She would guess he hadn't.

He had this thing about superior officers. He thought they had no right to tell him what to do, which, of course, was not the case.

Commander Okanata moved across the room to the door.

It opened.

He turned, then smiled and raised his hand in a wave.

Elaina raised her hand and smiled at him.

Okanata stepped out and the door slid shut.

"You're pretty tight with the commander."

Elaina's smile vanished. She turned to her husband. She shook her head. "No. He's just nice. Some of the commanders I've worked with have been real jerks. It feels good to have someone who's polite and friendly."

"Don't get too friendly."

Elaina put her right hand on her right hip and tipped her head. "Masal, why would you say something like that? You know I don't mess around."

"Just don't or you'll be damn sorry." He marched away across the conference room to the door.

It sucked open to the right and Masal stepped over the curved threshold into the corridor.

In the next second the door closed.

It occurred to Elaina that even though the commander's intentions were really kind when he placed Masal and her on the same shift, things between them were not going to change.

She had pictured Masal and herself walking down the corridor side by side toward the elevator and chatting like those couples she had seen in the malls in Memphis. That wasn't going to happen.

She sometimes wondered why she stayed in this marriage. She did have a furlough coming after this journey. Masal would be on duty again and have to leave.

Maybe she should see a lawyer and probably she shouldn't let Masal know. He might hit her or something. She should definitely see a lawyer during her next furlough.

CHAPTER TEN

"The Smile"

Starship Cygnus
Compartment 306
10M, Day 21, 6572
8:12 a.m.

Commander Seth Okanata had left Captain Tikal at the helm of the starship. He didn't like to do that, but he had received this coded message just after he had settled in for his shift.

He exited the elevator on Level 3 and moved down the corridor on the even number side. He had already passed 302 and was approaching 304.

Seth Okanata never liked these personal tasks, especially when they involved tragedies.

He stopped in front of Compartment 306.

One reason he was so unwilling to leave the bridge was that they were approaching the wormhole, the one which they hoped would provide access to the Orion Arm of the galaxy.

Nobody had been to that specific part of the galaxy in over a thousand years. The last journey to and from that solar system had been long before the MSA commanders had begun to use wormholes. Therefore, there was no record to use as a guide.

What the astrophysicists did was to choose an area which fit the "normal" pattern for wormholes and had access to particular parts of the galaxy. The problem was there was no normal pattern actually. It was all rather random.

Of course, once you had found a wormhole that worked, you marked it with your onboard electronics. Thereafter it became the regular access road to that place in the galaxy, so to speak.

Now he had to report bad news to one of his crew members. He hated this part of his duties as a commander – notifying people of tragedies. Besides, this man had just gotten off duty and would be settling down for some much needed rest.

There was no getting around tragedies, however. One had to face them and deal with them. He had learned that as a child when his parents had been killed in an aircraft accident on Hyksos.

Commander Okanata raised his hand to the black button to the right of the door to Compartment 306. He pressed the button.

There was a muffled buzzing sound.

Seth hoped this man wasn't in bed already. He heard the rhythmic thump of muffled footsteps. He was sure Copan was now at the peephole lens in the top half of the compartment door.

The door hissed and slid open into the wall on Okanata's left.

"Good morning, Sergeant."

The man saluted. "Good mornin' to you, sir."

Commander Okanata carelessly returned the salute. "It's too early for formalities, Sergeant. May I come in?"

The shorter man stepped aside. "Sure. Come in, Commander."

Seth Okanata stepped over the curved threshold into the compartment.

The door slid closed.

"Make yourself at home, sir." Sergeant Hector Copan motioned to the safety seats in the living room area next to the kitchenette.

"Thank you, Sergeant." Seth Okanata crossed the small room and dropped into the nearest of the four pedestal seats. He looked up at Hector Copan. "You may sit, Sergeant. This isn't formal."

The short dark-skinned man sat in the seat next to the commander.

"Sergeant, I don't know how to say this, except to get right to the point. I have received a coded message from Hyksos via our text messaging system. It took us several minutes to unscramble the message or I would have been here sooner."

Commander Okanata pulled himself together and looked directly into Hector Copan's eyes. "Your wife has been killed in an automobile accident on the driving range outside of Memphis. She was apparently with a man, a Cadmus Menon, I suppose a friend of the two of you. Both occupants of the automobile died instantly. The car apparently went out of control from excessive speed."

He focused on Copan's eyes. "I'm very sorry, Sergeant. If I didn't need you on duty during the next Orange Shift, I would give you leave, but I can't spare you."

"I understand, sir."

Commander Okanata looked at Hector Copan. "I'm really sorry to have to be the one to report this to you, Sergeant. You're a good man and a real asset to this crew."

"Thank you, sir."

"If you want to see the grief counselor, we can send Doctor Neleus to your compartment. Bokar Neleus is a very kindly man and might give you some ways of coping with this, Sergeant."

"I'm good, sir."

Seth Okanata was amazed that this man didn't seem to be showing any signs of grief whatsoever. Perhaps it was the shock of this event. After all, it was very sudden and he was sure it was totally unexpected.

The commander rose to his feet.

Sergeant Hector Copan stood up.

Commander Okanata held out his right hand. "My condolences, Hector."

Sergeant Hector Copan clasped the commander's hand and shook it once firmly. "Thank you, sir."

Commander Okanata walked across the small compartment to the door. Then he turned. "If there's anything you want or need, Hector, feel free to ask me directly."

"Thank you, sir."

Seth Okanata pressed his hand against the blue light panel to the right of the door casing.

The pocket door hissed and slid with a rattle to the right.

He stepped out into the corridor.

The commander was going to turn and wave or smile or something, but he was still stunned because of this man's almost passive response to hearing about his wife's death. He assumed that, probably, it was better just to leave.

The door rattled shut behind him.

Seth Okanata turned and stared at the door with the number 306 in large black figures directly above it. Perhaps he should send Bokar Neleus up to see Hector. He would have to give that idea some thought.

Seth Okanata walked with precise steps down the corridor toward the elevator. He would return to the bridge.

When he thought of going to the bridge these days, it made him smile. He wasn't smiling because he liked his job, although he certainly did. He was smiling because he would see somebody there, somebody who always smiled at him when he walked through the bridge doorway.

If she didn't, it almost felt like Seth was being chastised and, really, it would only happen because Elaina was so focused on her work that she hadn't noticed him coming into the bridge.

Yes, lately he had been thinking of her as Elaina, not Lieutenant Djoser. She was just so pretty and so charming. When he thought about her husband, Seth found it difficult to imagine this beautiful, elegant woman with that man.

Masal Djoser was a talented mechanic for sure, but he wasn't a very refined person. In fact, he came off as somewhat surly. Seth had no idea what that was about. He supposed some people were just that way.

Yes, he was looking forward to seeing Elaina's smile.

CHAPTER ELEVEN

"Somebody"

Hyksos
Memphis
4281 Aswan Street
10M, Day 21, 6572
9:32 a.m.

Niobe Lysander had stayed the night at the Copan house with the children and she had gotten both Charis and Aten off to school this morning.

She had no idea why Mrs. Copan hadn't come back last night. The woman had been gone all day. It would mean a really great chunk of money because Niobe had sat with the kids all day yesterday, but this was kind of weird.

Of course, Mrs. Copan had been acting kind of strange lately anyway. She had been running around with that guy named Cadmus, and she was married.

All marriages were not perfect. She knew that for sure. Her parents usually got along most of the time. Her mother wasn't the easiest person to live with. She was controlling.

Usually she and her mother got along fine, but sometimes Niobe had to play her to make sure things didn't get out of hand. Yes, she did things behind her mother's back. Why? Because sometimes her mother was totally unreasonable.

Niobe would probably get married someday, but it sure wasn't going to be to some controlling guy, no matter how cool he was.

She was taking classes downtown at Memphis University to become an elementary teacher and as soon as she had her degree, she was gone.

She wanted to move to Thebes. She had heard that the island city was really a cool place to live. People had warned her that it was expensive, but she didn't care. She wanted to live there anyway.

Why? Well, because it was a beautiful city. Memphis was all right in certain parts, but only okay down where she lived in the poorer section. Mostly it was because she wanted to be on her own, away from her mother.

If she was going to get married someday, she didn't want her kids growing up around her controlling mother. Sure she would visit her parents. Her father would be great with grandchildren. He was really sweet.

Niobe walked into the small living room and moved up to the front window. She had expected Mrs. Copan to teleport in last night and wake her up and tell her to go home.

It had never happened.

Outside the morning was sunny. The sidewalk was still wet from the morning dew.

Niobe had made a lunch for Charis and had stood at the front door while she teleported to Second Avenue Elementary. An hour later she had watched Aten teleport to preschool.

Now she was waiting for Mrs. Copan, and she needed to be paid. She could only wait so long. She had a math class at ten forty-five.

She might just have to lock up and leave and get her money later. She figured that Mrs. Copan owed her at least fifty dollars. Actually, seventy would be more like it. After all, she had been here all night.

She had lay down on the couch and covered herself with a blanket, figuring that Mrs. Copan would come at any time.

Actually she had slept on this couch, although it wasn't the best night's sleep she'd ever had. She kept waking every time she heard any noise. Then she would get up and check the kids, just to make sure they were all right.

In a way, she wasn't surprised that Mrs. Copan had become kind of weird. She always seemed unhappy, and Niobe couldn't understand why.

After all, Mrs. Copan was married to a guy who worked for the MSA. He was gone a lot but he was real nice, and kind of nice looking in a short muscular way, if you liked short muscular men. She didn't care about that one way or the other.

She just knew he was nice. Mister Copan was always nice to her and he would ask her how the college courses were coming. He treated her like she was somebody.

On the other hand, Mrs. Copan always seemed to be angry and she had been going away a lot lately, probably spending time with that

Cadmus guy. Niobe wondered if Mrs. Copan was cheating on her husband. That would be too bad because Mr. Copan seemed real nice.

Outside, on the teleportico a column of blue light appeared.

Niobe smiled. "She's here."

She moved away from the window and walked over to the front door. Then she pushed down the lever handle and pulled the door open.

Outside stood an elderly woman. The woman moved with deliberate steps to the screen door and pulled it open. "You must be Niobe."

"Yes, ma'am."

The elderly woman stepped inside.

Niobe moved out of her way.

"Can you stay the day?"

"No, ma'am. I have a college math class in less than an hour."

The old woman made a wan smile. "I'm Hector's – Mister Copan's mother, Themis Copan. I'm afraid somethin' terrible has happened, Niobe. Mrs. Copan, Lycia, was killed in an accident yesterday. It was out at the drivin' range. I don't mean to be disgustin', but I was told there was so little left of them that identification was real difficult and took some time.

"I was notified late last night and I knew you were here. I should have called but I knew the children would want to speak to me and then I'd have to tell them. I didn't want to do that over the phone. I thought it would be better to wait until today and do it in person."

"I'm really sorry, Mrs. Copan."

The woman made a brief smile. "Thank you. It's too bad. I don't think Lycia knew what she had with her marriage to Hector and their wonderful children. Apparently she was runnin' around with some guy." The old woman shrugged. "That's not important now – water over the dam."

She turned to Niobe. "Can you be back here at the house when the children come home? I may need some help."

"Yes, ma'am, I can come."

"Terrible thing this is. Those poor children. Their daddy's millions of miles away or he'd be here to comfort them."

"Yes, ma'am. I can help. They're really sweet children and I get along with them just fine. I'm sure they're going to be very upset so I'll be here to help, ma'am."

Themis Copan smiled. "Hector said you were a real nice young lady."

Niobe could feel her face flush with embarrassment. "I like the children."

"How much did Lycia usually pay you?"

"Fifty dollars – but I was here all night, ma'am."

Themis Copan nodded. Then she swung her small purse off her shoulder and opened it. She held out a small plastic token. "All I have is twenty. Will that be enough for now?"

Niobe didn't want to be shorted on this job. She needed the money, but things were hard for this old lady. "Yes, ma'am. You can pay me the rest later."

"I will do that, Niobe."

"Yes, ma'am." Niobe took the token. "Thank you."

"What time do the kids return from school?"

"Aten will be back at one o'clock. Charis will be home at two-thirty."

"Can you come back here at two?"

"Sure."

The old woman smiled at her. "Thank you and have a good day at the college."

"Thank you, ma'am." Niobe pulled open the front door and walked out to the teleportico.

She pulled the door closed behind her.

Now she had to go home. She never looked forward to that. If it wasn't her mother trying to run every detail of her life, it was her younger brother who thought he was going to conquer the world.

Agrius thought he was smarter than everyone else. He was ditching classes at the high school and expecting that he was somehow going to do something big in this world. The only thing big in his future was a surprise. The surprise? He was going to end up nowhere.

Niobe just wanted out of that house, and as soon as possible. The only person she would miss was her father.

It was time to head home for a shower and fresh clothes. Then to class.

Niobe swiped down the face of her wrist control until she saw 1922 Lake Street. She tapped it.

A column of hazy blue surrounded her.

CHAPTER TWELVE
"The Cow Picture"

Hyksos
Memphis
4281 Aswan Street
10M, Day 21, 6572
2:03 p.m.

Themis Copan was actually pleased that she could keep busy. This whole thing was so tragic for her grandkids.

She had never been a big fan of her daughter-in-law. Right from the beginning she had felt this instability about her, but Themis knew she had brought her son up right, so just maybe Hector could make it work. That's what she had hoped for, but not everything happened the way you wanted in this life.

Now there was this mess and somehow she was going to have to take care of the funeral arrangements and all of that terribly emotional stuff. She would do it for Hector and her grandchildren. That's who she was doing it for, not for Lycia. She would have to remember that and it would make everything better.

"When's Mommy comin' home?"

Themis turned to the small male voice. She made a smile. "Honey, not for a while, Aten. Why don't you go play with your computer game. I'll let you know."

She was going to say that she would let him know when his mother got home, but Themis couldn't bring herself to lie like that. She had done enough lying to him already.

"It's Charis!" Little Aten pointed toward the picture window which looked out upon the teleportico.

The figure in the blue column of light on the teleportico became clearer.

"It's Niobe!" the little boy shouted. He ran to the front door.

Themis had been wondering all day if she could make an arrangement with this nice girl.

Because of the funeral plans and such, Themis would be in and out of here a lot. She wondered if it would be possible for this Niobe to actually live here for a few days, maybe even a week. It would make everything so much easier if she could.

The door opened and Niobe Lysander stepped inside. She closed the door and crouched down in front of Aten. "Hi, little man. What did you do at school today?"

The small boy folded his arms across his chest. "Well, I drew pictures a lot and I drew a horse and a cow and even a chicken, but Mrs. Ajax said the horse was the best."

"Did you bring them home?"

The little boy turned and pointed. "Grandma put them on the fridge."

"Well, let's go look at them. I'd like to see your drawings, Aten."

"Mrs. Ajax said the horse was the best but I think the cow is good too. Maybe I'll become a drawer of pictures for the president someday."

"Sure, why not?"

"Niobe. . ."

The girl's smile vanished and she turned to Themis. "Yes, ma'am?"

"Can we talk for a minute?"

"Sure, ma'am." She crouched down to Aten again. "You go ahead into the kitchen. I'll be right there to look at your pictures. I especially want to see that cow you said was so good."

"Mrs. Ajax is wrong about the cow. She's pretty smart and she's nice but she's wrong about the cow."

"I'm sure she is, Aten. You go ahead, honey."

"Okay." He walked to the kitchen doorway. Then he turned. "Don't keep me waitin'."

Niobe grinned. "I won't, your highness."

"What's 'your highness'?"

"It's just a little joke, Aten."

"It isn't very funny."

"You're right. It isn't." Niobe motioned with her right hand. "You go ahead. I'll be right there."

"Okay." The little boy scampered into the kitchen.

"Niobe, I'm gonna be all caught up in arrangements for the funeral and such. I was wonderin' if you'd be willin' to move right into this house and help me with these kids."

The young woman stared at her. "Move in?"

"Yes. I mean – if you have to check with your parents, that would be fine, but it's just that I know I'm gonna be real busy with everythin' else and these kids need some kind of normal things goin' on. They need somebody here all the time, especially when they're not in school."

"I do have college classes, ma'am, so I'll have to work around those."

"I can call your parents if you need me to do that."

"That won't be necessary, Mrs. Copan."

"Niobe!"

Themis turned.

In the doorway stood Aten with his arms folded across his chest. He had a stern expression on his little face.

Themis would have broken out laughing if the circumstances had been different.

"Niobe, you've been keepin' me waitin'."

The girl crossed to Aten and crouched down. "I'm sorry, Aten, but you see your grandma and I have important things to talk about. As soon as I'm done talking with your grandma, I'll come into the kitchen and see your pictures – promise."

The little boy's head canted to the left and he squinted. "You're not joshin' me, are you?"

Niobe grinned. "No, sweetie. I'm not joshing. I'll be right in as soon as I'm finished talking with your grandma."

The little boy shook his right index finger in Niobe's face. "Just don't keep me waitin'."

She kissed his forehead. Then she grinned. "I won't, honey."

He placed his hands on his hips and his head canted to the left. "You sure?"

"Yes, Aten, I'm sure." She rose to her feet. "You go into the kitchen. I'll be there as soon as I'm through with your grandma."

"Okay." The little boy charged into the kitchen.

Niobe turned to Themis. "Mrs. Copan, I know how hard it will be for these kids. I really like them a lot and they're going to need some-body around, like you say. So I can stay. I'll have to go home and get my clothes and my books and everything."

Themis was touched by the obvious close feelings this girl had for her grandchildren. "That would be wonderful, my dear. It'll make things so much easier."

Themis thought a minute. "Maybe you can sleep in the office down here. It has a Murphy bed in the wall. I've slept there before. You can use the main closet for your clothes."

"That would be fine, ma'am. Little Aten will be real upset but I worry most about Charis."

Themis nodded. "Yes, she's older. It'll be hard for her. I just wish her father was here. She really loves Hector."

"I can stay as long as you need me, Mrs. Copan."

Themis found that she was smiling. This was a great relief. "Thank you, Niobe. That's wonderful."

CHAPTER THIRTEEN
"The Question"

Starship Cygnus
Bridge
10M, Day 21, 6572
10:21 p.m.

Commander Seth Okanata had been at the helm of the starship now for ten hours, but that was part of the plan. They had approached the wormhole that would take them to the Orion Arm of the galaxy – if they were lucky.

The rest of the wormholes he used were on his charts and were numbered. There were forty–three of them on record. This one was not on the charts. If it proved to be a portal into the Orion Arm of the galaxy, then it would become wormhole forty-four, officially. So far, nothing about this wormhole was official.

It had been detected years ago by the crew of another starship. If he remembered correctly, it was the starship Nova. But that was unimportant now.

He had kept his favorite navigator, Elaina Djoser, on duty with him because he liked her – yes, but also because she had backed a starship out of a wormhole three years ago. He needed her experience if they got into trouble. Seth wasn't expecting a problem, but out here, you never knew.

A wavering oval appeared on the screen of his console. "The portal is in sight. Check your screens."

"Sir, I would suggest deceleration."

Commander Seth Okanata turned to look. A pretty face made a smile at him. "Why do you suggest that, Lieutenant Djoser?"

"Sir, if we have to back out of the portal, it will take less time and it won't be as chancy because we won't be as far inside."

Seth nodded. "Good thinking, Lieutenant."

She smiled and then averted her eyes to her screen.

Seth had to forget that pretty face just now. He had other, more important things to focus on. She was right. It would be easier and quicker to back out if they decelerated.

The thing you worried about with a wormhole was if you, for some strange, unknown reason, lost your course monitor even for a split second. All it would take is one split second of a glitch in the power system of the starship, and you might lose thousands of kilometers of distance and direction in the memory of your navigational system.

So, what would that mean? That would mean simply that you would have to feel your way around to your old course to find the way back out of the wormhole. True, it would be for just that one split second and those few thousands of kilometers, but when you were in a place where there were no stars and absolutely no aids for direction or sense of direction, you needed your electronics to be exact to the millionth with absolutely no glitches – not one – not for one split second.

"Captain Tikal, decelerate to five hundred thousand kilometers per hour."

The pilot's face was now in his direction. Seth could feel it.

He turned. "Is there a problem Captain Tikal?"

The tall man shook his head. "No, sir, but that's awfully slow."

"This is a special situation, Captain."

"Yes, sir." Tikal turned away and punched a red button on the right of his console. Then he swiped his right index finger downward on the right margin of his console screen.

He turned to Commander Okanata. "Speed set at five hundred thousand kilometers per hour, sir."

"Very good, Tikal. Monitor the deceleration. We want to be at that speed when we reach the portal. Based upon my calculations, we should be reaching this portal in approximately fifty-three point seven minutes and counting."

"Yes, sir." Tikal turned back to his console.

Seth Okanata did like the adventure of commanding a starship. However, unlike some people, he considered WTNs, or Wormholes to Nowhere, to be spooky and frightening.

Eight years ago he had been in one. At the time, it had seemed to him that it was like dying. You entered an area of space where there was just that – space. There were no stars, no planets, no asteroids – nothing. There was only blackness.

And it wasn't like the blackness you experienced walking into a dark room. With that dark room blackness, eventually you began to see objects. Your eyes adjusted to the low level of light.

In a Wormhole to Nowhere there was nothing. Your eyes never adjusted because there was nothing to adjust to. Your instruments registered nothing. Your scanners picked up no pings. There was nothing to ping off from. Nothing was there. It was empty – devoid of matter and energy of any kind except your starship and what was inside that starship.

The idea of wormholes was to shorten distances. It was like driving down a boulevard and knowing that you would have to go another kilometer before you could turn and go back on the other lane to a street you could see now but couldn't reach, simply because you had to drive another kilometer.

The wormhole was like being able to cut right across the median to the street you could see now. You avoided the need to drive another kilometer down the street, and another kilometer back, to reach it. It was a shortcut.

Some of them, however, led to nowhere because with wormholes you couldn't see the place you were going to. You were only in the approximate vicinity of that place.

In this particular situation, Commander Okanata was sure that if this wormhole didn't work, they could find another.

"Speed down to nine hundred thousand kilometers per hour and reducing."

"Very good, Captain." Seth Okanata had never liked using wormholes where he wasn't sure of the territory. This was one of those cases. He just wished this was over – that they would know whether this one would work or not.

Seth watched his screen as the oval portal approached. He pressed the reset button to the left of his screen.

The picture became smaller again. He checked the distance in the upper right corner of his screen. It read eighty-nine thousand kilometers for one split second. The white numbers rolled downward at a dizzying rate.

"Six hundred, eighty-one thousand kilometers per hour and reducing, Commander."

"Very good, Captain." Seth waited a second. "How is our trajectory, Lieutenant Djoser?"

"Right on, sir. We should shut off our cloaking device, sir."

"I'm waiting until the last possible second, Lieutenant Djoser."

"Yes, sir. But I'd err on the side of caution, sir. The cloaking device could affect our instrument readings when we pass through the portal, sir, and we need accurate readings at that time."

"Copy that, Lieutenant." He knew exactly what the pretty lieutenant was saying. If they had inaccurate readings at the entrance to the portal, it was possible that they could never find their way out, if this turned out to be a WTN. How could you back out of a wormhole if you didn't know where you came in?

Commander Okanata decided that - given that they knew nothing about this wormhole - perhaps it was time to shut off the cloaking device.

He doubted there were pirates here anyway. This particular area of space had no star. There was only the occasional asteroid or cast-off planet, one that had somehow been thrown out of an outer orbit of a star and was drifting in interstellar space.

If there were not many planets or planets' moons, then there were not many places for pirates to hide.

He reached up to the right side of his console and pressed a yellow button labeled C O. "Cloaking off."

"Very good, sir," said a female voice behind him.

Seth Okanata found that he was smiling. Then he noticed that Captain Tikal had seen his smile. "Captain, what's our speed?"

The tall, blond man faced his screen. "Five hundred ninety-six thousand kilometers per hour and reducing, sir." He turned back to the commander. "Should I hold the throttle right here, sir? We're slowing at a fast rate."

"No, this is good, Captain. If we happen to enter this portal at less than five hundred thousand kilometers per hour, that would be fine. The slower the speed, the easier to reverse."

"Yes, sir."

Seth Okanata had convinced himself that he had kept Lieutenant Elaina Djoser on this night because she had the most experience with wormholes of the two navigators. However, there was that other thing. . . he just liked having her around.

He pressed the reset button on the left side of his console.

The oval portal grew larger.

"What is the speed now, Captain?"

"Five hundred thousand forty-two kilometers per hour and reducing, sir."

"Very good. We're twenty-two point four thousand kilometers from the portal." There were numbers to the right of the point four on the number register in the upper right corner of his screen, but Seth Okanata thought it was useless reporting those because once you moved over to the ten thousand parts of a second area, the numbers were moving as you watched them. Farther right they were moving so fast you couldn't read them.

"We will be entering the portal in a matter of minutes, ladies and gentlemen. Stay sharp."

"Yes, sir," said a female voice behind Seth.

At this moment something occurred to Seth Okanata, the commander of this starship. It was a question. Was he falling in love with Elaina Djoser?

"Entering portal, sir," said the female voice behind him.

"What's our speed, Captain?"

"Five hundred twelve point six thousand kilometers per hour, sir."

Without warning the windshield in front of them went black. There was no light, nothing.

"Reverse engines!" said a female voice.

CHAPTER FOURTEEN
"Withdrawal"

Starship Cygnus
Bridge
10M, Day 21, 6572
10:48 p.m.

Elaina Djoser focused on her screen with an intensity that made her neck ache. "Our course is following the line of our entry, sir."

She didn't want to see the windshield. In fact, she wished there weren't a windshield. She would rather see riveted aluminum in front of her than that awful blackness.

WTNs were empty and they were frightening. When Elaina had been inside of another Wormhole to Nowhere three years ago, she had wondered if even any gods were there in those awful places. Nothing else was.

Space – that's what was there, but that wasn't there either because space was nothing so it couldn't be there. It couldn't be anywhere because it was nothing.

On her screen she could see the uneven oval of the portal coming toward them. The trick here, as far as she knew from her former experience, was to stay on the exact course you had used to come through the portal from the other direction.

Sure - the time instruments in the starship would be fouled up and maybe she would have to double check their navigation instruments, but getting out of here was the big thing. It was the only thing.

Elaina Djoser would have been embarrassed about the fact that she was sweating inside her coveralls. That was only because she was in the same place as Seth Okanata, except that she had to concentrate on what she was doing.

These days she did think of him as Seth. She had to be careful not to use that address with him so when she was on the bridge she had to remind herself that he was Commander Okanata.

Right now, however, she had to forget about Seth Okanata and sweating and the fact that she found him attractive. She had to focus on the course of Starship Cygnus. Otherwise they might never get back to regular space. They might stay in this Wormhole to Nowhere forever.

What would you do if you were caught in one of these places for the rest of your natural life? Well, first off, you'd probably spend several years trying to get out. Every day would be an attempt to find a way out, and she was sure there would be one failure after another.

The scariest thing about it was something a pilot told her once. He said that it was possible, theoretically, to move from one Wormhole to Nowhere into another Wormhole to Nowhere, and if you had that misfortune, you definitely would never find your way back.

She didn't even want to think about that, especially now. She would never see Hyksos again if they couldn't get back. She would never see her grandmother again. Everything she cared about would be gone, except for maybe one thing – one person actually.

No, she couldn't think about him. She had to focus on the course map in front of her in the console screen.

Elaina stared at the line of the current starship course. She saw a slight variation. She gently gripped onto the large toggle switch near the top of her console and moved it ever so slightly in an upward motion.

In front of her the starship's current course moved just slightly so that the line of the course was exactly the line of the course of the starship when it was traveling into the WTN.

The portal became larger and larger. Elaina assumed they were within a few thousand kilometers of their entry point. Normally this would be a distance they would cover in a split second. Not in this situation.

Here accuracy was the whole focus. Speed wasn't even a consideration, unless it was going slowly enough to insure that they were truly retracing their exact path into this zone.

"Lieutenant, how far are we from the portal?"

"A few thousand kilometers, sir."

"Can't you be any more accurate than that?"

"Sorry, sir. In a WTN there are no reference points. Real speed and distance are hard to measure."

"Understood, Lieutenant. What will you do when we reach the portal?"

"Just try to guide us through on exactly the same path we used to come in, sir." She glanced up and the commander was staring at her.

When he saw her looking, he smiled.

She smiled back, then averted her eyes down to the screen. She might have a crush on Commander Seth Okanata, but she wouldn't be able to do anything about it unless they got out of this WTN.

She glanced up at the windshield of the giant starship.

Outside was blackness.

Elaina thought of it as the blackness of death. No light came back. There was no light. There was nothing – no energy, no matter – nothing. It was darkness like death itself.

In the next second they popped into interstellar space.

A cheer went up in the bridge.

Elaina could feel tears running down her cheeks.

Now Commander Seth Okanata was standing at her side. He put his hand on her left shoulder. "Good job, Elaina, damned good job."

She looked up. "Thank you, sir."

"You're crying."

"Yes, sir. I was scared."

"All of us were scared, Elaina. Thank you for saving us."

She smiled. "The pleasure was all mine, sir."

He grinned. "Well said."

The commander hurried back to the left seat at the pilots' console. He looked back at her one more time and smiled.

Then he dropped into the black padded seat. "All members at the bridge, let's set a course parallel to this last portal. However, before we move, let's mark this in our charts as a WTN.

"Thanks to our very capable navigator we are back in interstellar space in one piece. Before we use our instruments, please do check them thoroughly for any anomalies. It's common knowledge that WTNs foul electronics. Do check your systems."

Lieutenant Elaina Djoser began digging into the navigation system aboard the starship. She was looking for just anything that might be out of the normal range of information or performance data.

She did find that anything involving time was wrong. She checked her wrist control. It was nine minutes and some few seconds ahead of the time in the navigation system.

Her fingers rattled over the keys. She was checking time back on Hyksos. Yes, it was 11:13 p.m. there, the same as her wrist control.

She corrected the time in the navigation system. She wondered if they had traveled backward in time. It was hard to believe such a thing had happened, but the discrepancies in the times on the two clocks made her wonder.

"Commander, check the time in your systems. I think you'll find they don't match the time on Hyksos. We seemed to have lost nine minutes and some seconds in the WTN."

"That's impossible, Lieutenant. I mean – if you're trying to tell us we went back in time, that's not possible. There are certain laws of cause and effect which make it impossible to go into the past."

Elaina looked up at Captain Tikal in the co-pilot's seat. "I realize that, Captain, but I still suggest you compare your console time with the time back on Hyksos."

"Do it, Captain."

The co-pilot looked at the commander. "Yes, sir."

CHAPTER FIFTEEN
"Strange Behavior"

Starship Cygnus
Level 1
Recreation Center
10M, Day 22, 6572
12:22 a.m.

Captain Salathiel Tikal still didn't understand how the starship could have gone back in time. What was even weirder was that his wrist control was correct, but the time in the propulsion system was incorrect.

How was that possible? If they really had gone back in time, then their wrist controls should reflect that time change as well, not just the systems in the starship.

Maybe the best thing to do was to drink more beer and forget the whole damned horrible night.

He drank down some of the foamy beer. He had never gotten used to the way beer foamed right out of the bottle in this lower gravitation aboard the starship. The starship was at ninety-percent of the gravitation on Hyksos.

Sal Tikal understood that actually years ago on the first starship the artificial gravitation was only sixty percent. Now, that would be a challenge, especially when it came to beer. Of course, he didn't know if they drank beer back then.

Sal usually drank alone, but he liked to sit at the bar because sometimes bartenders were friendly. He especially liked female bartenders who were friendly. He didn't know why, except that they were female and were often reasonably good-looking. Talking to a good-looking woman was not a bad thing to do.

Next to him on his right was another crew member. He didn't know the man's name, but he was pretty sure he was one of the people in charge of maintaining the rocket propulsion system. All of them had been at the briefing back on Hyksos.

"Hi, I don't know your name, but I did recognize you as one of our rocket mechanics." Sal held out his hand.

The other, shorter man turned. "Hi. Hector Copan – Sergeant Hector Copan." He grabbed Sal's hand and shook it once. "Pretty busy on the bridge tonight, eh?"

"Very. As you know, we got into a WTN. The navigator, a woman, backed us out. She's pretty good – knows what she's doing."

"Elaina Djoser?"

"Yes."

"I work with her husband."

"She's married?"

Hector Copan shrugged. "Sure. I thought everybody knew that. She's been married to Masal for eight years."

Captain Sal Tikal was surprised by this information, considering what seemed to be going on between Commander Okanata and this navigator. "Are you sure we're talking about the same woman?"

"Yeah, I'm sure. Brown hair, real good lookin', 'specially when she smiles? 'Bout five feet four inches tall?"

"That's the same woman."

"You surprised she's married?"

Captain Tikal shrugged. "Actually I am rather surprised."

"Why do you say that?"

"Oh, I don't know. It just seems like she's really friendly with Commander Okanata."

"How friendly?"

Sal Tikal shrugged again. "Oh, I don't know. They just seem to be really friendly. At least that's what I see."

"I sure hope Masal doesn't find out."

"Why is that?"

"He has this temper. Doesn't like it when people cross him. Gets real mad."

It occurred to Captain Tikal that perhaps he shouldn't have spoken so freely to this man. Maybe he should have kept this information to himself.

Certainly, everyone on the bridge had to see it. The friendly relationship was really obvious. Of course it would only be himself and the other pilot, Chan Caracol and the guard who was on duty at the door to the bridge.

There was always a guard at the door to the bridge. Sal guessed it was some kind of tradition. He couldn't imagine there would be any danger from a crew member. In the old days there were many more civilians on starships. The bridge had to be guarded.

Of course, these days there was always the present danger of pirates. So maybe having a guard armed with an assault rifle on the bridge was still necessary.

Well, he had certainly spilled the beans. Somebody was bound to do it and, unfortunately, it had been him. Sal would imagine that the husband had to know what was going on. After all, the starship group only consisted of fifty or sixty people.

"You won't say anything to this Masal, will you?"

"I sure don't want to get into the middle of this shit."

"No, really Sergeant, I'm not sure anything's going on. They're just really friendly. That's all that I've noticed."

The shorter man's intense brown eyes looked at Sal. "She'd be real stupid to do somethin' right under his nose. She's in the MSA so she should understand what it's like travelin' around the galaxy like we do. "Some women don't get that – like my wife. She never got it."

"Is she back on Hyksos?"

"No, she was killed in a car accident."

"An old fashioned car?"

"Yeah, we belong to this club that goes out to the drivin' range outside of Memphis. She was out there with this guy and they had a car accident – real bad."

"When did this happen?"

"Few days back."

Sal Tikal wondered why this man didn't seem all that upset about his wife's death. "I'm really sorry to hear that, Sergeant."

Hector Copan shrugged. "Hey, they were speedin'. Can't speed in those old cars, 'specially when they're not rebuilt right."

At that moment Captain Sal Tikal had the sense that there was more to this story than he was hearing. He wasn't going to dig, but there was definitely something amiss.

However, the strangest part of this conversation was how completely unmoved this man seemed to be by his wife's recent death. That was truly a strange kind of behavior.

CHAPTER SIXTEEN
"Mister Bear"

Hyksos
Memphis
4281 Aswan Street
10M, Day 22, 6572
7:34 a.m.

Charis still missed her mother. It was like there was this hollow place in the house all the time. She didn't know where heaven was, but Daddy had told her that her mother was in heaven. Her daddy had sent her a text message about that.

Most of all she wanted her daddy home. She missed him so very much. She wanted him here so he could hug her. If her daddy was here, he could also read stories at night when she went to bed and he could just sit and talk with her like he did so many times before when he was home.

When her daddy was here at home and talked to her at night about what he did when he was a little boy, she would smile and snuggle into her bed with Mister Bear - her teddy bear - and she would go to sleep and dream nice things.

She wanted her daddy back so much. He was text messaging her about two times a week and that was good, but she still missed him.

It was good that Niobe had moved into the house. She read Charis stories too, but not as good as her daddy did. Niobe was really smart and she was so friendly and everything. Charis really liked her. If she could have a mommy besides her real mommy, she would want that mommy to be Niobe.

"Finish your cereal, Charis."

She looked up.

Niobe was standing at the kitchen stove. She was holding a mug of coffee. She smiled at Charis. "Honey, you have to finish your cereal. You're going to be teleporting to school very soon. You have gym classes this morning."

"I know." Charis didn't like gym classes because they made you all sweaty and, besides, you had to wear this really ugly gym uniform that made you look like a skinny chicken.

She was glad the boys weren't in her gym class. She knew some of them would laugh at her in her skinny chicken uniform, especially Borus Campaneus.

He was really cute but he always picked on her. Her daddy had told Charis that probably Borus actually liked her because sometimes boys picked on you when they liked you.

Charis didn't understand that. It seemed kind of weird, but a lot of things about boys were weird.

She finished her cereal. She had put too much sugar on it when Niobe wasn't looking. Now Charis felt really dumb about that because she knew it was wrong and she knew she would be hyper for about an hour, then she would have a headache and feel hungry again. Sugar did that to her.

Maybe she should start being smart about those things and not mess around with the sugar like that. Besides, she liked Niobe and she didn't like pulling stuff over on her like the sugar thing. It always made Charis feel guilty and stupid.

She slipped off the stool behind the breakfast bar and walked across the dining room. In the living room her little brother, Aten, was sitting on the wooden floor with his remote control. He was playing with his battery powered helicopter.

The little airship was buzzing around the far end of the living room.

Charis envied Aten. He had school for only half a day. He had it so easy and that wasn't fair.

She wondered about him sometimes because he had cried a lot when their mother died and he always wanted to see her. But Niobe had said that the casket would be closed because that's the way they did it when there was a bad accident.

Charis finally figured out why. She figured out that her mother would be all messed up and she didn't want to see her that way so she was actually glad they didn't open that casket.

But Aten had cried and cried that he wanted to see his mother. Charis knew that her little brother didn't understand that his mommy was gone for good. Charis knew that. She didn't really understand all of it, but she knew that part of it.

She tried to think of her mother up in heaven looking down at them and smiling. That made her feel better. She tried to not think about the accident because she had seen accidents before on the news, airplane accidents and you knew things were very bad with pieces of the airplane all over the place. She figured the car accident was probably like that.

Charis stopped in the foyer and bent down to pick up her backpack.

Niobe walked in and smiled at her. "Do you have everything?"

"Yes." Charis pulled her backpack up onto her shoulders.

Niobe bent down and kissed Charis's forehead. "You have a good day at school. If you have any problems, you know how to reach me. If I don't answer my wrist control, just leave a voice message. Okay?"

"Yeah, okay."

"And you know you can always call your grandma."

"But I want to call you."

"I know, honey, but you can call your grandma too, especially if it's an emergency."

Charis shrugged. "I know."

Niobe hugged her. "You have a good day, honey."

Charis felt better just then. She loved to be hugged like that. For just a little bit of time, this made the hurt about her mother go away. The hurt would come back, but at least for just a little bit of time, it was gone.

Niobe pulled open the house door.

Charis pressed the lever on the screen door and pushed the door back. Then she stepped out onto the concrete teleportico.

Once she was out to an area marked with a blue circle in the concrete, she turned around to face the house.

Before she teleported to school, she was looking at Niobe, who was smiling at her. She liked Niobe's smile. It made her feel warm and all cozy.

CHAPTER SEVENTEEN

"Power"

Starship Cygnus
Level 3
10M, Day 24, 6572
6:21 p.m.

Lieutenant Elaina Djoser stepped out of the elevator.

She was just a little late getting back to her compartment at the end of the Green Shift. Commander Seth Okanata had stopped her to talk.

He had begun the conversation by thanking her, once again, for her "very competent work" with regard to extracting the starship from the WTN. Compliments always made her feel good of course, but coming from the commander made it even better.

The only problem was that everyone else overheard him doing this and she didn't want to create any jealousy on the bridge.

The other thing at play was that he seemed to be quite taken with her. That was a compliment too, of course. She was finally able to admit that this thing existed between them. She could feel it every time he was near. It made her feel young and beautiful again. It gave her a whole new perspective.

There was problem, however. She was married to a guy who was very possessive and very jealous.

Elaina had pretty much made up her mind to divorce Masal, but she wasn't going to do it when he was around because he had a really bad temper. She would wait until he was gone on a mission and she was home on furlough.

He had hit her before several times. Well, actually she was kidding herself. It was eleven times. Yes, she had counted. How could you not remember something like that? It hurt, but most of all, it made her feel like she was nobody.

She would feel worthless. Maybe what was worse, however, was that she also felt powerless. That feeling was awful.

Elaina stopped midway down the corridor. She just hoped Masal didn't make a big deal about her being late.

Her mind moved to Seth Okanata and she found that she was smiling. She supposed that was why she absolutely ate up the compliments coming from him. They were reinforcing. They made her feel good about herself.

She moved down the corridor again.

Seth was such a nice man. The name, itself, had this clear, clean feeling about it. It was probably because she had a crush on him.

What was this crush about? Was it sexual? Well, actually everything about this was sexual in some way - or almost everything. But with Seth, what she loved was his real decency and his integrity and his kindness. He was a quality human being. She could absolutely sense that when she was around him.

She had had enough of men who were only so-so. She had dealt with that long enough. She had to admit that she had married a so-so male. However, she had married him because she had been very young and she had made a bad choice.

In the corridor of Level 3, Elaina looked up at the number above her compartment door, 317. On this journey into the Orion Belt she had dreaded returning to her compartment after every Green Shift. Masal would be here.

Usually when she was assigned to an interstellar journey, she was alone. Now that she considered the matter, she wondered if the fact that she was separated from him so often was part of the reason her marriage had survived as long as it did.

It was simple, really. She was away for months at a time by herself. That last part was the most important part - by herself.

When she was not around Masal, things were good. She functioned well and she enjoyed her work.

Many times she had dreaded going home to Hyksos. Those were the times when she and Masal happened to have furloughs at the same time.

"What are you doing? You're crazy to stay married to him," she whispered.

Yes, during this coming furlough when he was on an assignment, she would file for divorce and move out of their house. She didn't want to bring her grandmother into this, so she would live by herself some-where – maybe a condo complex.

The Green Shift was long over. It was time she arrived back at her compartment.

Elaina stabbed her plastic key card into the slot to the right of the door to Compartment 317.

The card slot glowed blue and the door rattled open to the left.

She yanked out her card and stepped over the curved threshold.

The titanium door rattled shut behind her.

"Where you been?"

Elaina's head jerked up. "On the bridge."

"What took you so long? I haven't had my dinner yet."

"You could have gone ahead without me, Masal."

"You been talkin' to your boyfriend?"

"My boyfriend?"

"Yes, your boyfriend."

She squinted. "What are you talking about?"

"Your boyfriend, Seth Okanata, the anointed one."

"He's not my boyfriend."

Masal stepped forward. "Don't lie to me!"

"I'm not lying. Why would you say that? Commander Okanata is not my boyfriend. He's my commanding officer on the bridge."

Masal grabbed her left bicep and squeezed. His hand was like a vise grip.

"What are you doing?"

"You're sweet on him, aren't ya?"

"Let go of me!"

"Not till I get a fuckin' answer!"

"Let go of my arm! You're hurting me!" Elaina stared into the angry brown eyes. She dreaded what was coming. Her arm ached from his grip. "Don't do this, Masal."

"Do what?"

"Get all angry over nothing."

"Nothin'?"

"Yes, nothing."

"Have you been sleepin' with him?"

"What?"

He squeezed the arm harder. "Have you been fuckin' him?"

"You're hurting me!"

"Have you?"

"What do you think?"

The brown eyes stared. "You have, haven't ya?"

"No!"

The hand came around so fast she didn't see it.

It struck the left side of her face. She saw red sparks and she could feel tears.

"Tell me!"

"Tell you what?"

"Have you been sleepin' with him?"

"No!"

"Don't lie to me!"

This time it felt different. Something hard like knuckles hit her left eye.

Then it was like she was floating downward. She was a heavy bird going downward so slowly.

She hit the floor. Then black.

Seconds later she came to. She was looking straight up.

Masal was leaning over her, staring down. "Now I'm gonna show you whose boss around here!"

She could feel the pants of her uniform being pulled down, then her underwear.

Her legs were forced open and something hard pushed into her vagina. It hurt.

She wanted to die.

CHAPTER EIGHTEEN
"Things to Consider"

Starship Cygnus
Bridge
10M, Day 25, 6572
4:02 a.m.

Commander Seth Okanata had called his best bridge crew in early for the Green Shift. His Orange Shift pilot, Captain Chan Caracol, had called him on his wrist control almost an hour ago and told him that they had found a new wormhole portal.

The commander was not one to take chances, especially with unknown wormholes. He, therefore, wanted his best crew on the bridge.

He had ordered Caracol to slow the starship's speed immediately. That was his very first order. He remembered what his favorite navigator had recommended before – five hundred thousand kilometers per hour.

He didn't rouse Captain Tikal. He figured the man would come onto the Green Shift at six o'clock anyway, but he did want his best navigator here early.

He had been telling himself that he wanted her here because of her skill in working these wormholes. Lieutenant Lindos Lycastus, the current navigator, was a competent man, but Elaina had the real experience he wanted on the bridge.

Of course, he liked seeing her pretty face as well. When she was around, it made his day better.

He really shouldn't be thinking those things. After all, the woman was married. On the other hand, he hadn't made any improper gestures or statements with regard to her. He was just being friendly. He hoped that was the way it was interpreted.

Commander Okanata had contacted her almost thirty minutes ago. He wondered why she wasn't here yet. He wouldn't proceed into this portal unless she was his navigator. Even though Lieutenant Lycastus was well qualified, Seth had unwavering faith in Elaina's ability to deal with this.

"Sir, what are we waiting for?"

Seth Okanata turned to Captain Caracol. "For my navigator."

"But we have one, Commander."

"Not the one I want."

"Djoser?"

Seth turned to face Caracol. "Yes. She backed us out of the last wormhole. Otherwise we'd still be there. I want her to handle this. She knows what she's doing when it comes to wormholes."

Captain Caracol leaned over toward the commander. "But Lycastus is very good, sir," he whispered

Commander Okanata nodded. "Yes, I know. However, you weren't here for that WTN event, Caracol. She was really good."

The young pilot shrugged. "Then, I guess she's the best choice, sir."

The door to the bridge rattled open.

Before he knew he was doing it, Seth Okanata rose out of the command seat and turned.

What he saw startled him.

His beautiful navigator's face was bandaged and the area around her left eye was black and so swollen that he was sure she couldn't see out of it.

He moved across to greet her. "Lieutenant, what happened?"

She glanced at him. "Sorry, sir. I got up during the night and tripped. Fell into the sink and bruised myself. I know I must look a sight, sir."

"Are you all right?"

She made a quick grin for him. "I can work, sir, if that's what you're asking."

Seth smiled. "Good. I wanted you at the navigation station because of your experience with wormholes."

Behind him, Lieutenant Lycastus spoke. "Sir, I've navigated through wormholes many times."

The commander turned. "Have you ever backed out of a WTN?"

"No, sir."

Seth Okanata nodded toward Elaina. "She's done that twice."

"Oh." The male navigator rose out of the seat in front of the console. He smiled at Elaina. "Sorry about your fall. That must have hurt."

Elaina didn't answer right away. "Yes, very much. Dumb accident." She sat down at the console.

"Can I observe Lieutenant Djoser?" The other navigator was looking at the commander.

Seth shrugged. "It's fine with me, as long as she doesn't mind." He turned to Elaina. "Would you mind?"

"It's hard to focus, sir, when someone else is around. I'd rather do this alone." Elaina didn't make eye contact. She seemed engrossed by the screen on the navigation console.

"Certainly." The commander turned to the other navigator. "Then you're relieved, Lieutenant Lycastus."

The navigator saluted. "Yes, sir."

Seth Okanata automatically returned the salute.

The male navigator walked across to the door.

Seth Okanata didn't move. It was as if he was waiting for the other navigator to leave the bridge. The reason? He wanted privacy for Elaina Djoser.

That was very strange. When he considered why he wanted the privacy for her, it was based upon this weird feeling about Elaina's so-called accident. It wasn't her blackened eye or the bandage on the side of her face that caught his attention.

No. It was something about the way Elaina was behaving. She was avoiding eye contact. It was almost as if she was ashamed.

Seth touched her left shoulder.

Elaina jerked away.

"Sorry. . . didn't mean to startle you. I was just going to say that it's good to have you here. I know you can handle wormholes of any kind."

This time she looked at him and held his gaze for several seconds.

Seth smiled. "Sorry about your accident."

A tear slipped out of the corner of her good eye. She turned away immediately.

"Carry on, Lieutenant. We've reduced our speed for almost forty minutes."

"Very good, sir." She focused on the computer screen.

The commander hesitated. He was about to ask her a question, but he stopped short of doing that.

Instead, he moved around the end of the navigation console and walked across to his seat. He dropped into it.

Captain Caracol leaned over close to him. "Sir, that's a hell of a shiner," he whispered. "She must have fallen pretty hard."

Seth Okanata glanced back at Elaina.

She was facing the screen and her fingers were rattling across the keyboard on her console.

He faced the pilots' console again.

For some reason, which he couldn't easily explain, Commander Seth Okanata felt this enormous urge to walk back over to Elaina and pull her into his arms.

But why did he want to comfort her? Did she really need comforting? The bigger question was why. Why would she need comforting – unless she didn't get that bruised eye from a fall? Another cause for the fall popped into his mind.

"What is the current speed, Commander?"

Seth's head turned and he looked at the bruised face again. He swung around to his screen. "Eight hundred seventy-three thousand kilometers per hour."

"We are approximately twenty-two thousand kilometers from the portal, sir. It is possible that we should pass it and circle back to insure our speed is low enough."

"It took us a while to find this one, Lieutenant. I would rather chance entering it at a higher speed than risk not being able to find it again."

"We can mark it as we pass, sir."

"We can, Lieutenant but, as you know, we're traveling pretty fast and passing by a point at this speed means a much sloppier location mark on the portal itself. If we were aiming directly into it and marked it, then we could depend on our accuracy."

"Yes, sir, I understand."

Commander Okanata had every faith in this woman, no matter what had happened to her. "What would you estimate our speed will be when we enter the portal, Lieutenant?"

"Give me a second, sir."

"Certainly." Seth could hear the rattle of the navigation console keyboard.

What stuck in Seth's consciousness was the possibility that Elaina had been beaten by her husband. That was a dark shadow in his mind. That was a grim possibility. As Caracol suggested, she would have to fall awfully hard to be injured that much. She couldn't be that clumsy. She was an agile, young woman.

When Seth Okanata thought about this, the anger that rose inside him was something he had never experienced before. He was sure this kind of anger led people to kill.

"We will be traveling at somewhere between six hundred thousand and seven hundred thousand kilometers per hour, sir."

Seth turned and made a smile and nodded. "Thank you, Lieutenant." The commander considered the next question before he asked it.

He swung his leather seat around. "Lieutenant, do you think you could back us out of this wormhole if we enter at that speed?"

The right eye blinked. Then it looked down at the screen.

Seth could hear the rattle of the navigation keyboard again.

It stopped.

Elaina's head came up. "Yes, sir, but it might take twice the time to accomplish."

Seth felt a sweep of warmth. That was his confident, talented Elaina speaking now. He smiled and nodded. "We will enter the wormhole on this first pass, Lieutenant."

"Yes, sir."

"Thank you, Lieutenant."

"Yes, sir."

Seth Okanata pivoted his chair around to face his console. He could feel Caracol looking at him. He turned.

Caracol's eyes blinked. He scribbled something on his notepad, then slid the pad across the console shelf to the commander.

Seth stared at it.

"She's been beaten by someone," said the note.

Seth looked up.

Caracol's handsome face was grim. "I'm sure of it," he whispered.

Seth nodded. "Destroy that note," he whispered.

"Yes, sir."

Seth Okanata found that he was staring at his console screen and seeing nothing. While he was doing this, he was aware that it was not actually a very wise thing to do. After all, he was in command of a starship that was going to enter an unknown and unmarked wormhole.

"Shut off cloaking, Commander."

Seth reached up to a black switch to the right of his screen. He flipped it down. "Cloaking off, Lieutenant."

"Copy that, sir. Entering the portal in a matter of seconds, sir."

Seth Okanata concentrated on the wiggling oval on his screen. He pressed the button to the left of his screen.

The wormhole popped to larger size. This was closer to what they would see out of the windshield, if they could see a wormhole out of the windshield. These things, however, were electronic phenomena.

"Entering the wormhole, sir."

"Got it, Lieutenant."

He didn't want to, but he couldn't resist. Seth Okanta raised his head and looked at the windshield of the starship.

This time he didn't want to see empty blackness. It made you feel like you'd come to the end of everything.

A commander was supposed to be unmoved by these experiences. He was supposed to be poised and in control of his emotions at all times.

Right now, Seth Okanata found that difficult. For just a split second he thought it was because he feared they were entering another WTN.

No, that was not the reason. The reason? He was in love with Elaina Djoser, madly in love with her. And right now when he thought of those terrible bruises on her face, he wanted to murder the person responsible.

There were also gentler responses. He wanted to take Elaina into his arms and hold her close. He wanted to protect her from whatever person or thing was harming her.

He knew who that was. In fact, he couldn't stop thinking about how much he hated that man.

"We're through, sir."

Seth Okanata smiled.

In the windshield was black space filled with stars. They were safe – no WTN this time.

Caracol glanced over his left shoulder. "Good work, Lieutenant."

"Let's mark it, Lieutenant."

"Already done, sir."

The commander swung around in the pilot's seat and smiled. "Of course. I should have expected that."

Seth rose out of his seat and walked back to Elaina. He put his hand on her left shoulder. "Well done, Lieutenant."

She looked up at him and her bruised face twisted into a distorted smile. "Thank you, sir."

Seth Okanata realized he had things to consider here. Obviously his wonderful navigator was being abused by her husband.

In a general sense, it was none of his business but, in this case, maybe he could do something. In fact, he was sure he could.

CHAPTER NINETEEN

"The Surprise Visitor"

Starship Cygnus
Bridge
10M, Day 25, 6572
5:51 a.m.

For Lieutenant Elaina Djoser it had been a tough morning. She had come in to the bridge a wreck. It was so embarrassing, so humiliating to have to show up on the bridge with her face a mess. That was especially true because Seth Okanata was here. That was the worst part of it.

What touched her so much, however, was Seth's kindness and concern. He knew what had happened. She could tell.

She needed help from someone and she had no doubt that the "someone" was Seth. But how was she going to approach him?

She couldn't let this kind of thing go on. She hardly dared go back to her compartment. There was one part of her mind that knew Masal might be capable of killing her.

She had to act. It would be better if the commander approached her, offering help, but she couldn't wait. She didn't know what Masal would do next.

A sparkling blue column appeared next to the navigation console. Then a figure of a tall man appeared. He was holding an assault rifle.

Captain Caracol rose out of his seat. "What the hell is this?"

The large weapon pointed at him. "Sit down, Captain Caracol. You have now been boarded. I am Captain Argo Calchus. Haven't you heard of me? I'm sure my reputation precedes me."

He swung around. "Ah, a beautiful woman who has been beaten by some thug. I will treat you better than that, my lady."

Elaina didn't move.

"Now, Commander Okanata, I want you to announce to the rest of your crew that you have been boarded by the Megall pirates, and you may certainly mention me by name. . . Argo Calchus."

Elaina saw Captain Caracol flip up the cloaking switch. She was sure Calchus didn't see it. He was staring at her.

There was the possibility that she would be captured by this thug and kept in his harem.

"Notify your crew this instant, Commander, or I will have to cut this woman's throat."

He spun around and grabbed Elaina by the hair.

The pain was terrible, especially on the side of her face that was swollen.

There was something about this moment that made Elaina calm down. She remembered that there was a pen somewhere on the long counter in front of her console.

The pirate pulled her hair so hard that her eyes ran tears.

Elaina moved her right hand ever so carefully up from her side to the edge of the counter.

The pirate was watching Commander Okanata.

"I'm waiting, Commander. The longer you stand there, the closer I get to cutting this woman's throat."

Seth Okanata sat down and pressed a button on the console.

Elaina could barely make out his figure with her right eye. It was running tears because of the pain in her scalp.

Her fingers moved methodically along the counter toward her computer screen. She knew she had to remain completely calm to do this. She had to move her fingers slowly so she didn't make a noise.

Calchus's head turned.

Her fingers stopped.

The pirate grinned. "Having fun, Lieutenant?"

She didn't answer.

"I'll bet you don't have any bruises where it counts, do you?" Calchus licked his lips.

He turned back toward Seth. "Commander, I'm waiting."

Elaina's fingers moved along the counter toward the computer screen. She began to move them too fast, then she deliberately slowed the pace. She didn't want to knock that pen onto the floor.

Seth Okanata flipped up a switch. "Good morning, this is your commander. We have been boarded by a Megall pirate. I ask you all to remain calm. We will let you know what you must do next. Standby for further orders."

"Very good, Commander."

Elaina's fingers found the pen. She would have to press the button to make the point stick out. She waited for a noise that would cover the sound.

"Now, Commander, I want you and your crew here on the bridge to remove your pistol belts one at a time."

Elaina jumped up and swung her right hand with all her might toward the right eye.

"Ugh!" Calchus dropped his assault rifle. He fell backward gripping the pen sticking out of his right eye. "Ahhh!"

Captain Caracol grabbed the man by the arm and swung him around so he was lying face down on the floor.

"Help me! Have mercy!"

Commander Okanata slipped a zip strip onto the pirate's wrists. "Flip him over."

Caracol grabbed the man's right shoulder and rolled him onto his back. He then yanked the pen out of the man's eye.

Blood spurted onto the pirate's face.

The commander swung around and ran to his console. "Everyone aboard Starship Cygnus, man your battle stations!"

He turned to Elaina. "Good work. Now we have to get out of here before we're destroyed." He knelt on the deck in front of the pirate. "Listen, Calchus. You are now our prisoner. I want to reach your people. What radio frequency do I use?"

"One hundred seventeen point nine. Aren't you going to bring a doctor? That bitch stabbed me in the eye!"

The commander grabbed the pirate by the collar. "Say that again and I'll let her finish the job."

The pirate's good eye stared at Elaina. He actually seemed afraid of her. She had never seen a man afraid of her before. It was liberating to know she had power.

She wondered if this had anything to do with the anger she felt toward Masal. She was surprised by the power she had put into the thrust of that pen. There had been a lot of anger.

"Captain, bring this man over to the console."

Chan Caracol reached down. "Stand up, scum." He pulled on the man's right arm.

Calchus scrambled to his feet. Blood trickled down his cheek onto the front of his camouflage shirt.

Holding him at gunpoint, Caracol led him to the console.

Commander Okanata flipped up a switch. "Pirate ship, hear this. We have captured your Captain Calchus. If you ever want to see him alive again, you will let us pass." He turned to Calchus. "Speak to them."

"This is Calchus. Don't leave me. I have been a good commander. We have taken much booty and we've had many women together. Don't forget that."

The commander flipped the switch down. "Enough." He turned to Elaina. "Turn our course at right angles from where it is now. See if you can detect any evidence of another ship nearby. That will be the pirates. Avoid getting too near them."

Elaina moved back to her console and sat down. She was covered with blood and her hair was a wreck, but right now she had to get this starship out of here. She studied the screen. Then she moved a large joystick below the screen to the right.

The picture of stars swept to the left.

She saw something.

The moving screen stopped.

The commander motioned to Captain Caracol. "Take him down to the brig, Captain. Where's Tikal? He was supposed to report several minutes ago."

"I locked the door to the bridge, sir."

"Good move, Caracol." The commander sat down. His right hand slid under the counter.

He glanced back over his left shoulder. "That should unlock it."

The pocket door leading to the corridor rattled open.

Captain Tikal jumped over the curved threshold with his pistol drawn.

"Everything is under control, Captain, but we have to move the starship out of here. Get to your station."

"Yes, sir."

Elaina glanced at Tikal, then focused on her screen. "Commander, may I take over the control of the ship, sir?"

"Certainly, Lieutenant."

"I've been sweeping starboard, sir and I've spotted the pirate ship."

She moved the joystick to the left. "I've lost the image, sir. Can someone please man the laser cannons."

"Of course, Lieutenant." The commander gripped onto a handle farther up the console.

The vague image appeared near the middle of Elaina's screen. "Look at the upper left middle of your screen, sir."

"Got it, Lieutenant." There was a pause. "Holding steady on target. Fire one!" The commander squeezed the trigger.

The starship shook.

"Fire two!"

It shook again.

The vague image on Elaina's screen vanished.

"Got it!"

Elaina looked over the top of her console.

"Let's get out of here, Lieutenant. There may be more."

"Yes, sir, turning starboard, sir." Elaina pushed the red joystick to the right and focused on the screen. "Is our cloaking device on, sir?"

"Yes, it is, Lieutenant. Why do you ask?"

"I just saw another image, sir. It may be debris from the ship we just destroyed or it could be a second pirate ship."

"I'll notify the crew." The commander flipped up a switch at the top of his console. "Now, here this. This is your commander speaking. I'm placing this ship on high alert.

"We have successfully repelled one attempt to board us, but it is possible there are additional pirates in the vicinity. Stay sharp. All crew members report for duty."

Elaina focused on her console screen. She knew her hair was a wreck and her face was horrible with that black eye, but she was here on the bridge with Seth.

Now she was sure. Elaina was going to divorce Masal. She had thought she would wait for the next furlough. No.

If she could just move out of that compartment, she would feel better. Sure – everyone would know, but she didn't care.

How can you live in a compartment when you dread going back at night? That's the way she felt right now. She was afraid of what Masal might do. He might even try to kill her.

Maybe Seth could help her with this. She needed help from somebody if she was going to get away from Masal.

This whole thing was terribly embarrassing. Her husband behaved like some kind of wild, crazed animal.

She felt something to her left. Elaina had to turn her head farther because she couldn't see anything out of her left eye.

Seth Okanata's face was near. He was crouched down. "You saved the day, Elaina. You were very brave."

"Thank you, sir. I didn't really think about it. I just did it."

"Whatever the reason, you're the hero. Are you okay?"

Elaina grinned. "I must be a terrible sight, sir."

The commander patted her on the back. "You look fine to me, Lieutenant." He rose to his feet. The commander glanced around. Then he leaned down close to her. "If you ever want to talk to me about any-thing, Elaina, you know you can."

The female navigator felt a surge of emotion. She was sure she was going to cry, but she held it back. "Thank you, sir."

CHAPTER TWENTY
"Emotional Element"

Starship Cygnus
Level 3
Compartment 317
10M, Day 26, 6572
2:38 a.m.

"That bitch had it comin'. She did and nobody can tell me anythin' different."

He pointed the remote at the TV screen and pressed the volume bar near the top.

The sound of grunting men filled the small room.

Masal watched the sweating, muscular bodies. His eyes would wander to the buttocks of one man in particular.

Then he would pull his eyes away and pretend he cared about the wrestling match. He knew how it was going to turn out. He had seen it before. Lycurgus would win.

Lycurgus had won the last time and this was the same fucking video so why wouldn't he win again.

When Masal mentioned this to the guy who worked with him, Hector Copan, he would tell Hector that he liked to watch wrestling. Then Hector always said that wrestling was too slow to be interesting to watch. Hector liked soccer.

Then they would get into a conversation about sport teams and Masal would feel better. He wouldn't feel so weird and different.

Masal didn't want to use that other word. His father had used it all the time. His father also used the word pussy to describe guys who were afraid of things.

Talaus Djoser was a tough man who hated sissies and pussies and that other word. That was the word Masal hated.

He knew why he hated it. He knew deep down inside he was one of those people his father hated. No, he wasn't a pussy because he was afraid of very little and, no, he wasn't a sissy.

Masal had fought all his life not to be that, not to be those things his father had hated and cursed whenever he saw them. But, you see, there were some things you couldn't fight. There were some things that were natural to you.

Because his father had hated those things, Masal was supposed to hate them too. Oh, he knew his father had been an ignorant man and ignorant men have ignorant ideas. Masal had reasoned through all of that.

Yet, there was that emotional side of things, and it was so strong and it clung to you and wouldn't leave. It wouldn't let you reason your way out of things. It wouldn't let you reason that if you just happened to be different from most other men, you knew that it was all right because the gods made you that way.

If the gods made you that way, then it had to be all right. But the thing was he couldn't finish with women. He couldn't get his climax. He never had been able to do that.

Masal had never thought much about it. He had just thought that at some point everything would be all right, but then it wasn't all right. It didn't change.

He began to realize that he could spot certain types of people in society who were sometimes called "queers." He could tell which ones.

He had been able to tell them from everyone else for a long time. At first, he just thought he was more observant than others, had a better eye.

Maybe his father had made him that way because his father hated "queers." The man spent much of his life condemning them and cursing them. It was like he had his own personal vendetta against those people.

Then Hector had said something once that caught Masal's attention. This was years back when he first met Hector. His friend had said that Masal's father, Talaus Djoser, might have been "queer" himself. He might have been a homosexual.

Masal couldn't accept this. He told Hector it was "a lot of shit." That's the way he had put it – "a lot of shit."

Yet, the longer Masal thought about it, the more it began to make sense. Was his father just covering for his own homosexuality? Was he covering because he was actually one of those horrible queers?

Then the way his father died was strange too. The man seemed all right after his wife had died. Then, without warning, he had hung himself.

Masal had found him in the shed behind the house, hanging from a rafter. A kitchen chair was overturned on the concrete floor. His father had brought it out there for that one purpose.

Masal had pondered this for days, trying to figure it out, but at the time, none of it had made sense.

It had been so hard, finding his father like that. He had always held the man in high regard, tried to live up to the high standards his father had taught him.

Suppose those standards were phony? Then what? Was everything about his father phony? Was the man living a lie?

Masal had spent many years wondering about that. Then when Hector had told him that these really macho men sometimes were covering up for their own doubts about their sexuality, it began to make sense.

After that, Masal had looked at his own life. Something was out of sync. Something just didn't add up.

He could accept that in his brain. He could accept the fact in his brain that maybe marrying Elaina wasn't the answer.

More important, though, was whether his emotions would accept it. He really knew why he watched men's wrestling, and especially this one guy. He found the guy physically attractive.

Yet there was some part of Masal that wouldn't accept that. Oh, he knew that it was probably the part that his father had carefully trained – or brainwashed.

But how do you wipe that away? How do you erase that from who you are?

You might think all of it away. You might reason for hours and know that the world your father created for you was a phony world. Yes, you could do that, but how do you take out the emotional element? How do you unburden yourself from that?

He had not meant to hurt Elaina, but she had cheated on him. So what if their sexual life was nothing. She couldn't do that to him. His father would never allow a thing like that.

Masal tapped his wrist control. The time appeared on the surface. It was almost ten minutes before three in the morning. Elaina hadn't come back. Probably she was with her boyfriend.

Right after he had thought this, Masal realized how stupid it really was. Elaina didn't have a boyfriend. She wasn't the type to cheat. He knew that. He had always known it.

CHAPTER TWENTY-ONE
"Last Hope"

Starship Cygnus
Level 2
10M, Day 26, 6572
3:01 a.m.

Elaina had been to the Recreation Center twice. You could only stay forty minutes at a time. Luckily the hostess had changed after eleven o'clock or she couldn't have gotten in a second time.

She hadn't drunk any alcohol tonight. She didn't want to fall asleep or become dizzy. She was so tired that she was sure alcohol would be a serious mistake.

Right now, she was up here on Level 2 outside Seth's compartment.

She was afraid to return to her own compartment. Maybe it wasn't so much that she was scared of what Masal might do to her. Maybe it was more about what she might do to him.

After she had time to think about how she had stabbed that pirate with the pen today, Elaina realized that she harbored a lot of anger. The pirate had been a convenient outlet.

What would she do if she were with Masal? It might be something much worse. He had virtually raped her. He had made her feel so used and dirty. The shower this morning couldn't begin to wash away that feeling.

She loathed the man and she didn't trust herself around him. But where could she go? She didn't have a girlfriend aboard this starship and she certainly didn't want to ask a strange man to share his compartment.

She was exhausted. She had slept poorly last night – maybe two or three hours. Then, of course, today had been really stressful. And, in fact, if she did get some sleep tonight, it wouldn't be much.

They apparently had cleared away from the location of the pirates, but even that wasn't a sure thing. The entire crew had been on high alert all during the Green Shift.

Right now, the Orange Shift was still on high alert, but the whole tone around the starship was much less stressed than it had been earlier. She was thankful for that.

And here she was on Level 2 outside Commander Seth Okanata's compartment.

She had waited and waited before doing this and she had done a whole lot of thinking, careful thinking. She had waited for many reasons besides taking a long time to think.

She was also slow to do this because of the pure embarrassment of seeking help from him and then maybe having to explain what had happened with Masal. That would be the worst.

What had encouraged her to take this step, finally, was that Seth Okanata seemed to be a kind, good person. In fact, she was banking on that.

With her right index finger Elaina tapped the surface of her wrist control.

Dark numbers appeared in the glowing face.

It was after three in the morning. God, this was an awful thing to do to anyone at this time of the morning. But where else did she have to go?

She looked up at the number 205 in clear black figures above the pocket door.

She stood for several seconds, reconsidering. This was it – absolutely her only choice.

She reached out and pressed the black circular button to the right of the door.

There was a muffled buzz.

She turned her right ear toward the door to listen.

Nothing.

Finally, she heard the muffled thump of feet on the titanium floor.

For just a second, she considered jumping aside so that her commander couldn't see her through the peephole in the door.

Instead, she stood right where she was and stared down at the bottom of the pocket door.

The door rattled open. "Lieutenant Djoser."

Elaina raised her head and stared at him. Her right eye, the one she could see out of ran tears. She started to open her mouth.

A hand pressed against her back. "Come inside, Lieutenant."

"Thank you, sir." She stepped over the curved threshold into the compartment.

The door rattled shut.

Her commander stood in front of her. He was wearing a thin blue bathrobe over blue stripped pajamas. There were brown soft cloth slippers on his feet. "You're afraid to go back to your own compartment, aren't you?"

She nodded.

"It's your husband, isn't it?"

"Yes." She looked up. "I'm really sorry. I should leave." She turned.

"No. You need some rest. It's very late. You have to be exhausted."

She nodded. "Yes."

"I have an inflatable mattress. It's not much."

She smiled. "That would be great, sir. Actually, I could just sleep on the floor."

"Certainly not. We can't have that." He walked across the short space to the kitchen. "I'll bet you could use a glass of wine to relax your nerves."

"You don't have to do that, sir."

He turned and smiled. "I know, Lieutenant, but you're a good officer and you've had a very difficult day."

"Yes, sir, I have."

"You can call me Seth here. Don't use that name on the bridge, of course."

"Yes, sir."

"Do you like white wine?"

"Yes. . . Seth."

He smiled as he poured wine into two goblets. "That name sounds good spoken by you."

His smile vanished and he walked across the room and handed her the wine goblet. "I'll get that mattress for you. I also have a pair of clean pajamas. I don't imagine they'll fit very well, but you're welcome to them."

"That would be nice, sir." She took the goblet of wine, tilted it up and sipped the nearly clear liquid.

The flavor was fruity and delicate. Just drinking this delicious wine made her feel better.

As she had expected, Commander Okanata was a gentleman.

Seconds later, her commander appeared in the living room with a vinyl mattress in a tight roll. He placed the roll on the floor in an open area, then inserted the black plug into the wall socket on his left. The plug was attached to a wire which was connected to a small electric motor.

Next he shoved the pointed end of the electric motor into a small opening in the side of the mattress.

When he flipped the black switch on the small electric motor, it made a low buzzing sound.

The mattress began inflating. Gradually, creases popped out and eventually, the mattress was puffed up to full inflation.

The commander flipped down the switch and pulled out the pump. Then the he shoved an attached plastic plug into the opening.

He rose to his feet. "I don't have any extra sheets. Will a sleeping bag do?"

"Oh, yes. That would be fine."

"Good." He unplugged the small electric motor from the wall and tucked it under a small table off to the side.

He hurried down the short hallway and into the bedroom.

Seconds later he stepped out carrying a military green sleeping bag. "It's clean."

"I really don't care, sir."

"Seth." He placed the rolled sleeping bag on the inflated mattress. "Do you want those pajamas?"

"If you can spare them."

"Of course." He went down the hall and stepped into the bedroom again.

She could hear a drawer close.

The commander stepped out carrying folded striped pajamas. These stripes were green, not blue like his.

He placed the pajamas on the corner of the inflated mattress. "There."

The commander walked across to the other wine goblet on the end of the kitchen counter. He picked it up and sipped.

Then he turned and smiled. "I'm sorry this kind of thing has happened to you. Perhaps we can set up some counseling for you and your husband."

Elaina stared down at the floor. Then her gaze came up. "This isn't the first time." She covered her eyes with her left hand. "It's so embarrassing."

"Let me guess. You don't think counseling will work." The commander looked directly at her.

She shook her head. "No. Masal has so much anger. I have to find somewhere else to live. I can't impose on you."

The commander nodded. "We'll find some place, Lieutenant. It may not be sumptuous, but we will find something. I have to find living quarters for my favorite navigator."

She smiled. Then she winced because it hurt the swollen left side of her face.

"Have you seen the onboard doctor about your injuries?"

Elaina shook her head.

"Perhaps you should."

"I haven't had the time."

"You were afraid to see a doctor, weren't you?"

She nodded. "Yes. I thought it might just make him angrier."

"I would do it. You could have injuries to the bone in your face or to your eye."

"Thank you for doing this."

"You'd do it for me."

She smiled. "Yes, I would."

Commander Okanata drank down the remainder of his white wine then turned and placed the goblet on the counter. "Just put your goblet here when you finish."

He started to walk away, then turned. "Oh. . . you can change in the bathroom. There's a lock on the door."

"Thank you. . . Seth."

He bowed slightly. "You're more than welcome, Elaina."

CHAPTER TWENTY-TWO

"Surprises"

Starship Cygnus
Level 2
Compartment 205
10M, Day 27, 6572
5:32 a.m.

Elaina could smell coffee and something else like toast. She wasn't sure what it was.

She opened her right eye. The left one opened slightly. It was all gummy. Maybe she could eventually see out of that eye today. She was looking up at a lighted overhead in the starship and she was lying on something spongy.

For just a minute, she didn't know where she was. Then she remembered Seth Okanata and last night.

She checked with both hands to make sure the loose pajama top was on her shoulders. Then she rose to a sitting position in the sleeping bag.

Seth was in the kitchen. He was fully dressed in his green coveralls and he looked fresh and clean. He smiled at her. "Good morning, Elaina. Do you want some toast?"

She shook her head. "No, thanks."

"Coffee?"

"Yes, please."

"How do you take it?"

"One sugar."

"Coffee with one sugar coming up."

Elaina smiled. She felt so comfortable here with Seth. Wasn't that strange? She hardly knew him, yet he made her feel comfortable.

He stepped around the counter carrying a white mug. "I put in one rounded teaspoon of sugar and stirred it in." He walked up to the side of the inflated bed, leaned down toward her and held out the mug.

"Thank you. . . Seth."

He pointed to her left eye. "The swelling's gone down and it's a tasteful green in color now."

Elaina grinned. "I'm sure it's just beautiful."

"Actually, you're a very attractive woman – well, normally you're very attractive."

Elaina was still grinning. "Thank you for the backhanded compliment."

"You're more than welcome." He moved back toward the kitchen. "I've made an appointment for you with Doctor Neleus."

"The psychologist?"

"Psychiatrist. She's also a doctor, of course. She's functioning as our therapist and one of our doctors aboard the starship. I wanted her to look at your eye – maybe take some X-rays."

"I really don't think I need that, sir."

The commander was near the coffee pot. He was holding a mug of coffee near his face when his head turned. "You don't have a choice, Lieutenant. That's an order."

She looked into the blue eyes. She felt pressure, but she also felt protected. In fact, she had never felt so protected before in her life.

"Do it the first thing this morning. I'll leave a little early to go up to the bridge so you can have the shower and the bathroom to yourself. There's a new toothbrush in a package on the counter. You'll see it. There's a clean towel there too. It's folded on the counter.

"You probably want to go back to your compartment to get some fresh clothes. I would wait until you're through with Doctor Neleus. That way you'll be late enough so you won't have to deal with your husband."

Seth Okanata's head tilted downward. Then he turned to her. "I'm sorry. Here I am telling you what to do, as if you can't think for yourself. I guess I'm just trying to protect you."

Elaina smiled. "I appreciate that. Thank you."

"If you want, you can bring some clothes back here." He looked away and stared up at the overhead. "Sorry, there I go again, trying to tell you what to do."

He faced her. "I don't want you to be hurt a second time. If your husband finds out you slept here, I'm sure he'll be furious. If I were in your shoes, I'd pack a bag and move out today. I'll find you a place to bunk, but in the meantime, if I were you, I'd pack a bag with your belongings and bring it here. I wouldn't think you'd want to take a bag to the bridge. I can give you a key card for this place."

Elaina leaned forward and folded her arms around her knees. She felt comfortable with this man. "Thank you, Seth."

"I'll keep Lieutenant Lycastus on at the navigation station and I'll tell him that you called me to say that you were stopping at the clinic this morning because of your injuries."

"Why are you doing this for me?"

The commander turned to face her.

What surprised Elaina was that he hesitated before he spoke. It was almost as if he was going to say something else.

"You're my best navigator. I need you in good health and safe from harm. I can't operate this ship without you." He grinned. "Besides, you were the hero who saved the ship from that pirate, Calchus."

Elaina averted her eyes.

"What's wrong?"

She didn't answer. Tears began to flow from her right eye. She was also aware that she was crying from her swollen left eye as well.

She could feel Seth near her. "What's wrong, Elaina?"

"I was stabbing Masal."

Her commander crouched down in front of her. "It's all right. Any woman would be angry with somebody who hurt her."

"He raped me." This slipped out before Elaina even knew she was going to say it.

"Oh, my dear, I'm so sorry."

She could not look at Seth.

She felt his hand on her left shoulder.

"It won't happen again, Elaina. I won't let it happen."

When she heard this, she was amazed. It was not only because she hardly knew this man, but also because he would make this promise. She wasn't sure what it meant. She could sense protectiveness in it, and strength.

It was his strength protecting her. He was her protector now. It felt strange and new, but it also felt good.

CHAPTER TWENTY-THREE

"Big Plans"

Starship Dragon Fire
Bridge
10M, Day 26, 6572
7:22 a.m.

"Nisos, go out into the corridor and don't let anyone inside the bridge. You too, Castor."

"But I'm the navigator."

"Set the course, Castor, then step out into the corridor."

Delos motioned with his hand. "Go."

"What if that Mayan starship spots us?"

"Nothing will happen. We're cloaked."

"Cloaks have limits."

"Castor, get your fuckin' ass out of here!"

The navigator stared at Delos. "I don't like this."

Delos pointed toward the pocket door where Nisos was standing. "Out, both of you!"

Nisos slapped the blue glowing pad to the right of the door.

It sucked open to the right. Half way back, it stuck.

Nisos slammed the side of his fist against the bulkhead and the door slid back into the cavity.

Delos waited for both men to be out in the corridor and the door to close. This door was one of the many broken items aboard this old starship. Maybe he should call Pelias down in the repair department.

The door closed part way. Then, a second time, Nisos slammed his fist against the bulkhead.

The door rattled shut.

Delos turned to the other men. He knew where the problem was here. Scarphe couldn't be trusted. Now that Calchus was gone, Delos was sure that Scarphe was planning some way to move up to commander, even if he had to kill to do it.

"Okay, here's why I told those guys to step out. I have this idea. We have to get Calchus back."

"You think you can get him out of that Mayan starship?"

Delos looked at Scraphe. "Yeah, I do."

"Fuck, man, that's the dumbest idea I ever heard."

"You of all people, Scarphe, should know that Calchus is the best leader we ever had."

"Yeah, but what the fuck happens if we don't succeed in this plan? Tell me that. We will have no fuckin' starship at all and we'll be floatin' around in space stone dead. We've lost one starship already. Now you're gonna chance losin' this one?"

Delos was beginning to have a bad feeling about this meeting. "Look – it's not gonna be easy, but just remember that Calchus would try to save our asses in the same situation."

Halios folded his arms across his massive chest. "Scarphe's right. This is not a fuckin' freighter full of dumbasses we're dealin' with, Delos. This is a military starship."

Delos turned to the giant man. "True, but I figure there are gonna be times when they're in a tough situation and when they're gonna have the whole crew focused on dealin' with that situation – like a deceleration flyby, for instance."

"We don't even know where they're goin', Delos."

He turned back to Scarphe. "I have a pretty good idea. From what we've figured out, they're goin' to Mars, the fourth planet in that small solar system of eight planets. It's somewhere near coordinates one hundred twenty-seven horizontal and three hundred five vertical. The Cygnus is a Mayan starship and that's where their ancestors came from."

Delos glanced at Halios, then turned back to Scarphe. "We don't know why they're goin' there."

"Then you can't be sure they're actually goin' to this planet, Mars."

"Look, Scarphe, they haven't been out in this quadrant of the galaxy for as long as I can remember. Usually Mayan freighters stay in the Sagittarius Arm of the galaxy. Mars is where they came from originally. I looked it up. I figure that's the only reason they came out here."

"That doesn't mean they're goin' to that planet."

"Hey, boss."

Delos turned to the youngest pilot in the group. "So, what's up, Dymas?"

"Well, maybe that would be the best time to hit them - when they're slowing down to establish an orbit around Mars."

Delos nodded. "That's a good idea, but that means we have to wait and track them a long time. It's gonna be about a month before they get to Mars. Who knows what might happen to Calchus durin' that time. They might even execute him."

Scarphe shook his head. "No. Those military types lock people up and then they court martial them, and then they execute them." His head tilted back and laughed.

Scarphe made fun of everything. As far as Delos was concerned, once in a great while this guy was actually funny. Most of the time he was just a pain in the ass.

Delos held up his right hand. "Okay - let's get down to business."

Scraphe shrugged. "Have at it. Nobody's stoppin' you."

"We gotta save Calchus. We owe him that. He's taken us on more goddamn good raids than anyone else in this business. With him as commander, I've been makin' more money than ever before."

Scarphe folded his tattooed arms across his chest. "So, how the fuck you gonna do this raid? Tell me that."

Delos looked at him. "I figure that you and I could teleport into their bridge durin' some critical time when they have a lot to deal with. With two of us, one can hold his auto laser on them while the other takes their weapons."

Scarphe nodded. "Okay, that sounds good if this was a freighter with a bunch of half-asses on the bridge. But this is a military ship, Delos."

"I know that."

"But you don't get the fuckin' point, Delos."

"What point?"

"We're gonna get our asses kicked."

"We'll have surprise on our side."

"Tell me this, Delos. How many men do these Mayans have on the bridge durin' a shift?"

Delos didn't like to be challenged. That's what he always felt from Scarphe – reckless challenge. The guy was a loose laser cannon. "Okay, there'd be the pilot and co-pilot. . . the navigator. . . and probably a guard."

"That's four people."

"Don't you think we can take four people?"

Scarphe shrugged. "It all depends on whether we can surprise them. If there's an armed guard, that might be a problem. And, remember, these guys are trained military."

"There'll be an armed guard for sure."

"We'd have to blast his ass right away."

"What am I going to be doing all this time?"

Delos looked at the young pilot, Dymas. "You'll be at the helm of this ship."

"I think we ought to teleport a third person."

Delos turned around. "Yeah, Halios, that might be a good idea. The only problem is gettin' three down to that bridge without hittin' somethin' gets real tricky."

"Send down two first, then lay down a wrist control to set the coordinates for the third."

"Would you like to be the third man, Halios?"

"Sure."

"Then, you're in." Delos thought for a minute. "Okay – there are two things we have to consider here. First off, we should try to contact Calchus and find out what we're dealing with. I mean – he's pretty smart so I wanna know how the hell they took him captive.

"Okay – also we've gotta try to intercept their radio chatter and see where the fuck they're goin'. Like – maybe they are goin' to Mars after all. That's a long wait. . . probably a month. And here's the problem - the longer we wait, the greater the chance they spot us.

"So, if they're goin' to Mars, then where are they gonna do their fly-by decelerations? If we find that out, then we know where to hit them."

"They don't have any cargo. It's not a freighter. There's nothing in it for us to fuckin' steal."

Delos turned around. "Think about it, Scarphe. That's a new ship, nothin' like this old piece of shit. That's the real prize here. We can also take some of the women – only the good-lookin' ones of course."

Scarphe grinned.

"You think you're gonna get lucky, Scarphe? What's your little girlfriend, Proto, gonna say about that? She'll wait until late at night and cut off your fuckin' balls."

"That bitch wouldn't dare."

Delos grinned. "Hey, you never know about women, Scarphe."

The real issue here was figuring a way to take this Mayan starship. It was a beautiful piece of machinery and was probably faster than shit, and Delos wanted it. They could sure use something like that in the pirate fleet.

"We gonna try to reach Calchus on his implant?"

Delos turned to Scarphe. "That's it, and he can send messages back to us by tappin' together those two teeth with titanium tips. We all have them. I've never used mine, but I guess they work all right."

Scarphe squinted. "He can only tap his teeth if he's still alive, asshole."

"Now, that was brilliant, Scarphe." Delos had to watch his back now that Calchus was captured. He didn't trust Scarphe for one minute. That's why this asshole had to be on this raid. If Scarphe was with him, Delos would know where he was and what he was doing.

This was not going to be an easy operation. Probably Calchus was locked in the brig. This was a military ship. Coded messages to his implant were the only possible way to reach him. They'd have to make up a good plan for boarding that Mayan starship.

Maybe waiting for the Cygnus to reach Mars was the best strategy. He'd have to think about that.

CHAPTER TWENTY-FOUR
"Threat"

Starship Cygnus
Bridge
10M, Day 27, 6572
8:42 a.m.

Seth Okanata felt unusually chipper this morning and Elaina wasn't even here on the bridge. She was probably still moving out of the compartment where she lived with her husband.

Lieutenant Lycastus was at the navigation console. He was covering for Elaina until she showed up for her shift. She shouldn't be too much longer.

There was also something which made Seth uneasy this morning - Elaina's husband. The guy was apparently like a loaded gun, ready to go off at any time.

Earlier Seth had checked in the records on the onboard computer. Lieutenant Masal Djoser was a very competent mechanic with years of experience with the MSA. In fact, there were never any incidents of violence or even misbehavior of any kind in his MSA record.

Of course, this record didn't reflect his personal life and this was the first time he and his wife had been assigned together. Seth had noticed this strange phenomenon in the submitted dossiers but it had been so near launch that he decided just to go with the crew he had.

He even checked their individual records to see which one he would eliminate. Because Elaina had been highly recommended by Captain Tikal, Seth knew she was very competent. Therefore, he would definitely have cut her husband, rather than Elaina. Now he wished he had done just that.

Of course, if he had cut Masal, maybe he would never have gotten this close to Elaina. That had been a strange advantage built into this problem in her marriage.

Commander Seth Okanata did not believe in cheating on a spouse. He would never encourage that. Yet here was this beautiful woman in trouble, a woman he found very attractive, and – now - he had established a relationship with her.

No, it was not an intimate relationship, yet he did have this connection to her. It was probably because she was so vulnerable and he felt this need to protect her.

Typically Seth had difficulty getting close to women. He was kind of afraid of relationships with females. He had been that way for as long as he could remember.

He had found women fascinating, but confusing. With Elaina, however, he felt this connection based upon his caring for another human being. That he could handle. It didn't seem confusing at all.

He was cheerful this morning to the point of being what he would consider idiotic, but should he let himself get this emotionally involved? Sure, at this point it was only a sympathetic, compassionate emotion, but he knew very well that he had a real crush on Elaina, and that had very little to do with sympathy or compassion.

Why not just let things happen? She was beautiful and charming, as well as very competent. Of course, she was also married.

Seth did not like interfering with other people's lives, but in this case, he hoped she divorced that brute. Masal Djoser had actually raped his own wife. Who would do such a thing?

The whole idea made Seth's skin crawl. One part of him wanted to keep Elaina in his compartment protected from harm. Another part was repulsed by his disgust for what had happened to her.

There was a buzz at the door.

Commander Seth Okanata swung his swivel seat around to face the door to the bridge. "Private Imhotep, see who that is, please."

The soldier at the door moved over to the peephole in the upper half of the door.

Commander Okanata had kept a soldier with an assault rifle stationed at the door of the bridge since the pirate incursion two days ago. They had apparently moved out of the pirates' favorite lair, but it was wise to play it safe.

The soldier turned around. "Sir, it's a male member of the crew. I don't recognize him. He's a lieutenant, sir."

"Ask for his name, Private."

"Yes, sir." The soldier turned around. He pressed a button up high on the wall to the right of the door. "State your name and rank and position on the starship."

"Lieutenant Masal Djoser, Fusion Rocket Mechanic," said a male voice over the speaker.

Seth Okanata rose out of his seat.

"Commander. . ."

Seth turned to the navigator. "What is it, Lieutenant?"

"Sir, I'm picking up some strange radio signals."

"Where are they coming from?"

"I'm not sure, sir, but they're low frequency so they can't be traveling very far. And they're not strong signals, sir."

"Can you understand what's being sent, Lieutenant?"

Lindos Lycastus shook his head. "No, sir. They're in some kind of code."

"Record them, Lieutenant, and we'll send them down to decoding. Maybe they can figure them out."

Lieutenant Lycastus punched a button on the console. "Recording, sir. "

"Very good, Lieutenant."

Seth turned to the soldier at the door. "Private, tell Lieutenant Djoser that I will meet him outside in the corridor."

"Yes, sir."

The soldier turned and pressed the black button. "Commander Okanata will be out to see you in the corridor."

"Fine," was the one word that came back over the speaker.

"Sir, do you want me to go with you?"

Seth turned to his co-pilot. "No Captain Tikal. I can handle this."

"I heard what happened to his wife, sir. I don't know if this is a good idea. . . if you know what I mean."

Seth nodded. "Yes, I know what you mean, Captain, and I do appreciate your concern, but I think we have to handle this quietly and discretely."

"I'll have the guard check on you, Commander."

Seth considered. "There's no need to do that, Captain Tikal. I can handle this just fine."

The brown eyes focused on Seth. "Sir, I don't want anything to happen."

"I don't either, Tikal, and I'll be fine." Seth Okanata moved with confident ease across the aluminum deck to the guard at the door.

"Is he armed, Private?"

"No, sir, not as far as I can tell. Do you want me out there?"

"No, Private, but if I need you, I'll call."

"Yes, sir."

"You may open the door, Private."

"Yes, sir." The young soldier reached over to the blue lighted panel to the right of the door casing.

The door hissed and rattled to the right into the wall cavity.

Seth Okanata stepped over the curved threshold into the corridor.

"Where's my wife?"

The door rattled shut behind Seth. He stared at the shorter man with disheveled brown hair and bloodshot eyes. "When you address me, Lieutenant, you may use the word, sir."

"Sure. Where's my wife, sir?"

"She's in my protective custody."

The man's right hand shot out and he pointed his index finger at the commander. "You have no right!"

"I suggest that you control yourself, Lieutenant. You're just about ten seconds away from ending up in the brig."

"You're screwin' her, aren't you?"

"You piece of filth! How dare you!"

"You're screwin' her!"

Seth unsnapped his holster and yanked out his pistol. He cocked the hammer back and aimed the barrel of the black pistol at Masal's face. "Apparently, you are totally out of control, Lieutenant." He looked into the brown eyes. At this moment Seth noticed they were larger.

For the first time since their brief encounter, Seth felt that this man was showing enough deference toward his superior officer. In fact, Seth could detect fear in the man's bloodshot eyes.

"Now that I have your attention, Lieutenant, I want to make several points clear to you. First, I have never slept with your wife. Second, by this time, she has moved out of your compartment. Third, she will be living in her own compartment without you. Fourth, if I ever hear about you hitting her again, I will personally see to it that you are locked in the brig for the duration of this starship journey. Is that clear, Lieutenant Djoser?"

The other man stared at the pistol. He said nothing.

"Is that clear, Lieutenant Djoser?"

The oily face slipped into a grin. "She's got you under her thumb already. Just like that. You don't know what a sneaky, stubborn bitch she can be."

"Let me make something very clear, Lieutenant Djoser. If it weren't for a whole starship full of witnesses, I would shoot you in both legs right now. Then I would drag you down to the decompression chamber and I would eject you into space, like one might get rid of some really nasty garbage.

"You are only facing time in the brig because there are witnesses to protect you. Just remember that. You see, Lieutenant, it is entirely possible that there may be just one little moment in the future when there will be no witnesses and at that particular moment, you might want to look over your shoulder. Keep that in mind, Lieutenant.

"Lieutenant Djoser, in my estimation, you are completely expendable. In fact, it would clean up things around here a whole lot if you disappeared."

"Are you threatin' me?"

"Yes. . . absolutely."

CHAPTER TWENTY-FIVE

"As a Friend"

Starship Cygnus
EVA Storage Room
10M, Day 27, 6572
10:16 a.m.

"**Y**ou know what that asshole did? He threatened me."

"The commander?"

"Yeah, his highness, Seth Okanata."

Hector Copan didn't like being around trouble. It made him nervous. He had been that way ever since the accident. He had been kind of waiting for something to come back from Hyksos about an investigation. It hadn't.

He figured that if there was something like that going on, his mother would text message him. She sent texts about everything else. And if his mother didn't text about it, then Charis would. His little girl was damn smart. She would text him.

"Don't you have somethin' to say about this?"

Hector looked up from the helmet he was cleaning. "Why should I have somethin' to say?"

"Hey, you're workin' for me and, besides, we're friends."

"Look, Masal, I don't want to get into this thing between you and the commander."

"You're afraid of him."

"Sure I am. Look, Masal, he's the commander, and you don't mess with the commander."

"He's just a man like everybody else. Besides, he's fuckin' Elaina."

Hector stopped his cleaning cloth. "Look, Masal, I know you're pissed, but Commander Okanata would not mess around with somebody's wife, and you know it."

"You're on his side."

"Masal, what the hell's your problem?"

The other man stood upright. "Okay, here's the short version. She moved out."

"Why'd she do that?"

Masal hesitated for just a split second.

Hector wondered about that.

"I have no fuckin' idea, except that she's messin' around with Okanata."

Hector shook his head. "That's not happenin', Masal, not in a million years."

"So, you don't believe me?"

Hector shrugged. "I believe you believe it, but it's not happenin'. I've worked for this commander before. He's so straight that one guy I worked with thought he might even be queer."

"Hey, don't use that word."

Hector raised both hands. "Sorry, I know it's not politically correct and all that shit. This guy named Mastor said he thought the old man was gay."

"Okanata?"

"Yeah, that's what he said. He said the guy was like a robot and didn't show any emotion and all that shit. Then he said he thought the old man was queer."

"Hey, I told you not to use that word."

"Don't be so fuckin' sensitive, Masal. That's the word that Mastor used." Hector shrugged. "And, hey, I gotta tell you Okanata's no saint, but he's not fuckin' anybody, believe me. And why the hell are you so sensitive about the word, queer?"

"I just don't like it is all."

"You must really be into this politically correct shit."

"No. I just don't like that word."

Hector looked into the bloodshot blue eyes. He was sure Masal had been drinking last night. He looked hungover.

"He's hidin' Elaina."

Hector's head snapped up. "What?"

"The old man's hidin' her."

"Why would he do that?"

There was no answer.

"What's goin' on, Masal? You're not tellin' everythin'."

Masal turned away and picked up a space helmet out of the netting hanging from the wall of the storage room. A label on the netting read, "Lt. Djoser."

Hector Copan was absolutely sure now that Masal wasn't telling him everything. He was covering up something. Why would the commander hide Elaina?

Then Hector remembered an event from a long time ago. They were at the driving range outside of Memphis and when Masal's Lynx teleported onto the teleporting pad, Hector noticed something about Elaina.

First, she was really quiet. Then he noticed she had a small bandage on her left eyebrow. But what had really caught his attention was how quickly she explained that she had bumped her head on the corner of the kitchen cupboard.

It had been so fast and without the usual details and humor that go along with those funny and stupid accidents. In fact, at the time, he was sure she was lying.

There was another incident when they were out for dinner together, both couples, and Elaina had bruises on her left arm.

Hector placed the clean helmet back into the netting with the label "Sgt. Copan." He turned around and faced Masal.

The lieutenant had his helmet on the floor again. Now he was using a small tube of lubricant on the valve fittings on the breathing apparatus on the front.

"You're not tellin' everythin', are you, Masal?"

The other man's head jerked up. For just a second his blue eyes revealed surprise, but seconds later it was gone – hidden beneath calm. Masal leaned back on his haunches. "What are you gettin' at?"

Hector held back for a few seconds. Then, he said, "Have you been hittin' your wife again?"

"What are you talkin' about?"

Hector stared into the bloodshot blue eyes. "No bullshit this time, Masal. Tell me the truth."

The other man's head tilted down and he leaned forward. He pressed the tube of lubricant against the threads of a small adjustment valve and squeezed. "Too much." He pulled away the tube and grabbed a rag from the floor with his left hand. He dabbed the lubricant off the valve.

"You've hit her before, Masal. I know that."

The other man continued to stare at the threaded adjustment screw. Then he vigorously wiped it with the rag.

"The commander's protectin' Elaina, isn't he?"

Masal turned the helmet and placed the tip of the lubricating tube on another adjustment screw's thread. He squeezed, then pulled back the tube and with his left hand used the rag to wipe away the excess lubricant.

"Masal, I'm tellin' you this as a friend. You ought to see a marriage counselor."

The head popped up. "I'm not seein' anybody."

Hector was surprised by the anger in Masal's eyes. He had seen flashes of that anger before, but this was deeper and nastier.

"Tell you what - if that bitch is messin' around with the commander, she will pay for it no matter where he's keepin' her. I'll just smash down the fuckin' door and I'll kill that bitch."

Hector stared at his friend.

Masal's head turned, and he grinned. "You say anythin' about this, Hector, and I'll tell how you messed with Cadmus's car. You'll be locked up for fuckin' murder."

CHAPTER TWENTY-SIX

"Personal"

Starship Cygnus
Bridge Corridor
10M, Day 27, 6572
11:58 a.m.

Seth Okanata stepped over the curved threshold into the corridor. The titanium pocket door rattled shut behind him.

He moved down the short corridor away from the peephole in the door.

Seth was supposed to be on his lunch break and he would go on his break very soon, but he had signaled Elaina to meet him out here.

The door to the bridge rattled open again.

Elaina stepped out into the corridor and turned left and moved toward him.

The pocket door closed.

"You wanted to see me, sir?"

"Yes." He reached into the right side pocket of his blue coveralls and pulled out a red plastic card.

He held it out to Elaina. "This will get you into Storage Room C. It has been emptied of food stuffs and kitchen supplies. It's your room now. It's down on Level 3 near the decompression room.

"I had some of the men I can trust to keep quiet put a bed in there. There's no plumbing in the room, but you can keep my compartment key and use my shower and bathroom. In fact, you can eat your breakfasts in my compartment if you'd like."

"You're being very kind, sir."

"How was your visit with Doctor Neleus?"

"He said there was a lot of bruising but there were no broken bones. He gave me something for the swelling."

Seth smiled. "The swelling does seem to have gone down some already."

"The soldier at the door said you spoke with my husband this morning."

Seth nodded. "Yes. I don't think he will bother you anymore. I told him that I'd lock him up if he did."

Elaina's head tipped down. She seemed to be avoiding his eyes. Finally she looked up. "I'm sorry I got you involved."

"Elaina, I would have done the same for any of my crew members."

After he said that, Seth Okanata realized that he was actually lying. He would do this for Elaina, although probably not anyone else except maybe other members of his crew on the bridge, but then he realized that he probably wouldn't do it for them either.

The elevator at the end of the corridor made a ding and the door rattled open.

Sergeant Hector Copan stepped out into the corridor. He saluted Commander Okanata.

The elevator door rattled shut.

Seth returned his salute. "Can I help you, Sergeant?"

"Sir, I have to speak to Elaina."

Seth sensed something. Then he remembered that Copan worked with Masal Djoser. "If you don't mind my asking, Sergeant, what is this about?"

The sergeant looked up at Seth. "Sir, this is personal."

"Does it have to do with her husband?"

"Yes, sir."

"Then I wish to hear it as well, Sergeant. Lieutenant Djoser is on probation as of earlier this morning."

"Yes, sir." Hector Copan turned to Elaina. "I just thought I ought to warn you that Masal said right in front of me that no matter where you were he would break down the door and kill you."

Seth Okanata could feel the muscles in his neck tighten. "He actually said that, Sergeant?"

Hector turned to Seth. "Yes, sir, he did."

Seth nodded. "That's unfortunate. Is that all, Sergeant?"

"Yes, sir, but sir. . . "

"Yes, Sergeant?"

"Elaina ought to be careful. He sounded real weird, sir, like he was really goin' to do somethin'."

"Thank you for telling us, Sergeant, and, by the way, we won't let Lieutenant Djoser know where we got this information."

"Yes, sir, thank you, sir." Sergeant Copan saluted.

Commander Okanata returned the salute. "Thank you, Sergeant."

"You're welcome, sir." The short man moved down the corridor to the elevator.

The door rattled open.

Copan disappeared into the elevator.

Seth turned to Elaina. "I want you to stay in my compartment. It will be safer."

"I can't impose on you like that."

Seth gripped the sides of her shoulders. "Elaina. . ." He released his hands. "I'm sorry. I didn't mean to do that. I have no right."

She smiled. "It's fine, sir. . . Seth. It's nice to have someone looking out for me."

Seth stared up at the overhead and collected himself. Then he looked at Elaina again. "I don't want you to be subject to any more of his violence. I've given him fair warning about that. I said I would lock him up."

He looked down, then his gaze came up. "The problem is that we need both Copan and him when we enter Earth's solar system. We will be using Saturn and Jupiter to break our speed and those are the moments when you have problems with the starship.

"As you know, we often have meteorite hits. Sometimes they're harmless. Other times they damage critical areas. I need both mechanics on duty. If that weren't the case, I'd lock him up right now."

"You don't have to apologize, sir."

"Really, you should stay in my compartment. It will be safer. Masal has access to a lot of places on Level 3 – not the food storage area, but my point is he's down there a lot. I just don't want anything to happen to you."

Elaina nodded. "Let me think about it, sir."

"Certainly. Now, I have to go to lunch and you should be getting back to the bridge, Lieutenant."

"Yes, sir." She smiled. "You're a really nice person."

CHAPTER TWENTY-SEVEN
"Romantic Designs"

Starship Cygnus
Level 2
10M, Day 28, 6572
5:42 a.m.

Elaina stepped over the threshold of Compartment 205 into the corridor.

The door rattled shut behind her. Now she felt ready for work on the bridge. She was clean and she'd had a great breakfast.

She had slept in Storage Room C last night. It wasn't bad. It did smell a little like cardboard containers, but it was quiet and she did have privacy.

She had stopped to use the rest room at the Recreation Center on Level 1 before heading down to the storage room to sleep. There weren't any facilities down there and she wasn't going to pee in a bucket, especially in this ninety percent gravitation. The stuff could spill all over the place.

She had come up here to Seth's compartment this morning to shower. As usual, he had been so nice. He had even made her powdered eggs for breakfast earlier this morning before he left for the bridge.

She was beginning to feel a real attachment to this guy. He wasn't dashing or anything like that, but he was attentive and really nice, and that sure went a long way.

She turned to face the elevator.

What struck her as unusual was that the number 2 above the door was lit. That should mean that the elevator door was open or would open any second, but it didn't.

She had never heard of these things jamming. Now she had this creepy feeling.

Elaina lurched backward.

At that second, the elevator door rattled open and Masal lunged into the corridor.

Elaina turned and ran. She didn't know where she was going. Seth's compartment wasn't this way. She just hoped that somebody – anybody – would step out of their compartment. She needed somebody right now.

Something hit the back of her head and she stumbled headlong down the carpeted corridor.

As she fell she tried to pull her mind together. Her wrist control!

When she finally landed, she played possum and tapped HELP on her wrist control and she tapped SETH and the SEND button.

Hands grabbed her and yanked her to a sitting position.

She kicked out with all her might.

She heard a grunting sound. She scrambled to her feet, jumped over the figure on the floor and ran the other direction. She ran with all her might.

At Compartment 205 she stabbed the plastic key card into the slot.

The pocket door rattled open.

She jumped over the curved threshold and slammed her hand against the lighted rectangle to the right.

Then she scrambled backward.

Masal's hand reached out, then it was caught in the door.

He yelled and yanked his hand out.

Fists banged the door.

Elaina moved back into the living room and cowered into a corner. She tapped her wrist control. Then "SETH."

"Elaina, where are you?"

"In your compartment! He's outside banging on the door."

"We're on the elevator. There's a pistol in my bedroom in the small table next to the bed."

Elaina jumped up and ran down the short hallway to the bedroom. She lunged inside and yanked open the drawer on the small bed table.

She picked up the black pistol and swung around.

The compartment door rattled open.

Elaina cocked the hammer back and held the pistol up in front of her right eye. She aimed at the opening to the hallway.

"Elaina?"

She lowered the pistol to her right side.

Seth stepped into the bedroom. "Are you all right?"

Elaina could feel her shoulders fold forward. She thought she was going to collapse.

The pistol was removed from her hand and she was held in somebody's arms.

She could feel her body shake with sobs.

"You're all right now, Elaina. You're all right. He won't hurt you."

The arms released her and she looked up.

Seth was standing in front of her. He smiled. "Are you okay?"

She nodded. "Yes."

He patted the side of her left shoulder. "Good. Masal's in custody. We'll put him in the brig and let him cool off. I still think you should move into my compartment. You could have your own bed in the living room."

She nodded. "Maybe I will."

"Are you sure you're okay?"

"Yes."

"I have to return to the bridge." He pointed at her face. "Maybe you should redo your face, or whatever women do."

Elaina grinned. "I will. Thank you, again."

"I was happy I could make it down here in time, although I think you can take care of yourself pretty well." He laid the black pistol in the drawer of the small table and slid it closed.

"Seth. . ."

He looked up.

"Why are you doing this for me?"

He averted his eyes downward. Then his gaze came up. "You're a good navigator and a good person. I'm just trying to help you out. If you weren't in danger of any kind, it might be different, but you're husband's out of control. He's dangerous."

Seth folded his arms across his chest. "I hope a couple of days in the brig will help him think this situation through."

Elaina nodded. "Thanks."

"You're welcome." Commander Okanata walked out of the bedroom into the short hallway and disappeared.

Elaina could hear the rattle of the pocket door at the front of the compartment. Then it closed.

She would love to believe that Masal would come around after two days in the brig, yet she was sure he wouldn't. He was angry about something, but she had no idea what that was.

She peeked around the edge of the bedroom doorway into the living room of the compartment. After she did it, she felt stupid.

Here she was playing hide and seek. She was afraid of who might be in the living room. That was ridiculous. This thing with Masal had to stop. She couldn't live this way any longer.

If she had to be assigned with Masal, she was certainly glad it was on Seth's starship.

She wondered how Seth felt about her. It would be too much to hope that he had romantic designs. No, that wasn't possible – not with Seth Okanata. He was just very kind.

Elaina stepped across the hallway into the bathroom. She had to make herself presentable and get up to the bridge.

She checked her wrist control. It was 5:54 a.m. She was on duty at 6:00. She had better get moving.

CHAPTER TWENTY-EIGHT
"Imminent Danger"

Starship Cygnus
Bridge
10M, Day 28, 6572
9:51 a.m.

Captain Salathiel Tikal was glad that everything here on the bridge had quieted down this morning. This business with Elaina Djoser's husband had been a huge distraction.

When he thought of distractions, however, Captain Tikal was more focused on this vague image that would appear like some kind of white ghost on his console screen. Here he was studying the functions of the fusion engine and he was getting this ghost-like white image popping in and out of the screen.

He had observed this same problem two days ago and had expected it was some anomaly in the electronic system aboard the ship – perhaps something left over in the memory of the computer or whatever. In any case, it was a little unnerving.

He had tried to create scenarios of what it might be, but nothing seemed to make any sense.

"Stay sharp, people, we are now entering the solar system Orion Four. We have bypassed the outermost planet of any size, Neptune. It was too far out of our trajectory to use it to brake our speed, as was the planet Saturn.

"We have begun deceleration with the fusion engine." There was a pause. "Captain Tikal, you've been monitoring the engine. What's the status?"

"Everything is nominal, Commander. . . with one exception."

"And what is that exception, Captain?"

"Sir, over the last two days, whenever I've been viewing this particular screen, I've been seeing a ghost figure in the upper left quadrant of the screen, sir."

"A ghost figure?"

"Yes, sir. It's a white shape that seems incomplete and it comes and goes on my screen."

"What screen are you watching, Captain?"

"Number four, sir."

The commander's fingers rattled on the computer keyboard. He leaned forward and stared at his console screen. "I don't see anything, Captain."

"It's there, sir."

The commander rose out of his seat and leaned over Tikal's left shoulder. "That's strange. There is something on your screen and nothing on mine." He rose to full height and turned. "Lieutenant Djoser, check screen number four."

"Yes, sir," said a female voice behind Tikal.

Fingers rattled on computer keys. "I'm getting a clear image, sir. No ghost."

Commander Okanata turned again. "Come up here and look at this, Lieutenant."

"Yes, sir."

Lieutenant Elaina Djoser rose out of her seat and walked around the navigation console to the pilot console. She leaned over Captain Tikal's right shoulder. Then she pointed at the upper left quadrant of the screen. "Is this what you're referring to, Captain?"

Tikal turned. "That's it."

Lieutenant Djoser rose to full height. "Commander, that looks an awful lot like the image of the pirate starship I was getting before we blew it out of existence."

The commander folded his arms across his chest. "I wonder if somebody's been following us."

"How could they do that, sir? We have our cloaking device on." Elaina touched her chest. "I put it on myself. I know it's on."

Tikal looked up at Commander Okanata. "They could have planted a locator on Calchus – maybe under his skin." Captain Tikal shrugged. "I suppose it's possible that they've been following us, sir, just waiting for the right moment to strike."

"Why wouldn't they have attacked us already?"

Tikal thought about this. "Maybe their ship is small, not well armed so they'll wait until we're really vulnerable."

"We'd be really vulnerable in our flyby of Jupiter."

Tikal nodded. "Yes, sir, we would."

The commander rubbed his chin. "They're probably waiting for that. I imagine they're intercepting our communications and they know exactly what we're doing and when."

"Yes, sir, that's possible – even probable."

Seth Okanata turned to Elaina Djoser. "Lieutenant, take a look at our proposed course through the outlying area of Jupiter. See if there isn't some way to trap these pirates."

"Yes, sir." The navigator hurried away.

Commander Okanata looked down at Tikal. "What I want you to do, Captain, is take Private Imhotep with you and go down to the brig. You'll need an electronic bug scanner. I want you to scan Calchus for that bug. Go to the usual places. I'd start with the soft tissue behind his ears – maybe his armpits.

"If you have to bring Doctor Neleus into this, he could shoot up Calchus with a tranquilizer of some kind. I don't imagine our pirate friend is going to submit to this without a fight."

"When I get that bug, what do you want me to do with it Commander?"

"Bring it to me."

"Won't they notice a change of location?"

"Sure. But I want to check it out up here. It might have a built in radio so that Calchus can communicate with them. The other day, Lieutenant Lycastus said he was picking up radio signals – weak signals from something nearby. This might be what he was detecting."

Captain Tikal rose out of his seat. "I'll get right on that, sir."

"Be careful, Captain. This man is smart and he's dangerous."

Sal Tikal moved across to the door. "Come with me, Private."

"Yes, sir."

Captain Tikal placed his hand on the lighted panel to the right of the door.

It rattled open.

He stepped over the curved threshold into the corridor.

The guard followed.

The bridge door closed.

Sal moved down the short corridor to the end and turned at the elevator. He pressed the DOWN arrow.

The elevator opened.

He stepped inside and Imhotep followed.

Sal pressed the 2 button. Then he turned to Imhotep. "We're going down to the brig. We're going to scan the pirate, Calchus for a bug. We have suspicions that a pirate ship has been shadowing us and using his bug as their guidance system."

"But, sir, you pressed the wrong button."

"I'm going to pick up Doctor Neleus in the clinic first. By the way, Imhotep, this is classified information, so do keep your mouth shut about all of what we're doing here. Got it?"

"Yes, sir."

Sal stared into the soldier's brown eyes. "We've got to handle this carefully or the pirates may catch on to what we're doing. That's why this has to stay classified, Imhotep."

"Sir, are they gonna attack us?"

"I'm sure that's their plan. But their ship has to be small or they would have attacked us already. They're probably waiting for us to be vulnerable."

"The Jupiter flyby."

"Exactly."

The elevator door opened on Level 2.

Sal Tikal stepped out into the corridor. "Keep the elevator right where it is, Imhotep."

Captain Tikal marched down the corridor to number 200. He pressed his hand against the blue pad to the right of the door.

It opened to the left.

Tikal stepped into the small reception area. "I have to see Doctor Neleus right now. It's an emergency."

"He's with a patient," said the young nurse at the desk.

"Look. . . either you go in and get him, or I will."

She stared at Tikal. "An emergency? What kind of emergency?"

"That's classified. Look. . . I'm the co-pilot on this shift. These orders come directly from Commander Okanata. If I tell you there's an emergency, you should get your fat ass out of that chair and get Doctor Neleus!"

The young woman jerked up to her feet, moved toward the pocket door to her left, then pressed a button on the wall.

The door rattled open and she stepped inside.

"What do you mean interrupting a session with a patient?"

Sal could see the psychiatrist sitting in a straight chair. Across from him was a male patient sitting in a soft lounge chair.

"It's an emergency, Doctor. The co-pilot of the starship is in the outer office. He says these are orders from Commander Okanata."

The tall wiry man rose out of his chair. He was wearing a white cotton doctor's jacket with his name tag on the left breast pocket. "Menon, we'll have to continue this next time. I'm sorry."

The man in the lounge chair rose to his feet and shuffled into the outer office. He looked up at Sal Tikal. "What's goin' on, Captain?"

Tikal made a brief smile. "Sorry, can't say."

"Classified?"

"That's it."

The other man nodded. "Figures." He shuffled across the small office.

Tikal heard a door rattle open behind him.

Doctor Neleus stepped into the outer office. "What is this about? It had better be good, Captain."

"I can't explain it here, Doctor. I'd just ask you to bring some kind of tranquilizer shot with you."

"Tranquilizer?"

"Yes, sir."

"For what reason?"

"It's for a man. That's all I'm allowed to say, sir." Actually Tikal had never been given those orders but he didn't want the doctor arguing with him.

The doctor stared into Sal Tikal's eyes. "There's no point in my asking anything else because you won't tell me."

"No, sir. If you please, sir, time is important here."

Doctor Neleus nodded. "Okay, sure. I'll get my bag. . . and some tranquilizer."

The doctor stepped into a small room behind the receptionist's desk.

The receptionist stared at Captain Tikal.

He met her stare. He knew she was trying to make a point about his being rude, but right now he didn't care. There was no telling when these pirates might attack.

Doctor Neleus walked out of the back office carrying a soft leather bag. "I'm ready, Captain."

"Very good, sir." Sal Tikal turned and walked across to the exit door. He placed his right hand on the glowing blue rectangular block to the right of the door.

It rattled open.

He stepped over the threshold and marched down the corridor toward Private Imhotep who was standing with three other people at the elevator.

There was a mumble of voices near.

Captain Tikal walked up to Private Imhotep.

"Sir, these people want to get on the elevator."

Sal turned. "This is an emergency. You will have to wait for the next elevator."

"But. . ."

Sal pointed at the woman. "Look, you can take it up with the commander or you can shut up and wait for the next elevator."

"Well!"

Sal Tikal turned. "Get on the elevator, Doctor. You, too, Imhotep."

"Yes, sir."

Doctor Neleus stepped into the elevator and Imhotep after him.

Tikal stepped in and punched the 3 button.

The elevator door slid shut.

As it did, Sal Tikal could hear the woman ranting.

Sal could care less. That stupid woman had no idea what kind of danger the starship was in.

At Level 3, the elevator made a loud ding. The door rattled open.

Tikal motioned to Imhotep. "You go first, Private."

"Yes, sir." He stepped out.

"All clear, Private?"

The young man looked up and down the corridor. "Yes, sir."

Sal stepped out. "Come on, Doctor Neleus." He turned right.

The doctor stepped out. "The brig?"

"Yes, sir."

"Why the hell are you taking me to the brig?"

"We can talk about that once we're inside, sir."

At door to the brig, Captain Sal Tikal pressed the black button on the right side of the casing.

There was a muffled buzz from inside.

"What is your name and what is your business?"

"I am Captain Salathiel Tikal, co-pilot of the starship Cygnus. I have come to question prisoner Calchus."

"Very good, sir."

The door rattled open.

Sal stepped inside. "What's your name, soldier?"

"Private Mases Astrides of Starship Security, sir."

The doctor and Private Imhotep came into the small room.

The door rattled shut.

"Everything I tell you is classified, Private Astrides. We have come here to see the pirate, Calchus. We assume that he has an electronic device on him somewhere, probably buried under his skin. We are going to remove that device."

Sal Tikal looked around at the group of men. "He will probably resist so I'm going to need your help." He looked at the psychiatrist. "Doctor Neleus, I want you to shoot him with some tranquilizer so that he will be easier to deal with."

He turned to Private Astrides. "You have a scanner around, don't you?"

"Yes, sir."

"Get it."

"Yes, sir." The tall man moved over to the side wall and opened a cupboard above his head.

"You said this was an emergency, Captain."

Sal turned to the psychiatrist. "This is classified as far as you're concerned too, Doctor. If you utter anything about this to anyone, we'll lock you up." Sal waited for that to sink in.

Sal continued. "Okay, Doctor, here's the scoop. We're being shadowed by a pirate ship. We're convinced that Calchus, this pirate we have in the brig, has a locator device on his body somewhere and that's how the pirates have been able to trace our direction."

"Why haven't they attacked?"

"Because, Doctor, we are assuming that they have a class C starship, much smaller than ours, and that they're no match for our firepower. They're just waiting for a moment when we're vulnerable."

The psychiatrist nodded. "That makes sense. How much does this Calchus weigh?"

"Somewhere over two hundred pounds, but I'm only guessing. You'll have to decide that for yourself, Doc."

"Is there some way I can see him?"

Private Astrides pointed. "Pull aside that little window over there, Doc."

The psychiatrist crossed to the door at the back of the room.

"He's the taller one," said Astrides.

Doctor Neleus slid a small, recessed rectangular plate aside in the top section of the pocket door. He leaned forward so his face was against the opening. He stood in that position for several seconds.

Then he pulled back and slid the small rectangular plate closed. "I'd guess two hundred forty to two hundred forty-five pounds."

He walked back to Sal Tikal. "The best way to handle this is for you to find some way to hold him against the bars and I'll give him a shot. I don't want to go into his cell. He could kill me."

Sal Tikal thought about this. Finally he said, "Okay, I'll hold him at gunpoint and ask him to place his back against the bars. You two. . ." Sal pointed to the two privates, ". . . grab his arms and hold them against the bars. Then the doctor, here, can give him a shot of that tranquilizer."

He turned to Doctor Neleus. "How long does it take this tranquilizer to take effect?"

"Oh. . . probably a minute or so. I'll give him the shot in his neck. That would be the easiest to reach, I should think."

The psychiatrist put his bag on the counter and opened it. He brought out a vial of clear liquid. He then unscrewed the top and plunged a hypodermic needle into the bottle.

He pulled back the plunger and stopped. He then studied the titrated side of the hypodermic. He pulled the hypodermic back farther and, finally, pulled the needle out of the liquid.

He placed the hypodermic on the counter with the needle out over the edge in the open. Then he twisted the cap onto the top of the bottle of liquid and placed it in the back in the leather bag. Next he brought out a bottle of alcohol and a gauze pad.

"Doc, I don't think we're going to have time for rubbing alcohol on his skin."

The psychiatrist made a grimace. "You're probably right, but I'll put some on this gauze, just in case." He opened the alcohol and tilted it against the swab of gauze.

Neleus twisted on the cap and put the bottle back inside the bag. He then picked up the needle and held it in his right hand. "Maybe I should stay out of sight until you're ready for me."

Captain Tikal nodded. "Good idea, Doc. We'll get him up against the bars. Then you come in and shoot the juice to him." He looked at the two soldiers. "Ready?"

Private Astrides nodded.

"I'm ready, sir," said Imhotep.

Sal pointed at the door. "Open it, Astrides."

"Yes, sir." The young soldier slipped a red plastic card into the slot to the right of the door.

It rattled open.

Astrides stepped inside.

Captain Tikal stepped in behind him and Private Imhotep followed Tikal.

"Hey, I want a lawyer!"

Sal ignored the voice. He walked toward the cage-like enclosure at the back of the room.

Calchus was standing at the bars with his hands gripping two bars at shoulder width. There was a white gauze patch taped over his left eye.

When Sal came near the cage, he pulled out his pistol and held it up in front of the pirate's face.

Private Astrides flinched.

Sal made eye contact. "Calchus, turn around."

"Why should I do that?"

"So I won't shoot you."

"Hey, I want a lawyer!"

Sal turned toward the other cage. "Lieutenant Djoser, I presume."

"I demand a lawyer."

"I would suggest, Lieutenant, that you shut up." Sal stared into the blue eyes.

Djoser didn't move.

Sal swung around and faced the pirate again. "Put your back to the bars, Calchus."

"Suppose I don't."

"Well, there are two ways to do this – the easy way or the hard way. I would suggest the easy way."

"I want a lawyer!"

Sal Tikal spun around and marched over to Lieutenant Djoser. He reached in through the bars and grabbed the man's disheveled hair in his left hand. Then he slammed the man's face against the bars. "Now, listen to me, Djoser, you will shut your fucking mouth or I will shut it for you. Do you understand me?"

The blue eyes blinked. "I just want a lawyer."

"You don't need a lawyer right now as much as you need to shut up," he whispered. "This starship is in danger and all of us will be dead in a matter of hours if you don't shut your big mouth and let me get on with this."

The man's blue eyes stared at him.

"Do you understand me, Djoser?"

"Yes."

Sal Tikal released the lieutenant's blond hair. He looked at the man. "We okay, now?"

Masal nodded. "Sure."

Sal turned and walked back to the other cell. He raised his pistol in front of the pirate's face. He was fully aware that this man was a lot bigger and probably a lot tougher. "Okay, Calchus, turn around and make this easy – all right?"

"Why should I?"

"Because if you don't, I'll shoot you in the leg." Sal cocked back the hammer of his pistol. He stared into the brown eyes. "There's no bullshit here, Calchus. This is real. Turn or I'll shoot you in the leg."

The pirate shrugged. "Shit. . . some fuckin' asshole tells me to turn around or he's gonna shoot me in the leg."

Calchus turned.

"Now raise your arms against the bars."

Calchus raised his arms.

Private Imhotep nodded at the other soldier and grabbed Calchus's right wrist.

The other private grabbed the left.

"Hey, what's goin' on here?"

Doctor Neleus scurried into the cellblock. He grabbed the back of Calchus's shirt at the neck, pulled it down and jabbed the needle.

The pirate struggled, flinging his large body backward and forward.

Imhotep leaned back and pulled against the wrist.

Doctor Neleus yanked out the needle. "Got it."

Imhotep looked over at the other soldier, then released the wrist.

The pirate lurched forward across the cell. He spun around. "What the fuck are you doin' to me?"

His eyes stared at them and he staggered forward. "Shit! What's in that needle?" His mouth jerked into a smile. Then his eyes glazed over.

CHAPTER TWENTY-NINE
"Generous Person"

Starship Cygnus
Brig
10M, Day 28, 6572
10:22 a.m.

"Okay, now that he's out, we'll go inside the cell. Astrides, do you have that scanner?"

"Yes, sir."

Captain Tikal turned to the psychiatrist. "Do you have a scalpel with you, Doc?"

"I believe there's one in my case."

"We're going to need that. I'm assuming that this tracking device is buried beneath his skin. We'll have to get it out, making sure not to damage it. By the way, there may also be a listening device in it, so don't talk." Captain Tikal glanced around. "Everybody got that?"

"Sir, do you want me to open his cell?"

"Yes, and stand by the door, just in case that tranquilizer doesn't last long enough."

Private Astrides stabbed the plastic key card into a box on the cell door.

The light on the top of the black plate flashed green.

Astrides pulled the door open.

"Give me that scanner, Astrides."

The young soldier handed the little rectangular device to Captain Tikal.

Sal moved into the cell, making sure he kept away from the pirate's feet and arms.

Private Imhotep and the psychiatrist followed him.

"Pull out your pistol and keep it on him, Imhotep."

The soldier unbuckled his holster and yanked out a black pistol. He moved up near the pirate's feet and held the pistol pointed down at the large man's chest.

Sal Tikal knelt down next to Calchus's head and held out the scanner. He pressed the button on the side.

A green light glowed on the front of the small device.

Sal moved it around the man's neck. He had seen implants put anywhere in the soft tissue in the recesses of the neck and ears. The translators the Mayan Space Administration implanted were behind the ears of all those who worked for them.

The chip was inserted with a large needle. The area was numbed, then it was cut open and the chip inserted. Afterward the area was taped closed and within five or six days it would heal and the implant was there for the whole career of the MSA officer.

When that officer retired, the chip was surgically removed. Again, it was a simple process, taking just minutes. All members of the Great Alliance used these devices. It made trade and other things so much easier.

Captain Tikal moved the scanner across the right side of the pirate's neck. When it reached the back of the neck a red light flashed.

Sal moved the scanner back around the neck.

The red light blinked out.

He moved it forward toward the jaw.

The red light came on.

Then he moved it upward.

The red light blinked on and off.

Sal moved the scanner up behind the ear.

There were three loud beeps.

He released the button and turned to the psychiatrist. "It's behind his right ear." Sal felt with his finger, then he lifted the earlobe up. He pointed. "Right here. You can feel it."

The psychiatrist knelt down and dug into his bag. He removed a black cloth case and unsnapped the front.

Inside were several knives.

He slid one out of its slot and put the case back into his leather bag. Then he lifted out the plastic bottle of alcohol and a cotton swab.

Doctor Neleus soaked the swab with alcohol. Then he placed the cap back on the bottle and turned it. Finally, he rubbed the alcohol on the area below the pirate's ear and once more on the blade of the knife. "When I cut him, he will bleed, Captain. At that point, please hand me two of those swabs from the plastic bag inside my case."

Sal crouched down next to the doctor's leather case. He picked up the plastic bag of cotton swabs.

Doctor Neleus cut into the area behind the ear with one deft, swift movement of the knife blade. "Hand me a swab."

Sal handed him one.

Doctor Neleus placed the swab against the stream of blood oozing out of the cut. "Another, please."

The psychiatrist put the second swab on the floor and laid the knife blade on it. Then he held the blood-soaked swab below the cut with his left hand and with the index finger of his right hand pressed the skin next to the cut.

A small, circular disk popped outward into the stream of blood. "Here it is."

"Be quiet."

The psychiatrist handed the small, circular disk over to Captain Tikal.

Sal wrapped a swab around it and slipped it into his right pants pocket. "Now we can talk. . . but quietly."

"Another two swabs, please."

Sal held out two swabs.

Doctor Neleus dabbed the wound. "I'll need some of that white tape. It's in the bottom of the bag."

Sal dug into the bag and found the roll of tape. He held it out to the psychiatrist.

The pirate made a groaning sound.

Sal pointed at Imhotep. "Keep that pistol on him, Private."

"Yes, sir." The young soldier held the pistol up in front of the pirate's face and cocked back the hammer.

Sal Tikal wondered how much time this kid had spent on the gun range. He looked pretty new at this.

"Okay, the cut is taped and the bleeding has been stopped."

Sal Tikal rose to his feet. "Then let's get out of here."

He turned to Imhotep. "You keep the pistol on him until we're out of the cell."

"Yes, sir."

There was another moan and the pirate's right arm moved.

Private Astrides slid open the cell door.

Sal stepped out, followed by Doctor Neleus.

Private Imhotep backed to the door, holding the pistol pointed at the pirate. At the door he lowered the pistol's hammer and stepped out.

Private Astrides slid the door closed and stabbed the card into the slot.

A red light glowed on the lock pad.

Captain Tikal turned to the psychiatrist. He reached out his right hand. "Thank you."

The man smiled and grabbed Sal's hand. "You're welcome, Captain."

Sal motioned to Imhotep. "Let's get this up to the bridge."

He crossed to the door that led out of the cellblock.

"Hey, Captain, when am I gonna get my lawyer?"

"I'll talk to the commander."

"See that you do."

Sal Tikal stared at the blond man inside the small cell. He was very tempted to say something to this piece of shit, but he decided against that. He wouldn't dignify that remark with a reply.

He turned away and stepped over the curved threshold into the outer guardroom.

"Hey, get me that lawyer!"

The other three men stepped into the guardroom and the door rattled shut.

"Are you gonna get him one, sir?"

Sal turned to Private Astrides. "No."

Astrides smiled. "I thought you wouldn't, sir."

"You thought right, Private. Thank you for your help."

"You're welcome, sir."

Sal looked around at the others in the small room. "Remember, this whole operation is classified. None of what happened gets beyond these walls."

"What about Lieutenant Djoser?"

"He'll be in there for a few more days. He won't be any problem."

"You can have him back anytime you want, sir."

Captain Sal Tikal turned. "Astrides, you are one very generous person."

The young soldier grinned. "Thank you, sir."

CHAPTER THIRTY

"Plans"

Starship Cygnus
Level 1
Conference Room #3
10M, Day 28, 6572
11:56 a.m.

" I t was wise of you to bring this down here to the Conference Room." Lieutenant Menelaus held up the small circular piece to Commander Okanata.

Seth clasped onto the device.

"There's no listening device, Commander. Obviously there's a locator in it and it acts as a primitive radio, so whoever had this implant could receive messages." He closed the hard plastic case on the table. "Where did you find this, Commander?"

"I'm sorry, Lieutenant, right now I'd rather not say."

"Is something going on here, Commander?"

"Let me put it this way, Lieutenant. What we have just done is considered classified. Keep it to yourself."

"I don't understand, sir."

"I'm afraid that's all I can tell you at this point, Lieutenant. You're dismissed."

Lieutenant Menelaus rose from his chair and saluted. "Yes, sir."

Seth Okanata watched as the man from Technical Support walked across the Conference Room to the door. There he pressed the blue pad.

The door opened.

The lieutenant stepped out into the corridor and the door closed.

Seth Okanata turned to his co-pilot. "We have to work out some sort of a plan, Captain. I'm willing to listen to any of your ideas."

"Sir, is there some way we could send this locator to a place where the pirate ship might get into trouble?"

Seth Okanata thought about this. "Well, I suppose we could load it onto a small rocket and fire it dangerously close to the planet Jupiter."

"I think they might catch on to that."

"Perhaps." Seth Okanata considered this for a moment. "Suppose we send this rocket on a trajectory that veers off our course, but with only a gradual change of direction, one that wouldn't be obvious. Do you think that would work?"

"It might, sir. I was thinking, sir, that we could always drug Calchus and put the implant back behind his ear, then put him into a rocket."

"I don't think so, Captain. I have a problem with taking a man's life."

"He was willing to take ours, Commander."

"I realize that, Captain Tikal, but we're not pirates. We live by higher standards."

"Yes, sir, I understand."

Commander Okanata was not totally convinced that his co-pilot did understand. That kind of thing was not something Seth would even think of doing unless it was absolutely necessary. So far he felt they were one step ahead of these pirates.

He held out the locator and studied it. Then he turned to Captain Tikal. "Let's have a chat with Lieutenant Djoser."

"I hope you're referring to our navigator, sir."

"Yes. How's the husband doing?"

"He wants a lawyer."

"Why does he want a lawyer?"

"I have no idea, sir."

"I suppose he thinks he's being mistreated."

"Frankly, sir, I think he's a real liability."

Seth nodded. "Yes, except that he's an excellent mechanic and we may need him at some point."

"Don't we have anyone else, sir?"

"Sergeant Copan."

"How's he to get along with?"

"Fine. He lost his wife in an accident back on Hyksos and he worked the next day."

"Maybe we should just keep Lieutenant Djoser locked up."

"Until we need him." Seth moved across the Conference Room to the door. He placed his hand against the blue lighted pad to the right of the door casing.

The door opened.

The commander stepped into the corridor.

Captain Tikal came out behind him.

Seth glanced back over his shoulder. "We have to deal with this pirate situation, Captain. We'll worry about Masal Djoser later."

"Yes, sir."

At the elevator, Commander Okanata pressed the UP arrow.

The door opened.

Seth stepped into the elevator and turned around.

Captain Tikal stepped in next to him.

Seth pressed the B button.

The door slid shut and the elevator jerked upward.

Seconds later, it jerked to a stop and the door opened.

Seth Okanata stepped out into the short corridor. To Seth this problem had many facets. First, if they were to send the locator on a rocket inward closer to Jupiter, it would have to be a convincing trajectory. Second, they would need a contingency plan if the pirates didn't fall for this. Also, they might need to deal with the pirates again if they happened to come out on the other side of Jupiter.

The commander stopped in front of the door to the bridge. He pressed the black button to the right of the door casing.

There was a muffled buzz.

"Who are you and what is your business on the bridge?"

"This is your commander, Private Imhotep. Captain Tikal is with me."

"Yes, sir."

The door opened.

Commander Okanata stepped into the bridge.

Tikal followed.

"Take the helm, Captain. I'm going to confer with Lieutenant Djoser to see if she's come up with an idea."

The commander walked over to the navigation station and sat down next to Elaina. "Lieutenant, have you come up with idea for getting rid of these pirates?"

"Well, sir, I thought we could send them off course into the asteroid belt between Jupiter and Mars. The problem is that we'd have to devise a way of misleading them."

"Captain Tikal and I have been talking about this. We wonder if we couldn't send a rocket with that locator on a trajectory that would lead the pirates dangerously close to Jupiter."

"That is possible, sir. On the other hand, I wonder if they can see us on their detectors like we can see them."

"Maybe they can."

"Well, sir, I had thought that if we led them inside the Belt of Moons that we might be able to get away from them by veering off behind one of the larger moons - like Europa."

Seth Okanata thought about this. "Yes, that might work, especially if we, at the same time, eject a rocket with the locator on a path inside the moons."

"Exactly, sir."

Seth nodded. "Of course, that's much too close to Jupiter for us. That would put us in a lot of danger."

"We could always fire our lasers at them, sir."

"I'd thought of that too, Lieutenant. However, that image we're getting on Tikal's screen is very vague and we're not getting it on the other two screens. I'm not sure I can trust the location of the image. That pirate ship could be hundreds of miles from that location."

"Is there any way of verifying where the pirate ship really is located?"

"I can't think of any at the moment, except dropping our cloaking device to draw their fire. Then we'd know exactly – if we survived."

"Yes, sir."

Seth leaned close to the small ear sheltered under the black hair. "Elaina. . ." he whispered.

She turned. "What is it, sir?"

"Your husband is not behaving himself. We're going to keep him locked up. I'm sorry it has to be this way, Elaina."

"Yes, sir."

CHAPTER THIRTY-ONE

"The Crunch"

Starship Cygnus
Bridge
10M, Day 30, 6572
2:18 p.m.

Commander Okanata knew this was going to be a big gamble, but how else were they going to get rid of this pirate ship?

They had been pulled into Jupiter's gravitation for the last six or seven hours. It was a strange phenomenon because at first it wasn't a constant thing.

Doctor Colonus Meander, the astrophysicist on board, had told him that this unevenness of the gravitation had to do with the other bodies orbiting the giant planet. He had said that they were like pockets of gravitational release.

Seth had the pirate's locator chip in his pocket again. He had taken it back to the brig two days ago, figuring that if it were a precise locator, then whoever was tracking this might know that Calchus had been moved around the starship. A man being held by his captors didn't move around much, so keeping it in the cupboard down in the brig was a good idea.

Seth had this vague idea about getting rid of this locator once they were close enough to Jupiter. It would simply be a matter of placing it on the deck and crushing it with his boot. Of course, when they were doing the flyby he wouldn't be able to move enough to crush the locator that way because of Jupiter's enormous gravity. That plan wouldn't work.

Elaina had laid out a course by Jupiter which took them toward the inner belt inside the multiple moons orbiting the planet. It would really be pushing things to the extreme if they actually maintained that course.

The starship shook violently.

Seth could feel his eyeballs shaking inside his head. He closed his eyes. He couldn't stand that feeling. He never had been able to deal with it very well.

They had known about the pirate ship shadowing them for two days now. It had made Seth feel strange. It was like somebody was peeking in his window. He was very uncomfortable with it, but it was a necessary evil in this situation.

Elaina was sure that if they controlled their trajectory, they could actually move slightly inside the belt of Jupiter's satellites and turn away on the other side of Europa. They had chosen that particular moon because it was the largest and they figured it would provide the most cover for their attempt to evade the pirate ship.

After much thought, Seth had finally convinced himself that really the only way to destroy this locator chip was to put it into his mouth and crush it between his teeth at the appropriate time. Trying to destroy it with one's boot would be next to impossible when the gravity was that extreme near Jupiter.

Yes, he had decided to put it into his mouth. He had asked Doctor Neleus if alcohol would destroy the chip because he was considering putting it into his mouth and he didn't relish having the pirate's blood there.

The doctor had warned him that the alcohol might, in fact, destroy it prematurely and, of course, if Seth did that, then all these plans for escaping the pirates would be for naught.

No, he would not clean the chip in alcohol. He would put the little, bloody thing into his mouth and tough it out. Well, it wasn't actually bloody, but the pirate's blood had been on it and probably was still on it.

The starship shook again.

The commander flipped up a black switch on the right side of his console. "This is Commander Okanata speaking. As you know by now, we are entering the gravitational field of Jupiter. At this time we would suggest that you buckle yourself into an approved safety seat and pull the restraining harness tight." He flipped down the switch.

Seth then turned his head to the left and peered over his shoulder. "Lieutenant Djoser, how is our course at this time?"

"We're right on, sir. I'm checking every five minutes to make sure our trajectory is correct."

"When we make that evasive maneuver, what will be our approximate speed?"

There was a rattle of computer keys.

"Approximately, seven hundred eighty-nine thousand kilometers per hour, sir."

"Can the starship stand a turn at that speed inside Jupiter's gravitational field?"

"Yes, sir. I've checked the data already, sir. The ship will change shape temporarily. It will flex with the strain because of the turn, but it will hold, sir."

"Thank you, Lieutenant."

"You're welcome, sir."

Seth Okanata was amused by how reassuring Elaina's voice was. Well, actually he wasn't so much reassured as he was pleased by hearing her voice. He had a thing for this woman.

The problem was how could he tell her? How could he, considering the circumstances, let her know he thought she was a marvelous woman whom he would like to start seeing?

Seth slammed forward against his safety harness.

He had thought he had tightened the belts, but now he knew that they were loose around his waist and across both sides of his chest because here he was hanging against them with space between his body and the seat.

"Speed increasing, sir."

"Copy that, Lieutenant." When Seth spoke the words he couldn't completely understand them. They sounded garbled. He wasn't sure if it was his hearing or he had actually garbled the words.

He reached into his right pants pocket and lifted out the locator chip. He then slipped it into the right side of his mouth, being sure to keep it close to his molars on the right. They were his strongest teeth.

The thought of the pirate's blood inside his mouth was disgusting. But he would force himself to forget that.

The pressure of the belts against his body increased. He seemed to be hanging in midair above his console screen.

In front of him on the console was a large orange ball of the planet Jupiter. It filled the whole screen. In front of the giant orange ball he could see several moons. They seemed to be approaching quickly.

Elaina's voice said something he could not understand.

Seth was convinced that he would know when they should turn. He would do that by firing one of the port-side rockets that was usually fired during a docking procedure at a planet's terminal satellite. This time, they were using these rockets to turn the starship.

"Approach!" the word faded.

Seth recognized Elaina's voice.

"Satellites!" This word was clear.

In his screen Seth could see the huge pockmarked grey sphere off to the starboard side of the starship.

He tipped his head upward and tried to focus on the windshield above the console.

Up there, Jupiter looked even larger. It filled the windshield from one side to the other. It was almost as if the starship was going to be swallowed up by this giant planet.

He wouldn't think about that. It was disturbing, to say the least.

The moon, Europa, seemed to float by on the right side of the windshield like a huge pockmarked shadow. Finally, it vanished from view.

"Fire port!" Nothing else came.

Seth stretched his left hand out toward the left side of the console. He pushed it farther.

Finally his index finger touched a red button.

There was an explosion.

He jerked to the left against the belts.

He slid his tongue to that side of his mouth and moved the locator chip up. He bit down, but missed.

He pushed the locator toward his teeth with his tongue. This time he bit down onto something like a hard candy.

Fragments of metal scattered inside his mouth. He spat.

The pieces spewed out on the left side of his lips and sprayed across his left cheek.

Now the pirates had no locator to follow.

It occurred to Seth that this might not work, that maybe they should try to find this pirate ship and blow it up with lasers. However, the problem was seeing it well enough to get a clear shot.

He had an idea. Maybe there was a way to see that pirate ship after all.

If this current maneuver worked, he wouldn't have to worry. Only time would tell. They would have to clear Jupiter and then see if the pirate ship was still around.

Europa appeared again to starboard, in the right side of the windshield.

Seth stretched his left hand out toward the red button.

"Cut engine!"

Seth stabbed the red button.

His body slammed back against the seat.

CHAPTER THIRTY-TWO

"Apologize"

Starship Dragon Fire
Bridge
10M, Day 30, 6572
2:52 p.m.

"No locator signal!"

Scarphe worked to move his head to the right and stared at his co-pilot, Balius. He would have said something to this idiot but it was too hard to speak with this pressure from the gravitation of this huge planet.

If there was no locator signal, then Calchus's implant was destroyed or damaged. He could have gotten thrown around during this flyby.

If they really had lost the signal, they had lost Calchus, the commander and captain of the Black Leopard, their other starship. Actually, it was their destroyed other starship. Now it was a bunch of debris, floating around in space.

Okay, they were all brothers in this business, but now it was possible that he, Scarphe, could move up to commander of the fleet. That wasn't all bad. Of course, there was only one starship in the fleet – this one.

There were other people who might plan on becoming commander - Balius and Casus, for instance, and the crew on the other shift, Delos and Halios. All of them would want to become commander of this one ship pirate fleet. Halios was too much of a grumpy asshole to lead anyone, so he was definitely not a possibility.

The one Scarphe was most worried about was Delos. He had lots of friends onboard. A bunch of dick suckers – that's all they were.

All of them would have to figure this out somehow – maybe just draw lots, or maybe some other way. But if Delos had an accident, then things might work out just fine.

"Where's that fuckin' starship?" Scarphe tried to speak it slowly so the words were clear, but they sounded strange in this heavy gravity – like some kind of garbled slow motion video or something.

Hey, if they lost this Mayan starship, then they lost a real chance at getting themselves some women to sell as slaves and most of those MSA starships had all kinds of equipment on them. They could just steal the whole starship. It was a hell of a lot better than this old piece of shit.

The Cygnus was a Class A starship, a huge mother of a ship. They could sure use something like that in the pirate command.

Scarphe figured if he could take the Cygnus in one piece, he'd be the hero of the whole fucking Megall Pirate Alliance. Wow, that would be the best goddamn thing in the galaxy – a Class A starship! He'd be a hero. Well, of course, he'd have to share the glory with Delos. Hey, nothing was perfect.

But there was always the chance that Delos could have some kind of terrible accident. Scarphe figured that he would have to think about that. Maybe he could come up with something.

Here he was thinking about flying that monster Mayan starship and they didn't even have it yet. Besides, these MSA guys didn't give up easily. They were well-equipped with lasers and they knew how to fight.

Scarphe could feel himself moving inside his harness. He had strapped himself in so tight that he could hardly move, but right now he was hanging away from the pilot's seat like some kind of giant bug flying through the air.

He wondered what these MSA assholes were up to. Were they really going in this close to this big-ass planet, Jupiter?

Scarphe wondered if this old pirate ship could stand the pressures this close to that monster planet.

"Leak port side!" ·

Scarphe recognized Balius's voice off to his right. Balius was generally a real shithead, but he did know how to copilot a starship.

It occurred to Scarphe what they were doing right now was dangerous, too dangerous. They had to change course and get out of here. At this point, he could give a good shit if they lost track of that MSA starship. He wasn't going to get killed just to track Calchus.

"Changin' course!" His words sounded garbled. He reached out with his right hand and stabbed a large button on the left side of the console.

There was an explosion.

The starship lurched to the right.

A large pock-marked moon loomed in the left side of the windshield.

As Scarphe hung in his harness, he wondered if this was the end, if this was the way he was going to die. When you were a pirate you couldn't think about dying because that made you cautious and when you were cautious, you made mistakes that got you killed. So you tried not to think about it.

But right now, he wondered if their starship was going to crash into this grey-colored moon off to their left. He supposed that would be all right. He didn't mind all that much as long as it was quick. A slow painful death was what he dreaded, especially if his girlfriend, Proto was around.

With Proto, there would be a lot of crying. Then she'd get over it and would start hanging around with some other guy.

Scarphe knew if he died, she would find somebody else before his body was cold. He accepted that. It was just that he didn't want to see her doing her thing with this other guy as he was dying. That would be one nasty way to go.

Seconds later, the image of the surface of that grey moon became smaller.

That made Scarphe realize that they were swinging away from it, and if they were swinging away from it – as long as this little starship didn't fall apart – they were going to make it.

He had always liked excitement, living on the edge, and he liked taking things from other people, especially people he figured were rich or privileged.

He hated those people. He always had. Scarphe lived to burst their arrogant bubble of confidence. He just loved it when his crew boarded a starship and everybody looked scared. All of those snotty privileged people were scared. That he loved.

It gave him a sense of power. Now he was their equal. Now, in fact, he was in control of them, so he guessed he was better than they were.

The changing pressure thrust Scarphe against the pilot's seat. In the console screen was black space and stars. Their Class C starship was headed out away from this big-ass planet, Jupiter, and they were still alive.

"Hey, Casus, check that fuckin' leak!"

"How the hell can I check the leak when I can't stand up, asshole?"

Scarphe grinned. "If it's a small leak, Casus, you can plug it with your pecker!"

To his right, a man guffawed.

Scarphe turned to look.

Balius pointed at him. "Shit, Scarphe, that wasn't nice!"

"Should I apologize?"

Balius laughed even louder.

CHAPTER THIRTY-THREE

"The Shadow"

Starship Cygnus
EVA
1M, Day 1, 6573
8:19 a.m.

Sergeant Hector Copan hadn't seen Masal for several days. This morning, early, they had let him out of the brig to do this EVA. Now they were floating side by side outside the starship.

Hector had always been aware that his friend had a bad temper, but what he'd been hearing lately wasn't good.

It was strange how that affected the way you saw somebody. His view of Masal had changed. Hector had always imagined the man was somehow superior to him – smarter about things. But now he wasn't so sure.

Yes, everybody had skeletons in their closets. He had some. It was a thing you learned to live with. But Masal's thing was his temper. That was a fact.

Hector realized that he had to stay focused. They were both out here on this EVA tethered to a metal ring on the side of the ship. Masal was welding.

Masal hadn't talked much this morning. He was all about work. That was fine. They had to get this leak plugged.

A meteorite had shot through the hull and was causing an air leak. It was a result of the Jupiter flyby. Luckily nobody was hurt. The meteorite had blown through a storage compartment. But it did cause air to leak out of the starship and losing air was a bad thing, no matter where it came from.

That trip by Jupiter had been tough. Hector was told to be on full alert but the commander had not said anything unusual about the flyby.

Then Hector found out this morning that they had been shadowed by a pirate ship right into the flyby. He sure as hell hoped the pirates were gone.

Hector was told that he was out here on this EVA to assist Masal and to provide security for him, in case something happened. He hoped it wasn't those pirates he was supposed to deal with. He was alone out here with Masal and he was carrying only a small laser sidearm on his right hip.

Hector pushed against the hull of the starship to turn himself away. He gazed out toward the giant orange and red planet in the distance.

There was Jupiter with all its moons. It was a monster, but it was good for a flyby. Well, maybe they shouldn't have gone in that close, but the commander today had hinted at the pirate thing being the reason they had taken that chance.

Hector grabbed onto his tether cable and pulled himself around. "Good to be out of that brig, Masal?"

Masal's helmet turned and the dark bubble of glass faced Hector. "She's been cheatin' on me, Hector."

This was the same old theme with Masal lately, but in no way did Hector believe it. "You're wrong, Masal. Elaina wouldn't do that."

"You're takin' her side."

"No. I'm just sayin' that you got her all wrong."

"Then, why'd she move out?"

Hector had a pretty good idea why, but he wasn't going to go there. "I don't know. Ask her."

The dark Plexiglas bubble turned away from Hector. "Got to finish this weld. Don't want to fuck this up."

"You're a good welder. What the hell you worried about?"

"Figure if maybe I do this right, the old man will let me out of the brig."

Hector didn't know what to say to that. He finally decided he wouldn't say anything. He pushed himself away from the side of the ship so he would pivot around again.

Hector liked looking out at the millions of stars. It was kind of exciting. This galaxy was so goddamn big. In fact, it was so big you couldn't travel across it in a whole lifetime.

The red-orange ball of Jupiter was now off to his right. He turned to look. That planet was real impressive.

As he was staring at Jupiter, a shadow passed in front of the planet. For just a second, Hector wondered what the hell that was. Then he recognized the shape.

It was a starship. "This is Sergeant Hector Copan callin' the bridge!"

"This is Captain Tikal on the bridge, Sergeant."

"Captain, I'm on an EVA outside the starship on the starboard aft section. I spotted the shadow of a starship passin' by Jupiter. It would be parallel to the aft section of our starship, sir."

"Are you sure, Sergeant?"

"Couldn't miss it, sir. Cloakin' or not, I saw the shadow, sir."

"Copy that, Copan. Thanks."

Now all Hector could see of the shadow was the tail section of that other ship and finally that disappeared.

He reached out for the cable and as he did, he heard a pop.

Something shiny flew by his helmet.

Hector swung around.

A stream of air and moisture was spraying out of Masal's regulator on the front of his helmet.

Hector grabbed Masal's backpack and ripped the Velcro cover off. He reached inside and grabbed the roll of tape.

With his heavy gloves he pulled tape off the roll and pulled himself toward the spray of moist air.

Now there was a narrow red stream shooting out of the hole.

Hector clamped his left hand behind Masal's helmet and with his right slapped the tape over the hole.

The welding torch floated near Hector's helmet.

He slapped it away. Then he pressed the tape tighter over the hole.

"Emergency! Need medics in the decompression chamber ASAP!"

Hector reached around to Masal's back and twisted off the oxygen valve.

The white torch flame flashed out.

Hector reached down for the end of Masal's tether and released the ring. Then he hooked the ring onto his own ring and released that from the loop on the side of the starship.

He grabbed onto Masal with his left hand and on the control arm sticking out from his right side he pressed his right thumb against the rocket button.

There was a subtle roar.

Hector floated along the starship toward the door to the decompression chamber.

Now he released the button.

The two men drifted toward the aft end of the giant starship.

Hector now realized that the pirate ship was at his back. Of course, they might not know the Cygnus was here. The cloaking device still enclosed this whole starship.

He wondered how Masal was doing. That blood spraying out of the hole made him nervous. "You all right, buddy?"

There was no answer.

Hector pressed the rocket button.

He felt the jerk from behind his back and he heard the subtle roar.

He was moving pretty fast, but he figured that if Masal was bleeding, time was important.

Up ahead, Hector saw the tether rings on this side of the door to the decompression chamber.

He felt off to his left with his left gloved hand. The back of his glove bumped into the tether line.

Hector's gloved fingers slid along the stainless steel cable until they found the ring.

He pulled Masal around in front of him so that he could see the ring.

The tape on Masal's regulator was still attached but it looked like it had peeled away on one side.

Actually, Hector didn't know if tape would seal that leak, but it was the only thing he had.

When the ring on the side of the ship neared, Hector moved out his arm and swung his hand hard.

The ring on his tether snapped onto the ring on the side of the starship.

He swung his body around by shifting himself inside the spacesuit. Then he fired the rocket.

There was a roar.

Hector could feel the jerk of Masal stopping for just a split second. He had to slow them down or the stop on that ring might be so violent that it would break his neck.

He pressed the button again.

There was a subtle roar.

He felt the jerk again.

Hector visually checked the side of the starship. It was still moving by him, but now it was much slower.

His thumb stabbed the rocket switch.

The jerk ended almost before it started.

Hector reached the end of the tether cable. He was whipped back and forth.

He closed his eyes so he wouldn't feel dizzy.

When the violent swinging subsided, he opened his eyes. Then he pulled himself back along the tether cable to the side of the ship. "Ready to enter the decompression chamber."

"Copy that," said a male voice.

The wide hatch slid sideways into the hull.

Hector unhooked the tether and reached inside the hatch for a handle. Once his glove found the large grip, he pulled.

Hector swung around almost one hundred eighty degrees.

Behind him Masal swung in a half circle into the decompression chamber.

Hector checked around. "All clear."

The wide door slid across the side of the chamber.

There was a loud hiss.

The end of the chamber opened and two medics wearing air tanks and facemasks rushed inside.

They hurried across to Masal.

One of the men gripped onto his helmet and twisted with a hard yank.

The helmet came free and blood blew out all over the front of Masal's spacesuit.

The medic slapped an air mask onto Masal's nose and mouth.

The other medic jumped onto him and began CPR. He thrust down on Masal's chest.

The other man was checking a gauge attached to the air hose.

The one performing the CPR kept pumping and pumping on the chest.

Finally the one with the gauge looked at the other medic and shook his head. Then he pulled off his air mask.

Hector reached up and twisted his space helmet.

The seal made a puff sound when it broke.

He lifted the helmet up off his head. Hector found that he was staring at Masal's bloody face.

"The air probably rushed out so fast his lungs burst."

Hector looked at the medic. "I tried to tape the hole. I don't know what else I coulda done. That's all I had was tape."

"Don't worry about it, Sergeant. He was a goner before you put the tape on."

"There was blood shooting out."

The medic nodded. "He was already a goner, Sergeant."

CHAPTER THIRTY-FOUR

"Friends"

Starship Dragon Fire
Compartment 266
1M, Day 1, 6573
8:26 a.m.

Dymas sat on the stool at the breakfast bar near the door. For sure, he knew exactly why he did this. He didn't trust Scarphe. He wanted to be near the door, just in case he had to get his ass out of here.

His attitude came from experience living in this pirate community. If you had friends around you, then you were okay. You were like your own little tribe. You covered each other's back.

In this situation, Dymas wasn't sure about anything. Halios seemed harmless enough, although he was a grumpy sonofabitch. But you never could be sure about people you didn't know.

He just didn't trust Scarphe at all. The man was ambitious, very ambitious. He wanted to be commander of this faction of the pirate fleet, but he didn't have the votes. He didn't have a lot of friends. Delos did and he had the votes to become commander. But that wasn't going to stop Scarphe.

"So, Scarphe, why the hell'd you ask me to come down here to your pad?"

Scarphe turned in the kitchen. He was holding a bottle of red wine. "I have somethin' to talk to you about, Halios."

"Well, let's get on with it."

Scarphe poured some wine into a cup, raised the cup and drank it down with one swallow.

Dymas glanced back at the door.

"What you lookin' at, kid?"

Dymas's head pivoted around. "Thought I heard somebody."

Scarphe put down the cup and the wine bottle, then crossed the space to the door. He leaned close to the peephole in the top. Then he stepped away. "Nobody there."

He walked back into the kitchen and turned around to face the two men. "Okay, the real reason I brought you two here this mornin' is I got this proposition to talk about."

He folded his tattooed arms across his chest. "See – right now when it comes to raidin' that Mayan starship, we're fucked. The reason we're fucked is we lost contact with Calchus's locator implant. We can't send messages or get them."

Scarphe leaned back against the counter behind him. "It happened during that time we were near Jupiter. I was at the helm and we were shakin' like we were gonna fall apart. So, it's possible Calchus was thrown around and the thing got damaged. But I don't think that's what happened."

He looked up at the overhead. Then his gaze came down again. "I think the Mayans found it and destroyed it. If that's what happened – and I think it is – they know we're close."

He pushed his back away from the counter and unfolded his arms. Then he moved over close to the counter where Halios and Dymas were sitting. "So, what does that mean? It means we're not gonna surprise those Mayans. They're just waitin' for us to make our move."

He folded his arms again. "And what does that mean? Well, you can figure that out for yourself. Think about it. If we try to teleport aboard that starship, we're fucked. They'll be sittin' there waitin' and we'll be done for."

Scarphe walked back into the kitchen, then he pivoted around to face the two men again. "So, our chances of boardin' that starship and bringin' Calchus back don't amount to shit.

"And that means we have to stop Delos from goin' through with this fuckin' idea about tryin' to get Calchus back. Believe me when I say - boardin' that Mayan starship would be a suicide mission." He looked down at the deck, then his gaze came up. "My crew, Balius, Casus and Tydeus are with me. I want you guys with me too."

"Have you told Delos what you think?"

Scarphe stared at Dymas. "Kid, would he listen to me? He's got this big hard-on to go into that Mayan starship with guns blazin'. It won't work."

"In your opinion."

"Kid - think about it. The locator's dead. That means either they took it off Calchus or they killed him and threw him overboard."

"I thought you said they would put him on trial first."

"Kid, I was just sayin' that."

"So tell me somethin'. Are you just sayin' what you're telling us now?"

Scarphe's eyes blinked. "I don't need no fuckin' smartass kid makin' fun of me. Maybe you should watch what you say 'cause you never know who's gonna be in charge around here now that Calchus is gone."

"You don't have the votes."

Scarphe's mouth twisted and jerked into a smile. "Watch your mouth, kid."

"I'm just stating a fact, Scarphe. Delos has more friends aboard this starship than you do. He's a shoo-in for commander."

"Who said anythin' about commander?"

"Like Delos said, Calchus has gotten us more wealth than anyone before him. But you don't want Calchus to come back, do you, Scarphe?"

The man across the counter squinted his eyes and he pointed at Dymas. "Kid, you're really askin' for it. People mess with me and they just disappear. They take a free ride out there into space, flying out of the decompression chamber with no suit on. That's not a good way to die, kid. Your lungs explode and your mouth fills with your own blood.

"They say it feels like you're on fire from the inside out. Hurts like a son of a bitch and it lasts much too long."

"Delos has my back, Scarphe."

"Not if Delos ain't around anymore, kid."

Dymas moved backward toward the door.

"It's locked, kid."

He was sure Scarphe was lying. When Dymas thought he was close enough, he reached out his left hand toward the door opener pad.

Scarphe was grinning and his grey-blue eyes were staring at him like Dymas wasn't even there – like he didn't even exist.

CHAPTER THIRTY-FIVE

"The Sound Solution"

Starship Cygnus
Bridge
1M, Day 1, 6573
9:03 a.m.

"That pirate ship is still out there, Captain Tikal."

"Yes, sir, it is, but the question is where."

"The bigger question is when it will strike."

The co-pilot's head turned and he focused on Seth. "I would think about the time we get to Mars to pick up those remains of that Gurab guy who died there fourteen hundred years ago. Frankly, Commander, if I were in charge, I would skip that part of the mission. I think we'll be putting ourselves in unnecessary danger."

"But what you forget, Captain, is that if the pirates don't strike there, they will strike when we arrive at Earth, which might even be worse. How can we establish trade with these Earth people when we bring pirates down on them?"

"Obviously, we have to find these pirates and wipe them out, Commander."

"I agree, Captain, but how?"

"Sir, I think I know," said a female voice behind them.

Commander Seth Okanata spun around his pilot's seat one hundred eighty degrees and faced the navigation station. He was going to ask his favorite navigator what idea she had. At that moment, however, Seth was startled by her almost cheerful demeanor.

Her husband had died less than an hour ago. She had accepted the news at her station and she had shed some tears, but then she had wiped them away and had gone back to work.

This was strange. What was stranger was that Masal Djoser's equipment had failed. That equipment was checked and double checked every time it was used. How could there be a faulty or loose adjustment screw?

Something crossed Seth's mind, something he would rather not think about. He dismissed it, however, because he had faith in Elaina. She was a good navigator, a good officer and a good person.

"Come here, sir, I'd like to show you something."

Seth rose out of the pilot's seat. He turned to Captain Tikal. "Keep sharp, Captain. Those pirates could strike at any time."

"Yes, sir."

Seth moved toward the end of his console and turned left around the end of the navigation console. "What is it that you want to show me, Lieutenant?"

Elaina looked up. Then she pointed at her screen. "Sir, I've been searching through our inventory of devices aboard the starship and I happened upon something that I think might prove useful."

Seth bent over her shoulder and stared at the screen. He was looking at a dish receiver. He pointed. "This is part of our mineral deposit search system."

Elaina looked up. "Yes, sir. But, sir, what's significant about this system is that it uses sound to find minerals – mostly metals."

"Of course – a starship is made out of metal."

"Yes, sir, and I don't believe that cloaking systems stop sound."

Seth Okanata could feel his face break into a smile. "I think I know where you're going with this, Lieutenant."

Elaina pointed at the screen. "Sir, if we were to send out low frequency sound waves in - say - an arc of one hundred sixty degrees, we might be able to detect metal objects in that arc."

"What screen are you on, Lieutenant?"

"Twelve, sir."

"Screen twelve?"

"Yes, sir. It's the one usually used by the onboard geologist."

"Let me set up the lasers, Lieutenant, and maybe we can get rid of our pirate problem." Seth hesitated. Then he leaned close to Elaina. "Are you all right?" He focused on her blue eyes.

She made a half-hearted smile. "I'm okay, sir."

"We can bring Lieutenant Lycastus up here to relieve you."

"That won't be necessary, sir. I'd rather be busy doing something."

Seth nodded. "I understand. If you need someone to talk to when this shift is over, I'd be more than willing, Lieutenant."

A smile slipped across the small mouth, then disappeared. "That's very kind, sir. Maybe I'll take you up on that."

Seth glanced over his right shoulder.

Captain Tikal was watching them.

Seth faced Elaina again. "You could always see Doctor Neleus, of course."

"The psychiatrist?"

"Bokar is a really nice man. He's a good listener, or at least that's what I've been told."

"I'd rather talk to you, sir."

Seth found that he was staring into the pretty eyes. The only evidence left of that bruise on the left side of her face was a small mark where she had been cut below the outside edge of her left eyebrow.

The commander rose to full height. "We'll talk later, Lieutenant. In the meantime let me set up the lasers. Maybe we can find that pirate ship."

"Yes, sir."

Seth walked around the end of the console and up to the pilot's seat. He sat down.

"How's she doing?"

Seth felt uncomfortable. "She seems fine." He turned to the co-pilot. "She's suggested using sound to find the pirate ship. It's really a very clever idea. We will be using screen twelve."

"That's the geology screen, sir."

"What do our geologists look for, Captain?"

"Minerals – metals." Sal Tikal's face broke into a smile. "Yes, of course – metal."

"Lieutenant Djoser and I are going to have to coordinate two screens. You bring up screen four, Captain, and monitor the starship's systems. We may get some return fire."

There was a rattle of computer keys.

"I have screen four, sir."

"Good, Captain." Seth's fingers flew across his keyboard. "And I have screen seven."

The commander turned his head and looked back over his left shoulder. "Are you all set, Lieutenant?"

"Yes, sir."

"I'll need specific coordinates, Lieutenant."

Seth checked his screen. "Canons are ready." He raised his right hand to a large joystick above the screen at the top of the console. His right hand gripped the stick.

To fire the canons he first had to punch in a small red button on the left side of the stick with his thumb, then pull the trigger with his index finger.

Seth studied his screen. At this point the virtual crosshairs on the screen were off to the left of center – exactly twelve degrees left and three point four degrees above center. He waited.

When the sound came, it was not something Seth heard. Instead he felt it through the soles of his boots, then going up the titanium post under his seat into the cushion and into his buttocks.

Finally his whole body vibrated and Seth could feel the flesh on his cheeks vibrate.

"Got it, sir."

"Give me the exact coordinates, Lieutenant."

"Eighteen point three degrees right, eleven point seven degrees above the center of the screen, sir."

Seth moved the joystick to the right then upward. He placed the crosshairs at eighteen point three degrees right and eleven point seven degrees above center. "All hands ready to fire."

Seth pressed his thumb against the red button then pulled the trigger.

The starship shuddered.

"Direct hit, sir!"

"Volley two." Seth pressed the red button a second time and pulled the trigger.

The starship shuddered.

"What do you see, Lieutenant?"

"Fragments, sir. I can't see the actual starship, but it is silver pieces, sir."

"Can you get a fix on their location, Lieutenant?"

"Yes, sir."

"We should change course briefly and do a visual check of the area."

"Sir, if you give me control of the ship, I can move us to within a few thousand feet."

"Yes, Lieutenant, move us in. I'll scan through the windshield for debris."

Commander Okanata had seen debris fields before. He wasn't really looking forward to this. Sure – it would be a confirmation that they had destroyed the pirate ship, but there would be everything floating in space.

When he had done this before, a human head had floated by the starship windshield. This was followed by other body parts and pieces of metal – junk.

Eventually the body parts would disintegrate, thankfully, but the bones would remain for quite some time. He had never seen that and, frankly, he never wanted to.

"We're getting close, sir."

"Very good, Lieutenant." Seth stared out the windshield.

A large piece of shiny sheet metal floated in the blackness in front of the windshield.

Then, far out from the ship, Seth could see the shape of a human figure. It looked like it was lying down with its arms stretched out.

He hoped they didn't get too close. He didn't want to see any details.

More debris passed the ship.

Seth turned his head to the left. "Lieutenant, take us out of here."

"Yes, sir."

The starship moved in a wide sweep toward the left.

Debris swept by in a stream toward the right.

There was a subtle "thump." Something had hit the starship.

Now Seth could see what looked like someone had flung the contents of a giant waste basket. In front of the myriad of stars floated space junk of all sizes and shapes. There were two more human bodies. Thankfully they were intact – no body parts floating around.

"Mark these coordinates, Lieutenant. We want to avoid this mess on the way out of this solar system."

"Yes, sir, Commander."

CHAPTER THIRTY-SIX
"Investigation"

Starship Cygnus
Level 1
Conference Room #3
1M, Day 2, 6573
6:28 a.m.

Lieutenant Elaina Djoser didn't like meetings like this, especially when they were in any way connected to her.

The one thing she held onto these days was the belief that Commander Seth Okanata was her friend. Maybe he was more, but at least he was her friend. That's what mattered.

How did she feel about Masal dying? She felt guilty, and that was mostly because she was relieved he wasn't around anymore. While he was alive she had lived in constant fear that somehow he would find her and hurt her. Actually, he might have killed her.

That's the way she felt now that he was gone. He was a very angry guy and she could never figure out why. It was just this thing with him – an angry man - and it seemed to be getting worse.

"I've called all of you here this morning, to inform you that there will be a thorough investigation." The commander motioned with his hand toward Elaina. "Lieutenant Djoser's husband, Masal Djoser, died during an EVA when an adjustment screw on his regulator blew out."

The commander's head turned and he seemed to be scanning the whole conference room. "All of us know that the EVA equipment is locked up. Also, it is inspected and serviced on a regular basis.

"Considering these facts, I am astonished that such an accident could actually happen. We are even looking into sabotage. Currently we are checking the video feed to the cameras that constantly scan the storage compartment for EVA equipment. We're looking at all possibilities."

The commander leaned his head forward and cleared his throat with his fist held in front of his closed lips. Then he glanced around the conference room again. "I would say at this point that if there are any of you who know anything, do come forward."

A hand shot up.

The commander nodded. "Yes, Sergeant?"

Sergeant Hector Copan stood up. "Sir, I've gotta say that both Masal and I inspected that equipment almost daily. I don't want to throw any rocks at anyone, but, sir, I've gotta say that I think somebody loosened that screw. There's no way that coulda loosened by itself."

"That's a pretty serious accusation, Sergeant."

"Yes, sir, I know. But you see, sir, Masal and I were on top of that thing because we were puttin' ourselves in danger out there in space. Right after he died, I had to go back out and weld that hole shut – the one he started weldin'. Out there, we put ourselves in danger, so we're not gonna be careless about our equipment."

"Is there anything else you'd like to say, Sergeant?"

"No, sir. That's all." Sergeant Hector Copan dropped into his seat near the end of the long table.

"Are there any other questions or comments?"

Another hand went up.

"Yes, Lieutenant Bucolus?"

The large man rose out of his seat. "Sir, we're goin' to do a thorough job. I just want to say that we're gonna be askin' questions of almost everyone before we're through. Sir, you're right that we can't have this kind of thing happenin' on our ship. So the Starship Security is already on it.

"We wish that screw had not been lost, but we realize Sergeant Copan was just tryin' to get Lieutenant Djoser back into the starship to save his life. If we could see that screw, we could tell whether it was tampered with or not.

"We'll be reporting to you on a regular basis, sir. Every five days we'll be sendin' you a written report, sir. And if you have any other questions or suggestions, you can always contact me, sir."

"You find out anythin' so far?"

The huge man turned to Copan. "No, we haven't, Sergeant. I do want to talk to you today if that's possible."

"Sure, Lieutenant."

Bucolus faced Seth. "That's all I have, Commander."

"Any fingerprints on the regulator, Lieutenant?"

"We can identify those of Lieutenant Djoser and Sergeant Copan. We expected to find them, but there is a third print. It's smudged. We figure somebody tried to rub the regulator clean, but missed this. It's only a partial print so that's goin' to make it difficult to identify."

The huge man swung around. "If any of you saw anythin' or heard anythin', we'd like to know. What you saw or heard could be meaningless, but you never know about those things. So you be sure to tell us if there's anythin' at all."

Lieutenant Bucolus dropped into his seat.

The commander looked around the Conference Room. "Are there any other remarks?"

He scanned the room one more time. "This meeting is over. You are dismissed."

The crew people in the room rose to their feet and saluted.

Seth Okanata returned the salute.

The hands dropped and everyone turned and moved toward the door.

The guard at the door, Private Imhotep, pressed his hand against the blue pad.

The pocket door opened.

The small crowd filed out. There was low talking. A woman in the corridor laughed.

Seth turned to Lieutenant Djoser. "How are you holding up after this meeting?"

She nodded. "I'm okay. I know I must come off as a cold fish or something like that, but I'm still in shock."

"We can have a funeral service before we cremate the body, if you want."

Elaina shook her head. "No. I might have some kind of service when we bury his ashes back on Hyksos. Right now, I'm still trying to believe he's gone. It happened so fast."

The commander leaned back in his chair. "I get the impression, Elaina, that you two weren't exactly close."

"Why do you say that?"

Seth shrugged. "It's just an impression I've had."

She nodded. "It's true. Masal always seemed to be so angry. I don't know what that was about. It drove us apart."

Seth Okanata glanced at his wrist control. "We're due on the bridge."

Elaina smiled. "Yes, sir." She was actually looking forward to being there, being occupied with something to do.

"If you ever want to talk to me, Elaina, I'm here for you."

"Thank you. . . Seth. That's very kind. I'm still working things out in my own mind. Maybe in a few days."

"Sure." The commander moved down the length of the table to the door. There he waited for Elaina.

When she reached him, Commander Okanata faced the guard. "You are relieved here, Imhotep. But I expect you to be up at the bridge within the hour."

The young soldier saluted. "Yes, sir. Thank you, sir."

Seth returned the salute. "You're quite welcome, Imhotep."

The young soldier slapped his hand on the raised rectangular plate, glowing with blue light.

The pocket door slid open.

Seth Okanata stepped aside to let Elaina go first. Then he stepped over the curved threshold right behind her.

Elaina waited for him. She always seemed to feel comfortable around Seth.

He fell in next to her. "I'm so sorry this happened to your husband, Elaina. There's no excuse for errors like this. We'll get to the bottom of it."

"Thank you, sir, but honestly. . ." Elaina knew tears were coming. "Sorry, sir."

She could feel his hand on her back.

"Elaina, this has been a strain. I know you and your husband were having problems, but this has to be very difficult, nevertheless."

Elaina dug a tissue out of her pocket and dabbed her eyes. "I guess I'm crying for the days in the distant past when Masal and I were close. In the last few years things have gotten pretty bad, sir." She stopped walking. "I'm so sorry. You don't want to hear about all my problems."

The commander smiled. "That's quite all right. I meant it when I said that if you need someone to talk to, you should see me as a friend. Obviously on the bridge we have to operate professionally, but after the Green Shift is over, I can be your sounding board – but only if you want, of course."

Elaina appreciated the support. Seth was more formal than most men were with her. At the same time, however, he was kind and considerate. Right now, those were really important qualities as far as she was concerned.

She'd been through a lot with Masal. Now, all that was over, except for the mourning. At least, she hoped it was.

CHAPTER THIRTY-SEVEN
"The Invitation"

Starship Cygnus
Level 3
Compartment 317
1M, Day 4, 6573
8:04 p.m.

S eth Okanata lifted a box off the small cart outside the compartment door, moved to the doorway and carefully stepped over the threshold.

When he did, his toe caught and he tripped.

The contents of the box flew outward and landed on the compartment floor.

Seth stood above the mess. "I'm so sorry, Elaina. I'm very clumsy sometimes."

She smiled at him. "And here I thought you were this perfect commander without any faults."

Seth shook his head. "Hardly. Look at the mess I've made." He dropped to his knees, righted the box and began picking up the items.

There were books and manuals and some photographs.

Seth picked up a photo. "These are really well done, Elaina. Who took these?"

"I did."

"They look like they were done by a professional photographer with a good quality camera."

"I've always been interested in photography. It's been one of my hobbies for years. I've been able to take some photos during my travels across the galaxy. It's wonderful to have access to all that raw material – star clusters, oddly shaped moons, some planets with unusual foliage."

Seth studied one photo of a moon close up. It reminded him of what Europa looked like when the starship passed during their flyby.

Jupiter had given them the braking they needed. They would be going at less than one hundred thousand kilometers per hour when they reached Mars. That would be slow enough to establish an orbit.

He studied another photograph of a cluster of stars. It was obvious that the photo was taken out of a port or the windshield of a starship.

That reminded Seth of Masal's death. It was always on his mind, mostly because of the investigation.

Seth had interviewed several people, including Sergeant Copan, Masal's companion. He was just trying to see if Copan remembered something.

This was all a repeated effort, of course, because Lieutenant Bucolus, the starship security chief had done the very same thing. It was just that Seth was a stickler for details.

Bucolus had discovered one thing. Someone had tampered with the video feed that covered the EVA storage room. There were videos, but Bucolus had discovered a slight irregularity.

The security chief had slowed down the video several times to a point where he was actually able to spot an overdub on the video storage device itself. Obviously someone had tampered with it.

It became clear to Seth Okanata as commander of this starship that he had a murderer in his midst. One of his crew people had killed Masal Djoser and had tried to cover his tracks, and Lieutenant Bucolus had caught him at it.

It really bothered Seth that there was this killer in his midst and he didn't know who it was. He didn't like not knowing, especially when it came to his crew.

The starship commander found that he was looking at his people in a new light. Every time he was around somebody he hadn't seen for a while, he would study that person. Of course, he was more subtle than that. He didn't want to unduly upset anyone.

Lieutenant Alto Bucolus had also said something to Seth that was unnerving. He had told Seth that someone who is murdered is, in fact, most often murdered by a person he or she knows very well.

That remark gave Seth the creeps. It pointed to Elaina. That's why he found it so creepy. Obviously Elaina couldn't do such a thing.

What Seth had wondered over and over again was how close Sergeant Copan was to Masal. Seth had gotten the impression they were friends and that they had worked together before, but those things did change. Sometimes close friends had a falling out.

Seth found that his mind continued to return to Sergeant Copan over and over again. Copan, of all people, had the easiest access to the EVA storage area.

Of course, Seth realized that he might just be trying to deflect his own doubts about Elaina. She did have a lot of reason to be very angry with Masal.

Seth supposed that Lieutenant Bucolus was focusing his investigation on Elaina. This made Seth somewhat uneasy. What compounded this feeling was that Bucolus was not consulting with him or keeping him abreast of what was going on, except for those reports.

He had received one so far and it was just a very basic tally of information to a particular point in the investigation. There were no statements of speculation or projected directions the investigation might take - nothing.

Seth had asked Bucolus what person he suspected had committed the crime, but the man refused to speculate like that. He had simply said, "I will go wherever the investigation leads me."

After placing the last of the photos into the box, Seth rose from the floor of the compartment and walked across the living room into the short hallway.

Elaina was standing in the bedroom, reaching up into a cupboard above the closet. When she saw him, she said, "Put that on the bed, Seth, will you?"

"Sure."

He placed the box on the end corner of the bed.

Seth had been bracing himself to say something to Elaina, but so often, when he planned too long, he would eventually run out of courage to say anything.

This time he didn't think about it. "Would you like to have dinner at my place?"

Elaina's head turned. She smiled. "Sure."

Seth's pulse was throbbing in his ears but he did hear that answer. There, it had been quite easy, after all.

He supposed that members of the bridge crew were not allowed to see each other socially, but maybe this could be one exception. Of course he could always reassign Elaina to the Orange Shift.

He would miss having her around, however. She was so smart and, of course, pleasant to look at. But, then, he was getting ahead of himself here. He had just asked her to dinner at his compartment.

Sure, it would be MREs but he did have some good wine. He assumed she was tired after moving all this stuff and there had to be an emotional component here as well. She was moving back into the compartment she and her abusive husband had shared. Yes, there was definitely an emotional component.

"Are you making something special for our dinner?"

"No."

Elaina touched her chin and looked up at the ceiling in a mock thoughtful pose. "Let me see. . ." She looked at him. "Are you preparing MREs?"

Seth could feel his face flush with embarrassment.

"You're blushing." She smiled and she put her hand on his shoulder. "I hope you have some wine."

"Of course."

CHAPTER THIRTY-EIGHT
"Big Assignment"

Starship Cygnus
Level 2
Compartment 218
1M, Day 5, 6573
7:22 a.m.

Captain Chan Caracol had invited his friend to dinner because he liked Alto and he knew the man was working hard to solve this apparent murder.

Alto Bucolus was one of those people who would tell you that everything was fine, when he was actually working long hours, pushing himself to finish some job. In fact, Chan knew his friend was not only working long hours, he probably wasn't getting enough rest or taking time off to relax.

"I can never get used to eating dinner at eight in the morning."

"Pretend it's eight in the evening, Alto. Actually in terms of the Orange Shift, that's the correct time."

Alto touched his right temple. "Up here, I know it's supposed to be evening, but my body tells me it's morning. I never get used to this late shift thing. You can call it the Second Shift or the Orange Shift or the Dog Shift or whatever, but it's still nighttime to me."

Chan shrugged. "It's daytime to me. I guess I adjust better."

The huge security chief grinned. "I'll bet part of it is that you spend so much time messin' around with chicks at night when you're back on Hyksos. You don't know what time of day or night it is because you're havin' fun."

Chan nodded. "Of course. So how was your freeze-dried bison steak?"

"Hey, it was great. Not as good as fresh, but real good."

"I kind of figured you'd like it. Sometimes I get worried about you when you're on a case."

"How's that?"

"Oh, I know you work hard and really get into what you're doing. I bet you're not getting enough sleep these days."

Alto raised his bottle of beer to a point near his mouth. Then his hand stopped. "I'm not gettin' much. This case has me baffled. Somebody really thought this one out. All we have is that partial print and it's not enough to match in the starship database."

"I thought you had a good print."

"I've kind of let people think that. I figured it might make the killer nervous so he'd do somethin' stupid. So far, no luck."

"Who do you think the killer is?"

Alto swallowed some beer. Then he looked up at his friend Chan. "I have several people in mind."

"If I know you, there's one person you're focused on."

Alto shrugged. "Yeah, kind of."

Chan came at this from another angle. "How many suspects do you have?"

"Three."

Chan thought a minute. "I would guess Hector Copan and Elaina Djoser. Who's the third?"

"Now, wouldn't you just love to know who that is?"

"Yes, I would."

Alto chuckled. "Sure you would."

"I can't think of a single other person."

"Chan - think about it. Who has been payin' special attention to Elaina Djoser?"

Chan suddenly knew the answer. "The commander?"

Alto nodded. "Yup. If he has a thing for Elaina and Masal was knockin' her around, then Commander Seth Okanata has a motive. He also has access to every compartment and storage room on this starship. Not many people have that kind of access."

"Hector has a key to the EVA storage room."

Alto nodded. "He sure does."

"Hector would be my prime suspect."

"But what's his motive?"

Chan shrugged. "I don't know. Maybe he didn't like seein' Elaina knocked around. He might even have a crush on her. She is one good-looking woman, Alto."

"Sure she is. But I just have this feelin' that the commander couldn't stand Masal, especially because he was whackin' Elaina around."

"He's a real gentleman."

"Masal sure wasn't a gentleman."

Captain Chan Caracol was a pilot on the Orange Shift. Now and then he had to work with Commander Okanata. He liked and respected the man. In fact, he even admired him to a certain extent.

Chan, therefore, had a hard time imagining that his commander could be guilty of murder. It was just too much to swallow.

Chan thought Hector Copan or Elaina would be much more likely to kill someone – especially Hector. The guy was a good mechanic but he was just a little rough around the edges. Hector would be his choice.

But he wasn't running this case. Alto was, and Alto would get to the truth. Chan was confident of that, if nothing else. "Want another beer?"

Alto shrugged. "Sure, if you're buyin'."

Chan pulled open the refrigerator door and pulled a beer bottle out of the lower shelf on the door. He carried it across the short space to the breakfast bar and placed it on the counter.

Alto looked relaxed. That was good to see. He was a good man. However, when he was working on a crime, he became intense and focused to the point where Chan sometimes didn't feel he even knew the guy.

Chan twisted the cap off the top of the plastic bottle. He held out his hand for the other bottle. "Give me your empty."

Alto tilted the empty bottle up and swallowed. Then he held it out to Chan. "Now it's empty."

"It's good to see you relaxed."

"It's good to be relaxed. This case is drivin' me nuts. I just can't get anywhere. It's like I'm sittin' around waitin' for the killer to make a mistake."

"You'll get him, whoever he is."

"Or she is."

"I just don't think it's Elaina."

"You'd love to get into her pants, wouldn't you? That's the reason you can't see her as guilty. A beautiful woman you'd love to screw."

Chan shrugged. "Could be. The thing I don't understand is why she hooked up with someone like Masal."

"Tell you what, Chan. What I've learned after workin' in this business all my life is that people do surprisin' things. Some of them don't seem to add up. But there's always a reason.

"Like – maybe when Elaina was young she wasn't such a confident person. Maybe she had low self-esteem or somethin'. That would make a woman marry some guy who, in no way, was her match socially or otherwise.

"This kind of shit goes on, Chan, right under our noses all the time. And then we get all surprised about it. Well, there's always a reason, whether it makes any sense of not."

Chan wondered about that. He had known a lot of women. However, he had never met one, no matter how cute she was, that he would want to live with for the rest of his life. Maybe the woman for him was out there and he just hadn't found her yet.

"This beer's makin' me real relaxed."

"Good. I was hoping I could take some of the pressure off."

"Now, you did me a favor. I have to do one for you."

"Find me that woman I want to marry."

Alto grinned and shook his head. "Now that is one damned big assignment."

CHAPTER THIRTY-NINE
"The Picketers"

Mars
Borealis Basin
1M, Day 23, 6573
10:06 a.m.

Lieutenant Alto Bucolus found this mission down to the surface of Mars to be a nice change of pace. He still hadn't solved that murder case and, now, everyone aboard the starship had seemed to lose interest. He was even having a hard time getting cooperation from some people.

He was down here with his assault rifle guarding these scientists. He was just trying to keep these jokers from doing something stupid.

The one he was least worried about was the astrophysicist, Doc Meander. That guy had his head screwed on tight. The rest of them? Well, that was another matter.

Meander had a two-foot long telescope and he was looking through it at the surface of the planet.

Alto could see the large man away from the others in an open space off to the southwest. Right now his telescope was pointed at that large mountain, Olympus Mons.

This planet wasn't exactly what you'd call a place to live. It was a big sand dune with rock outcroppings, at least here in the Borealis Basin that's what it was.

Alto was fascinated about being on this planet, though, because it was the place of his people's origin. The Mayan people had started from here almost seven thousand years ago. At least that's what the experts said.

It was strange here because the sky was slightly blue but the blue ended quickly and above it were black space and bright stars and planets, and this solar system's sun.

Doctor Eloi, the anthropologist stood up, holding a bone in his glove. "We have just found the elusive Lieutenant Gurab."

The geologist, Doctor Kan Naranjo was a few feet away. "Maybe we can carbon date those, Jak."

"No doubt, we'll have to if we're going to make sure this is Lieutenant Gurab. We do have family DNA with us for comparison. If there's any doubt, the DNA should clear it up."

Alto wiggled his air mask on his face. It was making his skin itch along the edges. He hated wearing these things. Probably that's why he had this itch.

He walked toward the two men digging in the orange sand.

Doctor Jak Eloi held up another bone. His sunglasses stared at the bone, then he slid it into a cloth bag hanging on a strap from his left shoulder.

When Alto neared a rock outcropping his left boot bumped into something. He stopped.

The chief of security wondered if it might be another bone. He crouched down and brushed the sand away from in front of his left boot.

It was nothing, only a small black triangular stone.

He rose to his feet and moved toward the two scientists. What he realized while he walked toward them was that he hadn't followed his own directive.

He stopped. Lieutenant Bucolus realized that he was being careless. They had read in the record of the previous Mayans on Mars that there were soft spots in the sand and sometimes even sinkholes.

Alto had been walking much too fast.

He moved forward again, this time at a slower pace. Just before he reached Doctor Eloi, the anthropologist rose to his feet again. He was holding a skull. "It's human for sure."

Lieutenant Bucolus had read about this Lieutenant Gurab. The man had been in the Starship Security detail just like Alto. However, Gurab had been lost in a sandstorm.

When Alto thought of that word, sandstorm, he straightened up and carefully scanned the horizon. Everything was calm – no sandstorms brewing, as far as he could tell anyway.

Lieutenant Bucolus had also read about the original people who had lived here. This whole area had been filled with giant plastic domes with buildings and parks inside. He had seen the ancient photographs. They were in the museum in Thebes.

He had been to the city of Thebes for a vacation seven years ago. It was a beautiful city on that island in the Poseidon Sea.

The museum was at the University of Thebes. That was the right place for it because the ancient historian, Agenor, had taught there. In fact, that's where he wrote his history scrolls about the ancient Mayan people who crossed the galaxy from this very planet.

The museum was fascinating. There were even videos of what the ancient cities here on Mars must have looked like when the Mayan people had lived here.

As Alto gazed off toward the southwest, he could clearly see the giant mountain, Olympus Mons. Now he could picture the domed cities of his ancestors along the orange sand in a staggered row crossing this planet just above its equator.

Their exodus from here must have been some huge event. He could not begin to imagine, and they set off for the solar system where he lived, CM Draconis, in an ancient rocket ship. It took them almost fifty years to make that journey.

These days they made that same journey in a little more than a month. Alto wondered at the courage of those ancient people, making that long, long journey with only the vague hope of finding a planet to live on.

"Here he is."

Alto swung around.

Doctor Eloi held up a ribcage, spine and set of hips. He studied the human skeleton held aloft in his right hand. "Yes, I'm pretty sure this is male." He carefully placed it on the surface of the orange sand.

He turned to Alto. "I've never had an assignment like this, Lieutenant. I can't say that I'm too comfortable with it, but of course this man should be returned to his family."

"Are any of his family still alive?"

"Yes, I do believe so. There are descendents of his living in the outskirts of Kadesh. They don't know much about him, of course, except what the rest of us know, but I should think they'd like to bury him anyway."

It occurred to Alto that he would want to be returned to his relatives if he had been lost like this. There was just something right about that.

Doctor Naranjo raised a vile of liquid up toward the sunlight. "I can't tell for sure, but based upon what I'm seeing here, I would think this planet would be a great source for iron. Plenty of it for the taking."

He glanced around behind him. "We could set up a mining operation here."

Jak Eloi stood up holding an arm bone with pieces of broken finger bones attached. "The Mayan Historical Society might object, Kan."

"Do you think they would?"

The smaller man shrugged. "They consider this historical real estate, I should think."

"Could be, but this place is loaded with iron. We could make some good money mining it here."

"You're going to have picketers standing on your teleportico, yelling unpleasant things at you, Kan."

"That's such trash. Nobody cares about this dead planet."

Jak Eloi's face crinkled into a grin around his breathing mask. "Don't ever say I didn't warn you, Kan."

Lieutenant Alto Bucolus was tired of these two. They would probably bicker about this historical society thing for hours. He was sure that Doctor Eloi liked to press Doctor Naranjo's buttons.

It was funny, in a way, but Alto was curious about what the astrophysicist was looking at through his small telescope.

Alto trudged through the soft sand back away from the two men toward the southwest. Doctor Meander wasn't too far away. He should check on the man to make sure everything was okay.

CHAPTER FORTY
"First Move"

Starship Cygnus
The Bridge
2M, Day 9, 6573
2:11 p.m.

There was a buzz at the door.

"Check to see who that is, Private Imhotep."

"Yes, sir." The young soldier walked over to the door and leaned his right eye against the peephole in the top section.

He turned. "It's one of the scientists that were down on Mars, sir."

"Let him in, Private."

"Yes, sir." The soldier slapped his hand against the blue glowing rectangle to the right of the door.

The pocket door slid into the wall cavity.

A small, handsome man with black straight hair, a black mustache and goatee stepped over the curved threshold.

The pocket door slid shut behind him.

Commander Seth Okanata rose out of his seat. He turned to the co-pilot. "Let me know when the drone disk is low enough to see anything, Captain."

"Yes, sir."

Seth Okanata moved by the navigation console.

Elaina's pretty face tilted upward and she smiled.

Seth nodded and smiled back.

Things with Elaina had progressed slowly. It was this whole situation surrounding her husband's accident - if that was really an accident.

The investigation had created a subtle tension in his crew. Seth hated that kind of thing. What didn't help was that the man in charge of the investigation, this Lieutenant Alto Bucolus, had actually bluntly told Seth in front of everyone that there were three suspects, Lieutenant Copan, Elaina Djoser and him.

That had been an unpleasant shock.

Seth stopped next to the small man who was standing in front of the door to the bridge.

"Good afternoon, Commander. I have brought you my report as soon as I was finished with it." Doctor Jak Eloi held out a thin booklet.

"Thank you, Doctor."

"I'm sorry it wasn't here sooner, Commander. Our DNA from the family on Hyksos was a match, but there were a lot of variables. When I finally did the math in the situation, which of course involved the time separation of some fourteen hundred years, it was close enough.

"Obviously if this is contested in court, some ambitious lawyer could prove that it's too inconclusive. However, considering the fact that we have found no other bones in that vicinity, which was clearly pinpointed during the last journey to this galaxy those many years ago, I don't see how it could be anybody but Lieutenant Gurab."

"We have visuals, Commander."

Seth Okanata turned to the sound of Captain Tikal's voice. "I'll be right there, Captain."

He faced Doctor Eloi. "Thank you for your work, Doctor. I will look at your findings. Have the descendants of Lieutenant Gurab been notified?"

"No, sir, we were waiting for your okay. Commander, are you having your first look at the surface of planet Earth?"

"Yes, as a matter of fact we are."

"Can I sit in on this, sir?"

Seth thought a minute. "Yes, in fact, that might be helpful. I will say, however, Doctor Eloi, that you shouldn't discuss any of what we've discovered on Earth until it's formally announced to the rest of the crew."

"Of course not, Commander."

"Come, you can sit up here." Seth saw an opportunity to sit next to Elaina. "Tell you what, Doctor Eloi, I'll put you in the pilot's seat. I want to sit back with the navigator. She's controlling the drone."

"That would be great, sir."

Seth held up the booklet. "I will look through this, Doctor Eloi, and I will get back with you. I'm just following procedures. I'm sure we could contact the descendants right now, but protocol specifies that I have to okay everything. You understand."

"Of course, Commander. Just get back to me when you're done and I'll notify Gurab's descendants." The small man moved across to the pilot's seat. He held out his hand to Captain Tikal. "Hello I'm Doctor Jak Eloi."

The co-pilot shook the small man's hand.

Commander Seth Okanata stared down at the thin booklet. This would be a matter of form, but he should look through this report anyway. He owed that to Lieutenant Gurab and his family.

Seth didn't remember the story in detail, but he did know that Gurab's death was an accident that had suspicious overtones because the lieutenant had been having an affair with the wife of the current commander of the starship Orion Four. It was a nasty situation.

That was history, however, and now they could return Gurab's remains to Hyksos and the man could be buried properly with a headstone in a proper cemetery.

Why was that so important? He wasn't sure. It just seemed the right thing to do. Everybody should have that right. It was a given, as far as he was concerned.

Now he had other things to attend to.

Seth moved over to Elaina's console and sat in the seat to her right. He caught the subtle scent of perfume.

Elaina looked over at him.

Seth was surprised that she did look. She was piloting the drone disk.

Seth smiled.

When he did that, Elaina seemed to come alive in front of him.

Seth could feel his skin heat up. He turned away and placed the thin booklet off to his right on the narrow counter. He would read Doctor Eloi's report this evening after dinner.

Actually that wasn't the most prominent thing on Seth's mind right now. It was the way Elaina had looked when he smiled at her. He wondered if he wasn't just imagining Elaina's response to his smile.

On the screen in front of Elaina was an area of countryside. In the upper right was what looked like a crowd of people on a long sloping hill.

Seth pointed. "What is that?"

She glanced at him. "I really don't know."

Seth looked into the brown eyes. "See if you can get closer to that crowd of people, so we can see what's happening."

"Yes, sir." Elaina moved a joy stick on the console next to the keyboard.

The crowd swept toward the lower left corner of the screen and finally there was a single man standing on the side of the hill, facing that same crowd. Around him sat other men on the ground. All were apparently listening to this one man.

Seth turned again. "Zoom in on that man who's in front of the crowd. Don't move the drone any closer. I don't want to frighten the people."

As he watched, Seth realized that these people were quite primitive. They were dressed in simple loose fitting robes. He would guess they were made of wool or cotton or maybe both materials were used.

Now he could clearly see the man who was talking. He was dark-skinned and had brown eyes. He was bearded and his face seemed to be wreathed in a soft smile. He looked to be in his late twenties, although it was hard to tell with these primitives.

"This is the beginning of the iron age."

Seth's head rose up over the console when he heard Doctor Eloi's voice.

"Their clothing is made of wool. Then some other items like shirts are made of cotton."

"What do you think this is, Doctor Eloi?"

The small man turned in the swivel chair. "I'd say some kind of meeting. By the look on the people's faces I'd say that they revere this man who is speaking."

"Is this a religious or political gathering, Doctor?"

"Could be either, Commander. If I were to make a guess, I'd say it's religious, but that's only a guess."

Seth studied the people scattered down the hill. "That's a good-sized crowd, Doctor . . . probably several hundred people."

"I'd say that's a pretty good guess, Commander."

"Maybe we should teleport some of our own people down there to see what this is all about." Seth leaned back in his seat. "Frankly, Doctor, I'm surprised that these people haven't progressed more than they have. It's been fourteen hundred years since we were last here."

"Oh, they've progressed, Commander. But, you see, with people living in these primitive conditions progress is very slow. Our society develops much faster.

"They have actually progressed. I would guess that there are still wars going on between tribal groups and city states. Maybe there are even wars between nations at this point. The people on Hyksos have gotten beyond all of that violence, of course."

"Tell me, Doctor, do you think we could set up trade relations with these people?"

The small man rubbed his bearded chin thoughtfully. "It would be limited. Frankly, it would be better if our geologist, Doctor Kan Naranjo, could discover some minerals here. I'm sure there are such things on this planet or in it. In fact, I would guess this place is rich in minerals. Of course, Kan would know much better than I."

"We'll have to send him down to take some samples."

"Could I go down, Commander?"

"Yes, Doctor Eloi, I would think that would be necessary to figure out what we can do with this society as far as trade and so forth."

"I could certainly help out, Commander. I'm really curious about this society – how it's put together and where they are in their development. Of course, I would submit a written report for the record."

Seth Okanata could see a problem with sending down too many people, but he was sure that both Doctor Eloi and Doctor Naranjo would be the most natural choices. Of course, he would have to send down security with them, maybe two men or so.

He was very much aware of Elaina sitting to his left. He could still smell that subtle fragrance of the perfume.

When she turned, he noticed that her lips seemed full.

She smiled. "This looks like an interesting place."

He stared into the intelligent brown eyes. "Yes, it does."

Elaina leaned close to his left ear.

Seth could feel her breath on his neck.

"Are you eating dinner alone tonight?" she whispered.

Seth was startled. "Yes."

"I'll be over, if that's all right."

Seth could hear his pulse thumping in his ears. He had been wanting to make that first move. As usual, however, he was timid.

Now, she had done it for him.

CHAPTER FORTY-ONE
"Reservations"

Starship Cygnus
Level 2
Compartment 205
2M, Day 9, 6573
6:43 p.m.

Seth Okanata had been reading Doctor Eloi's report about finding the remains of Lieutenant Coptos Gurab on the planet Mars. Actually it was easy to read and the information was very well organized.

One thing he did get from this report was that he would approve it. Doctor Eloi had been able to find all of the remains, except for some finger bones which had evidently become separated.

Seth could understand that. The bones were small and there was a lot of sand to sift through. However, they had most of the skeletal remains and the DNA had been close enough. With this amount of time since the man had died, anything closer would probably be impossible. Fourteen hundred years was, indeed, a long time.

Seth had put off having dinner because he was waiting for Elaina. Waiting was not one of his favorite things, but in this case it was probably going to be worth it.

He had no idea what was going to happen, but his hopes were high. He was not experienced in these matters. Therefore, he would let her take the lead.

He had avoided making a decision about who might be guilty of this supposed murder of Masal Djoser. In fact, he had gone over and over the evidence personally, looking for any indication that it might actually have been an accident.

He didn't want to think of the other possibility – murder. That's because there were only three suspects. He knew he didn't do it, although he wasn't particularly sorry to see that man die.

The two other suspects were Sergeant Hector Copan and Elaina. He would love to believe that Copan did it, but what was his motive? Copan was the man's friend. That left Elaina, and that's why he had avoided thinking about it, or at least he had tried to avoid thinking about it.

There was a loud buzz at the other end of the small living room. Seth jumped at the loud sound. Even though it had startled him and he had been anticipating Elaina coming to his compartment, he forced himself to sit in his living room chair for just a minute longer to collect himself. He didn't want to act like an idiot when he opened that door.

Finally he rose from his chair. He was going to put the report on the kitchen counter, but then he thought it might look like he was more in control if he walked to the door carrying the report. In other words, he would be trying to say to Elaina that he had really gotten involved in this report and almost forgot about her coming – or something like that.

Seth tucked the folder under his left arm and walked over to the pocket door. He was going to put his hand on the lighted pad to the right of the casing, but decided that, perhaps, it might be wise to peek outside.

When he leaned against the door, he saw her instantly. In fact, he received the impression that she might have stood there right in front of the peephole purposely. She was facing to his left, as if she were just standing there waiting. Of course, that could be her way of a posing for him.

She did, indeed, look beautiful. In fact, she was no longer wearing her regular uniform. She was wearing a white blouse and a pair of blue slacks. He could not see them very well, but from the waistband he could tell they were not MSA issue.

He stepped back.

A second buzz.

His hand moved instantly to the lighted pad, but then he stopped and waited for what he thought should be the appropriate time. Finally, he pressed his hand against it.

The door rattled open to the right.

"Elaina. . . you look absolutely beautiful." After he had said that, Seth realized that it sounded a bit sophomoric. The next time, maybe he should tone it down a bit.

She smiled. "Thank you, Seth. That's very sweet of you to say."

He moved over to the side and swept out his left hand. "Come in."

She stepped over the curved threshold.

The door rattled shut.

Now Seth could see the slacks clearly. They were slightly tight, he noticed. He pulled his eyes away. It wasn't polite to stare. "Would you like a beer or a glass of wine?"

"Wine would be nice."

"White or red?"

"Red, please."

"I have some red I bought from a farmer on Hyksos. It's really quite good. I like white usually, but this red is not as bold as most."

She smiled. "I'd like to try it, Seth."

He placed the report on the breakfast bar, then moved around the end of it into the kitchen and reached up to the cupboard above the refrigerator. He opened the door.

Seth knew the red wine was just inside because he had opened it already. He hoped there was enough left.

"I don't know about you, Seth, but I've been quite tense about this investigation."

He looked over his right shoulder. "Yes, I've been the same way." He pulled out the bottle of red wine.

He placed the bottle on the counter and re-latched the cupboard. Then he reached up to the larger cupboard to the right of the refrigerator.

On the top shelf were plastic wine goblets. He pulled out two, then latched that cupboard door.

He carried the goblets and the bottle across to the breakfast bar.

Elaina was standing on the other side. "I don't mean to bring up something which you might be uncomfortable to talk about, Seth, but it has been difficult for me to be around the crew on the bridge. Not you so much. We're in the same boat – suspects."

Seth had the feeling that Elaina was trying to ally herself with him. On one level, he could understand that. On another, more subtle level, he felt that she might be shoring up her defenses.

It was just an emotional response. Probably it meant nothing. After all, that's what tension on a bridge did to people who worked together.

He twisted out the rubber stopper and poured a plastic goblet of wine and held it out to Elaina. He made eye contact, then averted his eyes back to his own goblet. He poured the red liquid into his goblet. He pushed the stopper into the bottle.

The plastic goblets had been made especially for the MSA. They were as bulbous near the bottom above the stem as most wine goblets were, but the part above the stem was taller than typical goblets. That was to prevent splashes in this lower gravity.

Elaina held out her goblet toward Seth. "To friends."

"To friends." Seth found that he was trying to read her eyes.

One part of him wanted to have this woman as a lover. She was beautiful, bright and charming. There was another more cautious side, however, that warned him about what her motives might be. Of course, she wasn't guilty of this murder, so it was ridiculous to even think of such a thing.

He couldn't blame her for being angry and wanting to get back at Masal, but to loosen a screw on his regulator – that meant a sudden, violent and painful death.

Pressure inside your suit went to zero and your lungs bled profusely. According to what he had been told, that was very painful.

Elaina was sweet and kind. She could never do such a thing. "Taste it. I think you'll like it."

Elaina sipped from the wine. She swallowed and held out the goblet, apparently to look at the wine. "It's really good. It's sort of fruity, but it also has a lot of body."

Seth sipped some of his own wine. Yes, it was good. At least he personally thought it was. He hoped she really liked it.

Elaina sipped more of the red wine. After she swallowed, she said, "I can tell, Seth, that you're a little concerned about how this might look, but really I won't tell anyone, if you don't. Besides, this is just a friendly visit."

A weight suddenly seemed to lift off Seth's shoulders. Yes, he had to remember that they were just friends – at least for the time being. He had fantasized many times about this thing going further, but, after all, that was fantasy. "I don't think we have anything to worry about. Even if someone does find out, our relationship is quite harmless."

What Seth saw in Elaina's eyes at that moment was a sort of glint. It was as if something else was going on here. He wondered what that was about.

Obviously, he was a cautious man, yet when a man had feelings for a woman, caution sometimes was thrown to the wind, so to speak.

He put his partially empty goblet on the counter. "Well, perhaps I should get something started here." He turned to her. "It's going to be MREs, I'm afraid, Elaina."

She put her hand to her mouth and chuckled. "You looked so guilty when you said that. That's so cute." She placed her right hand on his arm. "Seth, don't feel guilty about serving me an MRE. They're actually quite good, except the pork and beans."

Seth folded his arms across his chest. "Well, I'm certainly glad you mentioned that fact because I was about to serve that very meal. What about steak and potatoes?"

"Excellent."

Seth crossed to the cupboard to the right of the refrigerator. He crouched down and opened the door. Then he dug around inside and pulled out an MRE package.

The cover read, "Steak and Potatoes." He raised it above his right shoulder and slid it onto the kitchen counter.

Then he dug into the cupboard a second time.

This time the package read, "Bison Stew." He placed that on the counter next to the other MRE.

He closed the cupboard and latched it. Then he rose to full height.

"You know, this is really nice. It's quiet and sort of domestic."

Seth turned to Elaina's voice.

"After all the pressure on the bridge lately, Seth, this is very nice."

He made a smile. "Yes, it is, isn't it?" He picked up the "Steak and Potatoes" package and moved over to the microwave. He pulled open the door, slid the package in and pushed the door closed.

Commander Seth Okanata had hoped this evening would be something special between the two of them. Now, however, he had reservations. He just couldn't help but feel that something was going on, that there was some kind of subterfuge.

It was only a feeling and maybe he would get over it by the end of the evening. Right now, however there was something inside that warned him to be cautious.

CHAPTER FORTY-TWO
"The Brother"

Earth
Galilee
2M, Day 11, 6573
7:48 a.m.

Captain Salathiel Tikal had just teleported down to the surface of Earth.

When the bubbles cleared, he checked the area around him. Yes, he was near a cluster of low trees with bushy tops. They chose this area because the trees would hide the teleporting process. They didn't want to frighten these primitive people.

Lieutenant Bucolus and Private Imhotep were standing a few feet away. They had been expecting him.

The two men moved over to where Sal was standing. Bucolus pointed toward a narrow dirt road. "Captain, that group of people is off to the east. Probably about 50 meters down that road."

Sal nodded. "So they don't know we're here."

"I'm pretty sure they don't, sir."

"Lieutenant, as soon as Doctor Naranjo and Doctor Eloi teleport, we can form up and move in that direction."

Commander Okanata seemed to be curious about this political or religious leader they had discovered.

Tikal was a bit interested himself, but he believed the most important thing was to find out what minerals were available on this planet. Actually the starship would have to do research in several locations.

They could also use the sound imaging from the starship. That would at least give them general clues about minerals.

Lieutenant Bucolus leaned close to Sal. "Imhotep and I have been scoutin' around. These people seem pretty harmless. One guy is sort of talkin' or preachin' to them. He has a small band of followers – maybe eight or nine. But I don't think it's political, sir."

"Good. We don't want to get involved in politics. Would you say he's a religious figure?"

"Yes, sir, it seems like that's the case."

"Well, maybe if we talk to him and his friends, we can get a sense of what this culture is like. Then we'll figure out if we can do business with them."

Bucolus turned. "Sir, if I may say so, these people seem really primitive. I don't know how we're going to do any trade or anythin' like that."

Sal nodded. "That's what I was thinking, Lieutenant."

Off to Sal's right a blue glow appeared. It was Doctor Kan Naranjo, the geologist.

Seconds later, another blue glow appeared farther away, near the orchard. It was Doctor Jak Eloi, the anthropologist.

To Captain Sal Tikal, this part about dealing with primitive societies was new. Most often he was in a delegation teleported down to a building where he would sit in a meeting with government and business representatives. They would discuss the mutual benefits of trading or setting up a business in that locality on the planet, etcetera.

In dealing with primitive societies, it was often wise to approach carefully. If you teleported down to the front door of a government building, you might find yourself locked up or killed. There had been incidents like that in the past. Tikal had read about some of them.

"Gentlemen, come over here, if you would." Sal Tikal beckoned to the two men who had just teleported.

Doctor Jak Eloi moved around his larger, pudgy companion, Naranjo, and stepped up next to Captain Tikal. He looked back. "Kan is getting his junk together. He always brings a lot of stuff. Kan does a lot of digging, so he always seems to have more gear than everybody else." A fleeting smile passed over the bearded man's face.

He glanced back over his left shoulder. "Kan, do you need any help?"

"No, I've got it. Thanks."

Doctor Jak Eloi looked at the captain. He shrugged. "I guess we just wait."

"Okay, I'm ready," said the geologist. With his right arm, he swung a large rucksack up behind his back. Then he slid his left arm through the left shoulder harness and buckled a strap across his chest. "All set."

He walked across to the group of men.

Sal glanced around. "Okay, here's how we're going to approach this. Lieutenant Bucolus, Private Imhotep and I are going to lead the way down this road.

"Lieutenant Bucolus has already checked-out these people visually and doesn't see any problem. In spite of that, they are going to be suspicious of us because of our clothing and our guns, and they're going to notice that, when we talk to them, our lips don't move the usual way."

"In fact, that may freak them out. I've seen that happen before with much more advanced people than this. So, what I suggest is that all of us be careful."

"Once we've established some kind of trust, we can start getting information from them." He looked at the anthropologist. "Doctor Eloi, it's very important that you figure out just where these people are historically. They seem pretty primitive to us laymen, but we want a closer assessment. That will give us clues about trade and such." He glanced around the group. "Any questions?"

"Not a question – a comment." Jak Eloi, the anthropologist folded his arms across his chest. "These are things to keep in mind. The people here are quite primitive, no doubt. That means they are suspicious of strangers. And by the way, you are not going to be warned by the sound of a pistol cocking or an assault rifle being raised. They have small daggers – knives, probably made of bronze or iron. Just be aware of that."

Lieutenant Alto Bucolus nodded several times. "I suppose the smart thing to do is keep your distance from them."

"Exactly." Doctor Eloi turned to Sal. "I didn't mean to steal your thunder, Captain. It's just that this kind of society is different. The people are generally local and they're suspicious of strangers. I thought you should be aware of that."

Captain Sal Tikal noticed that a man down on the road was staring at them. Then he took off running toward the east.

Sal pointed at the small figure running. "Our arrival is going to be announced."

Jak Eloi turned to look, then he said, "When we get to the group of people, I would be reluctant to mingle. Aside from the fact that the stench of sweat and filth will be terrible, it might be dangerous to mingle. I'd stay clear. I'm sure some of them have daggers and there might be pickpockets and other unsavory types among them. Some of them might even have leprosy and you don't want to come in contact with those people. That's a nasty disease."

Lieutenant Bucolus nodded. "Thanks for the info, Doc. We'll be careful." He flipped off the safety on his assault rifle.

Imhotep did the same.

Sal Tikal was carrying only a pistol in a holster on his right hip. But at that moment he thought it might be wise to make sure there was a round in the chamber.

He ripped the flap away from the Velcro strip on the side of the holster. Then he yanked out a black pistol and held it in front of his face, making sure the barrel was pointed away toward the empty field next to the orchard.

He pushed back the slide with the thumb and the index finger of his left hand.

Yes, there was a cartridge in the chamber. He released the slide slowly. Then he flipped off the safety, and slid the pistol back into the holster. He pressed the cover against the Velcro strip.

The captain turned to Bucolus. "Are you ready, Lieutenant?"

"All set, sir."

"Then let's do this." Sal Tikal led the small group through the cluster of low trees down the gradual hill toward the road.

To him, this country looked pretty rough. The ground was stony and sandy. He wondered what kind of trees were in this orchard. He supposed they might be some kind of olive trees. Actually he wouldn't know, one way or the other.

Once out of the orchard and on the primitive dirt road, Sal turned toward the east. Ahead of them along the side of the road was a small grove of wild trees.

He looked to his left. "Bucolus, when the road goes through those trees, keep sharp. It would be a good place for a group of people to hide and jump us."

Bucolus glanced over at Imhotep to his left. "You heard the captain."

"Yes, I did, sir."

As they approached the scraggly low, bushy trees, Captain Sal Tikal studied the area over and over again. Because this seemed to be a natural outcropping of trees, he wondered if there might perhaps be a water source right there, a natural well maybe.

If that were the case, it might be a place where people would congregate to drink or collect water in jugs, or whatever these people used.

At the grove trees, Lieutenant Bucolus held out his arm. "Captain, wait until Imhotep and I check this place out."

He moved forward with the private. Both of them held their assault rifles out in front of them.

Sal turned to the two scientists. "We'll wait here, gentlemen."

"All clear." Bucolus beckoned to them.

Sal moved forward and eventually stepped into the shade of the low trees. His impression of this area of the planet Earth was that it was poor and primitive. It had a kind of dusty, angular beauty. The sky was almost totally clear blue - a dry climate no doubt and it was very warm – hot actually.

As he had guessed, there was a flowing well in the midst of the trees. Next to that well were two men sitting in the scraggly green grass. They were wearing long off-white robes. The one worn by the man nearest to him had dingy stains around the bottom edge.

Sal was sure it was filthy.

That man pointed at him. "You are the leader. What country are you from? You have strange clothes. Are you Romans?"

Sal stopped. He noticed that the man was missing two teeth on the left side of his mouth – maybe from a fight. "We're Mayans."

"I have never heard of them."

"We're from far away."

The man pointed. "Your mouth moves funny when you talk."

"I'm sorry, but we are a strange people."

The man chuckled, then shrugged. "Everybody has his ways. They are all different. The great god of Israel has made us all different."

"Is this place Israel?"

"Of course. You didn't know that?"

"No, we have never been here before."

"That is strange. Everybody knows about Israel, especially since the Romans conquered us."

"Who are these Romans?"

"They are from a mighty city across the Mediterranean Sea, the city of Rome. That great city has conquered the whole world. People say it is a magnificent city where there are public baths.

"I will not say much about the Romans because you never know who is listening, but I will say that I liked Israel better before the Romans came."

"Who is the president of this country?"

"What is a president?"

"A leader."

"Oh, that would be Pontius Pilate. He was chosen by Rome to run all of Israel."

It occurred to Sal Tikal that perhaps at some point his commander should try to contact this Pilate fellow. For now, however, they had to get a reading on what this society was like.

"Of course even Pilate talks with the high priests and Pharisees." The man waved his hand dismissively. Then he glanced around. "They can all go to hell for all I care," he said in a lower voice.

Sal Tikal smiled at the man, trying to give him the impression he understood his attitude. "Thank you for the information, stranger."

The man waved at him. "Think nothing of it. Watch out for the Pharisees. They're everywhere."

"Thanks for that advice." Sal was somewhat relieved. That man didn't seem to be very unnerved by the translator situation. He did notice that Sal's mouth moved differently than it should, but that didn't seem to bother him.

On the other side of the small grove of low trees, Sal stopped.

Off on the right side of the road was a large crowd of people. He estimated that there had to be at least three hundred. And out in front of these people, far up the side of the hill was a single man talking to them. He was talking loud enough so that Sal could hear the voice, but he couldn't make out what the man was saying.

The man raised his hands up in the air and looked upward, almost as if he were talking to someone in the sky above him.

Many of the people in the crowd bowed their heads.

It occurred to Sal Tikal that this was the same thing the people did in the temples on Hyksos, when a priest uttered a prayer to the gods.

Seconds before, he was going to move up the hill, but now, he decided to wait.

"Captain, are we gonna move up and talk to him?"

Tikal held up his hand. "Just a minute," he said in a low voice. "I think he's praying to the gods." He pointed to the people in the crowd.

"See – they're bowing their heads. I think we should wait – show a little respect. That might help us gain their friendship."

"Yes, sir."

It occurred to Sal that perhaps waiting would also go over better with that leader farther up the hill.

Seconds later, he heard a chorus of voices, "Amen."

"I think we can go up now, Lieutenant." Sal turned to the two scientists. "Stay close, gentlemen. Doctor Eloi, why don't you walk by me. I may need your advice."

"Certainly." The small man moved up on his right.

Sal Tikal trudged over the uneven ground up the gradual slope of wild grasses. His pants legs brushed through the tall grass as he moved upward. He focused his eyes on the leader at the top. He didn't want to lose track of him in this crowd.

He noticed that some of the men around the leader had picked up baskets full of long tubular items of some kind. Sal didn't know what those things were.

The men were moving down the slope handing out the tubular items to various people.

"What are they handing out, Bucolus?"

"I don't know, sir."

"It's bread, sir."

Sal looked at Private Imhotep. "Really?"

"Yes, sir. It looks like the kind of bread my mom used to make, sir. The recipe was passed down from her great grandmother – my great, great grandmother."

"It's probably a staple of their diet."

Sal stopped and turned toward Doctor Eloi. "Bread?"

Jak Eloi nodded. "Yes, bread is often a staple in primitive cultures."

It dawned on Sal Tikal just how very primitive these people were. They had no idea about nutrition at all. With bread as a staple in their diet he wondered how long they lived.

He turned to Doctor Eloi again. "How can they live on bread?"

The other man shrugged. "Good question. They can't live as long as we do. They probably have a life span of thirty to thirty-five years."

Sal nodded. "Really backward."

"Yes, in terms of science and health. In other ways, it's hard to tell. Once we get to know them better, Captain, we'll figure out a lot of things."

The Mayans had reached the end of the crowd. Up ahead on the hillside was a small group of men. In their midst was the leader, the one who had been talking to the people.

Sal stopped and stared at the cluster of men, sitting in the grass on the hillside.

"When you approach them, be careful, Captain."

Sal turned to the anthropologist. He nodded. Then he looked at Bucolus. "Lieutenant, keep your eye on things. You and Imhotep stay behind and watch our backs. Doctor Eloi and I will go talk to this man who is their leader."

"Yes, sir." Bucolus motioned to Private Imhotep. "Stand over there, Private. I'll stay right here."

"Yes, sir."

"If anything happens, fire your assault rifle above their heads the first time. Got it?"

"Yes, sir, Lieutenant."

Satisfied that his back was covered, Sal Tikal began moving up the hill. He stopped suddenly. "Where is Doctor Naranjo?"

Jak Eloi turned around. He pointed down the hill a few feet. "He's picking up small rocks. He said that some of the them might have precious stones inside."

Sal checked Doctor Naranjo's proximity to Bucolus and Imhotep. He was just a few feet away from them. "I suppose he'll be all right."

"I think so, Captain."

Sal Tikal began to move up the hill again. When he neared the group of men, one of them stood up.

Sal stopped. "My name is Sal Tikal. I have come from another country. I would like to talk to your leader."

The man was holding a chunk of bread in his right hand. "I am Thomas and the man you are talking about is my twin brother, Jesus. We are from Nazareth."

"May I talk to your brother?"

"Why does your mouth move in strange ways when you talk?"

"Let me speak to your twin brother, and I will explain that to you."

CHAPTER FORTY-THREE

"Magic"

Earth
Galilee
2M, Day 11, 6573
9:46 a.m.

The bread was quite good. Captain Sal Tikal would not have eaten it except that accepting the bread seemed to be a gesture of acceptance of the person. Doctor Jak Eloi had accepted some as well.

Sal had also received the impression that for these people to offer the bread was a gesture of hospitality and even friendship. He was trying to make inroads here, so being polite might be important. It was difficult for Sal because he noticed that this man Thomas did not have clean hands and there was black grime under his fingernails.

He might suggest a round of immunity vaccinations and shots when they got back to the starship – just as a precaution.

Thomas nodded toward the man who did, in fact, look a lot like him. "This is my brother, Jesus."

Sal nodded. "How do you do, sir. I am Captain Sal Tikal."

The man, Jesus, didn't say anything at first. He just sat on the wild grass smiling at Sal. Finally, he placed a piece of bread in the lap of his loose fitting robe. "Thomas says you are from another country. I have the sense, because of your strange clothing, that this country is very far away."

"Yes, it is." Sal was intrigued by the intense brown eyes of this teacher or preacher or whatever he was.

"Is it beyond the powerful city of Rome?"

"Yes, much farther."

He pointed at Sal's mouth. "As Thomas said, your mouth does not move in the normal way when you speak."

Sal wondered if this man could begin to understand the translator imbedded in the soft tissue behind his left earlobe. Probably not.

"We can understand and speak the language of any people. We have that magic."

"There is no magic – only God and the angels and man. And I am the son of God."

Sal was startled by that statement.

"Being the son of God is a great gift and a great burden. Israel occupied by the Romans is a corrupt and violent place. God does not want Israel to be like that. He does not want His people to be spied upon and persecuted and overtaxed by corrupt officials. However, that is the way of life in Israel these days."

Sal could see that it would be difficult to arrange any sort of business with these people. He had come across corrupt governments before. It usually led to all kinds of problems.

"You have spent your whole life looking for something, Captain Tikal, haven't you?"

Sal's head jerked around and he stared at the dark-skinned man with the intense brown eyes. "How did you know that?"

"I can tell these things. Your soul is hungry for something."

Sal felt drawn in by the intense brown eyes. He had a sense of being somehow bonded to this man.

Thomas looked up. He pointed. "Are these your people?"

Sal turned.

Coming toward them were Doctor Naranjo, the geologist and Lieutenant Bucolus and Private Imhotep.

"Yes. That is the rest of my party."

"We will share our bread with them."

Sal was going to say there was no need to do that, but he refrained from saying it. This sharing of bread was a gesture of hospitality and kindness, apparently.

"Thomas, take care of these strangers. I want to talk to this man, Salathiel." Jesus rose from his resting place on the grass.

"Come with me." He motioned with his head toward the upper area of the hill.

Sal fell in step next to him on his right.

"I am interested in where you have come from, Captain Tikal." He turned to him. "Or should I call you Salathiel?"

"How did you know my name was Salathiel?"

The brown-eyed man shrugged. "I just knew. There are many things that come to me. God speaks to me. I know things."

He turned and faced Sal. "My disciples think it's wonderful magic." He looked down at the uneven rocky ground ahead of him. "I suppose it is. But with every power comes a responsibility." He turned to Sal. "You understand that, don't you?"

"Yes."

Jesus nodded. "I thought so." He looked up ahead at the clear blue sky. "Sometimes I wish I were a mere carpenter like my father, going into his shop each morning and cutting and fitting pieces of furniture for the people of the village."

Jesus turned to Sal again. "Joseph, my father, was a good man. He has been gone now for six years. He is with God the Father. I miss him very much. He was a wise and good man."

The Nazarene came to a stop at the top of the hill. "Joseph taught me well. He taught me to have a conscience and he taught me about the injustices in Israel. He brought me up in the Jewish faith and he taught me that it has been corrupted by the priests and the Pharisees. But you wouldn't know what they are."

He folded his arms across his chest. "Tell me, Salathiel, why have your people come here?"

Sal shrugged. "For trade mostly. We're also interested in what minerals and metals are in the ground. We might want to set up a mining company."

"Strictly business?"

"Yes. We have no interest in getting involved in politics."

"In Israel that would be a wise choice. The Romans now rule over us. The priests of our temples and the Pharisees hide in the shadows and plot with the Romans against their own people. Mark my words - Israel is going to come to no good because of this. The Jewish people will suffer horrible things someday. I have warned them."

He faced Sal again. "Enough of that. What about you, my friend? What about your life?" The intelligent brown eyes stared at Sal.

"I don't know what you're talking about."

"Of course you do, Salathiel. Your life is empty. You are looking for something. What you are looking for is God, my friend. If you come to Him, He will fill your heart and make your life whole."

CHAPTER FORTY-FOUR

"Motive"

C ommander Seth Okanata had called this meeting to find out in person what Captain Tikal's crew had discovered the day before down on the planet Earth.

He sat at the end of the table waiting. There was a hubbub of soft conversation at the long table in front of him.

Elaina wasn't here. She wasn't going to be. She was at the bridge with Captain Chan Caracol, the other pilot. He had agreed to stay on until this meeting was over.

The conference room door rattled open and Captain Sal Tikal stepped over the curved threshold.

At the table all four heads turned.

This was the person Seth was waiting for, Tikal.

There had been radio communication from down on Earth yesterday, of course, and there were the recorded conversations with some of the people of this country Israel. However, he wanted to know what the take was from the people themselves.

The commander rose from his seat at the end of the table. "Good morning, gentlemen."

The hubbub of voices vanished.

"I have brought you together to discuss your findings from your expedition down to the planet Earth yesterday. We have come here with the goal of establishing trade or other business arrangements. But you all know that. Let me call on individuals to fill in this information.

"By the way, this session is being video recorded. We need a record of these proceedings. Please use only appropriate language." He smiled.

There was a low chuckle in the Conference Room.

"First, I want to call on Doctor Jak Eloi, our anthropologist. Doctor Eloi, what did you discover?"

The small, handsome man rose out of his seat. He folded his arms across his chest. "Commander, this society in the country, Israel, is very primitive. These people have progressed far beyond the people in the reports about the city of Troy. As you know those reports were written over a millennium ago. However, the people on this planet are still primitive.

"One of the most important problems is that this particular country, Israel, has been occupied or conquered by a city state called Rome. Apparently these Romans are brutal and primitive. Honestly, I don't know how we could set up any kind of trade relations with these people in Israel.

"The country is occupied and that complicates things. Rome would be a possibility, but, again, we would be dealing with a late Bronze to early Iron Age society. In the past we haven't had a lot of success working with people at this level of development.

"First, there's too much violence and that leads to instability. Also there's the huge breach between their understanding of a trade relationship and our understanding of that kind of relationship. With these people, I don't think it's possible. That doesn't mean, however, that there won't be other societies on this planet that would work.

"When Captain Tikal walked up the hill with this religious leader yesterday, I had a chance to talk to several men in his group of friends. I got the distinct impression that their society is in complete disarray. That is not a situation we would want to be involved in." The small man glanced around. "Are there any questions?"

There was no response.

The anthropologist sat down.

"Thank you, Doctor Eloi. Now I call upon Doctor Kan Naranjo."

The large pudgy man rose from his chair. He had several sheets of disheveled paper in his right hand. "I had it all written out, Commander, but nobody wants to hear all my data, so let me just say this.

"Among the rocks I collected yesterday, and things I observed, I did notice some presence of minerals, although not in great quantities. Based on some of my soil samples and some of the rock samples, I saw the possibility of hydrocarbons deep down in the ground. Of course we don't use hydrocarbons anymore for fuels, so we have no real interest in them."

He glanced up the table toward the commander. "I did find some evidence of precious stones in the rock. That would always be a possibility, of course. However, after my own encounter with these people and listening to Jak's report, I doubt it would be worth our time to even consider mining precious stones in this region. There are too many political problems."

He glanced around the table. "I don't suppose there are any questions."

No hands went up.

The pudgy man slid down into the pedestal seat next to the table. It was obvious that this was not easy for him because of his girth.

When he had finally settled, Seth Okanata turned to his co-pilot. "Captain Tikal, what were your impressions?"

Sal rose to his feet. "I guess I had a more positive impression. I found this Jesus of Nazareth fascinating. He really has a lot of charisma – very intelligent man. He's trying to correct the wrongs in his country of Israel. It's a daunting task but I don't think that's going to stop him. In fact, he may have a huge impact on that society."

Seth was a little annoyed. "Captain, I'm sure he's a fascinating man, but what about the issue of trade?"

Sal Tikal seemed somewhat nonplussed for just a second. Then he said, "Probably what Doctor Eloi says is true, but I'd like to see this country after Jesus gets through changing it. There could be a revolution."

Jak Eloi turned around to face Sal Tikal. "'Captain, I got the distinct impression that this city of Rome is very powerful and nothing to fool with. I'm not sure this man has a chance against those odds. I'm sure this Jesus fellow is well intentioned, but he has a very steep hill to climb."

Captain Salathiel Tikal didn't answer that remark. Instead he shrugged. Then he stared off toward the side wall of the small room.

A hand went up.

Seth expected Captain Tikal to address the question. When he didn't, Seth responded. "Yes, Lieutenant Bucolus?"

"Sir, can I see you after this meetin's over?"

"Of course, Lieutenant." Seth didn't like the sound of that, but he had to wrap this up before he talked to Bucolus. "Any other comments or questions?"

A hand shot up.

"Yes, Private Imhotep?"

"Sir, are we goin' to try somewhere else on this planet?"

Seth made a quick smile. "Yes. In fact, Private Imhotep, we will check out some options and try several more places if necessary. I think all we have to do is find one good source of valuable minerals and that would justify establishing a colony. Then perhaps we could branch out from there."

Seth glanced around the small group. "Are there any other questions?"

No hands went up.

"In that case, this meeting is dismissed."

The men rose out of their pedestal chairs next to the table. The last one up was Doctor Naranjo, the geologist. He seemed to struggle to get out from between the table and his seat.

Seth remembered that the man had barely passed the body mass limit. He was obese, but they needed his skills, so they would just have to put up with the obesity.

The small group moved to the door.

Lieutenant Alto Bucolus lingered next to the table, watching the other men move up toward the door.

Seth stepped up next to Alto. "Lieutenant, you had something you wanted to discuss with me?"

"Yes I do, sir," the lieutenant said in a low voice, "but I want to make sure everybody's out of here."

Seth could feel his stomach muscles tense. He wondered what was coming. He certainly hoped it didn't have anything to do with Elaina. He was sure it did, but he was trying not to think that.

Imhotep turned at the doorway. "I'll wait for you outside, sir."

"No, you go ahead, Imhotep. Go down to the Security Center and log on the master computer to see if there were any problems yesterday."

"Yes, sir." Private Imhotep stepped over the curved threshold into the corridor.

The door rattled shut.

Lieutenant Bucolus waited several seconds. It was almost as if he expected Imhotep to come back into the Conference Room.

Finally he turned around and faced Seth. "Sir, I've discovered some new evidence in the Masal Djoser case."

Seth could feel his body tense. He was sure he was holding his breath.

"Commander, this came out of nowhere. Just for the hell of it, I figured I should check into the background of all the suspects – includin' yourself, sir."

Seth wondered how closely this man checked. He didn't really have anything to hide, at least as far as he could remember. "You apparently discovered something, Lieutenant."

"Yes, sir. When I was diggin' around I found out that Lieutenant Masal Djoser and Sergeant Hector Copan had established a business partnership back on Hyksos."

"That's not unusual, Lieutenant."

Alto held up his right hand. "Bear with me, sir."

"Sorry, Lieutenant. Please continue."

"Well, it seems that Masal Djoser stiffed Hector Copan as far as his share of the investment money in the partnership. In other words, they were legally partners and then Masal came up short as far as the amount of money he invested in an antique automobile restoration company."

"How much was he short?"

"Two hundred fifty thousand dollars."

Seth was relieved this had nothing to do with Elaina.

"You see, sir, the thing is that Hector had no way of gettin' Masal to ante up. He couldn't make him pay because they were already partners. He could go to court, but that would cost thousands of dollars."

"I gather, Lieutenant Bucolus, that you see this as a motive."

"Yes, that's right, sir."

Seth nodded. "Then I'd pursue this new information and see what you come up with."

"Yes, sir. It may not amount to anythin', sir, or it might get this case solved."

Seth felt greatly relieved. He had been sure this was about Elaina.

"That doesn't mean Sergeant Copan is guilty and it doesn't mean anybody else is off the hook. But I just thought I ought to tell you, sir."

"I'm glad you did, Lieutenant. Keep me abreast of what you find out."

"I will, sir." The large man turned away and walked to the door. With his huge, meaty hand he touched the blue rectangle to the right of the casing.

The door opened.

Lieutenant Bucolus stepped out into the corridor.

When the door shut, Commander Seth Okanata smiled. In just a matter of minutes he would be with Elaina up on the bridge.

CHAPTER FORTY-FIVE
"The Locked Door"

Starship Cygnus
Level 3
Compartment 317
2M, Day 12, 6573
7:38 p.m.

Seth Okanata stood outside the compartment door. He had thought this through thoroughly and had decided to act.

Though it was true that the MSA did not approve of "fraternizing in the ranks," as they called it, he had decided it was time to move this forward.

It was not easy for him. He was a man who believed in rules and order in the ranks. Yet, he also knew there were times in life where there were turning points.

At those turning points, if you didn't act with courage and conviction, you were left behind. He was totally convinced that was true.

His father had been a good man, a smart man, but he had never gotten anywhere with his life. He had remained a clerk in a shipping company for thirty-five years. Then he had retired on a meager pension.

It had frustrated his mother because she knew how smart her husband was, but she also knew that he didn't like to step out of what was safe and familiar.

Seth had seen glimmers of his father's intelligence and his skills, but they were almost always glimmers in the shadows. Balder Okanata had never launched out into the light and let his talents show. Balder had been afraid.

At this moment, Seth was afraid as well. What was he afraid of? It was simple – rejection.

Elaina was on the other side of that door, beautiful Elaina. And, after what Lieutenant Bucolus had said today, Seth was now sure Elaina was truly innocent. In fact, Seth was convinced that Hector Copan had killed Masal Djoser.

Back in the darker corners of his mind was that statement Bucolus had made – something about none of the suspects being "off the hook." But Seth was suppressing that remark. He was suppressing his own doubts.

Now was the time to act. In ten years he didn't want to look back at this moment and realize that he had let a great opportunity for happiness slip by.

Seth lunged toward the door to Compartment 317 and stabbed the black button on the right.

There was a muffled buzz inside the compartment.

He stood directly in front of that compartment door wondering what he had just done. He was breathing hard. Seth realized that, if he wasn't careful, he could hyperventilate. That would certainly be embarrassing.

He had to stop thinking about embarrassing mistakes and screw-ups. He had to remain positive.

There was a subtle thumping sound from inside the compartment.

Seth had this huge urge to run, but he forced his body to stay right where it was. Inside his casual clothes he had chosen carefully for this evening, he was now sweating. God, how he hated sweating like this! It was so embarrassing when you were sweating.

The door rattled open to the left.

Elaina smiled. "Hello, Seth." She stepped off to the side. "Come in."

Seth hesitated.

"Seth, come on. I'm not going to hurt you." She grinned coyly.

He could feel his skin heat up. Seth stepped over the curved threshold into the compartment.

Behind him, the door rattled shut.

Elaina looked into his eyes, then her gaze went down to the floor. Finally, her gaze came up and she focused on his eyes again. "I thought this was never going to happen."

"I've wanted to, Elaina. It's just. . ."

"You were afraid."

He smiled and looked into the blue eyes. "Yes."

"Were you afraid of me?"

He shook his head. "No. It was kind of a fear that you would say no."

"When I went to your compartment the other night I was going to say something, but I just couldn't say it."

Seth could feel his face break into a grin. "That's funny. We've both been trying to take the step."

She nodded. "Yes."

"I know the MSA wouldn't approve and I believe in rules, Elaina, but I just had to do this."

"I understand. Would you like to watch some television? I was watching a movie."

"Sure."

"Would you like some wine?"

"Yes, that would calm my nerves."

She leaned forward and kissed his cheek. When she pulled back, she said, "You don't have to be nervous around me, Seth."

He smiled. Seth suddenly felt a sense of release. He was beginning to feel comfortable with her. In fact, he could at this moment imagine living with her. It felt so natural.

Elaina crossed into the small kitchen and opened a cupboard. Seconds later, she turned around. She was holding two goblets in her left hand and a bottle in her right.

She placed the goblets on the breakfast bar, then she twisted the cork out of the wine bottle and poured red wine into one of the goblets.

She slid that goblet across the breakfast bar. "Here - this is yours."

Seth walked up to the breakfast bar on the other side and picked up the goblet. He raised it and took a substantial swallow.

Elaina poured wine in the other goblet and pushed the cork into the bottle neck. She took a sip, then looked down the breakfast bar at Seth.

When her eyes met his, she smiled. "We can sit and watch the rest of this movie, if you want."

He shrugged. "Sure."

Elaina walked toward the end of the breakfast bar. When she stepped around it, she stopped and reached over to the black switch next to the door. She flicked the switch down.

"Why did you lock the door?"

She shrugged. "Maybe I'm afraid of burglars."

"On this starship?"

She was standing in front of him now. "You never know."

"I don't think it's really necessary."

Elaina grinned. "You don't get it, do you?"

"What are you talking about?"

She looked down at the floor. Then her gaze came up. "Well, I thought we might sit in front of the TV and drink wine and hold hands and whatever. . ."

She put her hand to her mouth. "This is so embarrassing."

Something occurred to Seth. His pulse drummed in his ears. "You want me to stay."

"Why do you think I locked the door, silly?" She was smiling and her eyes were staring at him.

"May I kiss you?"

"As much as you want."

Seth put his goblet on the breakfast bar.

Elaina put hers next to his.

He stepped forward and pulled her into his arms.

CHAPTER FORTY-SIX

"Rebel"

Earth
El Meco
2M, Day 20, 6573
7:34 a.m.

Captain Chan Caracol had wanted to come down here to this planet Earth. He wasn't really into new things like this, especially wild and primitive planets, but Alto was with him, so he figured he was fine.

They had teleported onto a beach on the large bay that fed out into an ocean that covered most of the planet. They were probably a kilometer, or maybe less, from a small village next to the water.

Doctor Jak Eloi was with them. The anthropologist had said that this probably was a fishing village and because it was small, it was also probably peaceful. Apparently the larger communities were large because they declared war on other communities and swallowed up their populations.

In any case, their observations from the drone had suggested that these people were peaceful. But you never knew, really.

Off to his right, Chan could see the village next to the water. There were several small boats pulled up onto the beach and he could see a cluster of thatch huts shaped like tiny domes.

Doctor Eloi moved up on Chan's left. "These are probably very primitive people, Captain. They will have spears, knives and probably bows and arrows. Do you have any questions?"

"The only question I have, Doctor, is whether they're going to be hostile or not and I don't think you can answer that."

"They will probably be afraid of us but in a situation like that, don't do anything the least bit aggressive or they will turn on you."

Now Chan could see two people walking toward them. It looked like two women. He pointed. "Look."

Doctor Eloi moved out in front of the group of Mayans. He held up his hand. "Stop right here."

He turned around to check on the two people walking toward them. "Okay, I have a suggestion. Why don't two of us go up to these two women. . ." He glanced over his shoulder. ". . . and see if we can talk to them."

The anthropologist scanned the small group. He beckoned to Chan. "Captain, you come with me. You have your pistol. That will provide protection and I can give you insights into what they might do. Sound good?"

Alto Bucolus shook his head. "I don't know, Doc."

"Look, Lieutenant, you're a large person and you have that big assault rifle. They might see you as a threat." He nodded toward Private Imhotep. "The same with Imhotep, except he's not as big of course."

Alto Bucolus's eyes squinted, then he shrugged. "I guess you're right, Doc, but if anythin' happens, just yell and we'll come runnin'."

"Fair enough."

Actually Chan Caracol was the one in charge of this probe, but he was willing to let Doctor Eloi lead here. The man was an expert in primitive civilizations.

Chan wasn't usually assigned to these missions. The only reason Commander Okanata had chosen Chan was that the commander was having some doubts about Captain Tikal, the man who was usually his co-pilot. Tikal had been acting strange lately. Apparently something had happened when he went down to Earth earlier this month – something about some man he had met in that country of Israel.

"I'd make sure your pistol is ready to fire, Captain."

"Sure enough." Chan pulled up the holster cover and tugged out the black pistol. He turned the barrel away toward the water and pushed the slide back with the index finger and thumb of his left hand.

Yes, there was a cartridge in the chamber.

He let it slide back slowly. Then he flipped down the safety and slid the pistol back into his holster. Finally, he pushed down the flap and made sure the Velcro strip adhered. "All set, Doc."

The small man fell in next to him and, together, they moved along the wet sand bordering the water.

Chan preferred to walk out here because the footing was steadier and he felt more in control of his feet. He had no idea what kind of reception they would receive from these two females.

He could see, now, that they were dark-skinned and fairly short. He guessed they were less than five feet three inches tall – maybe shorter. He couldn't be sure at this distance.

As they moved closer, he could see that there was an age difference. The older one was talking intently at the younger one who seemed to be turning away occasionally.

As she did this, the younger one suddenly stopped in her tracks and pointed and said something to the older woman.

The older woman stopped. They stood, perhaps, a meter apart, staring at Chan Caracol and Doctor Eloi.

The older one yelled something and turned and ran.

The younger female started to turn, but then swung back and folded her arms across her chest and planted her feet wide apart.

Behind her the older woman stopped, turned around and screamed.

The younger one glanced back, then waved her hand dismissively.

The older one began to run again. She was screaming loudly as if she were trying to sound an alarm.

"Don't get too close to this one, Captain. We don't want to scare her like we did the other."

"Whatever you say, Doc."

When they reached a point approximately three meters away from the female, Doctor Eloi said, "Stop."

Captain Chan Caracol halted in the sand. He stared at the female. He thought she was really very attractive in a dark, small way.

She was wearing an ornately colored slit skirt and a simple loose blouse.

Chan moved forward one full step.

"Don't, Captain."

Chan held up his right hand palm outward. "We have come in peace."

"You are very handsome but your mouth moves in strange ways when you talk."

"I am speaking in my own language, but you hear it in your language. I am hearing what you say in your language in my language. It's because I'm wearing a translator implanted behind my ear."

"She sure as hell won't understand that, Captain."

The girl's head tilted. "What is a captain?"

"It's a rank in the MSA, the Mayan Space Administration."

"That's a very big name. What is your name?"

"Chan Caracol."

"Chan," she repeated. "Mine's Blanca."

"Who was the woman who ran away?"

"That was my mother."

Chan didn't know why he asked this next question. "How old are you?"

"I was born seventeen rainy seasons ago."

"How old are you, Chan?"

"A lot older than that."

"That's all right. In my tribe the girls marry older men all the time."

Farther down the beach, the older woman was coming back with two men. Both men had spears tilted back onto their right shoulders.

For just a second, Chan Caracol wondered if he should yell for Lieutenant Bucolus, but he didn't want to scare these people. "There are more coming and they're armed, Doctor Eloi."

"Your pistol will scare them away."

Blanca turned. "Oh, that's just my daddy, Montana, and our chief, Quelepa."

"I don't want them throwing those spears at us."

"They won't, especially when I tell Daddy I've found a man."

Chan felt a hand on his back. He turned his head. "What?"

"I think, Captain, that somebody has designs on you."

Chan stared at the little female, now looking back down the beach at the party of three advancing toward them. "Her?"

"I do believe so, my friend."

Chan looked at the anthropologist. "What should I do?"

"Don't encourage her." Then Jak Eloi faced Chan. "Of course, I don't think she needs any encouragement at all. She seems to have made up her mind already."

"You've got to help me out, here, Doc."

The anthropologist seemed to be considering the matter. "Well, her father is the one who will have the last say. Maybe you should explain things to him – or try at least."

Chan wondered how he could do that. Of course, she was really kind of cute. He wondered if they could have a casual relationship like he had had before with females, but then he wondered if primitive people like this knew what a casual relationship was.

The two men stopped with their spears cocked up above their right shoulders. The one on Chan's right spoke. "I am Montana and this is my daughter. You are strangers here. What do you want with my daughter?"

"We were just asking her about your tribe, sir."

"I am not this sir person. I am Montana."

"Sorry, Montana."

"Your apology is accepted, but I still want to know what you want with my daughter."

"Let me explain. . . Montana. We have come here from a long ways away. We have come here to discuss trade with your people."

The man named Montana pointed his spear at something behind Chan. "Who are they?"

Chan turned. "They are my security detail."

"I don't know what this 'security detail' is but they have strange spears."

"Daddy, I have found my man."

Montana scanned Chan and the others. Then he pointed his spear at them. "One of these ugly giants?"

Blanca pointed at Chan. "That one is not ugly. He's very pretty."

Montana looked up at Chan. Then he shrugged. "Okay, I guess, but he sure looks ugly to me and his lips move funny when he talks."

"That is because he's smart and has magic so he can understand our language and we can understand his."

"But he is so tall. He'll have a hard time getting into a hut and where will he sleep – outside the hut? His legs are so long his feet will stick out of the doorway."

The other man thought this was funny, evidently, because he chuckled.

"Don't laugh, Quelepa. Someday your daughter may come to your hut with an ugly giant. Then I will be laughing."

The other man waved his hand dismissively. "Shut up, Montana. That will never happen because my daughter is not this wild and a disobedient rebel like yours. My Izapa would never do this to her father.

Of course, if we let our daughters have their own way all the time, this is what happens."

"Why don't you stop with your shitty mouth, Quelepa, and let me take care of my own problems."

The other man shrugged. "Hey, I told you this would happen someday, but you wouldn't listen."

"Enough, Quelepa! Just because you are the chief of our tribe doesn't mean you're some kind of god with all the answers." Montana turned and stared at Chan. "Well, I suppose it would be rude not to ask these men if they would like some food."

He glanced around at the whole group. "You will have to leave your spears outside the village where we leave ours. That way if somebody like Quelepa begins to run off at the mouth, nobody will be hurt."

Doctor Eloi leaned close to Chan's left ear. "This is good."

Montana stared at him, then smiled. "At least one of you is normal height." He waved his hand. "Come." He turned and began walking.

Chan turned to Alto. "Come on, Lieutenant!"

As Chan walked down the hard sand behind Montana and his wife, a person stepped in on his right.

He turned.

The girl was next to him. She smiled. "You are almost too pretty for a man, but that's all right."

Chan was going to protest but decided that it might just be simpler to go with the flow. Besides, she was cute and she had beautiful brown eyes.

CHAPTER FORTY-SEVEN
"Starship Village"

Earth
El Meco
Early Night
of the
Last Moon

Blanca hated these situations. Here she was a grown-up woman and she had to listen to her parents talk about her in front of her. It was like her opinion didn't count at all.

After all, she was born seventeen rainy seasons ago, not eight or nine rainy seasons. That should make a difference.

And her father had pushed her and pushed her to find a man to marry. He had even brought some of the ugliest men in the tribe to her. Did he think she was going to marry some old, ugly man?

That really hurt, actually. Your father was supposed to love you and take care of you. All he ever did, it seemed, was yell at her. He said she was "stubborn" and "had a head like a rock." Those were not nice things to say about your own daughter.

Blanca sat near the door of the hut listening to the conversation.

"Why would she want to have a stranger for her man? He will go back to his own village so she will have to go with him and we will never see our grandchildren."

"At least she has chosen a man."

"But will this man have her?"

Her mother grinned and shrugged. "We will just have to see."

Montana threw his hands upward in a gesture of resignation. "I give up."

"Talk to her."

He nodded and rose from his place near the fire. Then he shuffled back to where Blanca was sitting. He crouched down. "As you know, your mother and I have been talking. This is what I have decided, my daughter.

"You may see this tall, ugly stranger. If he will have you, then we accept him. However, we want him to stay here in our village so that we may know our grandchildren."

"Suppose he wants to go back to his own village?"

"Then I cannot approve." He shook his finger at her. "Do not let him have his way with you, until you know this for sure. We do not want a pregnant daughter who has no husband. That would be a huge embarrassment.

"Quelepa would flap his lips at me for years about something like that. Of course, I should feel sorry for Quelepa. His own daughter is ugly and fat. She will never marry unless she's good at fucking." He shrugged. "And I suppose that is possible. Sometimes the gods even things out that way."

Montana rose to full height and looked down at Blanca. "Those are my terms, my daughter."

"I will try to keep him here, Father, but that may be difficult."

"You are a stubborn young woman, Blanca. You have a strong mind. Now is the time to use it."

Blanca rose to her feet. "I will go and talk to him." She turned around and ducked down. As she did, she raised her left arm up to push the leather flap over the entrance to the hut.

When she stepped outside, the air felt cool against her skin.

Up above to the east was the last sliver of the moon. Tomorrow night it would be gone and its magic with it. She always felt that this last phase of the moon was weak and dim. She sure hoped that had nothing to do with her chances with this Chan.

Whenever she thought of him, she could feel her heart race and her body tense. She knew what that meant. She had felt it the first time she laid eyes on him.

Why didn't she run on the beach this morning when she saw those men dressed in strange clothes and carrying strange spears? She was convinced it was fate and the gods. The gods worked in mysterious ways sometimes. Maybe this time they gave her the strength to stay and meet this beautiful man.

At the water's edge, Blanca turned and walked north. Up ahead she could see a campfire in front of the strangers' weird huts. They had made them out of some kind of cloth and silver sticks.

She was sure when she first met them that they did not have these weird huts with them. How did they get them? Well, these strangers did have some unusual kinds of magic. Maybe that was more of their magic.

Blanca felt that this was a time in her life when she would need to hold onto what she believed. Yes, she had always been that way, but now she was sure things were going to become difficult.

Her father wanted his own way. He was stubborn too. Maybe that's where she got her stubbornness.

Blanca smiled. She wondered if this was an example of the gods' sense of humor, giving a stubborn man a stubborn daughter. She had heard that the gods did play jokes on people. Maybe this was a joke on her father.

As she approached the fire of the strangers, Blanca could now make out the profile of the pretty one, Chan. Whenever she saw him, she knew she wanted him for her own.

Down deep, she knew she wanted him so much that she would do anything, even defy her father to have this man.

The very big, ugly man was sitting on the other side of Chan. They seemed to be talking.

Then she heard a third voice that seemed to be farther away. She wondered what that was – more of their magic?

When she stepped up next to Chan who was sitting in a strange chair in the sand, he raised his left wrist toward his mouth and said, "We have a visitor, Commander. Talk to you later."

He tapped his finger against the thing on his wrist and the bright thing went dark. "Hi, Blanca."

"Hello. We have to talk."

The huge man on the other side of Chan rose out of his strange chair. "I'll be leavin' you two alone, Chan."

Chan turned to the other man. "Alto, you don't have to do that."

"Oh, yes, I do." He made a finger wave. "Bye, bye, Chan." He looked at Blanca. "Take good care of this dude."

"What is a 'dude'?"

The big man shrugged. "It's a cool word for a man, especially a young, unmarried man." The big man laughed. Then he turned around and walked up the beach toward another of the strange huts. There was a fire in front of that hut also.

"It is smart for you to have fires outside your flimsy huts. Animals won't bother you if you have fires. If you had stronger huts, you would have more protection."

Chan smiled at her. "Thanks for the tip." He patted the bottom of the strange chair next to him. "Come over here and sit down."

Blanca walked around the fire toward the other chair. She did this so he would see her in the firelight. If you were a pretty woman you should show that to the man you want so he sees a good reason to want you as well.

She dropped down into the strange chair. Blanca was surprised that it was quite comfortable. There was cloth in the bottom and, apparently, it was wrapped around sticks. The sticks held up the chair.

"So, why did you come here tonight?"

"To talk to you."

"Is everything all right? You seem troubled."

"Well, there is no use pretending or beating around the bush. I will get right to the reason I came here."

She turned to face him. "You see – I want to marry you."

Blanca could see the surprise in his face. "I realize this is sudden, but sometimes the gods send us signs. They have sent me one this time. They are telling me that you are the man I must marry.

"We don't have to do this right away. We can wait several days before we do marry and there will be no sex until we are married. That's a tribal rule. The tribe doesn't want single mothers with babies to take care of and no man to provide for the baby."

She looked into his eyes. "You do understand that, don't you?"

The handsome man didn't answer.

Blanca continued. "My father approves of my choice, but there is one thing he wants for sure. Because you are a stranger from a faraway place, wherever that is, he is worried that I will marry you and go away to your village. Then he will not be able to know and love his grandchildren."

Blanca looked at the handsome man next to her.

He was smiling. "You're really cute."

"What is this 'cute'?"

The man seemed to be thinking. Finally he said, "It means beautiful in a special way."

"Oh, that's nice."

"Blanca, this may take some time and I have to report back to the starship tomorrow."

"What is this 'starship'?"

Chan seemed to be thinking. Finally, he tapped the surface of the band on his left wrist.

The band glowed.

He tapped it again. Then he held his wrist out toward Blanca. "Here's a picture of a starship."

Blanca stared at the glowing image of a long spear point on his wrist. "It is like a spear. But it is so small. How can you live there?"

Chan pulled his wrist away. He swung out his arms. "It's as big as this whole beach – actually bigger."

Blanca looked up and down the beach. She was trying to see this in her mind. Finally she shook her head. "I can't see it in my mind, but I know it would be big enough for you and your friends."

The next thing that Chan said surprised her. He nodded up the beach toward the other strange hut. "My friend, Alto, the man who was just here, has tried to get me married for years. I'm telling you this because I've had a hard time finding the right girl."

He looked directly at her. "You seem like a really nice girl."

"I am not a girl. I am a young woman. A girl is a female who has lived only ten rainy seasons and she is not bleeding yet. I have been bleeding since I was twelve rainy seasons old."

"Menstruating."

"What is that?"

Chan looked at her. "It happens when a girl becomes a grown up woman physically."

"When you start bleeding once every cycle of the moon."

Chan nodded. "Yes."

"You said this 'may take some time.' What is this 'time'?"

"Hours, days."

"Days, yes. It will take some days. But you can stay here next to the village and we can have a courtship together. We can spend long days talking and you can go fishing with my father to show him that you know how to provide for us."

Chan was sitting next to her staring down at the sand. Finally, he looked toward her. "I will have to take you up to the starship. That way you will have a sense of what my life is like."

"Yes, I can go there. I will tell my father. He may say no, but I will go anyway. It is only fair that I know about your starship village."

CHAPTER FORTY-EIGHT
"Tough Question"

Starship Cygnus
Conference Room #3
2M, Day 21, 6573
1:03 p.m.

Captain Chan Caracol sat near the end of the table in the Conference Room. He purposely chose this chair, away from the commander because he had some things to think over.

He knew very well that Commander Okanata was going to question him, but he needed some space. He was considering some big changes in his life.

The thing was that he couldn't get the image of the girl, Blanca, out of his mind. It was crazy. Hell, she was this little primitive girl from this island - yet that smile of hers. He just couldn't forget that smile.

Underneath it all, he wondered if this wasn't one of those crazy infatuations, like he had gone through before. You started out being absolutely captured by some woman because of a smile or a look or the eyes – something. Then, weeks later you got tired of her and wanted to move on.

This was probably much the same as that.

"I have called us together this morning to go over your findings." Commander Seth Okanata leaned forward on the table. "I have decided to make this less formal than the previous briefings.

"I would first like to have an overview by Doctor Jak Eloi." He turned to the small, handsome man on the left side of the table. "Doctor Eloi, what are your findings?"

"Well, Commander, these people are living back in a more primitive time period than the last people we dealt with, the ones in Israel. I would say this is definitely Bronze Age – probably middle Bronze Age more specifically.

"Consequently, you have societies that are centered in a city or village. The advantage is that they are less of a threat in any military sense.

The disadvantage is that they are going to be harder to train to work for us because they are farther back in their development."

"Do you think we could develop a business relationship with them, Doctor Eloi?"

The small man nodded. "Yes. The political system is less complicated. Of course this small village could be attacked by a larger community which might have some ambitious leader who wants more territory."

The commander looked somewhat puzzled. "Thank you, Doctor Eloi. Now I want to hear from Doctor Naranjo."

The large pudgy man looked up from a disorderly collection of papers. "Well, here's where it gets interesting, Commander. There seem to be large deposits of copper inland from this village. Some of it's almost pure copper."

He looked up from his papers. "If we could set up a mine and create enough security around the dig site, then we could have ourselves a real bonanza from copper mining."

"How many tons could we produce a year?"

"Oh, my gosh, I really don't know, but I do know it would be worth the effort. The purity of this copper is at almost eighty percent in some cases. Of course that varies, depending upon where and so forth, but there's plenty of it and it's good quality stuff."

The commander nodded. "Write that up, Doctor Naranjo, if you would, and make sure you include any recommendations based upon your personal reaction to this copper source."

He turned to Jak Eloi, the anthropologist. "Since this is the case, Doctor Eloi, I would ask you to write up an accompanying report with your observations of the primitive society you encountered down there."

"I'd like to do more research, Commander. I don't feel comfortable writing up a comprehensive report when I have so little data."

"Certainly. I would suggest that it might be wise to set up a temporary camp down in this area, near El Meco. We would provide a security detail, of course.

"It sounds like this area might be worth considering for a future copper mine. If we're going to recommend that to the Mayan Trade Association, then we'd better have plenty of data. I would also suggest photos or videos."

Doctor Eloi nodded. "Of course. In fact, I will interview Quelepa, the chief of the El Meco village, and some of the other people. I want the association to know that these people are peaceful."

"Perhaps, too, Commander, it would be a good idea to have some aerial photos of nearby cities and villages and some showing the topography of the area. I'm assuming that a drone could do that."

The commander nodded. "Yes, of course. In fact, we should do a preliminary map of the area and perhaps do some seismographs to determine where the copper deposits are. If the Trade Association is going to buy into this, we have to provide them enough evidence of plenty of copper, a controllable environment and a method whereby they can ship it out at a reasonable cost."

He turned to Chan. "Captain, any observations you want to add at this point?"

Chan had been daydreaming. He focused on the commander's face down the table. "These people seem really nice, sir. The village is peaceful."

The commander stared at Chan. "Are you all right, Captain?"

"Just tired, sir. Don't like sleeping in tents."

"Lieutenant Bucolus, would we be able to secure the area?"

"I think so, sir. If we begin minin', we're gonna have to fence in the area electronically. There's a lot of jungle with wild animals and there's probably some people who aren't as peaceful as these villagers."

The commander nodded. "That sounds reasonable. We'll send you down with some people to help set things up for your camp – probably our mechanic should go along."

"Can I make a request, sir?"

"Sure, Lieutenant."

"I'd like Captain Caracol to lead this next expedition."

"Why is that, Lieutenant?"

The huge man shrugged. "We know each other and work well together, sir."

"That sounds like a reasonable request, Lieutenant."

"Thank you, sir."

"Are there any other comments, questions or requests?"

Chan glanced around at the rest of the participants.

No hands went up.

"Okay. I would suggest, Captain Caracol, that you get your people together and plan on returning to El Meco tomorrow morning. You will need, I would think, perhaps five days of supplies. You might arrange for seven days, Captain, just as a precaution."

Chan nodded. "Yes, sir. I do have a question, sir."

"What is the question, Captain?"

"Sir, if we're going to send Doctor Naranjo out into the jungle to look for other copper deposits and Doctor Eloi out checking on other villages, shouldn't we have at least one more security person with us?"

The commander nodded. "Yes. I'll send Private Astrides along as well."

"Thank you, sir."

"While you gentlemen are down there, we will send down two drones to map the area and look for other copper deposits." The commander glanced around the table. "Any other suggestions or questions?"

No hands went up.

"This briefing is over. Very good work, people. This may have been the event that made this journey worthwhile."

The commander rose out of his seat.

Chan stood up. He had things to do today. He had to get focused – get his mind off that cute little native woman. God, she was only a teenager. Well, she was a grown woman, at least in their culture she was. Maybe he shouldn't mention her real age to anyone.

Alto Bucolus leaned close to his right ear. "I see you've been bitten."

Chan glanced around the room. Then he looked at Bucolus. "Does it show?"

"To me it does, but I know you. Don't worry about it."

At that moment the commander stepped out of the Conference Room into the corridor.

"I can't get her out of my mind," Chan whispered.

Alto smiled. "I'd think this was funny if it wasn't so serious. Tell me somethin', Chan. Is she gonna rocket away with us to Hyksos or are you gonna stay here?"

Chan nodded. "Yeah, that's one very tough question."

CHAPTER FORTY-NINE

"Much More"

Earth
El Meco
2M, Day 22, 6573
9:38 p.m.

They had set up camp with a good stock of supplies. Blanca had suggested putting their encampment farther back from the water than the last one because there might be a storm or sometimes there were what she called "high water times" or wind and that could wash the water far up onto the beach.

Chan had thought about this and he had concluded that, much like on Hyksos with the Man Moon and the Woman Moon, the waters of the seas on this planet were pushed around by the single moon, creating tides. Those were apparently the "high water times" Blanca had told him about.

As they walked along on the hard, wet sand, he tried to explain that to her. "The moon up there affects the huge oceans down here on the planet with its gravitation."

"What is gravitation?"

"That's the force that keeps us down here on Earth and not floating up in the sky."

"But you said your starship is up in the sky."

"Yes, it has a lot of power to work against gravitation."

"I would like to see where you live. You have seen my village and my father's hut, the place where I live. Are you going to show me where you live?"

Chan thought about this. He wondered if it would scare her terribly if she were teleported with him up to the starship. She had never seen them arrive by teleportation. He didn't believe any of the villagers had seen that either. "I have to think about it."

"Are you hiding another woman up there?"

Chan smiled. "Absolutely not. Let me tell you something. I will admit that I have been with other women, a lot of them – okay?"

"Did you have sex with them?"

Chan stopped walking.

Blanca turned and faced him. Her arms were folded across her chest. "Well, did you?"

"Yes."

"Do you have any children?"

"No."

"Then why did you have sex with these women?"

Chan didn't often become embarrassed, but right now he was. "Sex is fun – pleasurable."

"Of course. That's because the gods want us to have children. My father wants me to have children, too, because he wants grandchildren."

This kind of talk made Chan nervous. Of course, he knew that this was the fundamental reason you had that one real relationship with a woman. You planned on having children. It was just that he had lived with this freedom for so long. Could he really settle down and have a family?

"You are having deep thoughts?"

Chan nodded. "Yes."

"I know you like me and I know you want me. What is the problem?"

Chan looked up at the slender quarter moon in the black night sky. He wondered if this little woman could really be the one. Was such a thing possible? Could a man travel across the galaxy to some remote, primitive planet and fall in love?

"My mother says that sometimes thinking gets in the way of good choices." Blanca touched her chest. "She says you have to go with what's in your heart."

Chan smiled at the little woman. "You're mother sounds like she's pretty smart."

"Of course. She has lived a long time."

Chan motioned to her. "Let's walk."

She shrugged. "Okay."

"You see. . . I've been running around with different women all these years. That's what I'm used to."

"But what will you have when you are very old?"

Chan had to admit that this was a very good question. If you ran around all your life, what would you do when you got old? Would you run around with old women? There probably wouldn't be many of them who were still single, and probably those who were single wouldn't be worth spending time with anyway.

"You didn't answer."

"No, I didn't."

"Why?"

Chan breathed out heavily. "Well. . . to be very honest, I didn't have a good answer."

"My father says that if we have children, we have fulfilled the desire of the gods and they will be pleased. He says that it's our fate to have children so they can have children and their children can have children."

Chan stopped and faced Blanca. "Would you come back to Hyksos with me?"

"Where is Hyksos?"

The Milky Way was just above the southern horizon to the east.

Chan pointed at the Milky Way. "Do you see the outer band of that swirl?"

"In the sky?"

"Yes."

Blanca stared at him. "You came from a star?"

"Another planet like this place where you live. It's near one of those stars."

Blanca stared upward at the cluster of stars. Then she looked at Chan. "How did you get here? Did you fly through the air?"

"Not exactly." He thought a minute. "Beyond the air above this place where we're standing is space – nothing."

"Don't you breathe air?"

"Of course. There's air inside the starship."

"How big is this starship?"

Chan turned and looked down the long span of sand to a rock ledge that jutted out far down the beach. He pointed. "Do you see that rock ledge jutting out into the water?"

"Yes."

"It is bigger than from here to there."

Blanca stared down the moonlit beach. Finally she turned to Chan. "That is very big." She stabbed her temples with the tips of the index fingers of both hands. "It hurts my head to think about this."

"Would you like to go up to the starship?"

"It is where you live, isn't it?"

"For the time being."

"What is this 'time being'?"

"At the present time."

"What is time?"

Chan thought about this. Then he said, "It's a way of counting the parts of a day or night."

"I am very confused."

"Let's just say, Blanca, that I live on the starship."

"Why didn't you say that?"

Chan smiled. "You're very cute."

"Is that good?"

"Yes, very good." He reached out his right hand. "Do you want to hold hands while we walk?"

"Yes, very much. I want to touch your skin. I would like to kiss your lips, too, because they're pretty, but probably I should wait before I do that."

Chan clasped onto the small hand and began walking. When he looked over at Blanca, she was smiling. He turned away. This was more than he had bargained for, much more.

CHAPTER FIFTY
"Receptive"

Starship Cygnus
Bridge
2M, Day 24, 6573
7:08 p.m.

Commander Seth Okanata was disturbed by this event. This kind of thing just didn't happen aboard a Mayan Space Administration starship. It was unheard of.

He checked the screen on his console one more time. Then he tapped his wrist control. He punched in "Comp 219." This was the third time he had called.

He held up his wrist control near his mouth. "Captain Tikal, you're wanted on the bridge. You're late for your Orange Shift, Captain. You were due at six o'clock. It is now eight minutes after seven."

There was no response.

Seth rose out of his seat at the pilot's console. He looked back at the navigator. "Lieutenant Lycastus, do you know anything about this?"

The small wiry man shrugged. "Absolutely not, sir."

All Seth could think about was to contact Elaina, but that probably wouldn't look very good. Besides, how could Elaina help him with this?

Something lingered in the back of Seth's mind. Now, he remembered how distant Captain Tikal had been when he had returned from that country of Israel. It all had to do with this religious prophet – this man, Jesus.

Right now, Seth couldn't leave the bridge until he was relieved. That was a rule in the MSA, but it was also a very good precaution. If some problem occurred with the starship, there would be no one at the helm to deal with it.

He tapped his wrist control then swiped on the surface.

A list of names and compartments slipped across the surface.

When he saw "Teleportation," he stopped. He tapped the word.

"Doctor Rahotpe, teleportation," said a male voice.

"Doctor Rahotpe, this is Commander Okanata."

"What can I do for you, Commander?"

"In the last twenty-four hours, Doctor, have you teleported anyone down to that country of Israel?"

There was a pause.

"Yes - Captain Tikal."

"Do you still have the coordinates of that teleport?"

Another pause.

"Yes, I do, sir."

"Don't delete those, Doctor. We're going to need them."

"Of course, Commander."

"Tell me, Doctor, what did Tikal give as a reason for teleporting?"

Another pause.

"I believe, sir, he said something about a special mission."

"And you didn't challenge him?"

"Well, no. He's a captain – a pilot on this starship. I'm not privy to secret missions and such, Commander."

"Of course." Seth considered this for several seconds. "Thank you, Doctor Rahotpe, and do keep those coordinates."

"Absolutely, sir."

Seth Okanata tapped the surface of his wrist control. He stood, staring out at the scene in front of the starship's windshield.

On the left was a large blue ball with white clouds and an occasional area of green or light brown. It was rolling by the windshield in slow motion. On the right was black space and billions of white points of light.

He wondered what Captain Tikal was up to. In fact, he wondered if the man was in his right mind.

In a literal sense, Captain Tikal was AWOL, and that was serious. Seth was not going to make a production of this situation. He would try to take care of it quietly.

However, he did need an alternative pilot. The only other possibility was bringing Captain Caracol back to the starship.

He turned to the navigator. "Lieutenant, are we close enough to teleport Captain Chan Caracol up to the starship?"

The navigator's fingers rattled on the keyboard in front of his monitor. "No, sir, but we will be in range within three hours, sir."

Seth considered this. He would need Caracol up here, but he would also need someone to hunt down Tikal. He knew which one of the security people he wanted – Lieutenant Alto Bucolus. It might take an experienced man to find Tikal down there in that primitive country.

Seth tapped the surface of his wrist control.

It lit up.

He swiped his right index finger down the wide face.

A list of names passed. He stopped at Caracol and tapped the name.

"Captain Chan Caracol. What do you need, Commander?"

"Sal Tikal has disappeared."

"I don't understand, sir."

"Tikal has teleported down to Earth. I need you up here to help me pilot this starship, Captain."

"Yes, sir."

"Captain, also tell Lieutenant Bucolus that he has to return."

"I will do that, sir."

"We'll be in range within three hours, Captain. We will notify you at that time."

"Sir. . ."

"Do you have a question, Caracol?"

"No, sir."

"Very good. We will be teleporting you and Lieutenant Bucolus in approximately three hours."

"Yes, sir."

"Over and out." Seth Okanata had looked forward to spending some quality time with Elaina this evening, but that didn't look like a possibility now.

It would be long and tiring, waiting for Caracol to teleport up, but he could think about Elaina. That would help. Perhaps he should stop by her compartment later. He could always let himself in with the extra key and slide into bed with her. Sometimes when he did that she was very receptive.

CHAPTER FIFTY-ONE

"Resignation"

Earth
Israel
2M, Day 24, 6573
Afternoon

Captain Sal Tikal wondered what he was doing down here in this primitive society. At least sometimes he wondered that.

At other times it all seemed very natural, like it was meant to be. He didn't believe in fate or predestination or any of that, but there was just something about this that felt right. Besides, he wanted to be near Jesus. It felt right to be near him.

They had been in Jerusalem all afternoon. Jesus had openly defied the Pharisees and the priests. Sal could tell from the reaction of his followers, his disciples, that this was dangerous. His twin brother, Jude Thomas, had warned him.

Now they were on the road outside the city heading into the hills to eat, then rest for the night.

Sal was at the rear of the group, walking on the dusty road. He still wore his MSA uniform and carried his pistol in the holster on his right hip. He hadn't had time to change anything and he was still thinking about this.

"My friend, Salathiel."

Sal turned.

Jude Thomas was next to him. The resemblance to Jesus was striking. However, when you looked at the eyes, you could tell. With Jesus, there was this depth, a sort of resolution or determination. With Jude Thomas, you saw calmer, less resolute eyes.

"I was thinking, Salathiel, that the authorities are bearing down on us here." He glanced around. Then he leaned close. "I was thinking of going to Syria." He pulled back from Sal to check his reaction.

Sal said nothing. He wasn't sure about any of this.

Thomas leaned close again. "I could use a helper, Salathiel. I want to start a church in Syria. I want to spread the teachings of my brother in that country. Israel is much too dangerous." The shorter man glanced around at the people along the sides of the road in small encampments.

Sal supposed that Thomas was looking for Pharisees. They were the worst, and they were everywhere, or at least they seemed to be.

He turned to Thomas. "Let me think about it. I'm still getting used to this way of life."

The other man shrugged. "I understand, but if you do want to spread the word, Salathiel, I wouldn't do it here. It's much too dangerous."

"Yes, you're right."

When they came to a grove of trees, which Sal figured had to be about two kilometers from the city of Jerusalem, Jesus led them off the road up the side of a hill.

The shade of the trees was a great relief from the sun.

Thomas looked back down toward the road. "It is safer up here on the hillside. Not as many people around to listen to what you're saying. You never know who will go to a Pharisee and sell information for a few pieces of silver."

Sal saw a tree which looked like it might be comfortable to sit up against. He moved over into its shade.

"Do you want to come with me?"

Sal turned. "Where are you going?"

"To speak with my brother. I don't get many chances to do that. I want to tell him my idea."

"About Syria?"

"Yes. Maybe I can talk him into going there."

"Sure, I'd like to see him."

Thomas moved around the group of men talking and Sal fell in behind him.

A few of the men were still standing. Most of the others had succumbed to the heat and were sitting on the ground and leaning up against the rough bark of the small trees.

At the back of the group, Jesus was in earnest conversation with Peter and Andrew.

When he and Thomas approached the three men talking, Jesus turned. "Salathiel, you have joined us."

Sal smiled.

"Is my brother treating you well?"

"Yes." Sal found he was almost not able to speak with this man. It was as if he felt like he was in some kind of strange spell when he was around him.

Jesus placed his hand on Sal's right shoulder. "I know you will be there when I need you, Salathiel."

For Sal, there was an eerie quality of prediction in the way the man had uttered those words. He had no idea what it meant.

Jesus turned to his twin, Jude Thomas. "What did you want to speak to me about?"

"Brother, things are getting more and more dangerous every day. The Pharisees are everywhere. I know they are spying on us. We must leave."

"And where do you purpose we go, my brother?"

"To Syria. We will be well received there. In Syria there are no Pharisees."

Jesus smiled. "I know that is where you will go to preach to the people and lift them up. However, my brother, I cannot go to Syria. My fate is sealed. I must stay here. I have a destiny to fulfill and I must do it here."

"Is that destiny to die?"

"Thomas, why do you say such a thing?"

"Because the Pharisees are up to no good. The priests see you as a threat to Judaism and to them. They will not tolerate your criticisms forever. Right now, they are probably plotting against you."

"You are right, Thomas. They are plotting against me, but that's the way it is supposed to be. Many terrible things will happen to me. I know that. I also know that my people, the Jews, will suffer many things for years and years after I am gone. They will suffer these things in my name.

"I am the messenger of God. These priests and Pharisees don't want to hear that message. They don't want to know that even Moses, himself, would condemn them for what they are doing to their own people. But I am only the messenger of God's word."

Sal thought of a way out. "Jesus, I can help you."

The intense brown eyes focused on Sal. Then there was a smile. "You have a good, generous heart, Salathiel. You will help me when the time comes."

"Really, I can save you from any harm."

The eyes focused on his. "I know you can, Salathiel, but I will call on you when I need you."

Sal wasn't sure what this meant. However, he had a bad feeling about what was to come.

He saw in the face of Jesus a resignation and a calm. He wasn't sure what it meant. However, this was not the demeanor of a feisty rebel who was challenging the priests and rabbis.

This was a more philosophical man and, yes, there was a certain resignation. What was he resigned to?

Sal had no idea, but he didn't like the feeling of it. He had the sense that something awful was going to happen. He couldn't imagine what it would be, but he had the sense it was going to be awful.

CHAPTER FIFTY-TWO
"The Diplomat"

Starship Cygnus
Teleportation Room
2M, Day 24, 6573
10:32 p.m.

Captain Chan Caracol held the little woman against him as they were teleported. He could hear her scream, but he held on tight. "Don't move!"

The tugging stopped.

No one, as far as he knew, had ever been in motion during a teleport. The theory was that your molecules might come back together in some strange way on the other end, if you did move.

In many experiments with mice it had never happened that way, but nobody wanted to chance it, and he could understand why.

When they reached the platform in the starship, Chan was greatly relieved. He could make out the room now and the figure of Doctor Rahotpe at the controls.

The whole thing with returning to the starship was that you couldn't be off one iota. It was a much smaller target. This teleportation thing was refined, but mistakes did happen now and then. There were phenomena of weather and quirks in the system itself, things that no one had yet explained.

When the blue bubbles disappeared, Chan released Blanca. She looked up at him and smiled.

They were now in the teleport compartment on the starship.

"It's dangerous to move when that's happening."

"I want you to hug me the next time."

"We have to get off the platform so Alto can come up."

Doctor Rahotpe nodded toward the little woman. "I didn't know we were going to have three teleports. The commander just said two."

"I'll handle it, Doctor."

"I'd think of something, Captain. The commander will be very upset."

Chan stepped off the platform with Blanca.

She gazed around at the small titanium compartment. "This is very different. Is this really where you live?"

Chan wondered how to make this clear. "Not actually in this compartment, but this is part of the starship where I live. You'll see."

Blue light appeared on the platform.

Blanca grabbed onto Chan. "What is that?"

"Lieutenant Bucolus."

Alto Bucolus began to appear on the platform inside the blue light and gold bubbles surrounding his body. Then the bubbles vanished.

Blanca tugged at Chan's arm.

He looked down.

"You have great magic."

He shrugged. "I guess. It's called teleporting. It's how we get down to where you live and back up here. Now, we have to go up to the bridge and explain why you're here."

"Do we teleport there?"

"No, we go by elevator."

"You have many strange things in your starship. What is the bridge? Do you have water here?"

"No. It's not a bridge over water. It's a compartment on the starship, an important one. It's where the whole starship is controlled. It's where I work – where I pilot the ship."

"What is a pilot?"

"It's a person who steers, guides – like steering a boat – making it go in different directions."

Alto was standing next to them now. "We'd better go up and see the commander. How are you going to explain the little lady?"

"I'm still working on that."

Alto grinned. "If it gets bad, I can always say she's a diplomat."

"Thanks, Alto."

"You're more than welcome, Captain Caracol."

Chan took Blanca's hand. "Come. We have to go up to the bridge." He moved with her across to the door. Then he reached out and pressed the blue glowing pad to the right of the casing.

The door rattled open.

Blanca ran around behind him.

He turned and smiled. "It's only a pocket door. It won't hurt you." He stepped over the curved threshold into the corridor.

Blanca glanced back and forth between the door edge on her left and the pocket door in the wall pocket.

Chan reached through, grabbed her right hand. "Come on."

She stepped over the threshold, then stared back at Alto who also stepped over the curved metal threshold.

Chan led Blanca down the corridor.

The door rattled shut behind them.

Blanca's head jerked around.

Chan stopped next to her. "It's just a door. It closes off the compartment."

Blanca said nothing.

At the elevator, Chan pressed the up arrow.

There was a loud ding.

Blanca looked up at him and smiled. "That is a pretty sound."

The door rattled open.

She jumped back.

"It's okay. Just another door." He looked at Alto.

His large friend was smiling.

Chan motioned to Alto. "Go ahead."

The door started to close.

Alto grabbed the edge of the door.

The door rattled back.

Alto stepped inside.

Chan motioned to Blanca. "Go ahead."

"I want you with me."

"Of course."

"You get in first."

Chan stepped into the elevator. He pressed his index finger against the DOOR button. Then he smiled at Blanca. "Come on. We have to go up to the bridge."

She hesitated. Then thrust her right foot forward into the elevator and, finally, stepped in.

She was facing the back wall.

"Turn around. We'll be getting out this way."

Blanca turned around. Then she looked up at Chan and smiled.

He had to admit that she was very cute, but how was he going to explain her to the commander?

Chan released his finger.

The door rattled shut.

Blanca grabbed onto his left hand with both of hers.

The elevator jerked upward.

"We are moving."

"Of course. This is an elevator and it's taking us upward to the bridge."

Seconds later there was a loud ding.

The door rattled open.

Chan pulled Blanca forward with his hand. "Come into the corridor."

Blanca hesitated, then stepped out of the elevator.

Chan followed and took her hand again. "You have just ridden on an elevator."

"There are so many strange things."

"Yes." He nodded toward a door down the short corridor. "Now we'll walk to the bridge. It's right down here." He pointed. "Behind that door." He took her right hand and began walking.

The elevator door closed behind them.

Blanca glanced back.

It amused Chan that now she was becoming more confident.

"You figured out what you're gonna say to the commander?"

Chan glanced over his left shoulder. "Not really."

"Maybe you oughta tell him the truth."

Chan had wondered about that, but at this point he wasn't sure what the truth was, actually. It was somewhere between this cute woman was like a really great sister, but she wasn't quite a sister. She was more like a sort of girlfriend, but then she maybe was more than that. However the thought of this young woman from a primitive tribe on Earth traveling across the galaxy in this starship was kind of crazy.

He was trying to imagine her in his house back on Hyksos. It sort of worked, but then he would look at her and it didn't work at all.

Chan stopped in front of the bridge door. He dug into his pocket and pulled out a blue plastic card. He reached out the card toward the slot on the casing to the right of the door.

His hand stopped.

"I'll back you up, Chan."

He glanced over his left shoulder at Alto. "Thanks."

CHAPTER FIFTY-THREE

"Better World"

Earth
Israel
Jerusalem
2M, Day 25, 6573
3:23 p.m.

Alto Bucolus and his sidekick, Private Imhotep, had been searching across the usual places near Jerusalem where they had last seen this man, Jesus. They weren't looking for Jesus, of course. They were looking for Captain Salathiel Tikal.

Alto hated these assignments. He didn't like handcuffing and hauling away one of their own. It was just plain embarrassing.

It made him feel like he was working for a fucked up organization. Yes, even the MSA was fucked up some of the time, but he hated to admit it. After all, he had eighteen years with them. If you worked for something that long, you'd better believe in it. And he did.

To him, this Captain Tikal had always seemed pretty steady. Sure – he wasn't the most outgoing man he'd ever met, but there were a lot of quiet people who worked these kinds of jobs. However, Captain Tikal going AWOL was not okay.

You signed up for five years and you worked those five years, or you didn't sign up. You just didn't walk off the job right in the middle of things. That was unprofessional.

His buddy Chan had his faults, but walking off the job wasn't one of them. Alto smiled. He was remembering the commander's face yesterday when he first met Blanca.

"Sir, there's a crowd over there on that other street. Maybe Tikal is over there." Private Imhotep pointed down a narrow alley connecting two streets. "Down there."

Lieutenant Bucolus turned to look.

"Looks like some kind of crowd around somethin', sir. He might be there."

"I guess it can't hurt to look, Imhotep." Alto Bucolus was at a point where he was ready to quit this search for Tikal. It seemed pointless.

Obviously Tikal had shut off his wrist control, or had thrown it away. The starship would have been able to trace him if he was wearing it.

On the other hand, there was no signal. Probably he had destroyed it or had thrown it into a river or something. "Sure, let's have a look. I don't know about you, Imhotep, but I'm about ready to quit this pretty soon, if we don't find him."

A local man walked by them. "You two must be from out of town. You ought to see what's goin' on over there. This man claims to be the son of God and now he's gonna be crucified. Seems to me if he was the son of God he could figure a way of gettin' out of somethin' like that."

Alto looked at the stranger. "Who is this man?"

"He's Jesus of Nazareth. He didn't do any harm to anybody. But the Pharisees got him. Got Pilate to kill him. Don't know what for. Jesus was just preachin'."

Alto turned to Imhotep. "That's the preacher man we met."

"Yeah, I think that's him, sir."

"If you're goin' over there, I'd be careful of them Roman soldiers. They just as soon kill you, as look at you." Alto began moving down the narrow alley toward the crowd.

Private Imhotep fell in next to him.

In the distance Alto could see a huge crowd moving slowly along the street. He hated crowds like this, especially in a place where bathing was not a daily thing.

Alto was glad Imhotep was with him. When it came to a large crowd, two armed people were a lot better than one.

Before he actually reached the street, Alto stopped. He lifted the cover of his holster and pulled out his pistol. He twisted off the safety and slid it back down into the holster, then pressed the Velcro strip.

He glanced over at Imhotep.

The private pushed his pistol down into his holster.

"Stay close, Imhotep. This is gonna be a nasty crowd."

"Yes, sir. I'll be right next to you."

Alto moved forward.

When he reached the street, he could see that there was also a cluster of people on the other side. They were yelling at someone in the middle of the street.

As he moved nearer to the crowd, he caught the smell of body odor. A crowd of filthy people was the worst.

He pushed his way through to the street. He could feel Imhotep behind him.

What he saw next startled him. There was a man, naked to the waist and barefoot, hauling a huge T made of rough hewn wood.

The man's upper body was streaked with blood, apparently from whipping. On his head was a circular crown made of thorns. Apparently the thorns had been pressed into his skull because there were streaks of blood running down his face.

Behind him walked a Roman soldier carrying a whip.

This was not something Alto wanted to witness. These people were primitive and brutal. At this moment he really didn't want to be here.

He was about to turn to Private Imhotep and tell him that they should leave, when the man struggling with the large wooden T fell to the stone street.

Alto looked around at the crowd. His first impulse was to help this man. Then he noticed something. It was Jesus of Nazareth, that preacher they had met.

There was a commotion across the street and a man ran out of the crowd.

The Roman soldier turned to look.

Alto leaned close to Imhotep. "It's Tikal," he said in a low voice.

The Roman soldier stood by while Tikal helped Jesus to his feet.

Once he was steady, Jesus turned to him and his bloody, sweaty face smiled. He reached out and touched Tikal's shoulder. Then his lips moved.

Alto couldn't hear what the preacher was saying. The crowd was making too much noise. There was yelling and one woman with grey hair was wailing.

Jesus turned away from Tikal and continued dragging the cross down the stone street.

At a slow pace he shuffled by Alto, dragging the crudely hewn T resting atop his right shoulder.

The lieutenant wanted so much to help the man, but he remembered the commander's orders. Get Tikal and return him to the starship.

"Tikal's movin' back into the crowd, sir."

Alto turned to look.

Down the street, Captain Salathiel Tikal was staring toward Jesus and the crowd was moving by him up the street.

The lieutenant leaned close to Imhotep. "Let's slip around behind him."

He led Private Imhotep down the side of the street outside the stream of people moving behind Jesus.

When Alto next saw Captain Tikal, the man was standing as if in a trance, staring at the receding figure of Jesus.

Alto moved across the stone street behind Tikal. He grabbed the man's left arm and swung it around behind his back. "Captain Tikal, you are under arrest for being absent without leave."

Imhotep stepped up behind the captain and slipped a handcuff onto his right wrist. Then brought the right arm around behind his back and snapped the other handcuff onto the man's left wrist.

Captain Salathiel Tikal swung around and faced Alto. His eyes were full of anguish. "We have to save this man. He's the best thing these people have. He can change this entire world – make it a better place."

"Tell it to the commander, Tikal."

CHAPTER FIFTY-FOUR
"Black and White"

Starship Cygnus
Level 1
2M, Day 25, 6573
2:06 p.m.

They were standing in front of the elevator, waiting for it to rise to Level 1.

Lieutenant Alto Bucolus was having an internal struggle. This didn't happen very often because in most cases things were pretty much black and white when you worked security. Either the person was guilty or not guilty. That was it.

In this case he could not get the image of that man, Jesus, out of his mind. The thorns on his head had to be very painful. They had whipped him so much his back was lined with long cuts and there was more blood.

"Do you know what a crucifixion is like?"

He turned to the captain. "No, Tikal."

"They nail the palms of your hands and the arches of your feet to that T and raise it up and push the end of it down into the ground. You hang there until your body is so weak that you fall forward and the pressure against your lungs collapses them and you die of asphyxiation. It's painful and it's slow.

"This man hasn't done anything to anybody, Alto. The Jewish priests and Pharisees feared he would turn the people against them, so they're having him killed."

Alto turned to Captain Tikal. He looked into the man's blue eyes and he remembered the man on the cobblestone street dragging the wooden T.

It didn't seem right. He had seen these things before, but nothing this nasty. Things like this stayed with you.

He was a soldier by trade, but he had never understood why people were so brutal. Why couldn't people just get along with each other? He had never understood this brutality.

There was a loud ding.

The elevator door opened.

Alto nodded toward the opening.

Tikal stepped into the elevator.

Alto Bucolus and Private Imhotep followed.

Alto pressed the UP arrow.

The elevator door slid shut and the elevator jerked upward.

They were going up to the bridge to confront Commander Okanata.

Alto wondered what Tikal's punishment would be. He certainly wouldn't be nailed up on some wooden post like that poor bastard down there on Earth in the city of Jerusalem.

Alto thought about that man. He wondered how that poor beaten man was dealing with his horrible punishment. This Jesus had to know what was coming and there were all those people screaming at him from the sides of the street.

It had to be so terribly lonely. He was the spectacle for the day for those people. For some of them it was just macabre entertainment. For others who knew Jesus and loved him, it was a moment of ultimate anguish.

There was a loud ding.

The elevator jerked to a stop and the door opened.

"Go ahead, Tikal."

The man in handcuffs stepped into the corridor.

Lieutenant Bucolus and Private Imhotep followed him.

Alto Bucolus was a good soldier. He followed orders like a good soldier should, but this thing with Jesus of Nazareth bothered him. He wondered if he couldn't do something to help the man. It just seemed so wrong to kill a man like that for doing nothing.

At the bridge door, Alto slipped his red card into the slot to the right of the casing.

The red light blinked green.

The pocket door opened.

Alto yanked his card out of the slot and stuffed it into his pants pocket.

Inside, Commander Okanata rose from his seat at the console.

Tikal stepped over the threshold into the bridge compartment.

Alto moved in behind him. Then he turned to Imhotep. "Stay outside, Private. Don't let anyone in."

"Yes, sir." Imhotep moved to the right side of the door casing and pivoted around so his back was to the wall.

The door closed.

Commander Okanata crossed to Tikal. "So, Captain, what do you have to say in your defense?"

Tikal looked down at the deck in front of his feet. Then his gaze came up. "They're crucifying him, sir. They're crucifying Jesus of Nazareth. The man is a gentle, good person. He's done nothing wrong. We have to stop this."

"We can't interfere with these primitive societies, Tikal. That's a basic rule in the MSA."

What surprised Alto Bucolus was that normally he accepted what his commander said, no matter what. This time, however, he found that he was feeling a strong urge to object or to at least ask if there weren't exceptions to this rule about interference.

"Sir, he's the best thing that ever happened to that country, Israel. He's a man of peace, sir, in a violent world. He could change that whole world, sir - believe me."

The commander seemed to consider what Captain Tikal was saying. Then he nodded. "In spite of all of that, Tikal, we're going to have to put you in the brig. We can't have our crew members just running off and doing what they want, especially our officers. It sets a bad example."

"He'll die slowly, sir. They're nailing him up on this T-shaped wooden thing and he hangs there. Then he dies when his body collapses and puts pressure on his lungs so he can't breathe. It's slow and awful, sir. Can't we help him?"

"As Doctor Eloi would tell you, Tikal, we can't interfere with these societies."

"We do it when we set up mining operations."

"That's different."

"Because it means making money?"

Commander Okanata stared at Tikal.

To Lieutenant Bucolus, it seemed like the commander was actually thinking about what Captain Tikal was saying. Alto had always considered Commander Okanata to be a fair man. Maybe he was going to make an exception in this case.

The starship commander turned to Alto. "Lieutenant, take Captain Tikal down to the brig. Don't put him in the cell next to that pirate, Calchas. It might be dangerous. Put him in one of the other cells."

"Yes, sir."

"We have to save Jesus, sir. They're going to kill him."

Commander Okanata nodded. "I understand your concern, Tikal, but we have guidelines and rules for a reason. I'm sorry." He looked at Alto. "Take him down to the brig, Lieutenant."

Alto clasped onto Tikal's left arm and pulled. "Come on, Captain."

The tall pilot's shoulders seemed to slump forward and his face took on the air of a defeated man. He moved across to the pocket door.

Alto placed his right hand on the blue lighted pad.

The door opened.

Tikal stepped into the corridor.

Lieutenant Alto Bucolus followed. "Come on, Imhotep, we have to take the captain down to the brig."

"Yes, sir." Imhotep moved along next to the Lieutenant.

Alto Bucolus had every intention of taking Tikal down to the brig as ordered. However, somewhere in the process he began to realize that for the first time in his long military career, he might just act on his own, without being given an order.

CHAPTER FIFTY-FIVE
"The Savior"

Earth
Israel
Jerusalem
2M, Day 25, 6573
6:18 p.m.

Lieutenant Alto Bucolus had gone to his compartment tonight like a good soldier should, after he had accomplished his mission and he had even opened a new bottle of wine and was going to sit and watch some brain numbing television and relax.

There was only one problem. He couldn't relax. He finally had realized what he needed to do.

"Sir, are you sure the commander ordered you to do this?"

Alto turned to Private Imhotep. "Are you challenging me, Private?"

"No, sir. It's just that I thought this was somethin' we weren't supposed to do."

"That's correct, Imhotep."

"Then, why are we doing it, sir?"

"Don't ask so many questions."

Doctor Nestor turned to Alto. "This does seem a little off the mark, Lieutenant." He stopped and tightened the left shoulder strap of the large rucksack hanging from his back. "This equipment is getting heavy."

Alto pointed toward the hillside. "Here we are."

There was still one cross standing up against the moonlit sky. It was evening on the starship. Here it was night and things were quiet.

Alto now could smell the faint scent of rotting meat, or maybe it was human flesh. The man farther down the street had said this place was called Golgotha. It was the place where they did these brutal crucifixions.

Alto moved up the hill to a figure huddled at the side of the cobblestone street in the darkness. He stopped next to him. "Stranger, we have come here looking for this man Jesus."

The man looked up. "He is dead."

Alto's insides seemed to collapse. "Isn't he here anymore?"

The man turned and pointed. "No, just that thief over there. He's still alive, so they say." He faced Alto again. "Jesus is dead."

"Where is he?"

"In a tomb. Joseph of Arimathaea gave him his own tomb."

Now Alto noticed something. "You look like him – like Jesus."

"I am his twin brother, Jude Thomas."

"How long has he been dead?"

Thomas pointed at the Roman guard standing a few feet away. "The guard took him down a little while ago."

"Show us the tomb."

"You don't want to go there. The Pharisees put a guard in front of the stone covering the entrance. He will kill you."

"Take us there, Jude Thomas."

The man looked up. Then he shrugged. "I suppose it won't hurt. All is lost anyway. How can we go on without my brother?" He rose to his feet. "Follow me."

Jude Thomas led them down the low hillside to the cobblestone road. He shuffled along in silence ahead of them going east, away from the city wall.

Alto moved up next to him and he motioned for Doctor Nestor to flank Jude Thomas on the other side.

Alto turned to Thomas. "Tell me about what he was like when they took him down."

Thomas turned. "I wasn't there. I couldn't stand watching him die. We were very close. He was the strong one.

"I was told by the Roman guard that my brother muttered something about giving up his spirit to his god and then his head dropped and he died.

"The guard told me that he offered to thrust his short sword into Jesus to put him out of his misery, but Mary Magdalene said she didn't want his body mutilated."

Alto glanced around behind Thomas at Doctor Nestor. "What do you think, Doc?"

The short, muscular man shrugged. "I won't know until I actually see him and check his signs, Lieutenant."

When they had walked several hundred yards, Jude Thomas led them up a hillside to the right. It was a cemetery.

Up farther on the left, Alto could see a torch. He supposed that was the guard. He reached down and lifted the flap of his holster.

The sound of the Velcro rip stopped Thomas. He turned around. "What was that?"

Alto pulled out his pistol and cocked the hammer back. "It's nothing to worry about. It's a matter of security." He glanced back over his left shoulder. "Stay sharp, Imhotep. Is your weapon ready?"

"Yes, sir."

Alto touched Jude Thomas on the shoulder. "Hold it right here."

The man stopped.

The lieutenant motioned to Private Imhotep. "Come on," he whispered.

Up ahead the guard was standing next to a large rock. He was facing away from them, toward the southwest.

Alto stayed low and moved silently up the hillside. When he was right behind the guard, he pressed his pistol against the man's back and yanked his spear away.

The guard had evidently been dozing.

He was startled and jerked away. When he turned around, he yanked out his sword.

Alto fired his pistol at the ground in front of the man.

The loud pop echoed out over the hills.

The guard stumbled backwards and fell.

Alto jumped forward, stomped his left boot onto the man's chest and held his pistol aimed at his face. "Grab the sword, Imhotep, and pitch it away as far as you can."

"Yes, sir." The private crouched down, holding his own pistol. With his left hand, he yanked the sword out of the leather scabbard.

Then he turned around and flung it off into the trees.

There was a distant clanking sound.

Alto focused on the face of the guard. "The next time I will shoot you right in your face. Got it?"

The man nodded.

Alto removed his booted foot from the man's chest. "Now, get up."

The man in full leather armor struggled to his feet.

Jude Thomas pointed at a large rock. "This is the tomb."

Alto looked at the rock. "We can pull it away with this many men."

A woman appeared out of shadows under the trees. "Who is this? What are you doing?"

Alto turned. "We are going to try to save this Jesus of Nazareth, but time is important."

"You can save him?"

"We're going to try." Alto grabbed onto the guard's arm. "Come on and help us."

The guard tried to pull away. "No. They will punish me."

Alto raised his pistol in front of the man's face. "Would you rather I shoot you – kill you?"

The man shook his head. "No."

"Then grab onto the rock."

The guard wrapped his arms and hands round a portion of the giant rock that jutted upward on the right side.

Alto handed his pistol to Imhotep. "Keep an eye on the guard." He moved over to the rock.

The doctor unhooked the strap across his chest and lowered his rucksack to the ground in some bushes off to the side.

Thomas was the last to move.

They struggled with the giant rock.

After several minutes, finally the top began to pull away.

"Keep pushing!" Alto moved around into the small space behind the giant rock and pressed his back against the rock face of the large outcropping. He then pushed with all his strength against a flat surface above him.

Finally the top edge of the rock moved outward. It seemed to hang suspended for a second. Then finally teetered backward and rolled to the ground.

Alto pulled the small flashlight off his belt and ducked under the low ledge and walked into the tomb. He could feel someone behind him.

Ahead of him was a stone ledge and on the ledge was Jesus of Nazareth. The blood had been cleaned from his face, but there was still evidence of bleeding out of the sores on his head from the crown of thorns.

His arms were folded across his chest. His hands had apparently been cleaned but there was still blood oozing from the wounds.

Doctor Nestor dropped his case to the stone floor and ripped open the Velcro cover on the top. He pulled out a small respirator and placed the plastic mask on Jesus' face.

He then wrapped the elastic band around the Nazarene's head and flipped the small switch on the respirator upward.

It hummed in the silence.

The doctor placed his right index finger on the left side of Jesus' neck. He stared at the face of the man, then turned. "He's still alive. . . barely. I'll have to teleport him up to the ship."

"I want to go with him wherever you're taking him." The woman appeared out of the darkness.

Alto turned. "Who are you?"

"I am Mary Magdalene. I am his woman."

Alto looked at Doctor Nestor. "You teleport up with him. I'll bring up the woman."

Alto grabbed onto Mary Magdalene's arm. "Step back." He moved the woman toward the doorway.

Doctor Nestor tapped the surface of his wrist control. He then gripped on to Jesus' arm.

The area around them glowed blue.

Mary Magdalene lurched backward.

Alto held onto her.

The area around Doctor Nestor and Jesus turned gold. They vanished.

"You have taken him!"

"We will go there too. We just have to wait until Doctor Nestor gets help to move Jesus to the clinic. He will tell us when." He tugged on her arm. "Come. Let's go outside."

"But I want to be with him."

"You will. Just be patient."

She looked into Alto's eyes. "You are a good man. I will believe you. You people can perform miracles. I will trust you."

Mary moved out through the low opening.

Alto ducked down and stepped out into the night.

Private Imhotep was holding both pistols aimed at the tomb guard.

When Alto stepped out Imhotep handed the lieutenant his pistol.

Mary pointed at the guard. "Kill him or he will tell."

"No, we will keep him here until we leave." Alto lowered the hammer on his pistol, then shoved it down into his holster. He slipped a zip-strip out of his belt and walked around behind the guard. He grabbed the man's right hand and brought it around, then the left. He then zipped them together behind the man's back.

Alto's wrist control made a beeping sound. He held up his left wrist in front of his face. "The teleporting platform is clear." He turned to Mary Magdalene. "Do you want to see your friend again?"

She nodded.

"Then you're going to have to listen to me. I will hold onto you. We will glow blue, then gold. You must not move. Understand?"

"Your magic scares me."

"It's the only way you're going to be able to see him."

"Actually, Lieutenant, she could stay down here until he's back on his feet."

"Imhotep, that's not a sure thing."

"Yes, sir."

"Besides, these Pharisee assholes might kill her for stealin' his body."

"Yes, sir, I suppose so, sir."

"You hold your pistol on that guard until we transport. Then tell him to run if he wants to live. You might have to shoot a round in the air or somethin'. Then you teleport."

"Got it, sir."

Alto stepped over to the woman. He tapped the surface of his wrist control at the large letter T. Then he grabbed onto the woman's arm.

As the blue glow began he could feel the tension in her body. "Don't move."

CHAPTER FIFTY-SIX

"Impact"

Starship Cygnus
Bridge
2M, Day 26, 6573
7:04 a.m.

Commander Seth Okanata studied the four figures in front of him. One was his security chief, Lieutenant Alto Bucolus. The second was this strangely dressed woman, Mary Magdalene, from this country of Israel. Then there was Private Imhotep and, of course, Doctor Nestor.

He focused on Alto Bucolus's eyes. "Lieutenant, you have countermanded a direct order. We are not to interfere with the events of these people on this planet. In fact, we are mandated by the MSA not to interfere with any primitive society. Yet, you saw fit to do just that."

The commander stared into the large man's eyes. "Do you have anything to say for yourself, Bucolus?"

The lieutenant shrugged. "I saw the way they beat him and nailed him up, sir. It just didn't seem right."

Seth Okanata nodded. "Yes, I suppose so. But you see, Lieutenant, we can't have our officers disobeying orders."

"He saved Jesus. Don't yell at Alto. He is a good man. He has saved Jesus from dying. Jesus will save Israel from the Pharisees and the corrupt priests. He will save Judaism.

"This man, Alto, has kept this wonderful prophet alive. Now Jesus can go back to Israel and show those corrupt priests the error of their ways. Israel will be saved. That is all I have to say."

Seth Okanata studied Mary Magdalene's face. "It seems that, in your estimation, this man, Jesus, was important to Israel."

Mary waved her hand in a sweeping circle. "He will save the whole world because he is the son of God and his message is that the rabbis and priests and Pharisees should help the people, not steal from them and persecute them. They can do this because the people are poor and have no power.

"Jesus judged no one except those leaders who abused their power and cheated their people. The priests and the Pharisees are the ones responsible for his crucifixion – not the Romans. The priests and the Pharisees feared him because he spoke the truth. Jesus saw through their tricks and their lies."

"This Jesus of Nazareth sounds like a remarkable man."

"He is, sir."

Seth Okanata turned to Lieutenant Bucolus's voice. He had a difficult decision to make here. He couldn't have his officers disobeying orders, but he did realize that this Jesus of Nazareth must be truly something special because two of his good officers had been powerfully influenced by him.

Maybe it was time to meet this Jesus. Seth turned to Doctor Nestor. "How is the patient doing, Doctor?"

"He's in serious condition, Commander. He seems to be making progress, but it will take time. He has been brutally wounded. It is amazing that he was still alive when we found him."

"Doctor Nestor, I'd like to speak with this man when he's able."

"That may be a while, sir."

"How long?"

The doctor looked down to the titanium deck. Then his head came up. "I should think it will be, at least, three or four days. . . maybe longer. He's still on the respirator now, sir, and we're feeding him intravenously. However, we do see progress. Of course, things could change."

Seth Okanata nodded. Then he turned to Bucolus. "Imhotep was with you, Lieutenant."

"Yes, sir, but he was there under my orders. Imhotep had no choice, sir."

"I see." He turned to Imhotep. "Private, you may go about your duties. I would suggest, however, that the next time an officer does such an act as this, you must report that officer to me personally."

"Yes, sir."

Seth was not convinced that Imhotep would actually do that. Reporting your superior officer to the commander of a starship was a chancy act at best. "You're dismissed, Private Imhotep."

The young man saluted.

Seth returned the salute.

Imhotep did an about-face and marched to the door where Private Astrides slapped his hand against the blue lighted rectangle to the right of the door casing.

The bridge door opened.

Private Osiris Imhotep stepped over the threshold into the corridor.

Seth watched this young noncom leave because he needed time to think. He had to figure out a way to punish Lieutenant Bucolus. However, he didn't want it to be too severe because this man was a good officer and usually was a credit to his rank. Besides, this Jesus of Nazareth apparently had a magnetic and influential personality.

He turned to Alto Bucolus. "Lieutenant, you will have to spend some time in the brig, I'm afraid. I've decided this. On the other hand, I am considering not entering this in your record. As you know, such a thing can follow you your whole MSA career."

"Yes, sir."

"Private Astrides. . ."

The man at the door moved over to his commander. "Yes, sir?"

"Private, take Lieutenant Bucolus down to the brig and lock him up. Do not place him next to that pirate, Calchus. That man is dangerous."

"Yes, sir."

Seth made a dismissive motion with his hand. "Take him away, Private. No cuffs will be necessary."

"Yes, sir."

Bucolus saluted the commander, then moved over to the door.

Private Astrides slapped his hand against the glowing pad to the right of the door casing.

The pocket door opened.

Commander Okanata turned to Doctor Nestor. "I assume that you will be more careful next time, Orus."

"Yes I will, Commander. I thought it was somewhat odd that we would be interfering with these Israelites when it was against policy to do so."

Seth wanted to make a point here, but he didn't want to beat up this medical man for trying to do his job. "It was, Orus. That part is right. However, if you had come to me, you would have found out very quickly that this was not authorized."

"Perhaps I should have called you on my wrist control, but it all happened so fast."

"Next time, Orus, call me."

"I will, Commander."

"You're an educated man, Orus. Tell me - what do you think is the reason that two of my men have been drawn to this prophet?"

The short stocky man breathed out heavily. "Well, Commander, I would say it's probably his charisma - a really engaging personality – plus, of course, his message. He's a man of peace and, from what I've been told, he reaches people on a very personal level. At least I got that impression from Tikal."

"You gave Captain Tikal some tests, didn't you?"

The doctor nodded. "Yes, and he's fine physically. I don't know what Doctor Neleus had found out, if anything."

When Commander Seth Okanata originally brought both of these doctors into the issue of Tikal's AWOL, he was actually most interested in what the psychiatrist, Doctor Neleus would find. Seth was convinced that something emotional or psychological was going on.

He had talked over all of it with Elaina. She had become his sounding board on so many things. He was curious what she would say about this prophet, Jesus.

One thing for certain, Jesus of Nazareth had an impact on the people he met. There was no doubting that.

Seth was really curious about this man. He was looking forward to meeting him. Of course, there was the question of whether this Jesus would survive.

CHAPTER FIFTY-SEVEN
"In Hiding"

Starship Cygnus
Level 3
Compartment 300
2M, Day 27, 6573
3:06 a.m.

Captain Salathiel Tikal had no idea why he woke up. It just happened.

As usual during the sleeping hours, the brig had only dim yellow lighting. He supposed it was meant to be mellow and calming.

He found it irritating because if he read, he had to turn on the light near his bed. Then that seemed so bright it resembled a floodlight.

Sal sat up in bed. He felt strangely wide awake. Again, he didn't have any idea why he woke up. Usually he slept well, once he fell asleep. Sometimes that took quite a while, especially if his mind was working.

Lately, his mind had been on Jesus. There were so many things about this man that reached him on a very fundamental level. It was the kind eyes and this sense that the man knew what was in Sal's mind and even knew what he was yearning for in his life.

It was the kindred spirit thing and Sal knew very well that he was not the power behind this connection. It was this Jesus of Nazareth.

Sal looked over at Cell #5. That was Alto Bucolus, the man who had brought him into the brig from down on Earth. So, what was up here? Why was Bucolus in a cell? The guy was the head of security.

Sal still couldn't figure that out. Why would the security chief for the Starship Cygnus be in the brig? It didn't make any sense.

Something was going on here, but Sal had no idea what it was.

He had assumed when he was locked up, that at some point the commander would come down here to Compartment 300 and officially release him. Then Sal could go back to being a pilot again – back to the old routine.

Sure – he relished the idea of being free from this cell and returning to the old job. However, things had changed for him. It wasn't quite that simple anymore.

Did he really want to go back to the old routine? Actually, not. Actually, he wanted to go down to Earth and work side by side with this Jesus. But was Jesus alive? Sal didn't really know.

He wanted to believe that wonderful man was alive, but the cross was so heavy that day and Jesus had been bleeding so much. Some of the people in the streets of Jerusalem had told Sal what a crucifixion was like.

Since that day when Bucolus had arrested him, Sal had wondered about Jesus. He hoped the man had somehow escaped the crucifixion, but how could he?

Sal liked to believe if Jesus really was the Son of God, then certainly he could save himself from the horrors of dying that way. Yet, he had also seen this sort of resignation in the man's face. It was almost as if Jesus was destined to do this, no matter what, and that made Sal wonder if the crucifixion hadn't actually happened after all.

When he thought this way, his heart was broken. He had developed a kinship with this man, a connection. Sal had never felt that kind of kinship with anyone before in his life – not for his mother or father or brother – nobody.

It felt so wonderful, so fulfilling. It was as if this hungry place inside him had been fed.

He turned around again. He wanted to talk to Bucolus to see what this man's opinion was about Jesus. Also he would like to know why Bucolus was locked up in this brig.

When he turned to his right, his head stopped. He noticed something really odd. He could swear that his cell door was wide open.

His first reaction was that he was sure it was some kind of weird prank. That was a pretty nasty prank – and it was very strange.

Sal rose from his bunk and walked to the open doorway. If he walked out of here and into the guardroom, the guard would simply turn him around and put him back in the cell.

Sal stepped out into the narrow passageway and walked over to the door leading into the guardroom. He leaned close to the small window in the upper area of the steel door.

Inside the small room was Private Astrides, the guard. Everything seemed normal. Astrides was a pretty nice guy, actually. Right now the guard was leaning forward with his face resting on his forearms atop the desk.

It looked like he was asleep, really asleep.

Then Sal saw a wrist control lying on the desk next to Astrides' left arm. It probably belonged to Astrides. But why would he take it off?

Sal had a thought. He reached down and turned the doorknob.

It moved and the latch made a subtle click in the silence.

Astrides didn't move.

Calchus, the pirate, rose up from his bunk. "Hey, what you doin'?"

Sal didn't answer. Instead he pulled open the door and stepped into the small guardroom. Then he closed the door behind him and carefully released the lever so it wouldn't make any noise.

Astrides was still lying face down on his arms atop the desk.

Sal picked up the wrist control, slid it onto his wrist and pressed the Velcro strips together.

He stared down at Astrides. It occurred to Sal that this man had been drugged. He was really out cold. None of this noise had aroused the guy.

When Sal looked at the small screen on the wrist control, the letter "T" was already there. He touched the "L" for location.

"Jerusalem" appeared on the screen. He tapped the "T."

A blue haze surrounded him.

Sal stood rigid.

The next thing he knew, he was standing on a cobblestone street. He glanced around.

In front of a building across the narrow street a man was staring at him.

Sal moved away. He hurried down the next intersection of streets and turned into an alley. As he was walking, he pulled off the wrist control. He had to do something with it.

The easiest thing would be to drop it into a well or a river. That probably would mean the end of it. But what if he wanted to go back up to the starship?

When he reached the street at the end of the alley, he was in full moonlight. He stopped and opened the back of the casing of the wrist control. He then removed the battery and slipped it into his shirt pocket.

He snapped the rear cover back onto the device, slipped the loose strap onto his left wrist and pressed the Velcro strip.

Now he had to find Jesus and his disciples.

Sal looked up at the moon.

It was about halfway up into the sky from the eastern horizon. He remembered that the road Jesus had taken when he was carrying the cross was toward the southeast.

He would go in that direction. Sal was not terribly confident about what he would find, but he had to see for himself.

What dawned on him at this point was that someone had drugged Astrides, unlocked his cell and left that wrist control for him to find. In fact, that person had virtually set up the wrist control for this location. He wondered who that might be.

Were there others aboard the starship who were impressed by this Jesus of Nazareth? Did he have an ally? He wondered who it was and why that person didn't just come forth and tell him.

This puzzled him.

Sal made his way down the cobblestone street toward the eastern side of the city. When he reached the eastern wall, there was a gate. A Roman soldier stood guard.

He stopped in his tracks. If he was to get out of this city, he would have to approach this guard.

Sal moved toward the guard.

A hand grabbed his right arm.

He swung around. "Jesus?"

"No," whispered a man's voice. The man was wearing a hood. He put his index finger to his lips. "Don't mention that name." He tugged on Sal's arm. "Come."

Sal was led down the street, then into an alley on the left.

Now the stone buildings rising up from the sides of the alley hid the bright moonlight. The street was narrow and dark and it smelled of human waste and urine.

The man stopped and stared down the alley behind them. Then he turned abruptly and pulled Sal into a doorway.

They moved down a narrow passageway to a wooden door on the right.

The man stared back down the narrow passage, then lifted a wooden door latch and pushed the door inward. He grabbed onto Sal's arm. "Hurry," he whispered.

He closed the door. Out of the dim light in the room appeared a large man with his arms folded across his massive chest. "Who is this?"

The man with Sal turned. "He is one of the foreigners. He is a friend."

The man stared down at Sal. "He wears strange clothes. He must be a foreigner."

The man in the hood led Sal farther into the room to a table.

Around it sat a group of men.

The man with the hood pushed it backward.

Sal was startled. "Jesus?"

The man put his finger to his lips. "Shhh. No, I am Jude Thomas, his twin brother." He swung out his right hand. "These men are his disciples – all but one, Judas Iscariot. He is gone."

Thomas nodded toward the men sitting around the table. "All of these men are wanted by the Pharisees. Their lives are in danger – all of them. . . and myself."

He motioned to Sal. "Sit down, Salathiel, and have some bread and wine. We also have a small amount of goat cheese."

"I'm' not hungry, thank you. Where is Jesus?"

"He died on the cross, but then your people came in the night and took him out of his tomb. I don't know why they did this. He's dead. Why would they do this if he is dead?"

"Perhaps they were trying to fulfill the prophecy, or make it seem like it was fulfilling the prophecy."

Sal looked at a large man across the table. "What prophecy?"

"I am not afraid. I will say my name aloud. I am Peter. The prophecy was that he was the Christ, the son of God, and that he would rise from the dead."

Sal shook his head. "No. I'm sure they were trying to revive him."

"Bring him back? But he was dead."

Sal looked at Jude Thomas. "Maybe."

"I know he was dead. He was in the tomb for the whole evening right into the night when you foreigners came to take him."

Sal decided not to say anything more. These men wouldn't understand modern medicine and modern techniques for saving lives.

But something did occur to him. Maybe he would have to return to the starship. Someone had to warn Jesus about returning to Israel. It was much too dangerous here. "All I know is that Mayans do not believe in your god so they would not be interested in making him appear to rise from the dead."

Peter raised his arms in a gesture of hopelessness. "What does it matter? He is dead, and here we are hiding from the Pharisees in the city of Jerusalem."

Jude Thomas stepped forward and looked around at the group of men. "Listen to me. I am going to Syria to preach. There are no Pharisees in Syria. I would suggest that you all leave Jerusalem and go wherever you want. It might even be wise to leave Israel. The Pharisees are everywhere."

Something occurred to Salathiel Tikal. "Jude Thomas, we must talk. I have an idea."

CHAPTER FIFTY-EIGHT
"Surprises"

Starship Cygnus
Bridge
2M, Day 27, 6573
7:18 a.m.

Commander Seth Okanata had conducted many different interviews, but this one was certainly different.

Before him stood his pilot, Captain Chan Caracol, and a young woman from the planet Earth. Caracol had found a suitable pair of coveralls for her to wear, but the coveralls were slightly large, mostly because she was so tiny.

She had this charming, child-like air about her. What it came down to was that she looked out of place. At least he felt she did.

"Let me get this straight, Captain. You say that this young woman here, Blanca, wants to go back with us to Hyksos. Is that correct?"

"Yes, sir."

"Is she your wife or something?"

"No, sir."

"He needs permission from my father. . . sir."

Seth looked down at the tiny woman.

"Sir, that's why we need to go back down to El Meco."

Seth faced Caracol again. "You realize, Captain, that this places extra pressure on me. The only other pilot is in the brig. And even though I do eventually plan to set Tikal free so that he can help to pilot this starship again, I hadn't really planned on doing that in the next few days."

"I do understand, sir, that this is an imposition. But this shouldn't take more than a few hours."

Seth Okanata considered the request. He could set it up so that they went down to the planet during his shift at the helm. That way Caracol would be up for a possible sixteen hours, but Seth was sure this young pilot could handle sixteen hours.

"We would have to arrange this so it occurred during my shift, Captain. I would be the only pilot on the starship."

"I understand, sir."

"How are you going to be married?"

"Chan said you could do it, Commander, sir."

Seth didn't want to grin because he considered this to be a some-what serious matter, but he did grin, nevertheless.

Now Captain Chan Caracol was grinning. "Sir, she didn't mean to be presumptuous, sir."

Seth also noticed that Elaina, at her navigation station off to the left, was grinning.

Seth waved his arm. "No, that's fine. Your woman friend certainly speaks her mind." Seth cleared his throat. Then he faced Blanca. "I would be honored to perform such a ceremony, young lady."

"That's good because Chan said otherwise we would be illegal."

Seth found that he was grinning again. "Yes, I'm sure that's true."

He turned to Chan. "Captain, why don't you plan on going down tomorrow during my shift. You'll have to wait until we're within tele-porting range, but I would think that might work. If you're gone two or three hours, then it shouldn't be a problem. Do stay in contact with the starship, especially if there are any complications, Captain."

"Certainly, sir."

The door to the bridge opened and Private Astrides stepped over the curved threshold.

To Seth, the young soldier looked confused.

Seth saluted Chan Caracol. "Captain, you are dismissed."

Chan saluted the commander. "Thank you, sir."

"If you have any questions or there are any changes, Captain, please let me know right away."

"Yes sir, Commander." Chan Caracol led Blanca toward the door.

Private Astrides shuffled across the titanium deck and stopped in front of Seth. The young soldier looked terribly pale to Seth and his eyes seemed somewhat glassy.

Astrides saluted. "Sir."

Seth returned the salute. "What is it, Private?"

"Sir, somethin' happened durin' the Orange Shift, sir. I don't know for sure, but I think somebody drugged my coffee. The next thing I know, sir, is Imhotep's wakin' me up and one of the prisoners is gone."

"Which prisoner, Private?"

"Captain Tikal. I'm real sorry, sir. It was like I just went out an' I never knew what happened, sir."

Seth folded his arms across his chest. "Okay, Private Astrides, this is what's going to happen. You go down to the mess and get some coffee – clear your head. Then you're going to teleport down to that country Israel and bring back Tikal."

Private Mases Astrides braced at attention and saluted. "Yes, sir. I'm real sorry, sir."

Seth waved his hand dismissively. "Get some coffee and some food, Astrides. We'll deal with the rest of this later. Right now we have to get Tikal back."

"Yes, sir." The young soldier pivoted around and walked unsteadily to the door. He slapped his hand on the blue lighted rectangular panel to the right of the casing.

The door rattled open.

Astrides stepped into the corridor.

Commander Seth Okanata knew what he had to do. It was time to release Lieutenant Bucolus. This man was the only one on Security Team who was capable of finding Tikal.

Then he'd have to talk to Captain Caracol. This was bound to make the captain's request even more difficult to deal with.

Seth was getting a little concerned about his command. Things seemed to be falling apart. He didn't need any more of these surprises.

CHAPTER FIFTY-NINE
"Voices"

Earth
Israel
Jerusalem
2M, Day 27, 6573
8:26 a.m.

"How the hell did you get drugged, Astrides?"

"Sir, I don't remember. I just remember goin' into the cell-block because Calchus was actin' like an asshole – yellin' and everythin'. Then I calmed him down and went back to the guardroom. I was sittin' there lookin' at the news feed on my wrist control and drinkin' coffee. Then the next thing I know, Imhotep's wakin' me up."

"Maybe Calchus is behind it."

"I don't know, sir. I just know Imhotep was wakin' me up and Tikal's cell door was wide open and he was gone."

"How did he teleport?"

Imhotep tapped his left wrist. "He took my wrist control. This is a new one issued by the commander."

Alto Bucolus was glad to be out of that damned cell, but he hated being down here in Israel. This place could be dangerous.

He stopped next to the cemetery. This was where that prophet Jesus was buried. Obviously the body was gone, but he wondered if some of the guy's followers might be hanging around here.

Alto turned and stared back down the cobblestone road toward the area they had come from - the east wall of Jerusalem.

The road was empty.

There was a Roman guard to the right of the gate, standing with his back to the wall. That guard could easily see where they were going, if he paid any attention of course. It had been Alto's view, however, that lower level military people were not the ones who initiated things.

That soldier was probably the base grade, equal to a buck private in Alto's army. He might notice they were walking up into the cemetery to the place where that prophet was buried, but he probably wouldn't do anything.

Alto motioned with his hand. "Come on, Astrides."

"Why are we goin' into a cemetery?"

"Because we might find some people in here who know where Tikal is."

"Why would they be in here?"

"Because they believed in that Jesus guy. They believed he was the son of their god."

"Really?"

"No, I'm kiddin', Astrides."

"You shouldn't make jokes about things like that, sir."

"I have to say, Astrides, you are the dumbest man I've ever worked with."

The young soldier stared at Alto. Then he looked straight ahead.

Alto stepped into the cemetery and walked up the gradual grade. For just a second, he thought he could hear voices farther up the hill.

Then he couldn't hear them. Well, maybe he was just imagining those voices.

The longer he thought about this, however, the more he was sure he had heard voices.

When he and Astrides came to the area of the tomb where Jesus was buried, the stone was completely moved away and there were footprints in the dirt near the entrance.

What Alto concluded was that many of the followers of this man, Jesus, had come here to see for themselves that he was gone.

"I see that you are not Romans or Pharisees," said a deep voice behind him.

Alto pivoted around.

"I am called Peter. You are the foreigners."

Alto nodded. "Yes, we're looking for Captain Tikal."

Peter smiled. "Ah, yes - Salathiel. He has gone to Syria with Jude Thomas."

"Where is this Syria?"

Peter pointed. "It is a country far to the east of here." The large man moved close to Alto. He was tall enough to look straight into Alto's eyes.

Peter stood in front of him and smiled. "I know you want to bring him back to your people, but let me say this - Salathiel does not want to go back. He plans to preach the word of God to the people of Syria with Jude Thomas, the twin brother of Jesus.

"It is wise to leave Israel if you are one of us. Things these days are not very friendly here. That's why Jude Thomas moved away. But Thomas was never a very strong person anyway. He was always the weak one.

"I suppose every man does for God what he can. I, for one, have decided to stay here. Though it is true we are in hiding right now, eventually the Pharisees will get tired of hunting for us and they will move on to other ways of abusing the people of Israel.

"These are bad times in Israel, but unfortunately, Jesus saw worse times for the Israelites. I must stay here and minister to my people. I must do God's work among them."

He looked into Alto's eyes. "You will not find Salathiel. He is gone." The tall man turned away as if to leave. Then he stopped and looked back over his right shoulder. "I have to go now. If I were you, I would not stay near this tomb very long. The Pharisees send soldiers out here every so often to pick up people. There are rumors that the people they take from here are tortured." He shrugged. "I don't know if that is true, but I still wouldn't stay too long."

The tall man walked up the shallow grade into a stand of trees and moved into the foliage.

Seconds later, when he could no longer see this Peter, Alto heard distant voices. One of them sounded like the man, Peter.

Alto turned to Astrides. "We'd better get out of here." He started moving down the shallow grade toward the road.

Off to the left, he could see two men walking this way. They were wearing helmets and carrying spears.

He held out his arm in front of Astrides. "Hold it. There are soldiers comin'." Alto looked off to the right into the wooded hill. Alto pointed. "Let's go this way," he whispered.

"We can take care of them, Lieutenant."

Alto put his finger to his lips. "Be quiet. Sure we can take them, Astrides, but we don't want any trouble. The commander might not like that," he whispered.

He waved his arm. "Come on." Alto Bucolus led the young private up a steep slope toward the east. He was moving parallel to the road.

Alto figured that if they moved east, they could always try to follow Tikal. Of course, the captain might be several days ahead of them and they weren't getting any wrist control signal from him, so all of this was guesswork.

Once they were far up into the woods on the high knoll, Alto stopped and turned around. There was a lot of foliage between them and the tomb, but they were up high enough so that he might be able to see where those soldiers were.

He lifted the Velcro cover off his binocular case with his left hand, then pulled the small binoculars out and raised them to his eyes.

He adjusted the focus wheel between the two short tubes.

Now he could see the soldiers clearly. They were standing in front of the open tomb.

One ducked down and moved inside.

The other seemed to be scanning the hillside.

"Get down!" Alto whispered. He dropped into a crouch. Behind him, he could hear Astrides move.

"What's the matter, sir?"

"One of the soldiers is lookin' up here," he whispered. Alto waited. Finally, he turned to Astrides. "Stay down. I'm gonna look." He rose slowly with his binoculars up to his eyes. Now he saw the image of two soldiers with their backs to him. They were headed down the hill.

It occurred to Alto that now might be the time to radio the commander and tell him what Peter had passed on to them. He knew the answer the commander would give. Keep looking.

The two soldiers were far down the hill now.

Alto lowered the binoculars. He stuffed them back down in the small case on the left side of his belt and pressed the Velcro strip across the flap.

Then he turned to Private Astrides. "We're gonna head east and look for Tikal. To be honest, I don't think we're gonna find him, but then, who knows? We might just get lucky."

CHAPTER SIXTY
"The Best Man"

Earth
El Meco
2M, Day 27, 6573
7:48 a.m.

Blanca had done that teleport thing a second time. This one was not so frightening. These Mayan people and her handsome boyfriend, Chan, had some very strong magic. They could do all kinds of things.

They had those wrist controls. She was trying to learn to use one, but it was a very strange little thing. She liked to look at the pictures in the little square on it.

Chan had been teaching her how to read and write the Mayan language. It was very strange to have these symbols for things and people and places.

The people of El Meco had their own language but they never wrote those symbols. They just learned to speak the language from their parents who had learned it from their parents and on and on for many, many years. That was the proper and easy way. These symbols on what Chan called "paper" were hard to learn.

She would work at it because she loved Chan. He was so handsome and smart, and he was sweet too.

They had held hands and had kissed but that was all because she knew if they did the touching thing they would do the whole sex thing too. That wasn't allowed until you were married. Otherwise there would be children without fathers.

It was late afternoon here not far from El Meco. The sun was halfway down the western sky. It was the hottest part of the day. A breeze would come up when the sun went down and that would make everything feel cooler.

When she was a little girl playing out on the beach, her mother would come with a coconut and give her a drink through the hole in the shell. It was always so refreshing because she would be hot and on the beach there wasn't any water to drink. If you drank the seawater, you would just get thirsty all over again.

Right now, she was holding onto Chan's right hand with her left and they were walking along the beach toward El Meco. It seemed so natural to be with him, yet he was a foreigner with many types of magic.

Sometimes when she would look at him, he was a stranger from a faraway place. Then he would smile at her and maybe bend over and kiss her cheek, or maybe even her lips, and she would know that he could be from the moon up in the sky and she wouldn't care.

She had seen what Chan called "this planet" from the bridge of the starship. It was a blue and green ball with white clouds floating in the sky above it. And right next to it, there was that black place with all the stars. That looked like the sky at night, especially the sky during the dry season when you could see more stars.

Even though Chan was a stranger from a faraway place, Blanca had this feeling inside that he was the one. This is why she had to ask her father if she could marry him.

What would happen if her father refused? Blanca hadn't thought much about that. It was something she didn't want to think about. And, yes, her father could be very stubborn and with him, anything was possible.

As she walked along the beach with her man, Blanca began to think about what she would do if her father did refuse.

He would be angry if she defied him, but, yes, she might do that. She wanted Chan in the worst way. She wasn't going to give him up just because her father was stubborn.

If she defied him, it was possible that once she left with Chan, her father would have a funeral service for his only daughter and he would pronounce her dead. Blanca had seen that done before, and she had felt a chill down her back when she saw the girl in question walk off into the forest.

The next morning they had found her body at the bottom of a high cliff. She had jumped to her death.

Blanca would do no such a thing. If her father wanted to pronounce her dead, he could do that, but she wasn't going to die for him. She had a life of her own to live, and she wanted to live it with Chan.

"You're very quiet."

She looked up at Chan. "I was wondering what my father would say."

Chan turned his head away. He seemed to be staring down the beach toward the village. "He won't like it."

"Why do you say that?"

Chan turned back to her. "Because I'm a stranger from far away."

Blanca made a smile, but she was sure it wasn't a very strong smile. She wasn't feeling too confident about this either.

Chan stopped.

Blanca turned and looked at him. "What's wrong?"

He smiled down at her. "Before this begins, I wanted to say something I've never said to any other woman. I wanted to tell you that I love you." He looked over her head toward the water. Then his gaze focused on her eyes again. "I don't understand it, but I feel it. So. . . no matter what happens with your father, I want to marry you. Okay?"

Blanca could feel hot tears running down her cheeks. She couldn't clearly see him. "You are my man. I knew it when I first saw you." She touched her chest with her right hand. "I felt it here, in my heart."

She rubbed the tears off her cheeks with the back of both hands.

Chan was smiling at her. Now Blanca felt that she could face anything.

He grabbed onto her left hand. "Come on, let's talk to your father."

They walked hand and hand down the sandy beach.

Blanca felt now that everything was as it should be. Out to her right, she could see three small boats with sails moving toward the shore. That would be the fishermen.

Her father was on one of those boats. They went out every morning, except when there was a storm or the winds were too strong.

She knew his mood would depend upon how good the fishing was. It had been pretty good this year so there weren't many complaints, but there could always be a bad fishing day.

As she and Chan approached the village, she could see the women waiting along the shore with their knives. They would clean the fish and take the guts and the heads to the garden to use for fertilizer. All of that would stink for a while but they would put loose dirt on it to cover the smell and it wasn't so bad.

When the two of them came near the women, one dropped her knife in the sand and ran down the beach toward them.

Blanca looked up at Chan. "It's my mother. Her name is Sucia."

"I remember."

When her mother reached them she grabbed Blanca and hugged her. "Where have you been, little girl?"

Blanca looked toward the sky and pointed. "Up there in the starship."

"What is a starship?"

Blanca had to think about that. "It is a large tube up in the sky. It can look down upon this Earth from far above."

Sucia looked up at Chan. "You have taken my daughter from me."

He smiled. "I'm sorry, ma'am, but she came of her own free will."

"I am not this ma'am. I am Sucia."

"Sorry. That is a form of address that shows respect."

Sucia nodded. "Showing respect is good."

"We want to be married, Mother."

The woman's head snapped around. "Married to this tall foreigner?"

"Yes."

Sucia nodded several times, then shrugged. "We will just have to see what your father says. For your sake, I hope he's in a good mood and it has been a good fishing day."

Blanca was sure she couldn't have said it better. That was what she had been wishing for since they had teleported to a place farther up the beach.

Chan had told her that it would be better to do it that way because her people might be frightened by the teleport.

She could understand that. It was wonderful magic. You could go anywhere without even using a donkey and cart or a boat.

Sometimes their donkey was stubborn and her father had to bite his right ear when he harnessed the little guy just so the donkey wouldn't kick or bite. There was no need to harness anything with this teleport travel and you didn't have to bite a donkey's ear.

Her father hated to do that because he said he always got donkey hair in his mouth and had to spit it out. Her father would really like teleporting.

Sucia beckoned to them. "Come, you're father will be here on the beach. We must talk to him."

As they moved along, Sucia turned to Chan. "What dowry do you want with Blanca? That might make a big difference."

Chan looked at Blanca. "I have no idea. Why would I need a dowry?"

Sucia stopped walking. "It is customary. I suppose it made the bride more of a prize at one time. Now we do it because it is customary."

Chan shrugged. "I don't need a dowry. Blanca is a prize enough."

Blanca could feel her face break out in a grin. Her Chan was really smart and he sure must love her not to ask for a dowry. Although, she did wonder what her father would think of that. He was a person who believed in the old ways of doing things. This might not be a good idea.

The sails dropped down off the masts and now the boats were being rowed by the crews. A man aboard each boat wrapped the sail around the wooden boom above the low, deep hull.

When the boats rammed into the sand near the shore, the women rushed out.

The men inside the boats clambered out of the fish laden hulls into the water. Then each of them grabbed armfuls of fish and walked them up onto the beach where there were split logs jammed down into the wet sand.

There the women would drop to their knees and cut open the fish and remove the guts. They would fling them onto grass mats behind the logs.

When the mat was full of fish offal, two men would hoist it and carry it around the village back toward the garden.

"Montana!" Sucia stood with her hands on her hips.

Her husband jumped out of the second boat into the shallow water and waded up to shore. He stopped in front of his wife. "What is it, woman? We have fish to clean."

Sucia swung her arm around toward Chan and Blanca. "They have come back to ask for your permission to marry."

Montana stared up at Chan. Then he looked at Blanca. "Has my daughter behaved herself?"

"Of course." Blanca did not hesitate and she did not avert her eyes from her father's hard stare.

He made a grimace. "I can see why. This man is tall and white and ugly. I don't think any woman would want to have him – except my daughter."

"Don't insult my man!"

Montana's head snapped around. "You are insolent for a daughter who is seeking permission to marry."

"And you are insulting my man. That is not proper. Only a father who didn't care about his daughter would do such a thing."

Montana smiled and shook his head. "Why the gods gave me a defiant daughter I'll never understand." He looked at Blanca. "Why couldn't you just marry one of the men from the village?"

"I didn't like the men from the village."

"Ah." He nodded and smiled. "Not good enough for Blanca."

"I didn't like any of them. That is what I told you – nothing else."

Her father waved his hand toward her dismissively. "It must have been something I did to the gods." He glanced back. "I will think about it." He walked away toward the split logs on the beach where the women and men were cleaning the fish.

Blanca felt like she had been abandoned.

Her mother glanced back at her and shrugged. Then she followed her husband.

Blanca could feel tears rising in her eyes. She had tried to hold them back. She didn't want her father to see them. He might make fun of her for being weak.

At that moment something happened which really improved her mood. She felt a warm arm slip across her back and a hand squeeze her right shoulder.

She looked up into Chan's face. He was very sweet and he was her man, no matter what her father said.

Chan smiled. "You know what?"

"What?"

"After we have the commander marry us aboard the starship, to make it legal, I think we should have a huge wedding back on Hyksos."

"Back where you live?"

"Yes."

"Will you have to ask your parents?"

"I won't need their permission, but I will ask them to attend."

Blanca wiped the tears off her cheeks with the backs of her hands. She made a smile for her Chan. "What are weddings like on this Hyksos?"

Chan stared off toward the water. Then he looked at her again. "They're happy. Everybody gets together, friends and family, and they have a big party. They drink wine and beer and the hard stuff and they dance and laugh. It's a lot of fun."

"I want this Hyksos wedding."

"Good, because I do too." Chan turned around to face her. Then he leaned down.

Blanca knew what he was going to do so she closed her eyes. She wondered if her father was looking. She hoped he was because she had the best man of all and she wanted him to know that.

CHAPTER SIXTY-ONE

"Doubt"

Starship Cygnus
Clinic
2M, Day 29, 6573
10:06 a.m.

Commander Seth Okanata did not usually get involved in such issues. He had enough responsibilities here on the starship.

In this case, however, he couldn't let this man go back to his home country without fair warning. Lieutenant Alto Bucolus had just teleported back yesterday. He was the one who had seen things firsthand.

This young prophet, Jesus of Nazarath, was sitting up in bed. He had virtually fully recovered and was on the mend. Thankfully they had gotten to him soon enough. Doctor Nestor had told Seth that it was really close – touch and go the first few hours here in the clinic.

Next to the bed sat Mary Magdalene. What was she to this man? Seth wasn't sure, but he suspected that this woman had feelings for Jesus of Nazareth.

"Go ahead, Bucolus." Commander Okanata motioned for the lieutenant to go up to the bed.

Alto Bucolus moved closer and held out his hand. "Hello."

The other man gripped Bucolus's hand. "I understand, Alto, that you were the one, along with Doctor Nestor, who saved my life."

"Yes. That's correct, sir."

"Don't call me 'sir.' I am Jesus of Nazareth."

"Then I will call you Jesus."

"Yes, that will be good." The Nazarene looked away toward the wall of the small room. Then he faced Alto again. "There is just one problem. I was supposed to die on that cross. It was God's way of making a statement about how much he loved his people. He would let his son die on the cross for them."

"That's a strange god."

The prophet smiled. "Not so strange, Alto."

"Jesus, I was brought here by the commander because I went down to Jerusalem to find one of our officers who had gone AWOL . . . absent without leave."

The prophet stared at Alto. "What does that have to do with me?"

"When I was down in Israel, I met your disciple, Peter. All your disciples are in hidin', fearin' for their lives. Your twin brother, Jude Thomas, has gone to Syria where it's safer. Peter said Thomas will stay there and preach."

Jesus smiled. "I'm glad he's all right. Thomas was always the soft-hearted one. He is much better off in Syria."

"What I'm trying to tell you, Jesus, is that it's not safe for you to go back to Israel."

"But my people need me. They have no one to speak for them."

"That's up to you, of course, but it's not safe. All of your disciples are hidin'. They're afraid they'll be killed."

"Even Peter?"

"Yes, even Peter."

Jesus smiled. "He's so impetuous. I'm amazed he's being this careful. He won't stay in hiding long. I'm sure of it."

"But you can't go back, sir."

"I must go back."

"No!" Mary Magdalene jumped up from the straight-backed chair next to the bed. She clamped both hands onto Jesus' arm. "I have stayed silent long enough. You have given yourself for your people. Now it is time for us to live.

"I waited for you when you were carrying that cross to Golgotha. I waited by your tomb, hoping the old stories were true, that you would rise from the dead."

She swung out her arm. "These people, here in this strange place, have saved you from death. They have wonderful, magical ways and they have saved you.

"You have given enough, Jesus. Now it is time for us to have a life together far away from the priests and the Pharisees – some place where there is peace and some place where there are no Roman soldiers."

Alto turned to Seth. "Commander, could we put them down on Earth someplace else?"

Seth shrugged. "Certainly – if that's what they want." He moved over closer to the bed. What struck him was the bright and penetrating eyes of this man Jesus.

Seth was standing next to Alto. "Listen to the lieutenant, Jesus. He has been down there. He knows what is going on."

Bucolus nodded. "These Pharisees you talk about are trying to get rid of all of you. We tried to find your brother because our man, Tikal, was with him, and we wanted to bring Tikal back. But we had no luck findin' either one of them. I do know one thing; it's not safe for you in Israel."

"I will have to think about this." Jesus looked at Mary Magdalene. "I will have to think what the best thing is for the future."

Mary Magdalene was holding onto the prophet's arm. Jesus didn't seem to notice her. He appeared to be deep in thought.

The starship commander wondered what this unusual man was thinking. Seth hadn't been ready to be impressed by this prophet, but now he felt a certain bond with him. It was strange, but it was very real.

Right now, however, he had to get to the bridge and this man, Jesus, had some thinking to do.

The commander moved away from the bed. Then he turned around. "Lieutenant. . ."

Bucolus turned. "Yes, sir?"

Seth beckoned to him.

Alto Bucolus moved around Mary Magdalene and followed his commander across the small clinic room.

At the door Seth pressed the blue-lighted plate to the right of the casing.

The pocket door opened.

Seth stepped out into the corridor.

Bucolus followed.

When the door had closed, Seth turned to Bucolus. "Lieutenant, thank you for what you did in there. I'm not sure this fellow, Jesus, is going to follow your advice, but we had to try.

"I have to get up to the bridge. I would expect that you have your work cut out for you. You were gone most of two days. Things get behind. Get your work caught up, Lieutenant, and I'll give you a one-day pass."

Bucolus smiled. "Thank you, sir."

"Lieutenant, I was wondering. Have you uncovered any new information about the murder of Lieutenant Djoser?"

"No, sir, I have not. I've been pretty busy."

Seth nodded. He could understand that, but this murder was still unsolved. "Once your one-day pass is over, Lieutenant, I want you to get back on that case."

"Yes, sir, Commander."

"In fact, I will expect a report one week after you return from your leave."

"Yes, sir."

"Dismissed, Lieutenant." Seth saluted.

Bucolus returned the salute, then did an about face and walked away down the corridor toward the elevator.

Seth Okanata had been living with Elaina for several weeks now. He really enjoyed it. It was a life he never thought he would have.

However, there was this shadow lurking in the corner of his mind. There was just a tiny bit of doubt about Elaina's innocence. It haunted him constantly.

CHAPTER SIXTY-TWO
"The Reason"

Earth
El Meco
2M, Day 30, 6573
7:06 a.m.

Some of the men had come down to the fishing boats on the seashore. Some of the women had come as well, but not Montana and Sucia.

Chan stood by Blanca's side. He did not have a good feeling about how this would turn out.

Three days ago Blanca had left her father and mother telling them that she would be back in exactly three days, and at that time she wanted her father's answer. She and Chan then had teleported up to the starship to wait out the time. Chan was needed at the helm of the starship. Whenever he could take a break, he would check on Blanca to make sure she was all right.

Blanca had been angry, but she had held herself together. In fact, over time she had mellowed a bit. Being with him in the starship helped.

He had suggested keeping things as low key as possible. Chan told Blanca that sometimes controlling people like her father actually wanted you to argue with them. Then they felt they had control over you.

Now they were back at El Meco and Blanca's anger and resolve were obvious. Chan had a feeling of dread. This was not going to turn out well. He was quite sure of that.

They had walked the length of beach from where they had teleported down from the starship. Now, Blanca stopped several meters from the village. Her jaw was set. She was ready for battle. "I am not going to beg."

Chan slid his right arm around her shoulders.

She looked up at him and made a smile.

Chan could tell that the smile was difficult. She was bracing herself for rejection and she wasn't going to let her father see that she was hurt.

Montana and Sucia were moving toward them through the soft sand, ambling along, side by side.

It was obvious to Chan that they had no idea what was about to happen, or maybe they did and weren't revealing their own apprehensions.

He leaned close to Blanca. "I'll be right here the whole time, if you need me," he said in a low voice.

The little brown face turned to him and there was a quick smile. Blanca's eyes focused on his. Then she turned away.

Chan was sure she was on the verge of tears but she didn't want her father to see that.

As her parents approached, Chan squeezed Blanca's shoulder, then dropped his arm. He wanted to leave this for her to deal with. Blanca needed his support, but she also needed his respect.

When Montana reached the wet sand, Blanca stepped forward and blocked his way to the boats.

He stepped sideways, as if to walk around her.

She moved in front of him again. "Do not disrespect me by walking by me."

His head canted to the left and seemed to cock backward. "What is this? You are interfering with my fishing."

"I want an answer."

"An answer to what?"

"You know very well."

The small man focused on Chan off to his right.

Chan folded his arms across his chest and met the man's gaze. He didn't want any trouble with his future in-laws, but at the same time, he was not about to be pushed around by this little man.

Montana averted his gaze and focused on his daughter's face again. He shook his head. "I cannot do this. I cannot give you my approval when you want to run off with this tall, ugly man with skin as white as a fish belly."

"He is a good man and he is the man I want."

"If that is so, then I will declare you dead."

Blanca folded her arms across her chest. "You are being a fool, Father. Now you will never see your grandchildren."

Sucia touched her husband's right arm. "As she says, we will never see our grandchildren."

Montana shrugged. "The children will be ugly anyway."

Blanca's brown eyes were very intense. "You are being a stubborn fool."

Montana's head snapped to the right and he stared at his daughter. "Is this the way you convince your father to bless your marriage to this tall, ugly man?"

"You wouldn't approve of Chan anyway, Father. You are too narrow-minded to see what a good man he is."

Montana moved to his left and stepped around his daughter. "I have to go fishing." He moved across the wet sand to the water's edge and placed a coconut and a wooden container into the bow of the middle boat.

Chan moved closer to Blanca. He felt for her, but he didn't want to get in her way.

She apparently heard him move because she glanced back.

Her mother was standing in front of her. The woman's wrinkled face was full of anguish.

"Do you want to come with us, Mother? That way you will see your grandchildren and you will be able to hold them."

The woman stared down at the loose dry sand. She stayed that way for several seconds.

Then she looked up. "I cannot leave him. He would not know what to do if I left him. He might take up with some young woman in the village and get himself into all kinds of trouble. No, I cannot go."

"I will miss you, Mother. I will think about you often."

"I will think about you as well, Blanca. I will try to stop your father from declaring you dead, but you know what a stubborn man he is."

Blanca's face was sad. She nodded. "Yes, I know."

Sucia grabbed onto her daughter and hugged Blanca to her body. The eyes in her wrinkled face closed. Then she said in a voice just above a whisper, "May the gods go with you and may you have many children and prosper."

Just as suddenly as she had grabbed her daughter, she let her go. She stared at Blanca one last time, then turned and ran through the loose sand back toward the village.

Blanca walked over to Chan. "She will go back to our family hut and she will cry inside where nobody can see her."

Chan made a smile for Blanca. "Shall we go for a walk?"

"I want to go back to your starship."

"It's our starship now."

Blanca nodded. "That's true."

Chan grabbed onto her hand. "Let's walk."

Blanca tried to make a smile for him. Then she turned away and stared down at the sand as they moved southward down the beach.

He was going to suggest that they have the commander marry them soon, but right now he had to let her deal with whatever emotions she was having. "If you want to talk about it, I'll listen."

Her head turned and she smiled at him. "Right now I want silence."

"I'm good with that, Blanca."

"You know – there is one thing I'm sure about."

"What's that?"

"You are the man for me."

Chan grinned. "That's good because you're the woman for me."

"Are you making fun of me?"

"I wouldn't dream of doing that, especially not now." Chan stopped and turned to face her. "I will always be here for you no matter what happens."

She grabbed onto him and hugged him hard.

CHAPTER SIXTY-THREE

"The Escape"

Earth
Israel
Outside of Jerusalem
3M, Day 3, 6573
7:36 a.m.

Lieutenant Alto Bucolus could never get used to these time changes. Down here in Israel it was probably early afternoon. He could tell by where the sun was located in the sky.

Just as he had done when he was looking for Captain Tikal, he hung around inside the east gate of the city. He kept the two guards at the city gate in view all the time. He supposed they would pose the greatest threat, although he also wondered if the real threat could maybe be some of those thugs hired by the Pharisees.

He leaned his back against the wall and continuously scanned the square in front of the east gate.

Around him were people milling about. They often stared at him. He supposed it was because of his clothing. They were dressed in loose woolen robes. He was wearing a tan camouflage shirt, camouflage pants and leather boots. Of course, the ammunition belt, dagger and holster were odd as well.

His mission was to find Peter. He was to arrange for the disciples to go to a location outside the city to meet with Jesus.

Alto figured that if he hung out here long enough he would be spotted by someone who knew Peter and the man would come to find him.

Just in case there was a problem, he had set his wrist control for a location outside of Jerusalem. It would be his escape route. He would just teleport out there into what looked on his viewing screen to be a cluster of trees on a hillside.

"Don't turn around. The Roman guards will look at us if you do. I'm hiding behind you."

Alto recognized the voice. It was Peter.

"One of our friends recognized you and came to tell me. What do you want?"

"I have to speak to you in private."

"We will have to speak here. I cannot lead you anywhere. Someone may report us to the Pharisees. Then we are finished. What do you want? Make it quick."

Alto checked around the square. There were people milling about.

Some were buying fruit from a stand near the city gate. Others were at the well near the middle of the square with their large earthen jars. Small clusters of people were moving down the street toward the gate, one group leading a donkey that was harnessed to a two-wheel cart.

He saw no one who looked like a spy for the Pharisees. Of course, it was hard to tell.

He turned his head to the right and said in a low voice, "Jesus is alive. He wants to speak to all of you outside of the city where it's safe."

"Where is he now?"

"On our ship."

"In the sea of Galilee?"

Alto considered the issue of explaining what a starship was and decided against it. "Never mind that. Just choose a safe location outside the city and I will find you and send him there."

"Is he really alive?"

"Yes, but I wouldn't say anything about it to anyone. The word might get out then there might be a big problem. Just get the disciples out of the city to a safe location."

"It will take time. We will have to go out one by one or in small groups."

"How many?"

"Ten counting me. His twin brother, Thomas, is in Syria. Judas is dead, of course, but we don't speak of that traitor."

Alto spotted a man who seemed out of place at the far north side of the square. Something about his clothing looked more expensive than the rest of the people. "You'd better get out of here. Someone is watching us."

"I'll send the disciples out of the city. How will you know where we are?"

"I will know." Alto expected another question but there was none.

Now he noticed that the man he had spotted across the square was interested in something behind him.

Alto turned. He could see Peter moving up the sloping street toward the west.

He looked back at the man who appeared to be out of place.

The man had moved toward Alto into the square with the obvious objective of following Peter.

When he moved by Alto, he glanced back, but kept moving.

Alto figured this guy would come back for him. Right now, however, he was interested in where Peter was going.

The lieutenant waited until the man was far down the street weaving his way through the crowd of people, then he began to follow him.

Alto hustled along, dodging around clusters of people. His intention was to close the space between himself and the man. Now he was sure this guy was a spy for the Pharisees and was looking for the disciples.

Lieutenant Bucolus was armed with a pistol and a dagger. He didn't want to use either of them, but this guy was up to no good. Alto had done this kind of thing before and he knew that the only way not to lose this man in the crowd was to find some identifying thing about him and keep it in view. The guy was wearing a dark green skull cap. That was the only distinguishing thing about him.

Like all the rest of the people in the crowd, he was dark, with curly black hair. He did seem somewhat taller than most. That might also help, because Alto was taller and he could keep the man's head in view.

There was a yell off to Alto's right. He knew better, but he reacted. His head jerked in that direction. When he brought his gaze back, the green cap was gone.

Alto stopped in his tracks and studied the situation up the sloping, cobblestone street.

Seconds later, he saw something. It was at the beginning of an alley off to the left just about where he had last seen this man with the green cap.

He moved through the crowd over toward the wall on the left side of the street and followed it.

Just before Alto reached the alley, the man in the green cap bolted out into the crowd. Now he was in a hurry.

The man moved across the street and headed toward the east.

Just as he moved beyond Alto, he turned around and looked at him.

Alto pretended not to notice and stepped into the alley. He stood there and counted to ten.

Then he stepped out and looked toward the east.

The man with the green cap was far down the street, moving quickly.

Alto knew now what he had to do.

He lunged into the crowd and pushed his way to the far side. Then he broke into a jog, keeping the green skull cap in view.

He was sure the man had spotted where Peter and the other disciples were hiding, and he was going to report this information to his superior.

At the first intersection, the man turned.

This guy was going to check behind him.

Alto stepped into a doorway. There he counted to five and stepped out again.

The man's back went into a side street.

Alto jogged forward. At the side street, he turned left. He stopped and looked around. He didn't want to be attacked from a doorway.

Up ahead in the smaller cluster of people, he could see the man with the green cap.

Alto began jogging again. He wasn't sure what he'd do once he caught up to this guy but he did have to stop him.

Farther up this narrower street, the number of people diminished and there was less noise.

The man in the green cap turned. He broke into a run.

Alto made a decision. He stepped into the middle of the street and yanked his pistol out of the holster on his right hip. He flipped down the safety and aimed.

There was a loud pop.

A woman screamed.

The few people in the street turned.

The man with the green cap faltered and fell onto the cobblestones.

Alto ran forward.

As he approached, the man in the green cap rose from the pavement as if to move forward.

Alto was close now.

He stopped and raised the pistol. This time he aimed for the left side of the back.

He shot again.

The man lurched and fell to the cobblestones.

"Help!" screamed a woman's voice behind him.

Alto ran forward and knelt next to the man. He pressed his left index finger against the artery on the left side of the neck.

He was still alive.

This time Alto placed the barrel of his pistol at the back of the head and pulled the trigger.

There was a loud pop.

The ejected shell casing made a clanking sound on the cobblestones.

A pool of dark blood spread to the right of the man's head.

Alto heard feet moving fast. He stood up and turned.

A woman was running down the cobblestone street toward the east gate.

Alto moved around the body and walked farther up the street. He stepped into a wide doorway. There he lowered the hammer on his pistol, shoved it down into the holster and pressed the Velcro strap across.

He tapped his wrist control and slid his index finger down the small screen. An orchard of olive trees appeared on the screen.

He tapped the "T" on the margin of the screen.

The area around him glowed blue, then turned a bubbly gold.

CHAPTER SIXTY-FOUR
"The Resurrection"

Earth
Outside Jerusalem
3M, Day 3, 6573
10:03 a.m.

Alto studied the face of his wrist control. The coordinates appeared and there was a live picture of the ten remaining disciples in a cluster of olive trees on the side of a hill.

"I would teleport away from their location, Lieutenant. We don't want to scare them."

"Good idea, Doctor Rahotpe."

"Here are the coordinates I suggest, Lieutenant."

Alto studied the new coordinates. "How far away will I be?"

"About a hundred meters. There's a cluster of trees and brush between you and them, so I don't think they'll see you."

"Thanks, Doc."

"You're welcome, Lieutenant."

Alto touched the "T" along the right margin of the screen.

Seconds later he was standing next to a cluster of trees. Blue light glowed around him, then gold. Finally the light vanished.

He could not see the group of disciples. He assumed they were farther downhill.

He glanced around, then moved to his right into a clearing. Now he could see several men farther down the hill. He assumed it was the disciples, but to be sure he studied the group, looking for Peter.

For just a second he thought he saw the man but then he couldn't be sure.

He tapped the face of his wrist control. "Doctor Rahotpe, are the followers of Jesus north of me?"

"Yes, that's correct. By the way, Lieutenant, how do you want to do this thing with this man, Jesus?"

"I'm assuming he wants to make a grand entrance, so why don't I go to a location and tap the surface of my wrist control to signal you to send him."

"That would be fine with me."

"Just wait for my signal, Doc."

"I'll be right here, Lieutenant."

Alto began walking through the tall, dry grass down the steep hill. It was strange, but this man, Jesus, had the idea that he wanted to appear out of the sky before his followers.

The lieutenant assumed that the Nazarene had a reason for doing this. Based upon what he knew of Jesus, the man wasn't into dramatic appearances just for their own sake. He had some kind of plan up his sleeve.

Maybe he was thinking of his legacy. It was so true that people who left this world in a dramatic way might just have more impact than some guy who withered away at old age and died peacefully with his family at his side.

Frankly, as far as Alto was concerned, he preferred the last choice, but then, he didn't have any agenda either.

When he neared the group, Peter walked up the hill to meet him. "Where is he, Lieutenant? You said he would be here."

"He will be. Just give him time." Alto stopped. "Oh, by the way, there was a man in the square who followed you to your hiding place this morning."

"The authorities didn't come."

"No. I took care of that."

Peter stared at him. "I heard there was a strange killing of a man today in the streets."

"I had to do that. He would have gone to the Pharisees."

"Thank you, Lieutenant."

"You're welcome."

Peter turned around. "Let's go tell the rest of them that he will be coming soon. They have been very impatient. Andrew thought this might be some kind of trick to get us out of hiding."

Alto walked by his side. "Honestly, Peter, I wouldn't go back into Jerusalem. It's too dangerous."

The slightly shorter man turned to Alto. "But we have been hiding for many days without being discovered."

"It's only a matter of time before the Pharisees find you."

Peter nodded. "Yes, I suppose. And if we are all crucified, then who will preach God's word?"

As he and Peter approached, some of the men were staring at him.

"Who is this man in the strange clothes?"

"He is a friend, Andrew. He will bring our Jesus back to us. That is what he has told me."

"But we all saw Jesus nailed to that cross. He can't be alive."

Alto swung out his right arm. "Spread out, please."

The men moved back in a loose circle.

Alto tapped his wrist control.

It glowed.

Andrew pointed at Alto's wrist and whispered to the man next to him.

"Send him down, Doc."

"Where?"

"To my wrist control."

"You'd better take it off, Lieutenant."

Peter stared at Alto, as he unwrapped his wrist control and placed it on the ground in the center of the open area. "Okay, Doc."

Alto moved away from the wrist control.

A blue column of light appeared above it.

The disciples shrank back.

Peter pointed at the blue column. His mouth was wide open in wonder.

The column turned gold and bubbly.

Some of the disciples scrambled back farther.

A figure appeared.

Peter's hand went to his mouth and he stared in wonder. "It's him!" He pointed. "Look!"

The gold glow faded, then disappeared. Jesus of Nazareth stood in their midst.

Some of the men fell to their knees before him. Peter stood with his hands clasped together in a prayerful pose and his eyes focused on his master.

Jesus bent down and picked up the wrist control. He held it out. "Here, Alto."

The lieutenant smiled and took it. "Thanks."

Jesus turned and looked around at his followers. "It is good that you have come here today. I have important things to say to you."

He held out his wrists. "As you see, God has healed me. I am whole again.

"I have come down to you out of the sky to tell you that all of you must go abroad and preach. If you stay in Jerusalem you will be killed. You must remain alive and pass the word of God on to the people.

"Someday you can come back here to Jerusalem and preach the word to these people, some day when the Pharisees and the priests are gone and forgotten. For now, however, you must move on and do the will of God elsewhere.

"I will not stay among you for long, but I trust you to preach and do God's work. The people must be given hope so that they can move on with their lives. They must know that God loves them and will care for them, no matter what.

"They have lives of poverty and desperation. We must give them hope and faith in the love of God. They need this faith to carry on. They need this faith to do the will of God."

"Stay with us, Master."

Jesus turned to Peter. He smiled. "You will lead this crusade, Peter. You will be the cornerstone of my work here on Earth. The rest of the disciples will build this movement upon your strength."

Peter fell to his knees and clasped his hands together in front of his face as if he were praying to his God. "I will do as you say, Master."

The Nazarene tapped the surface of his wrist control with the index finger of his right hand.

A blue column of light appeared around him, then it gradually changed to gold.

Jesus vanished.

Peter remained kneeling with his hands clasped together and his eyes closed.

Then he opened his eyes and rose to his feet.

The rest of the disciples were talking among themselves in excited voices.

"Now, listen to me, brothers!"

Alto moved off into the trees. In the distance he could hear the resonant tones of Peter's voice. As he moved farther away the sound receded. However, it did seem to him that the man had gained a new strength and poise.

It occurred to Alto, just then, that it would be interesting to come back here in the future to see if this movement, this religion, had become something of importance.

Maybe he would ask the MSA for an assignment on a starship coming to this planet, Earth, a few years from now. Of course, he might not get it, but it would be worth the effort to try.

CHAPTER SIXTY-FIVE
"The Shadow"

Starship Cygnus
Level 1
Conference Room #3
3M Day 5, 6573
7:06 a.m.

"**B**y the power vested in me by the MSA, I now pronounce you man and wife." Commander Okanata nodded toward Chan Caracol. "Captain, you may kiss the bride."

Chan leaned forward and kissed Blanca on the lips.

Actually Commander Seth Okanata was pleased with the way the little ceremony had gone. Elaina had helped Blanca with the wedding dress. The poor girl had no understanding about what a proper wedding dress should look like.

Elaina had found a white dress of her own, which she had someone alter. Then she and Blanca cobbled together a white headband with artificial flowers and ribbons.

The little bride looked ecstatic when she came into the conference room for the ceremony.

Now she was standing in front of her new husband and she was crying.

Seth stepped forward. "Is everything all right?"

Chan turned to him. "She's upset because her parents weren't here," he whispered.

"We could have brought them up for the ceremony, Captain."

Chan Carocol shook his head. "No, sir. Her father wouldn't come. . . and her mother wouldn't do anything her husband didn't want her to do. It's complicated, sir."

Captain Caracol pulled his new wife into his arms and held her while she wept.

"Perhaps, Captain, once you get down to the Recreation Center, she will feel somewhat better."

"That's possible, sir."

Seth bent over to the side of the tiny bride's head. "Young lady, best wishes in your marriage."

The bride did not turn her head.

Elaina was standing off to Seth's right.

He walked over to her. "My, my, the bridesmaid looks absolutely beautiful."

Actually, Elaina did look striking, as far as Seth was concerned. She was wearing a light green dress with a light green headband, again with artificial flowers attached.

She smiled for him. "Why, thank you, sir."

"Shall we go up to the bridge, my lady?" Seth offered his arm.

"Sure."

They had planned this wedding for Seth's shift and had left Lieutenant Lycastus, the other navigator, in charge of the bridge. That way, Captain Caracol and his new bride, Blanca, could have a whole shift to themselves – a sort of short honeymoon.

When Seth neared the conference room door, the large security chief, Lieutenant Alto Bucolus, stepped up to the commander. "Sir. . ."

Seth turned. "Yes, Lieutenant?"

"Sir, I just want to thank you for doin' this."

"I was more than happy to, Bucolus."

"Well, you see, sir, this was a long time comin'."

"I don't understand. He just met this young lady, Blanca."

"No, sir, what I mean is that I've known Chan – Captain Caracol – for a long time, and Chan, he's been runnin' around with a lot of woman, sir." The lieutenant glanced at Elaina. "Sorry, Ma'am."

She grinned. "No need to apologize, Lieutenant."

"Well, sir, I've been worried about Chan settlin' down, and this sure makes me real happy. I just know this is the right woman for him, sir, and he's finally settlin' down."

Seth was quite touched. "So you and Captain Caracol are old friends?"

"Yes, sir. He's sort of like a younger brother to me. Has been for a long time and I've been worried about him." The lieutenant turned to look at the newlyweds. He faced the commander again. "Now everythin's good, sir."

Seth smiled. "Glad to hear it, Bucolus."

The other man grinned. "Yes, sir." He held out his meaty hand.

The commander clasped the large hand.

Lieutenant Bucolus shook Seth's hand hard twice. "Thank you so much, sir. . . for everythin'."

"You're more than welcome, Lieutenant."

Bucolus released Seth's hand and moved away to where Chan Caracol and Blanca were standing.

"I meant to ask him about the investigation." Seth turned to Elaina.

Her smile eclipsed.

"Is everything all right?"

"I was feeling all bright and cheerful until you mentioned that investigation. I thought it was done."

Seth shook his head. "Not until we find out who murdered your husband. . . former husband."

"Couldn't it have been an accident?"

Seth reached out for the blue-lighted pad to the right of the pocket door. He placed his hand on the pad.

The door opened.

He motioned toward the open doorway. "Go ahead."

Elaina stepped out into the corridor.

Seth followed her. He still marveled at how beautiful she looked in that green dress. She absolutely glowed – a beautiful woman. "It probably wasn't an accident because all that equipment is inspected almost constantly, and certainly before an EVA."

The door rattled shut behind Seth.

"Who do you think did it?"

The starship commander never liked to think about this. "I really don't know."

"You didn't answer right away."

He shrugged. "Just thinking about the question."

"Well, it wasn't either one of us."

"True." Seth wasn't absolutely sure about that.

"The only person left is the other mechanic, Sergeant Copan."

"I guess."

"Do you think there are other possibilities?" Elaina stopped in front of the elevator.

Seth pressed the UP arrow.

It glowed pink.

He looked at Elaina. "I don't think we've looked at this carefully enough. Copan is much too obvious. That would be like your cook poisoning your food. It's just much too obvious. Copan may be only a sergeant, but he's not stupid."

"Then who?"

That was the question which had plagued Seth Okanata since the day that Masal Djoser had died during the EVA.

Seth shrugged. "I don't know, but I think we're missing something."

"Like what?"

"Like the fact that the videos of the storage room were obviously tampered with. That raises the question of who had the knowledge and the skill to alter those videos."

He looked at Elaina. "I think we ought to go in that direction."

Elaina said nothing, but Seth noticed that her recent glow was gone. He hoped that was because she found this whole investigation tedious and, perhaps, even bothersome.

However, there was still this shadow in the back of his mind.

CHAPTER SIXTY-SIX
"Change in Direction"

Starship Cygnus
Level 1
Conference Room #3
3M, Day 7, 6573
6:30 p.m.

Commander Seth Okanata stepped into the Conference Room. The noise in the room abated and everyone rose out of their pedestal chairs around the table.

He moved down to the end of the table, where there was a lectern attached to its top, and swung around to face everyone.

Behind him was a video screen with a live picture of the bridge. Captain Chan Caracol was at the helm and the navigator was Lieutenant Lindos Lycastus.

"You may be seated."

There was the rustle of people settling down into the pedestal chairs around the table.

Seth Okanata unzipped his thin folder and opened it on the slanted surface of the lectern. "Good evening or morning, whichever the case may be for you." He looked up. "I have called this briefing as a method of clarifying where we are and what we will do next."

He raised his fist in front of his mouth and gently cleared his throat. "We will be departing from our orbit around Earth in five days." Seth glanced up and down both sides of the table.

"There are several issues we must discuss here before we can definitively plan for departure." He looked down the left side of the table to a very large man seated near the corner on the other end. "Lieutenant Bucolus, is there any change in the status of your investigation of Lieutenant Masal Djoser's death?"

The large man shook his head. "No, sir."

Seth now felt a certain nervousness. He raised his fist again, as if to clear his throat. Actually he was buying a little time to think.

He again looked down the table at the huge man. "Lieutenant, I would suggest that, perhaps, it would be wise to pursue this investigation from a slightly different angle. Namely, I would suggest you look for someone who had the skill and the opportunity to tamper with the video feed in the EVA equipment storage room."

Lieutenant Bucolus nodded. "Okay, sir, I will do that."

"I'm only suggesting that approach, Lieutenant, because other approaches haven't seemed to work."

"Yes, sir, I understand."

"Good." Seth looked down at his notes. Actually he was avoiding eye contact with Bucolus. "Now, as to the matter of Jesus of Nazareth and his friend, Mary Magdalene." He looked up. "We have their permission to send them down to the village of El Meco.

"It is a simple fishing village in the narrow land between the two continents in the west. I should certainly hope the prophet will be safe there. Captain Chan Caracol and his new wife will accompany them in the teleport."

Seth looked at Lieutenant Alto Bucolus. "That problem with her parents hasn't been resolved, has it, Lieutenant?"

Alto shook his head. "No, sir. I don't think so."

Seth nodded. "Too bad." He looked up again. "We have permanently lost our third pilot. Captain Salathiel Tikal is no longer a member of the MSA or a pilot of this starship. He is officially AWOL."

The commander glanced around the table. "With that in mind, I should add that if there is anyone who is interested in applying for pilot training, I would be glad to consider that person. You need to be at least a first lieutenant and you must have the commensurate education in engineering and mathematics.

"If you feel you are qualified, please submit a record of your MSA service and any military service and training to me. I may not get back to you right away, but I will get back to you. Needless to say, we are going to be quite busy once we are underway. That will slow down any appraisal of your qualifications, but I will, at some point, go over your records once you submit them to me."

He glanced up and down the table. "Now, with regards to the remains of Lieutenant Coptos Gurab we dug up on the planet Mars. We will be returning those remains to Hyksos and we will see that they are given to his descendants."

A hand went up.

"Yes, Doctor Eloi?"

"Commander, do you have the names of descendants on record?"

"Yes, we do, Doctor Eloi."

The anthropologist nodded. "Very good, Commander."

"As long as I have your attention, Doctor Eloi, is there anything to report with regard to the copper mine concept?"

"Yes, sir. We think the people on this peninsula where El Meco is located are malleable enough to be effectively utilized to mine copper. There will be some challenges, such as building roads to and from the mines and the offload sites. However, I think it can become a viable operation, Commander."

Seth turned to the pudgy geologist. "Do you have anything to add, Doctor Naranjo?"

"Only that there is a huge amount of copper and that it is often in a very pure state. These two factors, alone, make this a really positive opportunity for mining, Commander."

Seth nodded. "Very good, gentlemen." He turned around and faced the table again. "This starship will be departing from Earth orbit the twelfth day of this month. I expect that everyone will be prepared to leave at that time. We are planning to blast off at five fifty-nine that morning."

He scanned the right side of the table until his eyes rested upon a short, muscular man. "Sergeant Copan, can the propulsion systems be ready for departure at that time?"

"Sir, everythin' is ready now. I've been checkin' through all the systems and dealin' with any anomalies, sir."

"Very good, Sergeant. I do realize that you are doing the work of two men. If you need any help, just let me know, and I will try to find someone to assist you."

"Thank you, sir. I think, sir, that I will be fine."

Seth nodded. "Good." He glanced around the table. "We moved into this Orion band of the galaxy via Worm Hole forty-four. We have on record the coordinates for that portal for our return to Hyksos." His eyes focused on Elaina. "Is that correct, Lieutenant Djoser?"

"Yes, Commander."

"Very good."

Seth glanced up and down each side of the table. "Are there any questions?"

There was no response.

"Again, we will be underway at five fifty-nine the morning of the twelfth day of this month."

He glanced around again. "This briefing is over. You are dismissed."

Everyone rose from the pedestal chairs and saluted.

Seth Okanata returned the salute. Then he picked up his folder and moved around the right side of the table.

When he went by Elaina, she did not look up. He wondered if that had anything to do with his suggestion to Lieutenant Alto Bucolus about a change of direction in the investigation. He hoped not.

CHAPTER SIXTY-SEVEN
"The Injustice"

Earth
El Meco
3M, Day 8, 6573
7:02 a.m.

Captain Chan Caracol liked being married. With it came a new sense of responsibility. He felt very protective about Blanca. He realized that probably part of it was her tiny size, yet part of it was this strong connection he felt with her.

He was glad it was there. This woman was different than any other woman he had ever known, and he had known quite a few.

Chan looked down at the small person walking by his side. She was quiet this morning. He knew why. Blanca was afraid of what her father had already done or might do when he saw her. "Are you okay?"

She glanced up at him. "I will be fine."

"If you need my help, you have it."

She grinned. Then her eyes focused on his. "You are a good man."

"I try."

Her brown eyes blinked and she turned away.

Chan could detect a more deliberate movement in her walk today. She was nervous.

He glanced over his right shoulder. Jesus and Mary Magdalene were behind them walking on the wet sand. Jesus was talking to Mary and pointing out things inland.

This was picturesque country with majestic hills rising out of the thick forest inland. Here along the coast it was grassland and beach with some trees, most of them farther inland.

It was just after sunrise. They had come early so the men would still be around the village before they went out to fish for the day. Chan's specific assignment was to introduce Jesus and Mary Magdalene. Doctor Nestor had inserted translators behind the left ear of each one of them, so they would have no problem with the language of these people.

Up ahead to the east, Chan could see the three wooden boats run up onto the beach in front of the village. Beyond them the sun was a huge orange ball.

In front of the sun was a path of dark orange splayed across the shiny surface of the water. Eventually, as the triangular path became wider, the orange faded to a yellow, then to a creamy white.

Before he saw the men, Chan heard voices. The villagers were probably standing around eating corncakes and talking.

When Chan and Blanca came to the clearing in front of the village, Chan could see a group of men and women farther up the beach inland in the dry, white sand standing together and talking.

The voices stopped.

Chan put his hand on Blanca's back.

She turned.

"I will let you do the talking. He's your father. But if he gets nasty, I'm going to step in. I won't let my wife be bad-mouthed by anyone." He focused on the pretty brown eyes. "Okay?"

"Yes."

To Chan, Blanca's voice sounded very tense. He wasn't surprised. "Let me introduce Jesus and Mary Magdalene first."

Chan moved forward in the sand and stopped, perhaps, ten feet from the cluster of people. "Hello. I am Chan. You probably remember me. I have brought two new people to you. They would like to live among you."

He turned and held out his left hand, as if to point. "This is Jesus and Mary Magdalene. They have come here where it is safe from their enemies."

None of the villagers said anything.

Finally, a man pushed through the group and stepped out into the open. "I am Quelepa, chief of this village. Why do these people want to live here? They do not even look like us. They have ugly white skin. At least their eyes are brown like ours and their hair is dark."

"Jesus was a religious leader in his own land and some of the people feared him and what he was saying to the people so they captured him and tried to kill him."

"Does he know how to fish?"

Jesus stepped forward. "I have fished in the Sea of Galilee, but I am a carpenter by trade."

"What is a carpenter?"

"He is a person who makes furniture – tables, chairs, cupboards."

"I know about tables and chairs but I do not know cupboards."

"Once I can fashion some tools, I will make cupboards for you."

Quelepa folded his arms across his bony chest, then he smiled. "Ah, yes, this man may be of some use in the village."

He nodded toward Mary. "Does your wife know how to tend a garden?"

Jesus turned to Mary.

"Yes, I do."

Quelepa nodded and smiled. "That is good." He rubbed his chin thoughtfully. "Okay, this is what we will do. We will let you live in our village for one phase of the moon. We will help you build a hut and let you live here for that one moon. Then I and the village elders will meet with you and we will decide if this is working." He swung around and looked at the villagers. Then he faced Jesus and Mary again. "That is my decision."

A cool breeze brushed across Chan's right cheek. He turned his head to look. It was almost like a warning. He didn't normally believe in omens and such things, but when he turned, his eyes focused on a man in a cluster of people off to the right.

It was Montana, Blanca's father. He was staring at Chan.

"Welcome to our village."

Chan turned to the sound of Quelepa's voice.

The village chief stepped up closer to Jesus and held out both hands. "You must come fishing with us this morning. We go every day, except when there's a storm."

Jesus smiled. "I would be glad to help with the fishing." He turned to Chan. He was smiling. "I think this is going to work."

Quelepa stepped over to Mary and took both of her hands in his. "Welcome. You will go out into the garden with the women today and help with the weeding and harvesting."

She nodded. "Thank you, Quelepa."

Chan turned to say something to Blanca.

She was gone.

His eyes scanned the right side of the small cluster of people.

Blanca was talking to her mother. Her father was standing next to her mother, but his back was turned toward Blanca.

Chan crossed the soft, deep sand and stepped up onto the short rise where Blanca was standing.

Her mother, Sucia, turned and stared at Chan. "What are you doing here?"

"I'm here to support my wife."

"She is not your wife."

"According to the standards of my society, she is."

"She is living an unclean life with a man who is not married to her."

Chan shrugged. "I guess that's what you believe here in El Meco, but where I live, we're married." Chan nodded toward Montana's back. "You and your husband rejected her request. You have shown no respect toward her."

"I won't listen to this shit from a foreigner."

Chan ignored the remark and turned to Blanca. "Are you all right?"

Her pretty eyes were running tears.

"Do you really want to do this?"

She nodded.

"I'll be right here for you."

Blanca's small mouth made a brief, half-hearted smile. Then she turned to her father's back. "I am very much alive and I am married to a good man. I would have married in the fashion of our village if only you had accepted Chan as my husband. Because you would not do that, I married him the Mayan way on his starship."

"I will not look at my daughter. She is dead. I do not look at the dead. I bury them and if they have been good in this life, I remember them with love. If they have not been good, I forget them. I will forget my daughter."

"Why do you insult your daughter like this, Montana? You are her father."

"I will not address the questions of the non-being who says he has married my daughter."

"Have it your way, old man. You're being stupid. Now you will never see your grandchildren."

"I will not acknowledge the words of the non-being who says he has married my daughter."

Blanca's mother suddenly began to sob. She bent over and covered her face with her hands.

Blanca stepped forward and put her hand on her mother's back. "You can come with us, Mother. Then you will be able to hold your grandchildren and see them grow."

The woman shook her head, then turned away and stood next to her husband with her back toward her daughter.

"I can't believe that both of you are being this stupid. Your daughter only wants your approval and your support. She's a good daughter and you are rejecting her.

"Let me tell you something, Montana. Someday you will regret what you are doing now. That's all I have to say. I'm through with you."

Chan turned away from them and faced the water. He folded his arms across his chest.

He had never felt such anger before in his life. It was the injustice of this, the unfairness.

At that point, he realized that he was being selfish, only thinking about his own emotions.

He turned around, then walked over to Blanca's side.

She was standing bent over with her hands covering her face.

Chan slid his arm across her shoulders.

Blanca buried her face against his chest. Her whole body shook with sobs.

CHAPTER SIXTY-EIGHT

"Departure"

Starship Cygnus
Bridge
3M, Day 12, 6573
5:56 a.m.

Commander Seth Okanata had asked Captain Caracol to stay on the bridge for the period when they would be breaking away from Earth's gravity. It was only because he wanted another set of eyes monitoring the systems aboard the starship.

As far as shifts, he would let Caracol return to his compartment when this main event was over and they were moving off toward the outer reaches of this solar system.

With this fusion engine, they would need, perhaps, one flyby to aid in acceleration, but one should be enough. They would probably use that giant, Jupiter again. The next one, Saturn, was more complicated because it not only had a whole series of moons like Jupiter, it had a belt of debris circling it.

"Commander, I've checked all systems. I think we're a go." The co-pilot glanced over at Seth. Then he looked back over his left shoulder and smiled.

Seth didn't often break the rules of protocol, especially when they were ready to fire the rocket system and pull away from a planet. However, Captain Caracol had asked him if his new wife, Blanca, couldn't be on the bridge with the rest of them during the initial ignition and breakaway from Earth. She was frightened and he was afraid that she would get hurt.

Seth could understand that. This woman was from a primitive society and knew nothing about rockets or space travel.

He glanced back at the small woman. Seth always worried about his people being buckled in properly. She was buckled in.

He checked his wrist control. It was one minute after six. The launch was slightly late, but based upon their calculations, that wouldn't matter. They had a window of approximately eighteen minutes where they could pull away from Earth and establish a flyby course for Jupiter.

Seth turned to the co-pilot. "Captain Caracol, I'm going to announce to the whole ship that we will be launching in five minutes. Are all systems good to go?"

"Yes, sir, Commander."

"Very good." Seth reached up to a black switch on the upper right side of his console. He flipped the switch upward. "To the crew of Starship Cygnus, this is your commander. We will be launching in less than four minutes. Follow all safety procedures. Belt in and make sure all loose objects are tied down. May this be a safe journey."

He flicked the switch down. He glanced around the bridge one last time. Then he faced the console again. "We will be launching in ten, nine, eight, seven, six, five, four, three, two, one. . . fire." He stabbed a red button midway up the right side of his console.

There was a deep rumble. The starship shook.

Seth was focused on the systems readout on his console, but he spied a movement out of the corner of his right eye. He was sure that it was Captain Caracol checking on his wife.

The vibration became more violent and Seth could feel his body being pressed into the cushion of his seat. The mild pressure of his seat harness now felt loose and he knew there was space between his body and the straps.

Up in the windshield, just above the top of his console, he could see the blue and green of Earth slowly sweep away to the left.

Finally, it vanished. Ahead were myriads of white stars and black space.

The flesh on his face pressed back and he knew very well if he spoke, whatever he said would be garbled nonsense.

Some kind of fluid ran out of his right nostril onto his upper lip.

Seth was always disgusted by such accidents, but you learned to ignore them. There were more important things to focus on.

Now, because of the pressure, his eyes watered and the console screen blurred. He blinked, hoping the fluid in his eyes would go to the corners and then, perhaps, down his cheeks.

His left eye cleared. He closed the right and focused on the screen with just the one eye.

From what he could see, all systems were nominal. He always felt he had to monitor them, even though there were specialists aboard this starship doing the same thing during launches. It made him feel better to know what was going on.

As he sat there, plastered against the seat cushion, Seth wondered if that wasn't what bothered him about this very long investigation of Masal Djoser's death. He felt like he had no control over it. There was no beginning, middle or end.

He had worked before with this security chief, Lieutenant Alto Bucolus. The man was persistent and competent. Seth knew that to be a fact, both from Bucolus's record and from his own experience with the man.

However, in this situation, something was missing. Maybe the missing piece did have to do with the skills of a video editor.

Maybe that was it. He just wanted it to be over. Seth knew he had a special emotional relationship with this investigation. It was all about Elaina. The thing he wanted more than anything in his life right now was to know she was innocent. So far, he had never been absolutely sure about that.

The heavy pull of Earth's gravity began to ease. Ever so gradually the pressure let up.

He knew, of course, what was going to happen. Seth had done this hundreds of times before.

As he was waiting for the gravity to decrease, his mind drifted to Elaina again. He did love her, but it was a love that was somewhat conditional. He just didn't feel he could give himself to her fully.

On the surface, she seemed very relaxed about it all. Yet, he knew it had to be preying on her. Every so often he would catch a glimpse of that in her behavior.

It would be something in her face or the way she stood. Sometimes she would become very quiet. That quiet thing could be typical of her, but he wasn't totally convinced it wasn't connected to the investigation.

Seth had wondered over and over if all of these suspicions weren't just his way of telling himself that he could never be so lucky as to have someone as beautiful as Elaina Djoser as his lover. Yet, she was his lover.

They had been an item for almost two months. Well, actually before that he had been interested, but she had been married.

Now, here he was, doubting their relationship – more importantly - doubting her. Was it because he couldn't believe a beautiful woman like that would want him? On the other hand, was it because there was just something about her, something subtle, that said she had done it?

He hated thinking about these things. Mostly he hated it because he never came to any final conclusion. It made him uneasy and tense and he hated being uneasy and tense.

Finally he could feel the safety harness pressing against his chest. "We are free of Earth's gravity."

He glanced back over his left shoulder. "Lieutenant Djoser, are we still on course for the Jupiter flyby?"

There was a rattle of computer keys.

Elaina's beautiful blue eyes rose above the navigator's console. "Yes, sir, right on course."

"Very good, Lieutenant."

CHAPTER SIXTY-NINE
"Loose Ends"

Hyksos
Memphis
4281 Aswan Street
Memphis
6M, Day 23, 6573
(3 months later)
6:06 p.m.

Sergeant Hector Copan stood in the blue column of light on the teleportico in front of his own house.

He waited for the teleport to complete and even when the gold bubbles disappeared, he stood there. He wanted to see his kids so much but this was going to be hard. He just knew it would be hard.

What he saw next surprised him and made him happy too. He saw a small face in the sidelight window. It was his daughter, Charis. And to her right and slightly lower was his son's face. He could tell that Aten was crying.

The door opened. Charis ran out and grabbed him around the waist and hugged him. Aten charged out onto the concrete pad and clamped onto Hector's right leg.

Hector wrapped his arms around his children and pulled them up against him. He could feel tears running down his cheeks. Normally he would be embarrassed about this, but now he didn't really care.

In the blur of his tears he could see the babysitter, Niobe, standing in the doorway with her arms folded across her chest. She was smiling.

Charis looked up. "Daddy, I really missed you so much."

Hector grinned. "Me too, honey." He crouched down to Aten. "How's my little man?"

Aten wrapped his arms around his father's neck and kissed his cheek.

Hector picked up the boy in his right arm and took the hand of his daughter in his left. He moved over to the doorway.

"Hello, Mister Copan. Welcome back."

He grinned. "Hi, Niobe. Is my mother around?"

Niobe glanced back over her right shoulder. "She's in the kitchen."

When Hector stepped through the doorway into the house, he had the sense that there was a sort of shadow near him. He knew what it was – the presence of his wife. He could feel her near.

Lycia had been a beautiful woman, but she had gotten crazy. Then there was the accident. Hector liked to think about it as an accident. He didn't want to even consider that other thing.

The night he had gone into Cadmus's garage was a clear image in his mind. But he had convinced himself that he had done those things with the electrical cable just to scare Cadmus – give him something to think about. He had never counted on an accident. That's not the way he had planned it.

When Hector entered the living room, his mother moved through the doorway from the dining room. "My son! Hector, my son!" She waddled across the living room floor to where he stood and wrapped her arms around his neck. She kissed him over and over again on his right cheek.

When she pulled away, she was crying and she reached down and lifted her apron up and dabbed the tears from her eyes. "The gods have blessed us today. My boy is back."

She looked directly at him. "How are you, my boy?"

"I'm good, Ma." Aten was getting heavy, so Hector crouched down and placed him on the floor. He kissed a small wet, white cheek. "My good boy, Aten."

The boy's chest seemed to enlarge and he grinned proudly.

Charis still clung to Hector.

When he looked down, he was haunted by the sadness in her pretty blue eyes. He placed his left hand on top of her blonde hair and smiled at her. "It's been hard, hasn't it, baby?"

"Yes, Daddy."

"I was so sorry I was far away. I will never be that far away again." The thought of prison fleeted through Hector's mind.

He crouched down in front of Charis. "You have been my brave little girl and I am proud of you, but from now on Daddy is not gonna go anywhere. I'm gonna be right here."

"No more journeys, Daddy?"

"No more journeys. I'm quittin' the MSA."

"Are you really doin' that, Hector?"

Hector Copan rose to his feet and looked directly at his mother. "Sure am. Masal and I. . . I guess there's not gonna be any Masal anymore. We were gonna do it together."

"Somethin' happen to Masal?"

"He was killed in an EVA. I was right there with him. Adjustment screw blew out of his regulator."

"That's too bad. He was your friend."

Hector nodded. "Yup, sure was." He folded his arms across his chest. "Anyways, I'm gonna start an antique car restoration garage. There's good money in that business.

"That way I don't have to leave the kids and I don't have to travel all over the damn galaxy anymore. I'm real tired of that. Had too much of it."

"Then you won't be workin' for the MSA anymore."

"No."

"That's real steady work with a real steady paycheck, Hector."

"I know, Ma, but I just can't leave the kids anymore. All I do when I'm away is think about them and worry and everythin'."

"Oh, by the way, a Detective Clio from the police department has been here lookin' for you."

Hector tensed. "Yeah, I know. I talked to him already."

"What does a police detective want with you, Hector?"

"I don't know. Guess he's just followin' up on everythin' about the accident. I gotta talk to him again some time. Don't know when."

His mother nodded toward the babysitter. "Niobe's been stayin' here with me to take care of the children. She's been a real help. Says she'd like to continue to stay here, if it's all okay with you."

Hector turned to Niobe. "You really want to stay?"

"Yes, if it's okay. I'm going to college at night and sometimes I wait tables during the day. I need a place to stay and I can use a little extra money. You don't have to pay me much because I'm living here."

Hector remembered Lycia saying something about Niobe's mother being hard to live with.

Hector shrugged. "Sure. I know my mother can't do it all. If you wanna help and stay here, I'm okay with that."

"Thank you, Mister Copan."

He smiled and nodded. "Hey, we're good." He looked down at his children. "So, have you kids had your dinner?"

"No, they were waitin' for you, Hector. They knew you were comin' and I couldn't get them to sit at the table."

"Well, I'm sure hungry." He looked down at the children again. "You guys hungry?"

"Yeah!" shouted Aten.

Hector crouched down and swept the little boy up into his arms. "Well, guess we're gonna have to eat dinner."

Charis grabbed onto his left arm.

Hector rose to full height and with Aten in his arms he moved slowly into the dining room, then the kitchen.

It felt good to be back, in spite of the sense that something was missing, namely Lycia, his wife. He just had never figured on her going all wild like that and hanging out with that loser, Cadmus. Lycia had just seemed to come apart after all those years of marriage. Go figure.

When he sat at the table, Hector made sure he was between the children. Tonight there was no sitting at the end of the table, as he usually did. They wanted him right between them.

Then he would have to tuck them in tonight, when they went to bed. He was looking forward to that. Sometimes it was those little things that were the best part of life.

He wanted to get this situation with Detective Clio taken care of. He would call the man tomorrow.

The thought of it made him a little nervous, but he knew the real trick was to remain calm. Probably the man was just tying up loose ends. That's probably what it was.

CHAPTER SEVENTY

"Questions"

Hyksos
Memphis
City Building
1282 Main Street
6M, Day 24, 6573
1:06 p.m.

"Mister Copan, thank you so much for coming down on such short notice."

Hector shrugged. "Just wanted to get this all settled. Got a lot of time to make up with my kids. You know how it is when you're away."

"Actually I don't." The blue eyes focused on Hector. "However, I'm sure it presents its challenges."

"It's hard bein' away from your family."

"So how are the kids handling your wife's death?"

"They seem okay. Kids are pretty tough."

"Glad to have their daddy back?"

Hector nodded. "They sure are."

"Mister Copan. . . we understand that you are an expert in restoring antique automobiles."

"I know quite a bit." Hector noticed a pigeon landing outside on the windowsill. Its left eye blinked.

The detective shuffled papers in a folder. He was staring down at something. "It says here that you and a Mister Masal Djoser were supposed to start an antique car restoration business."

"Yup."

"But Mister Djoser was killed during an extra vehicular activity aboard the Starship Cygnus. Is that correct?"

Hector nodded. "I was right there next to him. Screw popped out of his air regulator. I tried to seal the hole with duct tape." Hector looked down. He suddenly felt sad about Masal. "I was too late."

"And yet, sir, you were able to go back out there and weld right after he died."

Hector shrugged. "Had to. I was the only welder besides Masal on that starship. You don't ever wanna leave holes in a starship hull."

"What killed Mister Djoser?"

Hector stared up at the ceiling and thought about this. Then he looked directly at the large man across the desk. "I guess it was somethin' about his lungs bleedin' out. I'm not sure. I had to get back out there and finish the weldin' job."

"I understand, Mister Copan that you and Mister Djoser were partners in a business venture."

"Yeah – restorin' antique cars."

"And he owed you money, didn't he?"

Hector shrugged. "Yeah, but I figured he'd come up with the money once the business got goin'."

"Did you like it when Cadmus hung out with your wife?"

Hector could smell a trap. "Would you like it?"

The detective's wide face broke into a smile. When he smiled, his mustache bent down on the right side. "No, Mister Copan, I guess I wouldn't." He leaned back in his chair. "You see. . . what we're lookin' at here is a strange coincidence."

"What coincidence?"

"Well, when we look at the fact that Cadmus and your wife died in an antique car accident and then we know that you are an expert in working on antique cars, it points to you."

"All I know about Cadmus's car is that he didn't take very good care of it and, besides, from what I was told, they were goin' awful fast when that car crashed."

"What are you trying to suggest, Mister Copan?"

"Well, it's pretty straight forward, if you ask me. Here he is drivin' this car that's not in good shape to begin with and then he's drivin' it too fast for where he is on the course. Seems to me – that's an accident waitin' to happen."

"Yes, I see what you mean." The detective seemed to be studying the file on his desk.

Hector felt that he had made a good point there. You can't argue with any of what he just said.

The detective looked up. "The fact remains that the accident was so awful, it's been difficult to find anything pointing to tampering at all."

Hector's first emotional reaction might have made him jump up and shout, but he had the feeling this detective was baiting him. Therefore, he was very careful.

Instead of showing any positive emotion, he just looked down at the floor, almost as if he was dealing with his sadness about losing his wife in that awful accident.

"The bodies were so mangled and so broken up, that they were almost unidentifiable."

Hector saw an opportunity. He looked up. "Detective Clio, do we have to talk about that part?"

The detective appeared to be surprised, but then he seemed to pull his emotions back and resume his cool, professional attitude. "It's all part of the picture, Mister Copan."

Hector's head went down. He found that he was on the verge of crying, so he let it happen.

His eyes ran tears. He did feel sad about Lycia. They had been in love at one time.

He wiped off his eyes.

"Here, Mister Copan."

Hector looked up.

There was a wad of white tissue in front of his face.

He reached out and took it. "Thanks." Hector dabbed his eyes. This time he had surprised himself. Maybe it was all that anger and sadness that he had pushed down inside. He wasn't exactly sure.

When he sat back, he noticed that the folder on the detective's desk was closed. He was tempted to make a lot out of that, but he resisted and focused on being cautious.

"If there is anything else that comes up, Mister Copan, I will call you. Are you going to be assigned to another starship soon?"

Hector wiped off his eyes and dropped his right hand into his lap. "No. I'm quittin' the MSA. Have to be with my kids. They don't have any momma now, so I have to be here for them."

The detective's large head nodded. "I see. Then you'll be around town?"

"Yup. Startin' an antique car restoration company. It's what I know – besides the MSA – so I figure it'll be somethin' I can do pretty good with."

The detective rose from his chair, towering over Hector. He held out his hand. "Good luck with you business venture, Mister Copan."

Hector stood up from the plastic chair and took the large, meaty hand. He made sure he shook it firmly twice. "Are we done, Detective Clio?"

"For now, Mister Copan. I may be giving you a call sometime."

Hector knew that was a way the detective was trying to make him nervous, on edge. "Be glad to help."

The detective seemed surprised by that remark. Then he face went deadpan. "We'll be in touch, Mister Copan."

Hector turned and walked toward the door. When he passed the end of the desk, he stopped at the large wire wastebasket. He looked back at Detective Clio. "Can I put this tissue in here?"

The man smiled. "Sure."

Hector dropped the used tissue in the wire wastebasket and walked across the small office to the door.

When he pulled it open, he was sure this detective was watching his every move, just looking for anything.

Once Hector Copan had stepped through the doorway and closed the door behind him, he felt relief. But he tried to remain deadpan and passive. He figured they could have video cameras all over this police building. Detective Clio might still be watching.

CHAPTER SEVENTY-ONE
"World of Ancient Wonders"

Hyksos
Memphis
27325 Sea View
6M, Day 24, 6573
6:05 p.m.

C aptain Chan Caracol could not believe that he was in his own backyard at his own grill. More importantly, this was a party after their wedding – no older folks, like his parents – just friends and fellow MSA people.

He had always imagined being back in his own yard, back in his own city. On some tough days aboard starships, that was what held him together.

However, to be here with his new wife – that was the best ever.

"You gonna cook those steaks right down to carbon bricks, Chan?"

The starship captain grinned. "Do you want yours raw, Alto?"

"Rare would be good."

"They're definitely not rare yet. They're raw." Chan slid the long-handled spatula under the steak in the right corner of the grill and lifted it out. He then moved it to the left front.

"Hot spot?"

He looked at Alto. "That's where it is. Right there in the corner." He nodded in that direction.

Alto took a swig from his bottle of beer and swallowed. He looked off toward a group of women talking. Among them was Blanca.

Chan was very proud of her. She was so adaptable. Obviously she was really intelligent and willing to learn because she had adapted quite easily to many of their customs.

"Gotta tell you, Chan, I couldn't be happier for you. Blanca is one fine woman and I can see that she's crazy about you."

"I know where you're going with that, Alto. No, I won't cheat on her and no, I won't go running around anymore. This is very different.

When I met Blanca it scared me because I knew I was going to either have her for life, or walk away. I just knew this was real, not some passing thing."

Alto nodded. "I'm glad it's finally happened. Couldn't happen to a better guy, far as I'm concerned."

Chan turned the steaks near the right corner, one at a time.

They hissed as he set the uncooked sides down onto the black grill.

After he had turned them over, he said, "I see things differently now. I'm even thinking about children."

Alto grinned. "No kiddin'?"

"Yup. I don't know. Everything's different. I've never felt this way before." He slid the spatula under one of the steaks at the back, lifted it and moved it forward.

Then he focused on Alto. "I don't mind being home with Blanca at night. Sometimes I'll sit and read a manual or something. She might be watching television. By the way, she's learning Mayan."

"That's great."

"Well, she figures that if a person isn't in the MSA and doesn't have a translator implant, she can't understand what the person is saying. I've given her an ear-clip translator. That should help her with people outside the MSA until she learns our language. She's also trying to learn how to write the language. Her own language was never written, just spoken, so the writing part is difficult for her."

"That would be weird for someone who never wrote a language before."

Chan lowered the lid over the grill.

The hissing became distant.

He turned to Alto. "She doesn't call it writing. She calls it pictures of words, but she'll catch on eventually."

"Sure she will." Alto turned. "Speakin' of the devil, guess who's comin.'"

Chan looked across the small yard.

Walking toward him was Blanca. She was wearing light green slacks and a white sleeveless top.

She was beautiful. Her dark skin really showed off the white top. What was more remarkable, however, was that she was wearing brown leather sandals.

That's what he had the most difficulty talking her into – wearing any kind of shoes. He had finally been able to convince her to try sandals. She seemed to like those, but she didn't like leather shoes. Tennis shoes might eventually be part of her footwear. She had put on a pair of those twice.

"Hi." She grinned at Chan. "You are cooking this bison very well, my husband."

He could tell that she was trying to use small-talk with him. He answered in kind. "I've done it before, my dear. Lots of experience."

Chan lifted the lid and checked the steaks, then lowered it again. He turned to Blanca. "I have a great idea for a honeymoon trip."

"I still don't get this honeymoon idea, my husband."

Chan looked at Alto and smiled. He was never going to laugh at her. She might feel insulted, and he wouldn't want to do that. "It's sort of like a vacation after your wedding in which you are given time alone to get to know each other better."

The small woman put her hands on her hips and nodded several times. "I guess I understand that." She looked at Chan. "Are we going down to the seashore?"

Chan chuckled. "You've been talking to the women, haven't you?"

"You told me to."

"No, no, honey. That's fine. Actually, I thought I had a better idea than the seashore - something very different. It's quite pricey, but, after all, you only have one honeymoon in your life."

"Some people have more, buddy."

Chan waved his hand dismissively. "None of that talk, Alto."

"Are we going to the seashore for our honeymoon?"

"No."

"Then where are we going?"

"Those women have been telling you to press me about this seashore thing, haven't they?"

"I don't understand this 'press.'"

"What I mean is they wanted you to keep asking me until I agreed to go to the seashore."

"Yes, that is right."

"Just a minute here." Chan grabbed the black handle on the grill lid and raised it upward. He checked the steaks inside. Then he glanced at his wrist control. "Couple more minutes." He lowered the lid.

"You must tell me."

Chan put the long-handled spatula on the shelf to the left of the tube-like, stainless steel grill hood. "Well, what I've decided to do – and, by the way, I've already bought the reservations – is take you up to the hotel and vacation spa that's attached to the World of Ancient Wonders."

"What is that?"

"Well, actually, originally it was a derelict spaceship orbiting the sun. It was left there by our ancient ancestors. We discovered it around fourteen hundred years ago. Now it's a combination of museum and vacation spa with a hotel and pool. There are several five-star restaurants and bars. There's a video screening theater, a dance club – even tennis courts and a golf course."

Alto moved over closer to Chan. "That must have cost you a fortune, buddy."

"Hey, nothing too good for the lady."

Blanca folded her arms, squinted her eyes and looked upward, as if she were considering this idea.

Chan was sure this was something she had seen Mayan woman do. He thought it was cute, but he wasn't going to make fun of her. He didn't want to hurt her feelings.

Finally Blanca turned to him. "Do we swim naked in the pool?"

Chan was shocked. "Ah. . . no."

"Then you have to buy me a bathing suit. If we went to the seashore, you'd have to buy me a bathing suit."

Chan grinned. She was just so cute. "I'll buy you two or three bathing suits. We can go downtown tomorrow to the mall."

Blanca moved up close to him. "I will wear them for you so I will be beautiful and you will love me even more."

"Blanca, I couldn't love you more than I do already."

CHAPTER SEVENTY-TWO
"Secondary Importance"

Hyksos
Memphis
1832 River Street
6M, Day 27, 6573
4:57 p.m.

Commander Seth Okanata waited for the gold bubbles to dissipate. Then he picked up his golf bag and stabbed the plastic key card into the slot to the right of the door.

The light on the pad blinked from red to green and there was a subtle clicking sound.

Seth twisted the doorknob, pushed the heavy door inward and stepped into the foyer.

The overhead light blinked on.

He closed the house door and crossed to the closet next to the staircase. There, he pulled open the narrow door and slid the golf bag inside behind the coats.

"Elaina!" Seth closed the closet door.

He could hear a TV set somewhere, probably the one in the family room. Elaina usually watched TV there.

Today he had felt the need to get away by himself to think.

Two days ago he had received an email from Lieutenant Alto Bucolus. It had listed the possible suspects in Masal Djoser's death and Elaina Djoser's name had been underlined, as had a statement below the list. The statement read, "Experience with photography and video editing."

For a very long time Seth had had his doubts about Elaina. They were not based upon any logical conclusion. It was just this intuitive feeling – strictly an emotional reaction. He did realize, however, that sometimes these intuitive feelings revealed the truth.

For instance, right at this moment, Seth was sensing something different about the house.

He moved into the hallway that led back to the kitchen. He was wearing tennis shoes so there was no noise as he made his way along the narrow hardwood floor.

As Seth approached the kitchen, the sound of the TV became louder. He recognized the practiced cadence of a male newscaster's voice.

When he stepped into the kitchen, the lights were on. He noticed that the green light on the coffee pot switch was still lit.

Elaina had forgotten it.

Seth crossed the white tile floor and flicked that off. When he did this, he noticed that the coffee was low and seemed to be bubbling – almost like it was boiling.

Obviously, this had been left on for a very long time.

"Elaina!"

He moved out of the kitchen through the small breakfast nook into the carpeted hallway leading to the bedrooms. When he passed the spare bedroom, he stopped.

He stepped back and looked inside.

Across the room, the pocket door in front of the walk-in closet was open. That was strange.

Seth stepped into the bedroom and crossed to the closet.

It was empty. There were plastic hangers unevenly spaced across the long PVC rod on the left. The three shelves off to the right were empty.

There was one hanger lying on the floor.

Seth stepped inside.

He could smell Elaina's perfume.

He bent over and picked up the white plastic hanger and slipped it up over the PVC rod.

Then he did an about face and moved out of the closet. When he passed through the doorway, he turned and grabbed the recessed hook in the pocket door and pulled it closed.

Seth was feeling very emotional just now. If Elaina's clothing was gone, she was gone.

Maybe she went back to her condo over on the other side of town.

Seth moved away from the closed pocket door. It felt like a barrier and he didn't like barriers at this moment.

He stepped out into the hallway, raised his wrist control and tapped the surface. He slid his finger down the right side of the screen until

Elaina's name appeared. Then he touched "SEND" at the bottom of the screen.

A bell appeared in the upper left corner of the screen.

Seth waited.

Finally a message filled the screen: "Elaina is not in. Would you like to leave a message? Yes? No?"

He tapped "No."

The screen went black.

Seth moved down the hallway toward the kitchen. His mind was going over recent conversations with her. He was looking for something – just anything – that would suggest why she had left.

Obviously she was not just leaving for the afternoon or staying overnight somewhere. She had taken all of her clothes.

When he stepped into the breakfast nook, he stopped.

There was a sheet of paper on the table with the sugar bowl placed on the upper right corner. He hadn't noticed it before.

Seth crossed to the table and bent over the sheet of paper. It was the email message from Lieutenant Alto Bucolus with Elaina's name underlined as well as the statement, "Experience with photography and video editing."

Seth stared down at the sheet of paper. He wished so very much that she hadn't left without saying anything. He wished she had talked to him about this.

But then, she had left. Perhaps it was not only because suspicion had been cast in her direction. It might be the other thing. She was feeling guilty.

Seth tugged the sheet of paper out from under the small white sugar bowl and moved toward the family room.

He stepped down off the tile floor into the deep carpet. Then he turned right and sat down on the grey leather couch.

His left hand dropped the sheet of paper to the smooth leather surface next to him.

He could remember so many lovely nights sitting here with Elaina, casually chatting and watching some mind-numbing, dumb program on TV. He had enjoyed that so much.

The news was on now. A handsome newscaster's face with intense brown eyes stared at the camera. "Now, closer to home. Today, the remains of Lieutenant Coptos Gurab were finally returned to his family."

The camera zoomed near the handsome face.

"Folks, this is an extraordinary story. Lieutenant Coptos Gurab was left for dead on the planet Mars in the Orion Belt of our galaxy fourteen hundred and seven years ago. He was on that planet as part of an expedition trying to discover the source of our origin.

"The details are sketchy, but apparently this lieutenant was having a liaison with the wife of Armant Zeus, the commander of the starship, Orion Four. Somehow Gurab was lost during a windstorm on Mars and because conditions were so bad on the planet's surface, he was left there. It was not until Starship Cygnus returned this year that his remains were finally recovered.

"Now we will go to Kadesh where a descendant of Lieutenant Gurab is receiving his remains. Amun Imhotep is on the scene right now. Amun. . ."

Seth reached down to the coffee table and picked up the remote. For some reason, which he could not understand, he pressed the MUTE button.

A second, younger male face appeared on the screen. This reporter was standing in front of a grey suburban house with a neat, green lawn and carefully trimmed shrubs.

The camera moved off the reporter and zoomed in toward the front porch of this grey suburban home. On that porch a young man in a military uniform was standing in front of the doorway, holding a shallow box, perhaps twelve decimeters long and seven decimeters wide.

Seth glanced at the black words crawling across the bottom of the television screen. He had actually been the one responsible for returning Lieutenant Gurab to his family, but that event was of secondary importance just now.

He had other, more important things to deal with.

CHAPTER SEVENTY-THREE
"Images"

Earth
El Meco
Early Night

Mary Magdalene stood outside the small hut. She was planning on entering, but she had to pull herself together first. There was something she had to tell Jesus, and she was a little nervous about it.

Finally, after waiting and thinking about this, she lifted the animal skin cover away from the entrance. Then she bent down and stepped into the hut.

Living here in this village was primitive, but the people were really friendly and, most of all, there were no Pharisees or priests.

The villagers had showed the two of them how to build this hut and had actually helped them. Mary liked that kind of attitude. These people here in El Meco seemed to cooperate and there were no accusers and nobody judging.

Once inside, she moved across the small space toward the fire where Jesus was sitting.

He was whittling again, working on another carving. The first one hadn't turned out so well, so he had thrown it into the fire one night, and that was the end of that.

Today, from early morning far into the afternoon, he had been out on Montana's fishing boat. According to what the villagers told them, the catch was quite good, and that seemed to be true because the boats were full of fish.

She and Jesus were trying to learn the villagers' language. At the time they were brought down here from the starship, the Mayans had told them that the batteries for these implants wouldn't last forever, whatever batteries were. In any case, they had to learn the language of this village because those translator implants wouldn't always work.

At the fire, Jesus turned to her. The firelight made yellow and black shadows on his face.

She pointed at a small wooden figure. "What are you whittling now?"

"Joseph."

"You already did a Joseph and then you threw it away."

Jesus nodded. "Yes. It was a very bad rendering. This time I got it right."

Mary sat down on the grass mat next to him in front of the small fire. "I'm happy here. How about you?"

Jesus shrugged. "I guess so."

"You don't want to go back to Israel, do you?"

His head turned and his deep brown eyes looked into hers. "I miss being among my people, and I often wonder what happened to my mother and Jude Thomas and the others."

"Just hope they all left Israel. It was too dangerous there."

"My mother wouldn't leave."

"I don't think she is in any danger – just your brothers and the disciples. They should definitely leave."

"I guess you're right."

"If the Mayan people hadn't saved you, you'd be dead right now, and what good would that do?"

Jesus looked up toward the low thatched grass roof. The firelight made ever changing shadows on his face. Finally he turned to her. "The things that were wrong in Israel are still wrong in Israel. I should be there, trying to change all of that so my people have a better life."

"I don't like hearing you talk like this. You tried to make changes, and the Pharisees were going to kill you. They almost succeeded. You've given enough for your people."

She turned to face him. "Besides, I don't think they really appreciated what you were trying to do anyway. I don't think the people understood."

"Some of them did. Look at the crowds I had when I traveled through Galilee."

"All they wanted, Jesus, was someone to save them from their miserable poverty. You couldn't do that."

He stared into the fire. "I guess not. I was just trying to change what was wrong."

"And the Pharisees and the priests were afraid you would succeed so they tried to kill you. And they would do it again without a second thought."

He nodded. "I suppose you're right."

"You know I'm right."

He looked at her. "My people need me."

"I need you more."

"You're a very strong woman. You don't need me."

"But I still want you with me."

He stared into her eyes. Then he turned away. "Here's my new Joseph." He held up the figure. "I've tried hard to get this to look like him. He was a very good father and a good man."

Jesus turned the figure in his fingers. "He taught me a trade, carpentry, but he also taught me about ideas and about God and about the world."

He turned to Mary. "I loved my father with all my heart. I felt so empty when he died. I still feel that emptiness. I have times when I really miss him a lot."

"Consider yourself blessed. You had a wonderful father. Not all children do."

"That's true." Jesus stared into her eyes. "I get the sense that there's something you're not saying that you really want to say very much."

She shrugged. "Could be."

"Please – don't be coy with me."

It seemed so simple the way Jesus put it, but it wasn't that simple. Mary didn't want him to feel that he was obligated to her, and had to stay with her. She wanted him to stay with her because he really wanted to stay with her.

He held up the small carved figure. "Don't you think that's a pretty good rendering?"

"It looks good to me. Of course, I never met your father, so how would I know?"

He studied the little figure in both hands. "It's really pretty good. I wanted to do it because I wanted to feel nearer to him."

"Aren't people in heaven supposed to be able to hear us and see us?"

Jesus turned to her. "That's what I've been told."

"And that's what you told the people, and they believed you. Don't you believe it?"

"Yes."

"Then your father should be close to you."

Jesus' eyes studied her face. "What did you want to tell me?"

Mary took in a deep breath. "I'm pregnant."

The brown eyes stared at her. "How do you know?"

"I know." Mary didn't really understand his reaction.

He turned away and faced the fire. "God has spoken."

"What does that mean?"

Jesus faced her again. "He's telling me to stay with you. He's telling me that my work in Israel is done."

"Aren't you even happy about this?"

"Of course."

"You don't act like it."

"I'm trying to get used to the idea of being a father."

"If it's a little girl, you can spoil her."

Jesus nodded. "Yes." He seemed lost in thought.

"And if it's a little boy, you can teach him to be a carpenter just like you and your father."

Jesus smiled. "Yes, I can teach him what his grandfather, Joseph, taught me. It will keep my father alive. Yes, that will be wonderful."

Mary wiggled over closer to Jesus on the grass mat. "Now, we will be a family."

"We should marry."

"Of course."

"But we can't have a Jewish wedding here."

"We can teach these people how to do it."

"But you'll be pregnant during the wedding."

"Nobody in the village will care, Jesus."

He held the carving of Joseph up in front of his face. "This grand-child will make my father very happy."

CHAPTER SEVENTY-FOUR
"Missing Person"

Hyksos
Memphis
1889 Bay Street
7M, Day 2, 6573
8:45 p.m.

S eth Okanata had called Lieutenant Bucolus before teleporting over here. He didn't want to talk over his wrist control. He wanted to talk to Alto in person.

He had tried to reach Alto during the day, but the man was out at some gathering of his family, and, of course, Seth didn't want to interfere with that. Family was important.

He, of all people, knew that. Seth had no family – well, except for his cousin, Otto, who lived in Kadesh. They had nothing in common, so he hadn't seen the man in over a decade. Sure, they were just a few years apart in age – Seth older by four years – but their lives were totally different. Otto was a farmer.

Seth took a deep breath. In so many ways, he wasn' looking forward to this, but he had to talk to Lieutenant Bucolus face-to-face. He wanted to know what was going on in the man's mind.

Seth pressed the doorbell button.

He heard the sound of muffled chimes. It was strange. He had never pictured Lieutenant Bucolus having chimes in his house. Of course, Bucolus was married. Probably his wife's idea, but, then, maybe not.

The door opened and a red-haired woman with a very pretty face smiled at him. "Commander Okanata – hello." She held out her hand. "You probably don't remember, but we met six years ago at a dinner party."

"Certainly." Seth shook her hand. "How are you, Mrs. Bucolus?"

"I'm good, Commander. You may call me Canace."

Seth smiled. "Very pretty name – unusual."

"My grandmother's first name. Do come in, Commander. Alto is waiting for you on the back porch."

Seth thought that was kind of strange, but maybe Alto had anticipated what Seth was going to talk about and wanted some privacy.

As he was following Canace Bucolus through the house, Seth began to feel a bit worried about how this was going to play out.

When Canace reached the door wall that led out to the porch, she slid the door open for him. "Alto, the commander is here."

The lieutenant rose up from a wicker chair and walked toward the door. He held out his hand. "Commander Okanata, good to see you."

Seth was trying to read the man's face. The face was friendly, but the eyes were wary. He didn't like the feel of that.

Alto swept out his hand. "Sit down, Commander. I was just having some wine. Would you like some, sir?"

"Yes, thank you. That would be very nice." Seth was sure it would help his nerves to have a little alcohol. He moved across the porch to the far side and sat down.

Alto sat where he had before, near the corner of the porch. Seth was at a right angle to the lieutenant.

"So, Commander, what brings you out here?"

Seth could see Alto's wife coming with a glass of red wine. He waited.

When she reached him, he stood up and took the wine. "Thank you, Canace."

"You're welcome, Commander."

He smiled again for her, then sat down.

The woman crossed the short space to the sliding glass door, stepped inside and pulled it shut.

Seth took a sip of the wine and held it in his mouth. He swallowed and nodded. "A very good red, Alto."

The lieutenant made a faint smile and nodded. "I thought so too, Commander. So what do you want to talk about?"

Seth sipped the wine again and swallowed. Then he placed the goblet on the small side table to his right.

He made eye contact with Alto. "I was wondering how that investigation was coming."

Alto shrugged. "I hate to tell you, sir, but it looks like it might be Elaina."

"Yes, I saw your note about experience with film and her name underlined."

Alto looked down at his hands folded in his lap. Then he raised his head and made eye contact with Seth. "I get the impression that you're not too happy with my conclusion."

Seth swallowed more wine and placed the goblet on the small table again. "You guessed right, Alto." He hesitated. "She's gone, you know. . . disappeared."

"Really?"

Seth nodded. "I'll have to admit, Alto, that I had strong feelings for her."

"Yes, sir, I figured that's what was happenin'. Beautiful woman. . . smart. . . lots of personality. Lots of men go for a woman like that."

Seth didn't like that last remark. "I never was one to spend much time with women. Maybe I was an easy mark."

"I might be steppin' out of bounds here, sir, but I think she really liked you."

At that moment, Seth Okanata thought he might come to tears. He was relieved and encouraged at the same time. "Do you really think so, Alto?"

"Yes, sir, I do. Remember, she was livin' with Masal and that guy beat her up pretty bad. I get the feelin' that it wasn't the first time either. You were kind to her."

Seth nodded. "She seemed like a good person." He turned around to face Alto. "If she came back, would you arrest her?"

Alto Bucolus seemed to be considering this question. "I'd probably have to, sir."

Seth nodded. He had expected that. "The evidence is that strong?"

"What I'm lookin' at, Commander, is the issue of film editing. Sergeant Copan said he hadn't had any experience with film editing. I checked his background in the records going back twelve years and, as far as I could tell, there was nothing about film, video or editing. So I figure he was tellin' the truth.

"Lieutenant Elaina Djoser took film classes in regular college before she went to the MSA Academy. When she was in undergraduate school, she even studied acting. She was planning a career in television and film."

"Really? How did she ever get into navigation, especially celestial navigation?"

"Don't know, sir. Just know that sometime after she finished college she did an about face and went back to school, studyin' navigation.

"The only unusual thing that stands out was that during her senior year in college, she requested a court order for her dramatics teacher to stay away from her, a Doctor Vaktor Silenus. He had, allegedly, made sexual advances toward her. He was over twenty years older."

At that moment, Seth Okanata began to see that Elaina had experienced a troubled past. Certainly not as bad as many people, but she did have that ugly event – and then, later, a very bad marriage.

Now, he was feeling sorry for her again. In fact, he was possessed by this painful need to protect her. Seth rose from his chair. "I've taken enough of your time, Alto. I should be going." He held out his hand. "Thank you for that information. I do appreciate it."

"You're quite welcome, sir." Lieutenant Alto Bucolus smiled.

The commander released his hand and began moving across the porch.

Alto followed.

They had reached the kitchen before the silence between them was broken.

"Commander. . ."

Seth turned. "Yes, Alto?"

"Sir, do you have any idea where she went?"

Seth shrugged. "I really don't know, Alto."

"There's that film company up in Nubia. If I was lookin' for her, I might ask around up there in the mountains. She probably wouldn't be usin' her real name."

Seth shrugged again. "I honestly don't know, Alto. She left no note. . . nothing. I came home from golfing and she was gone. . . just like that."

Alto made eye contact.

Seth wondered if the lieutenant was checking the veracity of what he had just said. Actually, Seth had nothing to hide. He really had no idea where Elaina might be.

CHAPTER SEVENTY-FIVE
"The Legal and the Moral"

Hyksos
Memphis
1889 Bay Street
7M, Day 6, 6573
11:07 a.m.

Alto Bucolus was, in so many ways, glad to be off that starship. Sure, it was interesting to go back to where their ancestors came from and he liked working for the MSA.

However, this last journey had been pretty tough. There was that damned case about Masal Djoser.

Personally, Alto did not like the man. First of all, he didn't like men who beat up their wives. And there was the fact that Masal had this sort of arrogant attitude. Sure he was a good rocket mechanic, but he wasn't the only good rocket mechanic. He certainly was the best rocket mechanic in the MSA.

When Alto was totally honest with himself, there was a part of him which believed that Lieutenant Masal Djoser had deserved to die.

Of course, there was another side to this thing. Alto had a job to perform. In fact, he had a duty to uphold the rules and the laws aboard any starship he was assigned to. Unfortunately, this time it had been the Cygnus and Masal Djoser had been aboard. Not only that, Masal Djoser had died under very suspicious circumstances.

This case was driving Alto crazy. The commander had come over here to his house just a few days ago and asked how things were going. Alto had definitely made progress, but not the kind he wanted to make.

He guessed what bothered him most was that, of all the people he had as suspects, the one who looked most guilty was this really terrific woman, Elaina Djoser. She was Masal Djoser's wife. Alto absolutely hated the idea of hunting her down and arresting her for murder. Yet, he had to do it.

Maybe to feel better he should go down to the basement and begin some woodworking project. He needed to get away from this thing and, besides, his wife, Canace, had told him she wanted a new table for the back porch. Maybe he could come up with something.

Alto loved handling wood. Touching and smelling it always made him feel better. And the thing about woodworking was when you were done, you had something beautiful and physical that might even be useful.

Alto stood up from the kitchen table and carried his coffee mug across to the sink. He had gone through four cups of the stuff already this morning.

Sitting around and worrying about how he was going to handle Masal Djoser's murder was driving him nuts. He would be better off doing a woodworking project.

The door chime clanged in the front foyer.

Alto's head turned. "Now, who the hell is that?" He really wanted to change his clothes and go down to the basement and start that table. But now he had to answer the damned front door.

The chime sounded again.

"Hey, don't get your underwear in a knot!" he muttered.

He wiped off his hands on the hand towel hanging from the bar on the front of the oven. Then he moved across the kitchen and into the hallway that led to the foyer.

At the front door, he leaned to look through the peephole. "Wonder who the hell he is. . . big sonofabitch."

The chimes clanged again.

Alto grabbed onto the deadbolt, turned it, then pressed down the thumb lever on the handle and pulled open the door.

"Hello, Lieutenant Bucolus. I'm Detective Balder Clio with the Memphis Police Department." He held up his police department shield.

Alto moved back into the foyer. "Come in, Detective."

The huge man moved by him.

Alto closed the door. "What can I do for you, Detective?"

"Can we sit down somewhere? I don't want to take a lot of your time, Lieutenant, but I do have a few things I'd like to talk over with you. Is there anyone else in the house?"

For just a second, Alto wondered why this man had asked that question. "Nobody's here. My wife's at work and the kids are in school."

"Good." The large round face broke into a smile. "I realize you're off duty now and furloughs are something we all really value. So I won't take too much of your time, Lieutenant."

"No problem." Alto pointed toward the living room. "We can sit in here."

He led the large man into a long, narrow room and nodded toward the chairs next to the bay window. "Sit down anywhere."

The big man swung around and sat in the nearest of the two chairs.

Alto took the other chair beyond the circular marble-topped table.

"Lieutenant Bucolus, I'm going to be recording this, if you don't mind. By law, I have to let you know." The detective pulled a small rectangular device out of the side pocket of his suit coat and placed it on the table. Then he punched a button.

Alto was beginning to wonder what the hell was going on. "Detective Clio, I don't understand. What's this about?"

"Well, what it comes down to, Lieutenant, is that you and I are investigating the same person."

"And who is that?"

"Sergeant Hector Copan."

Alto shrugged. "Yeah, he's one of the suspects in a case I'm workin' on."

"This may actually help you out and I may receive some benefit as well."

"Okay. . . sure."

Detective Clio made eye contact with Alto. "I understand, Lieutenant Alto Bucolis, that you work in security on MSA starships."

"Yes. I've been with the MSA for eighteen years."

"And I also understand that Sergeant Hector Copan was on the starship Cygnus with you on your last assignment."

"Yes, that's correct."

"There was an accident on that starship and a man died. Hector Copan was there when it happened. Am I right about that, Lieutenant?"

"Well. . . partly. Actually, it looks like it was an intentional act. . . murder, not an accident."

"And Hector Copan was somehow involved."

"As you said before, he was present when the event happened. But at this point I don't know that he was actually involved."

"Tell me about this event, if you would, Lieutenant."

"Lieutenant Masal Djoser and Sergeant Hector Copan were doin' an EVA. . . extra vehicular activity. We had been hit by a small meteor durin' a flyby to decelerate our starship and those two men were outside the ship makin' the repair. It involved weldin'. Lieutenant Djoser was doin' the actual weldin'. Sergeant Copan was assistin' him."

"So what happened?"

"Well, apparently a bolt was loose on Djoser's air control unit and it blew out. . . probably from him movin' around. Air escaped from his lungs at a high rate and, from what the autopsy showed, a main artery popped open because of the lack of pressure and he bled to death. It happened in a matter of seconds. Sergeant Copan tried to tape the bolt hole, but by that time, Djoser was already dead."

"Copan tried to save him?"

"That's right."

"He should have known it wouldn't work, Lieutenant. Even I know that."

Alto shrugged. "I guess he just reacted."

"Was this Sergeant Copan's first EVA?"

"No. He has probably done fifteen or twenty, at least."

"Then he should have known it was pointless to try and save this other man."

Alto nodded. "You're probably right."

"You said you're still doing an investigation?"

"Yes and I have three suspects, Lieutenant Djoser's wife, Sergeant Copan and the starship commander, Seth Okanata. Copan is on my list of suspects because he and Djoser had set up an antique car rebuildin' business. The problem was that Djoser had not come up with the money he was supposed to supply for startin' the business. Copan was not happy about that. . . not happy at all."

"How much money did Lieutenant Djoser owe?"

"Two hundred fifty thousand dollars."

The detective's large head nodded. "That's a lot of money for these guys."

"You see, Detective Clio, we figured that it was murder because that EVA equipment is inspected regularly and there is no way a loose bolt would not have been spotted by Djoser or Copan. . . unless somebody messed around with the equipment just before the EVA."

The detective leaned forward. "So. . . you figure somebody deliberately loosened that bolt."

"Yes, that's correct."

Detective Clio nodded. Then he looked directly at Alto. "Well, this case I'm working on was originally thought to be a car accident. It happened on that driving range south of town."

"You see. . . Copan's wife was killed in that accident. She was with another man, apparently her boyfriend. It seems that she was cheating on her husband. . . Sergeant Copan.

"Now, this event looked like an accident because the boyfriend, Menon, was driving so fast. Then we found out that someone had messed with the wiring on the electric car.

"Our men in the lab downtown who checked over the car said it was rigged to give the driver shocks through the steering wheel, and you're talking two hundred twenty volts, not one hundred ten. So this boyfriend, Cadmus Menon, must have been getting zapped pretty hard.

"In fact, a doctor I talked to said that, because it was two hundred twenty volts, it might have actually affected Menon's heart rhythm.

"I can't say much more about this because it's a pending case. I'm here only because I figured you must know something about Copan. You've been on the same starship with him for several months.

"However, I will tell you this much. . . Hector Copan is in real deep, Lieutenant. And let me say this. . . if I was in your shoes, he would be my red-hot suspect for that murder during the EVA you were telling me about."

"But he tried to save Djoser."

Detective Clio shrugged. "Maybe he was just covering his own ass. Look, Lieutenant, I'm not trying to hang both murders on this guy, but I think Copan might be capable. In fact, I have sometimes wondered if he might actually have intended to kill his wife and her boyfriend. It doesn't look like that, but there is always that possibility."

Alto grimaced and shook his head. "That's not the Hector Copan I know, Detective."

"His wife was cheating on him, Lieutenant. When things like that happen, people do crazy stuff." The large man shut off the recorder and slipped it into his suit coat pocket. Then he rose from his chair.

Alto stood up.

"Thank you, Lieutenant. You've been very helpful. I won't take any more of your time. I can imagine how you must look forward to these furloughs."

Alto smiled. "Oh, definitely. Bein' home is nice. Workin' in security on a starship is really interestin'. On the other hand, there are those times when you think you're never gonna solve a case. Those are real frustratin'."

Alto began leading the detective toward the front door.

"Oh, I certainly know about that, Lieutenant. The ones I can't solve haunt me. . . sometimes for years. It's sort of like having a ghost in your closet."

Alto nodded. "Yup. I've had a couple of those myself."

"The thing is that real life is crazier than movies or TV specials. There's a lot of weird shit that goes on out there, Lieutenant."

Alto stopped in front of the house door. "It's the same on a starship, Detective Clio. With this case, I have those three suspects, and I'm not sure where it's goin'."

"If I were you, Lieutenant, I'd look closely at this Hector Copan." The detective held out his hand. "Thank you for your help."

Alto shook his hand. Then he pulled open the house door.

Detective Balder Clio moved by him and opened the screen door.

Once outside, he turned and waved. "Thanks again, Lieutenant."

"You're welcome." Alto pushed the door closed and twisted the deadbolt.

Right at that moment, he remembered reading a book years before, in which this religious leader – he couldn't remember the man's name – said that there was sometimes a huge difference between what was legal in a particular situation and what was moral.

And look what he had done on planet Earth just two months ago. Alto had killed a man, had shot him – the man in the green hat. So what was legal about that? Sure, that guy was going to reveal the location of Peter and the other followers of Jesus, but was shooting him legal?

At the time it seemed the right thing to do, but it wasn't legal. Alto was sure of that. Okay. . . probably it was the moral thing to do.

Alto had always thought of himself as a person who did things the legal way. After all, he was in charge of law enforcement aboard a starship. Yet what he had done back there in that city of Jerusalem had been illegal. He had committed a crime.

Right now, he remembered something else - Elaina Djoser's face after her husband had beaten her. Here was this pretty and, actually, very nice woman who had been beaten so bad that you could barely tell it was her.

Did she have the right to be angry? Absolutely. Did she have the right to kill her husband? The law said no, but maybe it wasn't all that simple.

How many other times had Masal Djoser beaten her? Alto hated to think about that. He clearly remembered how Captain Salathiel Tikal had reacted to Elaina Djoser's beating. Tikal had told Alto that Masal Djoser should be gutted and shoved down the garbage chute into space.

Alto had always thought that was extreme, but then he wondered how he would feel if his daughter was the one who had been abused. If his daughter, Clova, was being beaten by some asshole, Alto knew exactly what would happen. He would kill the sonofabitch.

The lieutenant folded his arms across his chest. Then he nodded. "Yup. Got to do this."

He tapped his wrist control.

It lit up.

Then he tapped the phone symbol.

A list of names and numbers appeared on the screen. He swiped his right index finger down the length of the screen three times.

Now he was in the O's. He swiped carefully down the list until he came to the name Okanata. He tapped it.

The light in the wrist control flickered. "Hello, Lieutenant. What can I do for you?"

"Commander, I have good news. I just found out that Sergeant Hector Copan actually did have experience with film and video. He apparently photographed and videoed antique electric and gas-powered automobiles. A detective workin' for the city police department was just here talkin' to me and that's one thing he told me about."

"Then that means. . ."

"Yes, sir. This detective also told me that Sergeant Copan was responsible for the death of his wife and his wife's boyfriend out at that drivin' range south of the city. I'm sure you remember that his wife and a man were killed in a car accident?"

"Yes, I do remember that."

"Well, sir, it seems that Sergeant Copan had tampered with the boy-friend's car. So he's bein' investigated for murder."

"Really? I never would have expected that."

"Me either, but I remember, sir, that he didn't seem too worked up when he was told about the accident and his wife bein' killed."

"This changes everything, Lieutenant. Thank you so much for this call. I can't thank you enough, actually."

Alto smiled.

"I may be out of town for a while."

"Nubia, Commander?"

The other end of the phone was silent. Finally the commander said, "Yes, I had thought of that. . . beautiful place with all the mountains. . . very scenic."

"If not there, I'd go down to Kadesh, but I think Nubia is your best bet, Commander." Alto waited. He was expecting some reference to Lieutenant Elaina Djoser.

"Nubia's much more scenic."

"Yes, sir, that's true."

"Thank you, again, Alto."

"You're more than welcome, sir."

There was a subtle beep.

Alto Bucolus checked the surface of his wrist control. The light was out.

He moved over to the bay window and stared at his lawn and the street beyond.

The statements about Sergeant Copan and photographing cars was something he had made up, of course. That would eliminate any doubts the commander might have about Elaina Djoser.

Alto hoped the commander didn't talk about any of this. Somebody might challenge him or ask where he had heard that particular bit of information about Copan.

Of course, Sergeant Hector Copan was in trouble enough with the city police. Copan was in the city's jurisdiction right now. The city had control, not the starship.

Alto would just sit back and see what happened. He was pretty sure that because Copan's wife was cheating on him, the prosecutors would go for manslaughter. They could get a conviction that way.

Now, there was no reason to pursue this investigation of Masal Djoser's murder. Alto was damned glad about that.

CHAPTER SEVENTY-SIX
"Dreaming"

Hyksos
Nubia
Mountain View Mall
1181 View Avenue
7M, Day 10, 6573
2:03 p.m.

Commander Seth Okanata had put an ad in the Nubian Banner, the local newspaper. Also, he had placed the same ad on every social website he could find on his wrist control.

The message had simply said, **"Elaina, you're innocent. Meet me at the Mountain View Mall on Day 10 at 2:00 p.m. I'll be on the lower level in front of the T. J. Best clothing store. Love, Seth"**

At this moment he was standing in front of the T.J. Best clothing store. There were women going in and coming out in sporadic clusters of two or three and, occasionally, a man.

The mall was crowded today because it was a weekend and T.J. Best had a special one day, thirty percent off sale. He had chosen this day because Elaina would not be a standout in a crowded mall. Therefore, she would probably feel safer.

Seth checked his wrist control. It was after 2:00 p.m. He sure hoped she showed up. He had missed her terribly and now that Lieutenant Bucolus had told him about Sergeant Copan's skills with film and such, he was sure she was innocent.

He was pretty sure he could have lived with her, knowing that she had killed her husband. That man was a beast. Masal Djoser had beaten her terribly. It was only a matter of time before he would have killed her.

But Seth didn't even like to consider that possibility. Well, now Masal Djoser was gone. Sergeant Copan had done Elaina - and him – a huge favor.

Seth checked his wrist control again. He had been here nearly fifteen minutes. He had come early, just in case she showed up early.

"Seth," said a whisper behind him.

He spun around.

Her hair color was lighter, but the face was the same. "Elaina." He grabbed onto her and hugged her hard. "I've missed you so."

She pushed away and looked into his eyes. "Am I really innocent?"

Seth glanced around. Then he leaned close. "Sergeant Hector Copan is an experienced photographer and videographer. That's what Lieutenant Alto Bucolus told me. Apparently Alto got that information from a detective who works for the city. Hector Copan is being investigated for murdering his wife."

"But she died after he was onboard the starship."

Seth nodded. "Yes, she was in an automobile accident on that driving range south of town. However, Sergeant Copan had tampered with the car his wife's boyfriend owned before he left. That's what he was being investigated for. This city detective stopped by Alto's house and talked with him."

Elaina grinned. The tears began to flow.

Seth grabbed onto her and hugged her close. "It's all right now, my dear. I'm so glad to be with you again. My life has been empty with you gone."

"I've missed you too. It's been so hard, Seth. I haven't been accessing my bank account back in Memphis because I was afraid somebody would find me. I was beginning to run out of money."

Seth leaned back and looked at her. "You should have stayed, Elaina. I would have helped you, no matter what."

"But if I was arraigned for murder, your reputation - your whole life - would have been ruined."

He grinned. "We don't have to worry about that now."

She looked down and shook her head. "It's so hard to believe. I feel like I'm dreaming."

"You're not dreaming. This is real." Seth slipped his arm behind hers and clasped onto her hand. "Have you eaten lunch yet?"

"No. I was too nervous to even think about eating."

"Tell you what. I'll buy you lunch. Does that work for you?"

Elaina smiled. "Absolutely."

As Seth was walking with Elaina down the main corridor of the giant mall, it did occur to him that it was a strange coincidence that both Hector Copan and Elaina Djoser were well versed in the use of film and video.

Yes, in fact, there would always be this little shadow, this tiny scintilla of doubt, but there were a lot of things in life where there were doubts. No, it wasn't that he didn't have doubts about Elaina. Of course, in this case he had the convenience of a very good target for blame, a good prospect for conviction. That really helped with the doubts.

He could live with that. In fact, he definitely would live with it. And then there was the fact that she was a good woman who was brutally abused. Even if she was the one, didn't she have the right to fight back?

He wondered what that prophet, Jesus, would say about this. Of course, Seth would never get the chance to ask that man. Besides, he had to go on with his life, and he was with Elaina again. That, in itself, was enough.

THE END

Dear Reader,

I hope you enjoyed reading *Emmanuel* as much as I enjoyed writing it. This novel is the seventh in the series, *Birth of the Gods*. *Forever*, novel number eight, is the only one remaining.

Preceding this are *The End of Days*, *Constellation Draco*, *Darkness Visible*, *The Tales of Agenor*, *Orion Four* and *Spaceport Atlantis*, in that order.

You can find these novels at my website, j-r-bacon-author.com or at Amazon under J. R. Bacon. In fact, soon there will be other novels outside of this series available at my website and Amazon. Some will be science fiction. Others will not.

Feel free to visit my website or Amazon and check out my novels.

Warm regards,

J. R. Bacon